FALLING FOR THE SECRET PRINCESS

KANDY SHEPHERD

To Elizabeth Lhuede, good friend and my
first critique partner on my romance writing journey.

She's still there, with wise and informed feedback
not only on writing but also on the quirks
of human behaviour.

Thank you, Elizabeth!

FALLING FOR THE SECRET PRINCESS

KANDY SHEPHERD

THE MARINE'S FAMILY MISSION

VICTORIA PADE

MILLS & BOON

First Published in Great Britain 2019
by Mills & Boon, an imprint of HarperCollinsPublishers,
1 London Bridge Street, London, SE1 9GF

Falling for the Secret Princess © 2019 Kandy Shepherd
The Marine's Family Mission © 2019 Victoria Pade

ISBN: 978-0-263-27261-1

0919

CHAPTER ONE

NATALIA KNEW SHE should have eyes only for her friends, the bride and groom, as the deliriously happy couple exchanged vows in the grounds of a waterfront mansion on Sydney Harbour. The correct etiquette and protocol for every possible social occasion had been drummed into her since birth. *'You must always follow the rules, Natalia.'* She could almost hear the commanding tones of her parents. But, although she knew it was an impolite no-no, she could not help her gaze from straying to the tall, darkly handsome guest on the opposite side of the informal garden aisle. He was hot. Unbelievably hot.

What *was* it about Australia? Since she'd arrived in Sydney, five days previously, she'd never seen so many good-looking men. But none had triggered her interest like this one.

She'd noticed him as soon as the guests had started arriving—broad-shouldered and imposing, black hair, wearing an immaculately tailored charcoal tuxedo. Spanish? Middle Eastern? Greek? It was difficult to tell from this distance. She'd sneaked more than a few surreptitious glances since, each lingering longer than the last. This time he must have sensed her gaze on him because he turned to meet it.

Mortified, she froze. For a long second her eyes connected with his and he smiled, teeth dazzling white against olive skin, dark brows raised in acknowledgment. She flushed and quickly averted her gaze, looking down with feigned interest at the Order of Service card in her hand.

Despite her reputation in the gossip pages, Natalia wasn't a flirt, or a ruthless breaker of men's hearts. In fact she could be cursedly shy when she encountered an attractive man. But there was something about this fellow wedding guest that made her want to smile right back boldly. To flutter her eyelashes and let him know how drawn she was to him.

Instead she twisted the card between her fingers, determined not to look up again. Breach of protocol aside, she'd been warned to stay right under the radar so as not to take attention away from the bride and groom by her presence. That *didn't* mean conducting a public, across-the-aisle flirtation with a handsome stranger.

But then she remembered with a giddying rush of excitement that she was here incognito and in disguise. Those constricting rules need not apply to her alter ego. *She could do whatever she liked.*

No one but a select few were aware that she was Princess Natalia of Montovia, second in line to the throne of a small European kingdom, notorious for her six refusals of proposals of marriage from royal suitors and her seeming determination to stay single.

Her presence could draw unwanted media attention. The press intrusion was here, even in far-away Australia. Her brother Tristan, the Crown Prince, had married a Sydney girl, and every move they made was newsworthy. The condition of Natalia being allowed to accept the invitation to this wedding, where her brother was a groomsman and his wife a bridesmaid, was that she—Princess Heartbreaker—stayed out of the gossip pages.

So Natalia had chosen a full-on disguise for her stay in Sydney. Her shoulder-length dark brown hair had been straightened, lengthened with extensions and lightened to a honey-blonde that complemented her creamy skin. She'd tried coloured contact lenses to darken her blue eyes, but they'd hurt so she'd abandoned them. Her exclusive designer clothes had been replaced with a wardrobe purchased from a smart high street chain—she'd picked outfits that a regular, non-royal twenty-seven-year-old woman would wear—and her priceless jewellery was locked in a safe back home at the palace, save for a single pair of diamond ear studs.

So far, to her delight, no one had guessed her secret. And the more she knew she was getting away with her disguise, the bolder she'd become at testing it.

Not-Princess Natalia—at this moment not bound by her kingdom's rules—lifted her eyes and turned back to face the handsome guest, to find him still looking at her. She smiled, sure and confident, though she was racked with nerves inside. His answering grin made her flush grow warmer and awareness shimmer through her body.

Natalia had a sense that he was assessing her, in a subtle yet thorough way. Daringly, she did the same to him. On longer examination he was every bit as hot as he had appeared at first glance. Her smile danced at the corners of her mouth and she angled her shoulders towards him, scarcely aware that she was doing so. His grin widened and he nodded almost imperceptibly in acknowledgment of their silent exchange.

Her heart started beating in excitement. What next? Should she—?

At that moment the celebrant declared Eliza and Jake man and wife, and the newlyweds exchanged their first married kiss, to the accompaniment of happy sighs and cheers from their assembled family and friends. Natalia automatically turned towards the flowered arch where her friends were kissing, and watched as the couple started their march back down the grassy aisle. The bride was flaunting a neat baby bump, which was cause for great celebration.

'Don't you want to have children?'

Natalia's mother, the Queen, had asked that question— for what must have been the zillionth time since Natalia had turned eighteen—as she'd reluctantly said farewell to her only daughter.

Of course she did. And she wasn't averse to marriage. But she wasn't going to couple up with a man she didn't love just so she could have children and ensure further heirs to the throne. Besides, at twenty-seven she wasn't panicking. She simply hadn't met a man who thrilled her, either before or after the lifting of the edict that royals had to marry royals. In theory, she could now marry anyone she liked. That was if she ever fell in love.

Was it because of the men or herself that she'd never felt that giddying elation? Maybe she had to face up to the fact she wasn't a 'falling in love' person. Perhaps she didn't have it in her to trust someone enough to fall in love. Certainly there were very few examples of happy relationships in her family to inspire her.

She believed with all her heart that Tristan and Gemma's happy marriage would last the distance, but it was an exception. Her other brother's arranged marriage had been trumpeted as a 'love match', but his wife had turned out to be cold-hearted and greedy. Her selfishness had, in fact, contributed to her husband's death. And then there were the King and Queen... As a teenager she'd been devastated to discover her parents' marriage was a hypocritical sham.

But this wedding here in Sydney was the real deal, and it gave Natalia a skerrick of hope that true love could be found—among non-royals, anyway.

The bride shone her a special smile as she passed between the rows of white chairs set out on the lawn of the mansion. Eliza was one of the few here who knew her real identity. Eliza and Jake were friends of her brother Tristan. And Eliza and Tristan's wife, Gemma, along with their friend Andie, who was married to the best man, Dominic, ran Sydney's most successful party planning business, Party Queens.

Gemma now lived in Montovia and participated in the business from a distance. Her new sister-in-law had become a close friend, and Natalia had met the other two Party Queens on their visits to Montovia.

She had been thrilled to receive an invitation to Eliza and Jake's wedding. Not just because Eliza was a friend, but also because she'd wanted to see Sydney—the place where Tristan had met his wife Gemma, the place where he had spent a glorious few weeks as an anonymous tourist. She'd wanted a rare chance to be anonymous too. To be herself. Possibly even to find herself.

After the rest of the bridal party had passed by, she looked over to the handsome stranger with bated breath, only to see an empty chair.

Finn was caught up in a swell of well-wishers, all rushing past him to congratulate the bride and groom. As they thronged around him he lost sight of the beautiful woman across the aisle. By the time he'd elbowed past the other guests he could only see the back of her head as she hugged Eliza, her long blonde hair glinting golden in the afternoon sun. Then he himself got caught up in conversation with the best man, Dominic.

Weddings tended to bring out the grouch in Finn. He was what people delighted in calling 'an eligible bachelor'. He'd even, to his horror, been included in a well-publicised list of 'Bachelor Millionaires'—but he was a private person and loathed being in the spotlight. A wedding seemed to bring out matchmaking efforts in even the most unlikely of his friends and acquaintances, all keen to introduce him to potential spouses in whom he had no interest whatsoever. Marriage was not on the cards for him. Not in the foreseeable future.

Thankfully, property developer Dominic wanted to talk business, not potential brides, but real estate was the last thing on Finn's mind. He ground his teeth in frustration at the effort of being polite when all he ached to do was find an opportunity to see her again—the gorgeous sexy woman in the dark pink dress that hugged her curvaceous form. He had to see if she'd felt the same zing of attraction. That instant awareness that hadn't struck him for a long, long time.

After Dominic went on his way Finn politely but impatiently brushed off a stranger who wanted to gush about how romantic the wedding was and headed for the veranda of the beautiful old Kirribilli house where the reception was being held. He had one thing on his mind—to find that lovely woman before some other guy did.

Where was he? Natalia searched the throng of guests, the women wearing a rainbow of dresses, the men in shades of grey and black. No hot guy.

Eliza had ridden up the makeshift aisle on a pony, and a cluster of people had gathered to admire the little mare tethered under the shade cast by the late-afternoon shadow of a towering fig tree. Hot guy wasn't there either.

Natalia was five-foot-five in bare feet. Her stilettos gave her some height advantage over the crowd, but not enough to locate him.

She headed for the mansion where the meal was to be

served. Then climbed the short flight of wide, sandstone steps to a veranda that gave a view of the garden to the harbour beyond.

From her new vantage point she scanned the throng in the garden below. *Dignity, Natalia, dignity.* A princess did not chase after a man—no matter how devastatingly attractive she found him.

She rested her hands lightly on the veranda railing, so any onlooker would think she had paused to admire the view of the Opera House with its white sails on the opposite shore of the harbour. Then she tensed at the sudden awareness that tingled along her spine. All her senses seemed to scream an alert.

Him.

Slowly she turned around. The hot guy stood behind her, framed by the arched sandstone windows of the mansion. Just steps away he looked even more handsome than at first glance. Sculpted cheekbones, and his eyes... Not the dark brown she had expected but lighter—hazel, perhaps. A sensuous mouth that lifted in a half smile.

He held a flute of champagne in each hand, tiny bubbles floating rapidly upwards like the excitement rising in her. He stepped forward and offered her a glass. 'I snagged these from a waiter heading out to the garden.'

That voice! Deep, resonant, husky... The tone sent shivers through her. Her hands felt suddenly clammy with nerves. But it would be most un-princess-like behaviour to wipe them down the sides of her dress. She reached out for the flute, hoping it wouldn't slide out of her grip. The movement brought her closer to him, so close that she caught his scent—spicy, fresh, *male*—so potent it caused her pulse to quicken.

She wanted to close her eyes and breathe him in. Instead she took a breath to steady herself. 'Thank you,' she murmured.

'Most welcome. You're a friend of the groom?' he said.

How did he know that? Panic seized her voice, choking any possible reply.

'You were on the groom's side of the aisle,' he prompted.

'Yes. Yes, of course. Jake is a family friend.'

Tristan, Jake and Dominic had been friends for years, having met on the ski slopes of Montovia long before their Party Queens spouses had come along. Jake had been Tristan's best man at his wedding to Gemma.

But Natalia didn't want any questions about their connection. 'You, of course, were on the bride's side.'

'I went to university with Eliza. Since then I've done business with her party planning company.'

'I met her quite recently,' Natalia said.

Eliza had been one of Gemma's bridesmaids at her brother's spectacular wedding in the grand cathedral the previous year. Just the kind of wedding her parents intended for *her*. Dread squeezed her at the very thought. Marriage Montovian royal-style seemed more like a trap than a gateway to happy-ever-after.

'Eliza's lovely, and she seems so happy.'

'Yeah,' he said. 'And Jake's a good guy.'

Natalia had devised a cover story for her alter ego, but it didn't go very deep. Stalling, she gulped some champagne as she tried to keep the details straight in her mind.

Hot Guy seemed to have no such hesitation. He transferred his glass to his left hand and offered his right. 'Finn O'Neill,' he said, by way of introduction.

Natalie stared at him, spluttered over her champagne, and coughed. Then she quickly recovered herself. 'I'm sorry, I—'

'You were startled by my name? Don't worry. You're

not the first and I'd lay a hefty bet you won't be the last. Irish father; Chinese grandfather and Italian grandmother on my mother's side.'

So that was where those exotic good looks came from. 'No. I…er…' She started a polite fib, then thought better of it. To conceal her identity she was being forced to fib. No need to do so unnecessarily. 'Yes, I was surprised. Your name doesn't match your looks. Not like the Irish guys I've met, that is.'

'I'm a fine example of Australia's multicultural population,' he said lightly.

He was a fine example of a male.

Before she could dig herself in any further, she took his hand in a firm shake. 'Natalie Gerard,' she said. Natalie seemed a less memorable name than Natalia; Gerard was her father the King's name. She actually didn't *have* a surname—she was simply known as Natalia, Princess of Montovia.

'By the sound of your accent, you're English,' he said.

'Er…yes,' she said.

She didn't like to lie. But she'd promised her family not to blow her cover to anyone, in case of leaks to the media. Princess Heartbreaker in disguise at a wedding would be the kind of thing they liked to pounce on. So lie she must—though she'd rather think of it as tactical evasion.

Thank heaven for the English-born tutor married to a Montovian woman who had taught her perfectly accented English from the time she'd started to speak her first words. She also spoke impeccable German, French and Italian, with passable Spanish. So for today she would be English.

'Do you live here?' Finn asked.

She shook her head. 'Sadly I'm just visiting on vacation. I wish it were longer. Sydney is fabulous.'

'Spring is a good time to visit,' he said.

'Yes, it is,' she said. 'I'm loving it here.'

Just plain Natalie, a tourist, had spent the last three days riding the ferries, visiting the beaches, taking in a concert at the Opera House. She'd revelled in her freedom and anonymity—even though her two bodyguards were always at a discreet distance. As they were here now, masquerading as waiters.

Perhaps Finn had snagged the champagne from one of them. She was so used to the constant presence of household staff and bodyguards she scarcely noticed their presence.

'Where do you live in England?' Finn asked.

'London,' she said.

The royal family had a house in Mayfair, where she'd lived for a while when she was studying. Until the paparazzi had snapped her staggering out of a nightclub after one too many cocktails and she'd been recalled in disgrace to the palace before she'd been able to finish her degree in architecture.

'Whereabouts in London?' he said. 'I visit there quite often.'

No need to get too specific… Natalia chose to answer the second part of his question instead. 'What takes you to London?'

'My import/export business,' he said.

Which could, she thought, mean anything.

'What do *you* do?' he said.

Nothing she could share with him. Being Princess of Montovia was pretty much a full-time role. She wasn't allowed to be employed—rather had thrown herself into charity work.

Her main occupation was with the charity she'd started, which auctioned worn-once designer clothes and accessories donated by her and others in her circle to benefit her particular interest—the promotion of education for girls wherever they lived in the world.

Her online fashion parades and auctions had taken off way beyond anything she'd anticipated. Donations of fashion items now came from wealthy aristocrats and celebrities from all over Europe. Bids came from all around the world. The administration was undertaken by volunteers, so profits went straight to where they were needed. She was proud of what she had achieved through her own initiative. But that had nothing to do with Natalie Gerard.

The fact was, she'd been destined for a strategic marriage rather than a career. Especially after the tragic accident nearly three years ago that had robbed Montovia of her older brother Carl and his family, and pushed her up to second in line to the throne after Tristan, now Crown Prince.

Her life had changed radically after the tragedy, with her parents now obsessed with maintaining the succession to the throne. She'd had to work within their restrictions, not wanting to add to their intense grief in mourning their son and two-year-old grandson, still reeling from her own grief, not to mention the outpouring of grief throughout the country.

But she was beginning to weary of doing everything by the royal rules. She wanted her own life.

She couldn't share any of that with Finn. Instead she aimed for impartial chit-chat. 'I work in fashion,' she said.

That wasn't too much of a stretch of the truth. Organising her high-end fashion auctions *was* a job, if not a paid one.

'Retail or wholesale?'

'Retail.'

Her role often required several changes of formal clothing a day. That involved a lot of shopping in the fashion capitals of Europe. In fact, that had kicked off her idea for the auctions—she and other people in the public eye were expected by fashion-watchers to appear at functions in a different outfit each time. That meant expensive garments were often only worn once or twice.

'You fit the part.'

His eyes lit with admiration as he looked at her simple sheath dress in a deep rose-pink overlaid with lace. It wasn't silk, but it was a very good knock-off of a French designer whose couture originals took up considerable hanging space in her apartment-sized humidity-controlled closet back at the palace before they were moved on to auction.

'Thank you,' she said, inordinately pleased at the compliment. 'What do you import and export?' she asked, deflecting his attention from her.

'High-end foods and liquor,' he said. 'It takes me all around the world.'

She nodded. 'Hence your work with Party Queens?'

'Exactly,' he said.

She finished her champagne at the same time he did, then placed her glass on the wide veranda railing. Someone would be along to pick it up.

But Finn reached for it. 'I'll put that glass somewhere safer,' he said.

Mistake, she thought as he took the glasses and placed them on a table just inside the doorway. Regular girl Natalie would *not* be used to household staff picking up after her.

Finn was back within seconds. 'Tell me, Natalie, are you here with a partner?'

He glanced at the bare fingers of her left hand—without realising he did so, she thought. She did the same to him. No rings there either.

'No partner,' she said.

'Good,' he said, with a decisiveness that thrilled her. 'Either here at the wedding or in my life.'

'Me neither,' he said. 'Single. Never married.'

Her spine tingled at this less than subtle trumpeting of his single status. She was single and available too. For today.

Maybe for tonight.

'Likewise,' she said.

This handsome, handsome man must be thirtyish. How had such a catch evaded matrimony?

'D'you think they've put us at the singles table for the meal?' he asked.

'I have no idea,' she said. 'I…I hope so.'

'If they haven't I'll switch every place card in the room to make sure we're seated together.'

She laughed. 'Seriously?'

'Absolutely. Why wouldn't I want to sit with the most beautiful woman at the wedding?'

She laughed again. 'You flatter me.'

He was suddenly very serious. 'There's no flattery. I noticed you as soon as you walked across the grass to take your seat. I couldn't keep my eyes off you.'

She could act coy, not admit that she'd noticed him too, flirt a little, play hard to get… But she'd never met a man like him. Never felt that instant tug of attraction. And time was in very short supply.

'I noticed you too,' she said simply.

For a long moment she looked up into his eyes—up close a surprising sea-green—and he looked down into hers. His gaze was serious, intent, totally focused on her. The air between them shimmered with possibility. Her heart set up a furious beating. She felt giddy with the awareness that she could be on the edge of something momentous, something life-changing. He frowned as if puzzled. Did he feel it too?

'Natalie, I—'

But before he could say any more Gemma came up the steps, Tristan hovering solicitously behind her. Her sister-in-law smiled politely, as if Natalia were just another guest, although her eyes gleamed with the knowledge of their shared secret. Tristan's nod gave his sister a subtle warning. *Be careful.* As if she needed it. She was only too aware of her duty.

Duty. Duty. Duty. It had governed her life from the moment she was born. Duty to her family, to the Crown, to her country. What about her duty to *herself*? *Her* needs, *her* wants, *her* happiness? She was twenty-seven years old and she'd toed the line for too long. If she wanted to flirt with the most gorgeous man she had met in a long time— perhaps ever—she darn well would, and duty be damned.

She took a step closer to Finn. Smiled up at him as Tristan went past. The rigid set of her brother's shoulders was the only sign that he had noticed her provocative gesture. But Finn mistook her smile for amusement.

'I know,' he said. 'It isn't every day you go to a wedding where the groomsman is a prince and the bridesmaid a princess and everyone is pretending they're regular folk like you or me. That's despite the security detail both out on the road and down on the water to keep the media scrum at bay.'

'Bizarre, isn't it?' she said lightly.

In fact, it was rare that she went to a wedding where the bride and groom *weren't* royalty or high-ranking aristocracy. This wedding between people without rank was somewhat of a novelty.

'Bizarre, but kinda fun,' Finn said. 'When else would our paths cross so closely with royalty? Even if the Prince is from some obscure kingdom no one has ever heard of.'

Obscure? Natalia was about to huff in defence of her country. Montovia might be small, in both land mass and population, but it was wealthy, influential and punched above its weight on matters of state. But for today she was just plain Natalie—not Princess Natalia. And she wanted to enjoy the company of this very appealing Aussie guy without getting into any kind of debate that might give the game away.

'A prince is a prince, I guess, wherever he hails from,' she said.

'And a princess always adds a certain glamour to an occasion,' Finn said drily.

'Indeed,' she said.

A smile twitched at the corners of her mouth. *If only he knew.*

'Talking of fun…let's go inside and swap those place cards if we need to,' she said.

'Yes, ma'am,' he said.

Startled, she almost corrected him. *Ma'am* was a term of address reserved for her mother, the Queen, not her. But of course he was only using the word generically. She really had to stay on the alert if she were to successfully keep up the act.

She went to tuck her hand into his arm but decided against it. If she touched him—even the slightest touch— she wasn't sure how she'd react. She'd only known Finn O'Neill for a matter of minutes but she already knew she wanted him.

He could be the one.

population, but it was likely to be horrific that function above its usual quarters of state. But for today, she was just plain Natalie—not Princess Natalie. And she wanted to enjoy the company... the company of Aussie-boy without guards in a tidy kind of detail that might give the game away.

CHAPTER TWO

FINN FOLLOWED NATALIE along the veranda towards the ballroom of the sandstone mansion where the formal part of the wedding reception would shortly take place. He couldn't take his eyes off her shapely swaying hips. How could she walk so surely and confidently in those sky-high heels? Maybe it was the sexy shoes that gave her bottom that enticing little wiggle. Maybe—

She stopped abruptly, so that they collided.

'Sorry,' he said automatically. Although he wasn't sorry at all to be suddenly in such close proximity to this enchanting woman.

'No need to apologise,' she said, not moving away from him.

Her blue eyes glinted with mischief and her lush mouth tilted on the edge of laughter. He was close enough to catch her perfume...sweet, enticing and heady. She didn't seem in the slightest bit disconcerted by the sudden intimacy. Whereas he was overwhelmed by a rush of sensual awareness. He ached to be closer to her. *To kiss her.*

He took a step back from temptation, cleared his throat. 'Why did you stop?'

'I believe this is the room where the meal is to be served,' she said in a conspiratorial tone, gesturing to where wide French doors had been flung open to the veranda. She glanced furtively around her in an exaggerated dramatic way.

'Coast is clear,' he said, amused by her playfulness.

Drinks were still being served in the garden. They

had time before the other guests would flood into the ballroom.

He followed her as she tiptoed with dramatic exaggeration to the threshold of the room. Over her shoulder he could see circular tables set up for a formal meal, with a rectangular bridal party table up top. All elegantly decorated with the Party Queens trademark flair.

'No one in there,' Natalie whispered.

'Okay. Commence Operation Place Card Swap. We'll make a dash for it. You—'

She put her finger up against her lips. 'Shh… We have to be covert here. No bride likes her arrangements to be tampered with. We can't be caught. You go in—I'll guard the door.'

Finn found Natalie's place card first and filched it from its silver card holder. Then he searched for the place that had been assigned to him. As anticipated, he had not been seated anywhere near Natalie—four tables away, on the other side of the room, in fact.

Predictably, Eliza had placed him near Prue, a friend of hers from university, who was an attractive enough girl but who didn't interest him in the slightest—in spite of Eliza's matchmaking efforts. There was also the fact that Prue often played fast and loose with the truth, and if there was one thing Finn loathed it was a liar. Yet Eliza persisted.

That was the trouble with weddings. There was some kind of myth—promulgated by women—that a wedding was the perfect place to meet a life partner. Love being in the air and presumably contagious. As a result, weddings brought out their worst matchmaking instincts. As if, at the age of thirty-two, the combined efforts of his Italian, Chinese and Irish families to try and get him to settle down weren't enough, without his friends getting in on the act.

Marriage didn't interest him. Not now. He'd lost the urge when his first serious love had broken both their engagement and his heart. No one he'd met since had made him want to change his mind. Besides, he was in the midst of such a rapid expansion of his business, opening to exciting new markets, and he did not want the distraction of a serious relationship. International trade could be tumultuous. He had to be on top of his game.

He removed Prue's place card and deftly replaced it with the one that spelled out *Natalie Gerard*. Things were definitely looking up. Now he'd be sitting next to the only woman at the wedding who held any appeal for him. The only woman who had sparked his interest in a long time.

'I'll put this place card where yours came from and no one will be any the wiser,' he explained to his accomplice, who had now stepped cautiously into the room.

'Except Eliza,' Natalie said.

'Who I doubt will even notice the swap,' he said.

Natalie, for all her bravado, seemed unexpectedly hesitant. A slight frown creased her forehead. 'Is it really the right thing to do?'

'To sit next to me? Without a doubt.'

'I mean to mess up the seating plan.'

'A minor infringement of the wedding planner's rulebook,' he said.

'An infringement all the same. I...I usually play by the rules.' She averted her gaze, looked down at the pointy toes of her shoes.

'Perhaps it's time to live dangerously?' he said.

Her frown deepened. 'I'm not sure I know how to do that.'

'Live dangerously?'

She looked back up to face him. 'Yes,' she said uncertainly. The mischievous glint in her blue eyes had dimmed to something distressingly subdued.

'Then let me be your tutor.'

'In the art of living dangerously?' she said.

'Exactly,' he said.

She sighed. 'You can't imagine how tempting that sounds.'

The edge to her voice surprised him. 'Don't you ever give in to temptation?' he challenged.

Her smile returned, slow and thoughtful, with a sensuous twist of her lips. 'It depends who's doing the tempting.'

She was so tempting. Finn held up his hand. 'Consider the position of your tutor in Living Dangerously for Beginners to be officially filled,' he said.

She laughed, low and throaty. 'I hope you find me an apt student.'

He hoped so too.

'We'll start by finishing the place card swap. Why don't you do it? Your first "living dangerously" challenge.'

It would be a step towards others infinitely more interesting.

'That's not so dangerous,' she said, with a dismissive sweep of her perfectly manicured hand.

There was a touch of arrogance to her gesture that surprised and intrigued him. 'You think so? The sun is setting and I think I can hear people coming up the steps to the veranda. You'll have to be quick if you don't want to be caught in the act and bring down the wrath of the bride on your head.'

Any hint of haughtiness gone, Natalie made a sound somewhere between a squeal and a giggle that he found delightful. Without another word he held out Prue's place card.

Natalie snatched it from him. 'Mission accepted,' she said.

He watched as she quickly click-clacked on her high heels—hips swaying—to the table where she'd originally been seated and slid the card into place. When she returned she gave him a triumphant high five.

'Mission accomplished.'

'Well done. Now I won't have to find excuses all evening to visit you at your table.'

'And I won't need to take any opportunity to seek you out at yours.'

She coloured, high on her cheekbones, in a blush that seemed at odds with her provocative words.

'Would you have done that?' he asked. 'Seriously?'

'Of course,' she said. 'You are by far the most attractive man here.'

She seemed such an accomplished flirt, and yet her blush deepened and her eyelashes fluttered as she voiced the compliment.

'Thank you,' he said.

Considering the men of the bridal party were all good-looking billionaires—one a prince—Finn could only be flattered. And gratified that the instant attraction wasn't only on his side. He wasn't a fanciful man, but insinuating itself into his mind was a thought, wispy and insubstantial but growing in vigour, that this—*she*—was somehow meant to be.

'You know I intend to monopolise you all evening?'

'Monopolise me all you want,' she said slowly.

She was looking up at him with what he could only read as invitation, although there was an endearing uncertainty there too.

'You won't be able to escape me.'

'Do you see me running?' she murmured.

Her gaze met his for a long moment, and he wasn't sure of the message in those extraordinary blue eyes.

Then she smiled. 'Talking of escape—thank you for rescuing me from the table of people I don't know at all but who I suspect are Eliza's elderly relatives.'

'Don't speak too soon. We don't know who we've got sitting at my table.'

'Yes, we do,' she said.

He frowned. 'How did you—?'

She spoke over him. 'Each other. And that's all that counts.'

The words hung between them, seemingly escalating their flirtation to a higher and more exciting level of connection. Finn felt a buzz of excitement and anticipation.

'Quite right. Your first exercise in living dangerously has paid off. I don't care who else is on the table so long as your place card is still next to mine.'

Attending this wedding solo was more duty than pleasure, fond as he was of Eliza, and keen as he was to keep up his contact with Party Queens. But he wasn't one for wasting time on social chit-chat with strangers he might never see again.

An evening spent in the enchanting Natalie's company was a different matter altogether. Enjoying the pleasure of her company was now at the forefront of his mind.

Finn was about to tell her so, but there was a sudden burst of chatter from outside on the veranda. 'The other guests are starting to arrive. We shouldn't be seen in here.'

Natalia's eyes widened in alarm. 'We've got time to get out through that connecting door.'

He reached out his hand and pulled her towards him. 'Let's go before they realise we've been up to no good.

Then we'll march back in with the other guests and take our places at the table.'

'Innocent of any crime of swapping seats,' she said.

Not so innocent were his thoughts of where he hoped the evening might lead.

Natalie couldn't have borne it if she had been forced to sit on the other side of the room from Finn. She didn't want to waste a minute of this wedding away from him.

Tristan had probably had a hand in where she had been placed in the seating arrangements and might not be pleased at the switch. Too bad. Princess Natalia might have to sit dutifully where she was directed—not so just plain Natalie. She was going to grab this chance to be with Finn, no matter if she got dressed down for it later.

Tristan took his role of Crown Prince seriously. That meant protecting her. Since the loss of their brother, she and Tristan had looked out for each other. But sometimes she had to remind him that she didn't take kindly to being bossed around by her brother.

With Finn holding her hand, she made it safely out of the room without detection. Just the casual touch of his hand clasping hers sent shivers of anticipation through her. Never, ever had she felt this kind of thrill.

She was pleased when he didn't drop the connection after they'd made it to safety. Then, together, they strolled casually back into the ballroom alongside a group of other guests.

Each time she looked up to catch his eye she had to suppress a laugh, and saw that he did too. She felt like a naughty schoolgirl. Although in the private all-girls school she had attended there hadn't been anyone as handsome as Finn to get into mischief with.

Their surreptitious work had paid off—the swapped

name cards were still in place. Finn was hers for the duration of the celebration. She was scarcely able to believe
that this gorgeous man was real and seemed to want to be
with her as much as she did with him.

'We did it,' he said in a low undertone after they'd
taken their seats at the table. 'I caught Eliza glaring at
me, but there's nothing she can do about where we're sitting from where she is, way up there on the bridal table.'

'Clever us,' Natalia said, holding his gaze and revelling in the warmth of his smile.

So this is what it's like to be really attracted to a man.
Her thoughts were filled with nothing but him. *Insta
lust.* That was what her English-speaking friends called
the sudden overwhelming desire to be close to a man. But
it wasn't just a physical attraction. She liked Finn more
than she could have imagined she could like someone in
such a short space of time. Yes, she ached to touch him, to
feel his smooth olive skin under her fingers, and wondered
what it would be like to kiss him. But she also wanted to
talk with him, listen to him, laugh with him, find out all
she could about him.

She had never felt like this about a man before. Certainly never for any of the six men of noble birth she had
rejected as potential husbands. Not even for the boy she'd
had a crush on as a teenager in London.

It hadn't just been her being caught out at a nightclub
that had seen her recalled home to Montovia. She'd also
been seen kissing Danny—a fellow student definitely not
on the palace-approved list. It had hurt when she hadn't
heard from him again, and part of her heart had shut
down, never to recover. It hadn't been until much later
that she'd discovered he'd been paid off by the palace to
disappear from her life.

Her family's betrayal had added a whole new level of hurt.

Back then, the law that forbade her and her brothers from marrying someone not of noble birth had still been in place. She'd discovered they'd done the same thing to Tristan—paying off the parents of an English girl he'd loved and moving her to another part of the country. Tristan had been understandably bitter at their interference. Especially considering what a sham their parents' marriage was—the King still had a long-time mistress.

The history of unhappy, loveless marriages in their family had made both her and Tristan deeply cynical about marriage. Fortunately Tristan had found Gemma. For Natalia there had been no one.

On a trip to Africa the previous year, to visit a girls' school that her charity had funded, she had travelled with an attractive photographer. Sparks had flown between them—not the kind of powerful attraction she'd felt instantly for Finn, but sparks just the same. But he had made it clear he would never get involved with her. Not when he knew his life would come under scrutiny and he would have to play second fiddle to a princess. Natalia had appreciated his honesty but had felt wounded because she hadn't even been given a chance.

That had been back then. Now Natalia wanted to shut the rest of the world out, so it shrank to just her and Finn. She resented the time spent chatting with the other six guests at their table. But politeness dictated that she distributed her time evenly. All that royal training in graciousness and good manners didn't go away just because she was in disguise.

The other guests were all pleasant people from Eliza's pre-Party Queens life. Natalia made it a point to chat with each of them. Finn joined in too, charming and thoughtful in his conversation. The others seemed to assume she and Finn were a couple, and neither of them did anything to make them think any differently.

One of the women was Chinese, and Finn surprised Natalia by exchanging a few words with her in her own language. 'You sound fluent in Chinese,' Natalia said when he turned his attention back to her.

'Thankfully, yes,' he said. 'One of my biggest new export markets is mainland China,' he explained. 'It's a great advantage to be able to speak Mandarin.'

'I can imagine,' she said.

'My grandfather spoke to me in Chinese when I was a child and my mother insisted I study the language formally when I was older. I studied Italian to please my grandmother—also useful for the business. And my sister Bella studied both languages too.'

Natalia wanted to tell him she was also multilingual, even chat to him in Italian, but it was too risky in case she tripped up over the details of a made-up background. The less she said about herself, the better. Pretending to be someone else, denying the truth about herself, wasn't as easy as she'd thought. Not when she really wanted to impress Finn.

'Sounds like your grandparents were very influential in your life,' she said.

Hers had been too. Her late paternal grandfather had been King when she was a child and had ruled his family like a tyrant, although he'd been seen as a benevolent ruler of the country. She'd been terrified of him. Thankfully her mother and father, despite their differences and the restrictions of their royal duties, had been united in being loving parents to her and her brothers.

'My wonderful grandparents are both still around, fortunately,' Finn said. 'I have them to thank for my start in the business.'

Natalia hadn't mourned the death of her grandfather, and her grandmother had remained a distant, disapproving figure. She'd never known her mother's parents.

'Really?' she said, fascinated to know every detail of his life in the short time she had with him. Through him she could view life through a very different lens. 'I'd love to hear about it.'

'My grandfather and grandmother met each other in high school. It was like *Romeo and Juliet* set in the western suburbs of Sydney. His family owned the local Chinese restaurant—her family the Italian. Neither family was happy for their child to marry out of their culture—the old migrant story.'

Natalia leaned closer, sensing a real-life romance very different from her own family history of loveless arranged marriages. She was better off being single than being pushed into that kind of marriage—although to be fair to her parents, they had not pressured her, even when she'd said no to each of the unsuitable and unlovable six.

Anyway, how could you be sure of love? Her late brother Carl's marriage to Sylvie, the daughter of a duke, had supposedly been a 'love match'. Carl had been head over heels with her, and she'd seemed the same with him. But once she'd had her lavish wedding in the cathedral she'd proved to be greedy and avaricious, more in love with the wealth and status of being Crown Princess than with her husband. And there was no divorce for Montovian royalty. Make a bad choice and you were stuck with it for life.

'It must have been difficult for them if they had to defy their families,' she said.

'They say it only made them all the more determined

to be together,' said Finn. 'Once they were twenty-one they could marry without their families' consent and they did. Fortunately they were both passionate about food, and my grandparents ended up running both restaurants. Their parents imported authentic ingredients from Asia and Europe, supplying other restaurants too. My *nonna* was a canny businesswoman and she soon grew the import side of the business so that it eclipsed the actual restaurants and they sold them.'

'So where did you come in?'

'I inherited their interest in food. However, my family also had a passion for education. I did a business degree at university, but worked all my vacations in the business. I went full-time when I graduated. I soon saw the opportunities for export as well as import. My grandparents handed the business over to me and I expanded it way beyond its original parameters. They still have a stake in it, but they're enjoying their retirement. I take all the risks.'

'Didn't your parents and your sister feel they'd been passed over?'

The rules for inheritance were very strict in Montovia— for everyone, not just royals.

'Not at all. My mother is a pharmacist. My father has his own construction company. My sister works with him. Seems we like keeping things in the family.'

'Sounds like your family is very close.'

'Yeah. It is. But that's enough about me. What about you?'

'My family story isn't as interesting as yours,' she said.

Of course it was—an unbroken line of rulers stretching back hundreds of years—but she couldn't share that.

'Just ordinary, really. I have a brother.' It was too painful to mention her other brother, whom she had adored; his loss still cut too deeply. 'My parents take rather too much interest in my life—which is annoying, considering I'm twenty-seven—but I guess that's okay.'

'It would be worse if they didn't take an interest, wouldn't it?' he said with a smile.

'True,' she said, returning his smile and gazing into his green eyes for rather longer than was polite on a shared table.

Their heads had been bowed closely together, their voices low for the duration of the conversation. Reluctantly she broke her gaze away and returned her attention to the other people at the table, as good manners dictated.

A pleasant middle-aged couple sat opposite them—Eliza's neighbours. Natalia and Finn chatted with them about how much they were enjoying the meal.

Once the plates for the main course had been cleared, the woman—Kerry—sat back in her chair. Her narrow-eyed gaze went from Natalia to Finn and back again. 'So, is all the romance of this lovely wedding giving you two ideas?' she said.

'I beg your pardon?' said Natalia, completely taken aback.

'You and Finn. Any plans for a wedding of your own?'

Natalia wasn't often lost for a diplomatic reply to an unexpected question. But the Australian woman's blunt questioning had her floundering. She looked up to Finn for help, only to see him struggling too.

'No plans yet,' he finally choked out.

'You haven't popped the question?'

'No!' he said.

'How long have you been together?'

'We...er...we only just met,' Natalia said, flushing hot with embarrassment.

The woman frowned. 'Really? Forgive me. It's just that...'

'Just that what?' Natalia prompted, suddenly curious.

'I've been around a while, and I can usually tell a perfectly matched couple. You two look so right together.'

Natalia gasped. She didn't dare look at Finn, and was at a complete loss as to what to say. But Finn diplomatically came to the rescue.

'I think we're right together too,' he said smoothly. 'But it's very early days.'

Natalia wished she could sink through the floor.

The woman smiled. 'I see a wedding and I'm never wrong,' she said, before turning her attention to her husband, who'd been trying to shush her.

Mortified, Natalia kept her eyes on her plate.

'Don't worry about her,' Finn murmured in her ear. 'She seems harmless. Unfortunately I seem to attract matchmakers. Weddings bring out the worst in them.'

If he only knew the level of matchmaking that had gone on—and continued to go on—when it came to Princess Natalia of Montovia. Finn O'Neill from Sydney, Australia—a merchant—would seem, in the eyes of her parents and the royal court, like a very unsuitable match indeed.

She was glad when the speeches started and she was able to turn away from the odd woman and any talk of matchmaking and marriage to face the top table.

CHAPTER THREE

THE SPEECHES WERE over and the bride and groom were dancing their first dance together. All the guests had been invited on to the dance floor to share the bridal waltz. At last Finn had Natalie in his arms—if only as a dance partner.

There was something intimate about an old-fashioned waltz. With her hand on his shoulder, his arms around her waist, she was kissing-distance close, her flowery perfume already familiar but no less alluring. Her body so near to his was warm, soft, sensual, and her innate rhythm kept them perfectly in step.

'You dance very well,' she said.

'I tried to get out of lessons at school but there was no escape.'

'You learned to waltz at *school*?'

'Private boys' school. Ballroom dancing was seen as a social skill. But I only waltz at weddings.' He twirled her around the room until she was breathless and laughing. 'You're a good dancer yourself.'

'I also had lessons,' she said.

Finn noticed she didn't elaborate in any of her answers. Perhaps her life really had been ordinary, even dull, although he wondered how someone as poised and vivacious as Natalie could come from dullness. Maybe she hadn't had the same opportunities in life he had been fortunate enough to have. Or the truth might be that her life hadn't been very happy and she was reticent about reliving an unhappy past even in social conversation.

Sometimes he was guilty of taking for granted the happy

and supportive family life he enjoyed. This wedding—the happiness Eliza had found with Jake—had got him thinking. He wasn't as immune to wedding fever as he'd thought. Now, at the age of thirty-two, perhaps he did need to shake himself up, settle down and start a family of his own.

His *nonna* certainly thought that was the case. His broken engagement was ten years behind him—he could not in all reason continue to blame it for his aversion to marriage. He had to name it for what it was: an excuse—one he used to convince himself as well as others. The truth was that he hadn't met the right woman. Not one he could contemplate sharing his life with. When he did, he would willingly make that walk down the aisle. But he wouldn't compromise. And it wouldn't be any time soon—not when the business took up all his energy and time.

Perhaps...

He couldn't let himself think there was any chance of Natalie being that woman. No matter what that crazy Kerry had said. No matter how he'd found himself agreeing with her that he and Natalie did feel right together. Not when Natalie was English. A tourist. Her home a twenty-two-hour plane ride away.

Long-distance dating had been a disaster with his former fiancée Chiara, the girl he'd met in Italy ten years back. Her level of treachery had left him bitter and broken.

The frequency of their phone calls had decreased. He'd been preoccupied with exams. But the day exams finished, on impulse he'd decided to make a surprise visit to Italy and booked a flight for the next day.

Chiara had been surprised, all right. Not only had she found herself another guy, she was pregnant. But she'd still hung on to Finn's engagement ring. He had vowed never, ever to try long-distance again. This—Natalie—was purely for the short term. He had to keep telling himself that.

'Those lessons paid off,' he said to Natalie now. 'You're very graceful.'

It felt as if they were dancing together in their own bubble of awareness. But the reality was that they were dancing alongside other guests. When would he be able to get her alone?

She looked up at him. 'That woman… Kerry. It was kind of weird, what she said.'

'Yes. But I wasn't lying when I agreed with her that something seems right about us being together.' He could hardly believe he was saying this to a woman he had only known for a matter of hours.

Her blue eyes widened. 'You meant that?'

'About the rightness? I feel it. Do you?'

Her forehead pleated in a frown. 'Yes. I…I think I do. But I don't understand—'

Finn felt a tap on his shoulder and turned to find a beaming Eliza and Jake cutting in on him and Natalie for their obligatory dances. He had no choice but to relinquish his intimate hold on the most gorgeous of women. He cursed under his breath that he hadn't got a chance to hear what Natalie had been about to say.

Reluctantly he let her go and watched Natalie waltz away with Jake, smiling up at him. A spasm of jealousy shuddered through him at the sight of his beautiful dance partner in the arms of another man—even though Jake was a newlywed husband who adored his new wife.

What was happening here?

He'd only just met Natalie. He hardly knew her. But he'd never felt such a connection with a woman—if that was what you called something so compelling. He'd dated. He'd had steady girlfriends. He'd been engaged. But none of those relationships had started with a lightning bolt from nowhere.

'Surely you can take your eyes off her for long enough to speak to me?' said Eliza drily as he danced with his friend the bride.

'What do you mean?' he blustered.

'You're mesmerised by Natalie. She's beautiful. Charming. I get it. But you need to back off from her, Finn. She's not for you.'

'This is about Prue, isn't it?' He gritted his teeth. 'How many times do I have to tell you I'm not interested?'

'Even so, it was rude of you to change those place cards. What on earth got into you to do such a thing?'

Eliza had always been an outspoken kind of friend.

He shrugged. 'Sorry.'

But he wasn't sorry at all, and Eliza's sigh told him she knew it.

'This can't end well. That's all I can say.'

In spite of himself, he felt a chill of foreboding. 'Are you telling me that Natalie has a criminal record or—?'

Eliza looked aghast. 'Of course not. Don't be ridiculous.'

'Is she after my money?' he joked.

Ever since that Sunday newspaper had included him in a list of the most eligible young millionaires he'd been plagued by women whose interest in him was purely mercenary. Which had made him even more cynical about relationships.

'I very much doubt it,' Eliza said. 'She's just not for you. You'll have to trust me on this.'

He snorted his disbelief. 'You're warning me off? In the meantime, your neighbour Kerry is suggesting I propose to Natalie because we seem so perfect together.'

'What?'

'Yeah. In fact she asked if we'd made wedding plans.'

'Really?' Eliza frowned. 'Kerry reckons she's psychic.

She… Well, she wouldn't say that if she didn't believe it was true.'

Finn rolled his eyes. 'Psychic? *Huh!* She seemed nice enough until she came out with *that* nonsense.'

'What's stranger still is that her predictions often come true. The first time she met Jake she told me I'd marry him. It seemed highly unlikely at the time.'

'Coincidence—a lucky guess,' Finn said dismissively.

'Superstitious nonsense?' Eliza said.

Finn agreed. The trouble was, he came from three cultures where superstitions were taken seriously. By the older generation, that was. Not by him. He was a facts and numbers man.

'But it was disconcerting,' he admitted.

'In this case she's got it wrong,' Eliza said. 'I'll say it again—back off from Natalie.'

'You're seriously warning me, Eliza?'

'As a friend. Yes.'

'And as a friend, I appreciate your concern—although I don't know where it's coming from. But I'd rather you wished me luck than tossed a bucket of cold water over me. Because I like Natalie and I'm going to continue to enjoy her company for the rest of the evening.' He kissed her on the cheek. 'Thank you for the dance. Again, congratulations to you and Jake. Now I'm going to march over there to your husband and claim my dance partner back.'

Natalia couldn't remember when she'd so enjoyed a man's company. Dancing with Finn, their steps perfectly matched, was magic. Chatting with him, laughing with him, deepened the spell.

But the enchanted evening was winding down. The bride and groom had left to a chorus of good wishes for their honeymoon and a long life together. Other guests were starting to disperse and the band had announced the last number for the evening.

Soon the big room would echo with emptiness. Her bodyguards would be discreetly waiting to escort her back to the harbour-side hotel where she was booked in under her Natalie Gerard name. She would never see Finn again. She felt plunged into gloom at the thought.

The last dance was a slow one and they danced it close together. She breathed in the scent of him, felt his warm breath ruffling her hair. All sorts of potential conversations were running through her head. But all she managed was to look up at him and stutter. 'I...I don't want the night to end.'

His green eyes met hers. 'Neither do I.'

Too many hopes and possibilities were trembling on her lips for her actually to articulate the words *I want to be with you*. But finally she managed to choke out an invitation of sorts—although not the one she really wanted to communicate.

'I'm staying at a lovely hotel. It has a very smart bar, open all hours. Would you like to come back for a drink? Or a coffee? Or...?' Her voice trailed away. She was articulate in five languages, yet she was stumbling on a simple offer to extend the evening with a drink in a bar.

He tilted her chin, so his gaze met hers. 'Yes—to whatever you're offering.'

'I have a car and driver booked,' she said. And there would be another car with the second bodyguard following.

'Cancel it. Let me drive you in my car,' he said.

For a moment she was tempted. There was nothing she would have liked better than to be alone with Finn in his car. But 'living dangerously' had its limitations. The helicopter accident that had claimed the lives of her brother, his wife and their toddler son had been an accident, not an assassination. But after such a tragedy, security for the remaining heirs had become an obsession with the royal family. She could not dismiss her bodyguards.

'I can't do that, I'm afraid,' she said. She held her breath. Would that be a deal-breaker for Finn? 'You would have to come in my car. Or we could go to the hotel separately and meet there.'

'I'll ride with you.' Did he, like her, not want to waste a moment of the limited time they had together?

She sighed her relief. 'Good. My driver is outside. I'll call him and tell him we'll have an extra passenger.'

Would Finn wonder why she should do that? Most hire car drivers wouldn't have to be notified of an extra passenger.

'I'll have to go back to the table and retrieve my handbag. My phone's in it,' she said.

'As long as you come straight back to me,' he said, in that deep husky voice.

'Count on it,' she said, thrilled by the look in his eyes.

She called her bodyguards and provided Finn's name. She knew they would immediately run a security check on him. Perhaps she was being foolish, but she felt sure nothing untoward would come up on the check. She scarcely knew him, but she felt she could trust him to be who he said he was. It was she who was twisting the truth about herself right out of shape.

'Ready to go?' Finn said when she returned to his side.

'The car will come around to the front to pick us up,' she said.

He put a possessive arm around her as they headed outside. She leaned into him, loving the closeness to his strength and warmth. Then felt bereft when she moved

away from him for the sake of appearances as they
reached the main doors.

The street level entrance to the grand old house was
bracketed by tall palm trees and large old-fashioned carriage lamps. Cars and taxis inched forward on the circular
driveway to pick up the departing wedding guests. Natalia
spotted the unobtrusive dark sedan driven by her bodyguard in the line-up. The other bodyguard wouldn't be far
away. Their orders were to be close by always.

She could not fault her parents for taking such good
care of her, even if it did seem irksome at times. The ter-
rible loss of her brother and his family—not just Carl, but
precious two-year-old Rudolph, whom they'd all adored,
and his mother Sylvie—had thrown them into despair.

Tristan had been forced to step up into a role he'd felt
ill-prepared for. Natalia had been thrust into being second
in line to the throne and her freedom had been severely
curtailed.

Becoming second in line to a throne after a sudden
death was a different matter altogether from being fourth
in line behind three male heirs. She'd gone from being
relatively independent to being cosseted. And the cam-
paign to get her married to someone suitable and bearing further heirs had been stepped up. She'd begun to feel
trapped—albeit in a golden cage—stifled, and more than
a touch rebellious. She'd been determined to get permission to leave Montovia and attend this wedding.

Much as she railed against the stepped-up security,
she could see the reasons why. But nothing was going to
stop her enjoying every minute available to her with Finn.

She followed him to take their places near the cluster
of guests waiting for their cars. Thankfully, Tristan and
Gemma were not among them to see her looking so cosy
with Finn. Her brother and his wife had left early because

Gemma hadn't been feeling well. On the dance floor, Natalia had done nothing to earn her brother's disapproval. That might not be the case by the time the evening was through.

It soon became obvious that they were going to have to wait a few minutes for her car. She didn't want to wait a second longer to be alone with Finn.

He seemed to feel the same. 'We don't have to get caught up in banal conversation about why the traffic is backed up,' he said. 'C'mon.'

Just a few steps took them away from the other guests until they stood shoulder to shoulder by the side of the portico, away from the lamps that lit the entrance, private in the shadow of a large camellia tree studded with luminous white blooms. Huge tubs of exotic flowering orchids hid them from general view—plants she would only see in a greenhouse back home. The air was rich with the scent of jasmine, romantic and intoxicating.

Everything about Australia was so different from her homeland of snow-capped mountains, vast lakes and the sharp scent of pine needles. And Finn was so different from any man she had ever met. Different in such an exciting way.

So far away from home she wasn't bound by the rules.

She shivered—not just because of a gust of cool, early spring air but because she felt a sudden nervousness about finally being alone with him and what she hoped that might lead to.

He turned to face her. 'Are you cold?'

'Just the breeze,' she said, wrapping her arms around herself, not wanting to betray how she was feeling about him.

Finn stepped closer, his gaze intent on her face. In the poorly lit gloom his eyes gleamed green. She forgot to shiver, almost forgot to breathe, seeing the expression in his eyes, the sensual set of his mouth. Her heart started thudding so erratically that surely he could hear it.

He gently disengaged her arms and held her hands by her side, his hands warm on her bare skin. For a long moment he looked into her eyes, and questions and answers were silently exchanged. Her lips parted in anticipation as he lowered his mouth to hers and she sighed with pleasure as he kissed her.

At last.

His mouth was warm and firm on hers in a kiss that was sure and demanding while gentle at the same time. Her eyes closed as she savoured the closeness of him and she kissed him back.

She was just getting into the rhythm of kisses given and returned when he broke the contact. She swallowed a whimper of dismay at the loss—she didn't want to sound needy.

'I've wanted to kiss you for hours,' he said, in that so-sexy deep voice.

'Me too,' she said. 'Kiss *you*, I mean. Please…please don't stop.'

He laughed, low and triumphant, and then kissed her again. His touch ignited the hunger for him that had been brewing since the moment she'd seen him. She'd been without a man in her life for a long time, but this wasn't just hunger for a man's touch—it was hunger for *him*, this man, Finn.

His tongue slid between her lips to meet hers. He let go of her hands to put his arms around her and draw her closer. She wound her arms around his neck and returned his kiss, loving the feel of his tongue, his lips, the taste of him. Starbursts of sensation seemed to ignite along every pleasure pathway.

He certainly knew how to kiss. And the fact that he was experienced was a point in his favour. She wanted a man who knew what he was doing.

Yes. Finn was the one. There was no doubt in her mind. Tonight, she wanted to lose her virginity to Finn.

CHAPTER FOUR

NATALIA COULD NOT get enough of Finn's kisses. *She could not get enough of Finn.* But did her kisses, so enthusiastically returned, betray her lack of experience? Could he guess at her untouched state?

The thoughts plagued her as the sound of her name being called—her fake name—made her reluctantly break away from his kiss to see that her car had reached the head of the line.

She had to take a moment to compose herself, and noticed with a secret thrill that Finn had to do the same. Then, with a gentlemanly hand on her elbow, he steered her to where the driver, cap firmly down to shield his face, held the door open for her.

She hoped the remaining guests waiting for their transport were too busy chatting among themselves to notice the signs of recent passionate kisses on an incognito princess slinking out from the shadows—her flushed face, her lack of lipstick, her tousled hair... Then she realised that because she was incognito no one would care. She was just another guest at a wedding.

The anonymity thrilled her.

Of course she'd been kissed before. Mostly by frogs, but also by a few genuine princes. But she'd never gone much further than kissing. Duty again. It was expected that a royal Montovian bride would be a virgin. Her marriage would be more about alliances and political strategy than passionate love. There had to be no doubt that any children born to the union were her husband's legitimate offspring.

The necessity for her to stay chaste until marriage had been drummed into her from the time she'd understood what it was all about. But she hadn't expected to still be a virgin at age twenty-seven. It was a situation she was beginning to find onerous. Most of her friends were married—mothers, even—while she was still wondering what it was like to make love with a man.

In the hours since she'd met Finn, she'd found herself even more curious.

She'd been expected to marry young to a suitable man of noble birth chosen for her by her parents. Her refusal to marry any of the palace-approved contenders had meant she had stayed single—and celibate—for far longer than might have been expected. She'd also had a full year in mourning for her brother, and had been uninterested in dating during those dark days.

In retrospect, it was fortunate that she hadn't allowed herself to be talked into marrying any of those 'suitable' men who'd proposed. Tristan had recently had the rules changed to allow Montovian royals to marry commoners, so he could marry Gemma, an Australian chef. The new rule hadn't really been tested, though, as Gemma had discovered a connection to British royalty. But Natalia was now, in theory, allowed to marry who she wanted.

However, the King and Queen were resisting that idea when it came to their daughter. The ace they held in their hand was that she had to get their permission to marry, whether the man was royal or not. So had Carl. As had Tristan. And Natalia knew they had a nerdy twenty-two-year-old duke lined up for her to meet when she got home. She'd promised to be nice to him, as the only other aristocrat on offer was his widowed uncle the Grand Duke, who'd just had a double hip replacement.

Now, she squirmed in her seat with the effort of keeping a discreet distance from Finn in the back seat of the car. She wanted more kisses. More caresses. *More Finn.* Her nipples tightened at the thought of it. And when he reached across the seat to take her hand in his she nearly jumped through the roof of the car at the sensual thrill that simple touch ignited.

There was another reason she was still a virgin at twenty-seven. She hadn't met anyone who had tempted her. If she had, she might have defied duty and lost her virginity before. But no man had aroused her desire.

Until now.

Finn prided himself on his ability to stay in control under any circumstance. He didn't permit himself to be distracted by emotion. His cool level-headedness in negotiation was one of the reasons he was so successful in business. Plus, he had an instinct to know when to take a strategic risk—perhaps honed by all those childhood games of mah-jong with his grandfather.

But the feelings that surged through him now, just holding hands with Natalie, had him stymied. He wanted her so badly he ached. As a rule, he was cautious about trusting strangers. He'd learned that in both his business and personal life. But in Natalie's case caution simply didn't come into it. He didn't know her, and yet he felt he knew all he needed to know.

However Eliza wouldn't have warned him off her without reason. Every instinct shouted that Natalie might not be telling him everything about herself. But he didn't care.

He just wanted her.

In the back seat of the limo it was all he could do to stay a respectable distance from her. Her fingers entwined with his was their only contact. Her dress had ridden up over her knees, despite her efforts to keep it modestly tugged down, treating him to an enticing glimpse of bare, slender thighs. When the driver took a corner sharply she slid closer, so her thigh nudged his. He had to invoke every ounce of restraint not to reach out and put his hand on her bare skin, push the skirt higher.

Lustful thoughts fogged his brain, but another insistent thought wound its way through the want and the need. *This woman was special.* It wasn't just about sex. She fascinated him. He hadn't believed the so-called psychic when she'd predicted a future for him and Natalie. Yet one crazy, unrestrained part of him wanted to.

It was all he could do not to pull her into his arms and take advantage of the privacy the back seat allowed. But he'd noticed Natalie's quick, nervous glances at their driver. The back seat was not private enough for her and he respected that. This had happened unexpectedly. He would let her lead the way. Whatever she was willing to give, he was willing to take.

He was surprised when the car pulled up in front of a five-star hotel in one of the best locations in the city—right on the edge of the harbour, situated between the icons of the Sydney Harbour Bridge and the Opera House. Somehow he had expected more modest accommodation—but then this limousine was hardly a budget ride ordered from an app.

It seemed the world of fashion was treating Natalie well. Which, to his relief, put paid to any lingering thought that she might be interested in what he had rather than who he was. As far as he knew, they were total strangers who had met by chance at a wedding. How could she know the extent of his wealth?

She thanked the driver graciously as the man held the door open for her. Then turned to wait for Finn to follow her out of the car. He nodded his thanks to the driver, but in truth he hardly noticed the guy. And he scarcely took in the elegant hotel entrance, the glass walls that looked directly through to the water, the uniformed doormen…

Natalie. She was the only sight that interested him and he could not keep his eyes off her.

She was flushed high on her cheekbones and her mouth, swollen from his kisses, was parted in an enigmatic half-smile. Her gaze was as focused on him as his was on her. Her eyes were the most extraordinary shade of iris-blue—he had only seen eyes like them before on one other person, although he couldn't for the life of him remember who it was.

Not that it mattered. Natalie's eyes were the only eyes that interested him. Ditto Natalie's face. Natalie's body. Natalie's soul. He wanted to discover more about her, to know what made her tick, nail down what it was about her that he found so extraordinarily appealing. He was tense, coiled—impatient to be alone with her. And not just for this evening. For the remainder of her stay in Sydney.

He could not let himself think beyond that, much as his thoughts strained to go there.

Gritting his teeth against his impatience, he followed her through the foyer of the hotel, all marble and glass and luxury appointments. 'So, what's it to be?' he asked, forcing himself to sound laid-back. 'The bar? Coffee?'

Her flush deepened and she looked down before she looked up. Natalie was a hot, sexy woman, and he suspected she would give as good as she got in bed. Yet there was a reticence in her that made her even more appealing.

He would enjoy peeling back the layers of her personality as much as he would enjoy peeling that pink dress from her body. It closed with a long zipper at the back— he'd done a recce on it when she had been kissing him so sensationally behind those pots of orchids.

'I thought, perhaps, my room,' she said. 'We could order room service. Whatever you want.'

He pulled her close enough to whisper in her ear. 'I don't want coffee. I only want you. Your room sounds like a great idea.'

Finn felt a shiver go through her. It wasn't the cold this time. With a rising sense of elation he realised her shiver was one of anticipation.

He was exalted by a feeling that had nothing to do with reason, rationality, common sense. Tonight might be the start of something that switched him to a different track. Despite the odds—and her living in another country—Natalie could become someone so much more than a time-stamped encounter at a wedding.

'Let's go, then,' she murmured as she slipped her hand into his.

They had the elevator to themselves. He only let her go long enough for her to tap the key card for her room number before he pulled her to him in a hungry, urgent kiss. With a murmur of need and pleasure that made his heart thud she kissed him back with equal urgency, looping her arms around his neck and drawing him closer.

Three walls and the ceiling of the elevator were mirrored, and he could see her reflection in all of them—sexy, vibrant Natalie, in her clinging pink dress, all curves and blonde hair tumbling untamed down her back.

He felt his life had been lived in black and white until she had flashed into it in a glorious kaleidoscope of glittering blue eyes and shiny red lips and the flash of diamonds from her earrings. He was enveloped by her as she pressed her curves against him, as he breathed in her heady scent—all his senses were invaded and overwhelmed by the urgency of his need for her.

When the elevator doors glided open they were both

momentarily stunned by the interruption. She broke the kiss, looked up at him from the circle of his arms, and started to laugh—a delightful sound that prompted a smile from him in response. He didn't let her go, rather walked her out of the elevator, mumbled a question about the direction of her room, and then kissed her again.

He joined in her laughter as they kissed and stumbled their way up the corridor. Alternating laughter with kisses, they staggered to her room—a spacious suite with glass doors to a balcony framing a view of the harbour and the night-lit Opera House. An enormous bed dominated the room.

They were finally alone, and their laughter faded, vanquished by kisses of increasing intensity, their breath coming in gasps and sighs.

'I…I haven't done this before,' Natalia murmured, somewhere between him caressing her through her dress and locating the pull of her zipper.

Hadn't taken a man back to her hotel room on such short acquaintance? Something about the edge of nervousness to her voice led him to believe her.

'You don't have to do anything you don't want to,' he said.

'Er… I—I haven't lived this dangerously, I mean,' she said, stuttering a little.

'Let me help you enjoy life on the edge,' he said, tugging on her zipper.

'You're still my tutor?'

'Always,' he said.

He pulled down the zipper, the sound of it echoing in the empty room, and started to push her dress off her shoulders, making each movement a caress. He kissed along the delicate hollows of her throat, across her shoulders, down towards the swell of her breasts.

She gasped with surprised pleasure. Then shrugged her shoulders to help him free her of her dress. It slid to the floor, where it pooled around her feet before she stepped out of it, leaving her in a lacy pink bra and panties. He drew in a breath of admiration and excitement. Her body was perfection—creamy skin, curves in the right places, long slender legs.

She went to kick off her stilettoes. 'Leave them,' he said, scarcely able to choke out the words. He had never seen a sexier, more beautiful sight than Natalie clad in just her underwear and her high-heeled shoes.

For Natalia, being stripped down to her underwear in front of a man was something new, but she found she wasn't nervous. Instinctively, she trusted Finn to guide her through this momentous journey. Besides, she was too caught up in the moment to worry about what might come next. Kissing Finn, she was overwhelmed by sensation, by the promise of his hard, muscular body intimately close to hers, the pleasure his clever hands and mouth were giving her.

Even his most fleeting touch ignited starbursts of sensation, made her throb in places she hadn't known could throb. She wanted more. So much more. *Finn.*

'We need to even the score here,' she murmured, impatient with the feel of his jacket against her exposed skin. She ached for skin on skin.

With hands that weren't quite steady she pushed aside his jacket. He took over, sliding his arms out of the sleeves, tossing the jacket without aim so that it fell discarded on the carpet. She went to unfasten his dress shirt and found not buttons but fiddly studs that presented a momentary setback. She fumbled through with a semblance of confidence—she didn't want him to guess this was the first time she'd undressed a man—then got the bow tie unfurled and discarded.

Silently Finn held up his hands and she saw that his sleeves fastened with cufflinks in the shape of tiny compasses—white gold with black stones she realised were black diamonds. No tossing *those* on the floor. She hastily placed them and the bow tie on the narrow table set along the wall, impatient to strip him of his shirt.

As she pushed his shirt off his shoulders and to the floor Natalia gasped. She had to quickly disguise her sudden intake of breath as a cough. Finn bare-chested was even more impressive than Finn fully clothed. Broad shoulders, sculpted arms, chest firmly defined, his belly flat and taut, with just a dusting of dark body hair. His olive skin was smooth and warm beneath her touch.

She took a step back to feast her eyes on him. 'You are the most beautiful man,' she murmured, scarcely able to get the words out with the quickening of her breath. She felt almost faint with desire.

'Beautiful?' he said, with a quirk of his dark brows. 'That's a word I'd apply to you, the most beautiful woman at the wedding. Now I have you all to myself.'

'A man can be beautiful, can't he? But I'll say handsome if you prefer. Though even handsome isn't enough to describe your…your perfection.'

'I'm blushing,' he said.

But he wasn't. He was smiling. And his eyes narrowed further with a look of intensity that let her know she was about to be kissed again. Eager for his touch, she parted her lips to welcome him, pressed herself closer to him, her softness against his strength.

When he cupped her breast in his hand she almost screamed with the pleasure of it. In turn, she explored him, his skin smooth and warm over hard muscles, his reaction letting her know he enjoyed what she was doing. She kissed a trail down his throat and he moaned his appreciation. His reaction excited her, taking her to heights she hadn't known existed.

There wasn't much clothing left between them, and as she felt Finn grasp the fastening of her bra she realised there soon wouldn't be even that. She plucked up the courage to find the fastening of his belt, with the aim of undoing it, but it wasn't as straightforward as she'd thought. It was impossible to concentrate on anything other than the sensations Finn was arousing in her.

Her legs were beginning to buckle beneath her from the intensity of her pleasure, the ache of anticipation. That big bed was beckoning.

She broke away from the kiss. Finn followed the direction of her gaze. 'Yes,' he said.

Effortlessly, he swept her up in his arms.

'You...you're going to carry me to the bed?'

She'd thought this kind of thing only happened in movies. The thrill was immeasurable. She couldn't wait to be initiated by Finn into the mysteries of making love.

'That's my intention,' he said. He paused. 'But first, protection.'

Protection? For a moment she didn't realise what he meant. Protection in case he dropped her? Then it dawned on her. She hadn't ever been in need of the kind of protection he meant.

She couldn't meet his gaze, rather looked out over his shoulder at the view of Sydney Harbour. 'I...er... I'm not protected.'

He groaned. 'I wasn't expecting... I don't have anything.'

'Then we can't—?'

'No. But no doubt the hotel stocks—'

'You…you mean order them from room service?' she said faintly.

'Or visit the concierge,' he said.

Natalia stilled in his arms as the full impact of what they were discussing hit her. *She couldn't do this.* What had seemed romantic, rebellious and rather racy suddenly seemed very, very foolish. There would be consequences if she flaunted the rules. Protection was called protection for a reason. Protection against pregnancy being one of them.

She was a royal princess. What if she got pregnant from a vacation fling—for that was all it could be with Finn. What if she were recognised? What if someone saw Finn go down to the concierge to buy protection and then go up to her room?

She wanted Finn. Wanted him so badly that for a moment there she'd almost been prepared to take the risk of saying yes to no protection. *But she couldn't have him.* Not like this.

Duty. Honour. Responsibility. *Doing the right thing.* They were values ingrained in her very being. How could she ever have thought she could evade them? She was the Princess of Montovia and as such she did not have flings. She might be pretending to be just an ordinary girl but she wasn't.

The rules and restrictions were there for a reason—and she had to live by them. Not play risky games. It might seem terribly old-fashioned, but that was the way it was in Montovia. She and Tristan and Gemma were working together to stretch the boundaries when it came to contemporary life—but they weren't there yet.

A sob rose up in her throat and she swallowed it. To make love with Finn was too much of a risk for her to take—no matter how much she wanted him. No matter how much she liked him. This wasn't the way to lose her virginity.

She remembered the security guards in the adjoining room. They would be aware she had invited a stranger to her room. They might very well be listening via some device to ensure she was safe. Nausea struck her at the thought of them hearing what she and Finn had been murmuring to each other. But even if they were not, a full report of her behaviour would go back to the King and Queen.

What if she didn't care? What if she decided to make love with Finn completely on her own terms? *And then never saw him again?* The answer—emotional agony. She wanted to lose her virginity with a man who would be part of her life for more than one night.

Finn still held her aloft in his arms. But she couldn't stay there. Not now.

She wiggled to be let down. Finn immediately released her and held her until she was steady on her feet.

'You okay?' he asked with a puzzled frown.

How could she have this kind of conversation while standing in only her bra and panties and a pair of high heels?

She took a deep breath in an effort to steady her racing pulse. 'Not really. No. I…er… About the protection… I… I…don't think we'll need it. We need to stop. You see, I—'

'This is moving too quickly for you?' His voice was gruff, but not unkind.

She nearly collapsed with gratitude at his understanding. For just plain Natalie, it had been going just fine. She ached for more, to discover what making love to Finn would be like—utterly, mind-blowingly wonderful, she suspected. But for Princess Natalia, this had gone too far already. She had stepped right out of bounds.

Mutely, she nodded. 'Er…yes,' she finally managed to choke out, wary of his reaction and unable to look at him, focusing on the toes of her stilettos instead.

She'd heard what men called women who led men on

and then said no and it wasn't pleasant. She was still throbbing with desire for him, and he must feel at least as frustrated as she was.

'It's not that I'm not enjoying this—I am, very much—but—'

He reached out to her, placed his fingers under her chin and tilted her face up so she was forced to look at him. 'It's too soon. I get that. I want you, but only if you're ready.'

No calling her a tease. No frustrated anger.

'I... I...' How could she explain when to do so would mean having to untangle the web of lies she'd woven since the moment she'd met him? 'As I said earlier, I haven't done this before.'

She hadn't done *any* of this before. She could only imagine how surprised he would be if she admitted to her virginity.

Finn stood there, unbearably handsome in just his trousers, the belt looped where she had attempted to tug it loose.

'No need to explain,' he said. 'You're worth the wait, Natalie.'

'Th...thank you. But you...you should probably go,' she said.

'If that's what you want,' he said.

He looked around for his clothes, so joyously removed by her in anticipation of what she now would never experience with him.

Mutely, she nodded. Suddenly self-conscious, she reached for the luxurious velour robe provided by the hotel and shrugged into it. She went to wrap it around her waist.

Finn watched her, his eyes half hooded in sensual awareness. 'No need to do that robe up. I like the view with it open so much better.'

'Oh...' she said, blushing. 'I'm glad. That...that you like the view, I mean.'

She took a step towards him. He took a step back.

'Don't tempt me, Natalie. I might not be as strong-minded if I have you too close.'

'Of course,' she said.

She really didn't know how to behave. This was all new territory for her.

'Have you been sailing on the harbour?' he asked as he put on his shirt.

She was taken aback by the sudden change of subject. Then she realised the effort it was taking for him to turn the conversation to something other than their thwarted sexual escapade.

'I've ridden the ferries,' she said. 'I took the Manly ferry all the way to Manly.'

He laughed. 'Not quite the same. How about I swing around here tomorrow and pick you up? I'll take you out on my yacht—we can have lunch on the water.'

'You have a yacht?' she asked, stalling.

She couldn't in all honesty accept his invitation. Yet to outright decline it would entwine her in a more knotted tangle of lies. She realised she was twisting her hands together, something she did when agitated, and forced herself to stop it.

'A very beautiful yacht.'

He shrugged on his jacket, swept up his bow tie and cufflinks and shoved them carelessly into his pocket. Such a shame to cover that expanse of splendid male body, she thought with fleeting sadness.

'The best place to see Sydney is from the water. You'd love it.'

She couldn't call herself a sailor, but there was nothing

she would like more than to be on a boat with Finn. If it were in any way possible she would jump at the chance.

'I'm sure I would,' she murmured.

'I'll see you at ten tomorrow morning,' he said. 'I'll call to confirm.'

'That would be nice,' she said.

It *would* be nice. But she would not be here at ten o'clock tomorrow morning.

She looked up at him. At his open shirt collar, his thick straight black hair dishevelled by her caresses, his handsome, handsome face, his intelligent, kind eyes…

'Finn, I'm sorry about tonight. How things ended. Or… or didn't end. I—'

'No apologies. No explanations. It moved too fast for you. We have tomorrow.'

'Er…yes.'

Tomorrow would come, but not for them.

He took her in his arms, kissed her swift and hard on the mouth. 'I wasn't keen on going to the wedding— I expected it to be insufferably boring. But it turned out to be anything but boring. Because of you.'

'The wedding was…magical. Because of *you*.'

She reached up to trace her fingers down his cheek to the corner of his mouth, frantic to store his face in her memory.

He caught her hand and kissed the centre of her palm. It was almost unbearably pleasurable.

'Tomorrow can be magical too. There's something very special about being out on the harbour. You'll see.'

'Yes…' she said, the word trailing away.

'I have to go, or I might be tempted to talk you out of your decision. Goodnight, Natalie,' he said, and turned towards the door.

'Wait.' She reached up, cradled his face in her hands. 'Thank you, Finn. Thank you for your patience with me.

Thank you for...for everything. The best thing I ever did was switch those place cards. I had the most wonderful time with you. More wonderful than you can imagine.'

She kissed him on his mouth, slow and lingering, for the last time.

'I...I don't know how to say goodbye,' she said, choking up.

'Then don't,' he said. *'Alla prossima*, as we say in Italian.'

'Until we meet again,' she translated.

'You speak Italian?' he said.

She nodded.

'There's so much I don't know about you,' he said slowly.

If only he knew just how much.

She would cry if he stayed any longer. Sob and beg him to stay, spill the truth about her deception, beg him to forgive her for her lies.

But she had sworn to her family to tell no one in Australia the truth of her identity. And the habits of duty and obedience were impossible to break. Especially with the fragile state her parents had been in since Carl's death.

'And me about you,' she murmured.

'We'll have to remedy that,' he said, looking down into her face, a slight frown creasing his brow as if he guessed that all might not be as it seemed.

She put up her hand in farewell. *'Ciao, bello,'* she murmured. *Farewell, beautiful man.*

'Ciao, bella,' he said. 'The most beautiful girl at the wedding.'

She smiled shakily. 'I don't know that the groom would agree.'

'It's what *I* think that counts,' he said. 'See you in the morning.'

He turned, opened the door and walked away, turning back once for a final smile.

Natalie watched him go until he disappeared around the corner of the corridor. Then she let the door slam loudly behind him in frustration and anger at herself— and to make it clear to her security guards that her visitor was not staying. Scandal averted.

Immediately she regretted letting him go. Realised she might have made the biggest mistake of her life.

She would never see Finn again.

When he got here tomorrow morning he would be informed at the desk that Ms Gerard had checked out. What the hotel wouldn't know—what Finn would never know—was that Princess Natalia of Montovia, along with her brother the Crown Prince and his wife the Crown Princess, had flown out of Sydney early in the morning on the royal family's private jet and headed home to their ancestral palace.

She dragged one foot in front of the other back into the room, now achingly empty of Finn's presence—but stopped when she noticed something glinting on the carpet. A cufflink. One white gold cufflink in the shape of a compass, its face picked out in tiny black diamonds. It must have slipped from his pocket.

She picked it up. Was it fanciful to think that it still felt warm from his body?

She held it to her heart and let the tears of regret and lost opportunity flow.

CHAPTER FIVE

Three months later. Royal palace of Montovia.

NATALIA DRESSED FOR dinner with her family almost automatically. She had her own private apartment within the palace, as did Tristan and Gemma. But she was expected to attend the regular receptions, rich with the trappings of royalty, in the state dining area, where the King and Queen entertained dignitaries both from Montovia and other countries.

Increasingly, Tristan, in his role as Crown Prince, invited people of strategic importance to their country, and also to the business interests he oversaw. Natalia hadn't requested an invitation for anyone since she'd got back from Australia. It seemed too much effort.

She slipped into a full-length gown in midnight-blue silk, embellished with embroidery and crystals, beautiful in its simplicity and perfect cut. She teamed it with elegant stilettos covered in silk dyed the same shade of blue and scattered with crystals. She fastened earrings glittering with sapphires and diamonds and a matching bracelet. But she took little joy in her outfit.

Since her return from Australia she'd had to invest in a new wardrobe as she'd dropped two dress sizes. To someone with her interest in fashion, and the almost unlimited budget of a princess, shopping should have been a delight. Not so.

She was too down in the dumps to appreciate how lucky she was to be replenishing her wardrobe in the fashion capitals of Paris, Milan and London. Too un-motivated to appreciate what a boost her now too-large wardrobe would give to her next auction. Too darn exhausted to put 100 per cent into working alongside Tristan in promoting Montovia's export business—something she'd wanted to do for ages. Too heartsore to engage in anything much but endless agonising about 'what might have been' with Finn.

To her friends who asked about her weight loss secret, what diet she'd followed to get so skinny so fast, she had no reply. Not an honest one anyway. She had sworn to keep her incognito visit to Sydney a secret. That meant she couldn't confide in anyone the exhilaration of being Natalie Gerard, or the consequent deep dip in her spirits since she'd returned home.

Gemma knew about the trip, of course, but she couldn't talk to her either, because that would mean confiding in her sister-in-law the emotional rollercoaster of her time with Finn. The high of her powerful attraction to him, the shared laughter and the fun. The soaring excitement of his kisses and caresses. The plunge into misery as she'd watched Finn walk away.

No, the regret, self-recrimination and guilt were all hers to suffer on her own, often in the restless, sleepless hours after midnight. She had not wanted to lose weight, but her 'diet secret' could be put down to loss of appetite, trouble sleeping and the thoughts of Finn that plagued her like a repeat cycle she couldn't switch off, making her feel on the edge of anxiety.

She had run away from the only man she had ever wanted. Over and over she had relived that scene in her hotel bedroom. Wondered again and again what it would have been like if she had let Finn carry her to that bed. Regretted more times than she could count that she hadn't gone all the way with him. Only to realise that if she had, how much worse leaving him would have been.

Or what if she hadn't left? Why hadn't she even entertained a plan of simply informing Tristan she would not be flying back in the royal jet but rather staying to enjoy a day's sailing on the harbour before going home on a commercial flight when she was ready.

Because she would have had to tell the truth about her identity.

She sighed as she gave a final smoothing to the back of her hair. Her day-to-day life was fulfilling, what with her charity duties and her work with Tristan. Although somehow, caught up in her grief over Carl and her parents' obsession with the line of succession, she had gone backwards in terms of personal freedom as she got older rather than moving forward. But that was her life right now, and she wasn't sure what she could do to break out of it.

Other than run away to Sydney and find Finn...

Now, she headed down in the elevator to the state rooms, weary at the thought of having to divide her time equally between the person on her right and the one on her left, making polite, diplomatic small talk that would advance the interests of her country.

When had the thrill gone out of such occasions? Had they ever been more than endless duty and obligation?

Mentally she chastised herself for such ungrateful thoughts—she led a life of unimaginable privilege and should be unquestioningly thankful that she had won the lottery of noble birth. But a nagging thought kept intruding—the happiest days of her life had been those when she'd roamed incognito around Sydney, her only real obligation being to hide her identity. The happiest hours of all were when she'd been with Finn.

It always came back to Finn.

Natalia pasted on her most regal smile. As both Princess and dutiful daughter, her role was to be gracious and charming to the guests while cocktails and canapés were served before a formal dinner. She chatted to both people she knew and people she didn't, switching from one language to another as required. She felt her parents' approving glances upon her. This was what she'd been trained for, but since her time in laidback Australia she sometimes felt like an outsider, looking in on the rituals that she had been part of since birth.

Her smile was beginning to feel forced by the time she caught sight of Tristan walking into the room, deep in conversation with another man in black tie. Good, her brother could take over some of the work they were meant to share. But as they moved closer she froze. His companion was tall, broad-shouldered, with thick black hair. Something about the way the man held himself caught her attention, and for a crazy, breath-stealing moment she thought it was Finn.

She gave herself a mental shake. *Don't be so ridiculous.*

Was her heart going to jolt every time she saw someone even vaguely resembling the Australian man she was unable to forget? She thought she saw Finn everywhere: getting out of a car on Bond Street in London, striding along the Rue du Faubourg Saint-Honoré in Paris, even on the streets of the Montovian business capital, St Pierre.

Of course it was never him—never the man she wanted. When they turned around they didn't resemble him at all and she felt deflated and embarrassed.

Finn had become an obsession.

And now her feverish imaginings had conjured up a phantom Finn, right here in the palace.

She headed towards Tristan, just to be sure. Tristan's companion, as if he'd sensed her gaze on him, turned around to face her.

Him!

Natalia had to grab on to the plinth of a nearby piece of priceless sculpture—irreplaceable if it wobbled and fell. She didn't care. She had to anchor herself or she might slide into a faint. She felt light-headed, dizzy, over-whelmed by a wave of sheer joy and exultation.

Finn. It was really him. There could be no mistaking his dark good looks.

Finn. Here in Montovia.

It was as if all her hopes and dreams of the last three months had materialised into six foot two of solid, hand-some Australian male. Had he discovered who she was? Come after her? Had he longed for her as she'd longed for him?

Panic tore through her like a whirlwind. What could she possibly say that would make sense after the way they had parted? She had treated him with unforgivable rudeness, leading him on, standing him up and then dis-appearing. She wanted to throw herself into his arms and thank him for seeking her out. Apologise. Beg his forgiveness. *Grovel.*

He looked over and caught her eye. She attempted a smile, but it was as if her mouth had had enough of smil-ing that evening and she could only manage something that was more grimace than grin. His expression in re-turn was polite, restrained—the kind of look she often saw on the faces of strangers in such a social situation, when commoners encountered royalty.

Her mouth went dry. All this angst for nothing.

He didn't recognise her.

* * *

Finn guessed the elegant dark-haired woman in the glamorous gown must be Tristan's sister, Princess Natalia. He was predisposed not to like her. Irrational, he knew, but the name was too uncomfortably close to the name of the girl who had so cruelly played him in Sydney and left him high and dry.

Tristan confirmed his guess as to the woman's identity. 'Come and meet my sister,' he said now, with an amused sideways glance that Finn did not understand.

'With pleasure,' Finn said, letting Tristan guide him across the room.

When he'd made fun of Eliza having a real-life prince at her wedding, he'd never imagined he would end up doing business with him. Or that he'd *like* the guy. He'd been briefly introduced to Tristan at the wedding, and then had been surprised to be contacted by him when Tristan was renegotiating the contract for the distribution of Montovia's renowned chocolate and cheeses into Australia, New Zealand and the Pacific region.

Finn had won the lucrative contract. He had also proposed to Tristan that he work with one of his other clients to develop a prestige Montovian chocolate liqueur. Tristan had been very taken with the idea and had invited Finn to visit his kingdom.

He'd flown in that morning via London, to the small town of Montovia, which took its name from the country. Stepping off the plane had been like stepping through a portal to a totally different world. The place was like something from a movie, where witches and wizards might suddenly appear. A fortified medieval castle was perched high on a mountainside above a lake, looking down on cobbled streets, gingerbread-style houses and the spire of an ancient cathedral. And now here he was, inside the grand stateroom of the glittering palace that Tristan and his family called home.

The Princess waited regally for them to approach—as, Finn supposed, a princess would. She was lovely—very slender, with dark hair twisted off her face in a severe up-do, as befitted the formality of the evening. She didn't smile, rather she looked serious, perhaps somewhat snotty. Again, he supposed that might be typical princess behaviour. But she did manage a tentative hint of a smile.

He frowned, chasing a memory. There was something familiar about her smile... But then the smile was gone, and so was his moment of fleeting recognition.

As he approached she held out her hand—pale, slender, with perfectly manicured nails. He hesitated. Was he meant to kiss it? Bow down before her? No. It appeared that a formal handshake was all that was required.

'My sister, the Princess Natalia,' Tristan said.

'Finn O'Neill,' Finn said in turn.

He took the Princess's hand in a firm grip and was surprised to find it trembled. How could she possibly be nervous? She must shake many strangers' hands on occasions like this.

Tristan briefly explained his business connection with Finn. 'You two might have already met,' he said, looking from one to the other.

Huh? No way would he have forgotten meeting a beautiful young princess. 'I don't believe so,' he said.

The Princess's long pause began to seem awkward. Did she speak English? Because he sure as hell didn't know a word of Montovian.

She cleared her throat, gave a little cough before finally she spoke. 'Hello, Finn,' she said. 'I...I'm as shocked to see you here as you must be to see me.'

Her English-accented voice was immediately familiar,

and plunged him back into a million memories of the enchantress back in Sydney who had made an utter fool of him. The woman who had bailed on him without a goodbye or any word of explanation.

He seethed at the mere thought of her. Maybe he really had fallen into a place populated by witches and warlocks, because *this* woman was claiming to be *that* woman and it could not possibly be true.

He decided to test her. 'Natalie Gerard?'

The Princess bit her bottom lip, avoided his gaze. 'There's actually no such person. But I called myself that when I was in Sydney. When…when we met at Eliza and Jake's wedding. I was incognito and in disguise.'

Finn stared at the woman who stood before him in the glittering dark dress. *This was not the person he had known in Sydney.* Natalie had long, thick blonde hair. Princess Natalia's hair was dark, almost black, and put up in that severe style. Natalie was curvaceous; Natalia was very slender. She wore an elegant, modest gown; the last time he'd seen Natalie she'd been wearing only her pink lace underwear.

Hell, Natalia was an uptight Montovian princess, who lived a life of immense privilege in a lavishly appointed palace. Natalie was a sexy, uninhibited English girl on vacation in Sydney, who had made him laugh and been out-and-out naughty. *This was crazy.*

And yet there was something hauntingly familiar about the expressions that flitted across her face.

'I don't believe you're Natalie. Are you her sister? Her cousin?'

This must be some kind of scam. Or real witchy stuff.

'No.' Princess Natalia's dark eyelashes fluttered and her lips curved in a tremulous smile, as if that was the most ridiculous of suggestions.

Natalie's smile.

The same curving of lush, beautifully shaped lips... the same perfect white teeth. Yet the smile seemed subdued, of lower wattage, not lit by the vivacity of Natalie. Finn looked closer, not caring that the intensity of his examination might breach some royal protocol. The eyes. Those beautiful iris-blue eyes.

He glanced back to Tristan. Not that he was in the habit of staring into another guy's eyes but, yes, they were the same blue, just a shade darker than his sister's. That was where he'd seen that colour before—when he'd been briefly introduced to Tristan at the wedding. Before the beautiful stranger across the aisle had captivated his attention.

'I really am Natalie,' the Princess said. 'We sat at the same table. We...we swapped the place cards.'

'You danced with my sister,' said Tristan. 'More than once.'

He'd done a whole lot more than dance with Natalie Gerard. But this woman? *He didn't know her.*

An older man in military uniform passing by caught Tristan's eye and he turned to acknowledge him. In the moment when Tristan was distracted, the Princess stepped closer.

'Don't you remember? You were my tutor in living dangerously,' she whispered.

Only Natalie could know that.

Finn reeled, shocked not just by the intimacy of her words but by her closeness, her floral scent—so achingly familiar that it jolted him with memories he had battled to suppress.

Tristan turned his attention back to them. The Princess rolled her eyes so only Finn could see and in a flash she was the mischievous Natalie he'd known.

What the hell...?

Natalie and Princess Natalia were like light and shade. Yet the more he looked at the Princess, the more he could see Natalie. Until they morphed into one and the same person. Was she a natural blonde or a natural brunette? Her deception sickened him.

He clenched his fists by his sides. 'I can't get my head around this. Why the disguise? Why the deception?'

'It was the only way I was allowed to go to Eliza and Jake's wedding and get a chance to see Sydney. If the media had known I was there, it might have deflected attention from the bride and groom.'

'Why would the media be so interested in *you*?'

She flushed. 'Because I—'

Tristan interjected. 'Because she is a beautiful European princess who isn't yet married. That's reason enough for their interest.'

'Did Eliza know who you were?' he asked. Then he answered his own question. 'Of course she does. She warned me off Natalie Gerard. Now I see why.'

Princess Natalia's eyebrows rose—they were black, Natalie's had been light brown. 'What did she say about me? Eliza and the other Party Queens were sworn to secrecy.'

'Eliza did not betray your trust,' he said, tight-lipped.

How right Eliza had been to try and steer him away from Natalie out of concern for him. That beautiful girl in the pink lace dress had been a liar and a fraud. And he'd been fool enough to have been taken in by her.

He cringed when he remembered how fascinated he had been by her. How genuine she had seemed. How achingly he'd wanted her. How he'd started to wonder if she could be more than a fling.

'My sister's escapade in Sydney must be kept a secret,'

Tristan said. 'No one must know about her time pretending to be a commoner.'

A commoner? Who used such terms in this day and age? A hereditary prince like Tristan, Finn thought grimly. And a hereditary princess like his sister. A woman who had made a game out of slumming it with the commoners in Sydney.

He was her dirty little secret.

'I would appreciate it if you kept that confidence now we are doing business together.'

Finn didn't miss the warning in the Crown Prince's words, or the appeal in the Princess's eyes. The Montovian deal was both lucrative and prestigious. He didn't want to jeopardise it.

'I won't spill any beans,' he said through gritted teeth.

This situation was utterly unreal. As if he was trapped in a dark spider's web.

'I appreciate your discretion,' said Tristan. 'I didn't make the connection with the man Natalia was dancing with and the owner of one of the biggest food import and export companies in Australia until I actually met you face to face.'

'Your sister looked very different then. I really didn't recognise her.'

He wanted to tell Tristan's duplicitous sister exactly what he thought of her. Which would hardly be appropriate, considering their surroundings. He took a breath to steady himself. Inhaled that exciting Natalie scent. Wanted to spit it out.

'My sister did a good job in keeping under the radar,' Tristan said.

'I was under strict orders not to let anyone know who I really was,' she said, with an undertone of pleading in her voice. 'There are three important rules a Montovian princess must follow: she must never attract attention for the wrong reason, never be the focus of critical press and never be seen to reflect badly on the throne.' She paused. 'Of course there are a whole lot of other rules too.'

'And by following those rules she enjoyed her vacation and avoided any scandal,' said Tristan, looking approvingly at his sister.

Tristan obviously had no clue that he and Natalie had done much more than chat and dance. Finn suspected that in Tristan's eyes her behaviour on the evening of the wedding would have been considered highly scandalous for a princess.

He remembered how passionate she had been. How intrigued he'd been by her. How gutted he'd been when he'd gone to the hotel the next morning to find she'd checked out and left no forwarding address. How furious.

She'd made a total fool of him. He wanted nothing to do with Natalie/Natalia. Yet his glance kept returning to her, and he was fascinated that this woman was the same one who had enchanted him in Sydney. She was, without a doubt, a mistress of disguise, totally without scruples—and a very good liar.

She looked up at him with those beautiful blue eyes that could lie and lie and lie. 'Finn, I'm sorry I wasn't honest with you. I had no choice.'

Everyone *always* had a choice whether to tell the truth or lie. He wanted to explain that to her. But in the interests of diplomacy and doing business with her family he could only nod tersely. Her behaviour had been unforgivable. The sooner he could turn on his heel and walk away from her, the better. That was if he was allowed to turn his back on her. He was a 'commoner' and she was royalty. Perhaps she expected him to walk backwards from her presence, bowing and scraping all the way.

No matter how lucrative the Montovian contract, he would never, ever agree to do that.

Tristan didn't seem aware of the tension between him and his sister. 'It is good that you two have reconnected,' he said. 'Because unfortunately an emergency calls me away from here tomorrow. Natalia, can I ask you, please, to stand in for me in my meetings with Finn?'

The Princess looked as disconcerted as Finn felt. 'What meetings?' she said.

'Tomorrow morning I have organised a meeting for Finn with our master chocolatier at the chocolate factory.'

'That's always a pleasure,' she said.

'And then a meeting with the Chocolate Makers' Association over lunch.'

She nodded. 'You will need to brief me on the agenda.'

Tristan turned to Finn. 'Natalia has her own interests, with her auctions and other charity work, but she also keeps her finger on the bigger picture of Montovia's trade interests, and works with me when required.'

What choice did Finn have but to agree? 'Fine by me,' he said.

'Natalia is also an expert on the castle and the old town. Natalia, could you please give Finn a tour of the castle in the morning and the points of interest in the town in the afternoon?'

'Of course,' she said.

Tristan gave a slight bow. 'I must attend to my other guests. I shall leave you to carry on your conversation. Finn will be our guest for three days. There will be other opportunities for us to introduce him to our beautiful country during that time.'

CHAPTER SIX

NATALIA HAD TO keep shooting glances at Finn to make sure he was real—actually here in Montovia, working with her brother, and now with her, to further her country's interests.

She wanted to reach up and touch him, to check he was indeed solid flesh and blood and not some hallucination she had conjured up out of her hopeless longing for him. But she didn't dare risk it—not a hand on his arm, not a finger trailed down the smooth olive skin of his cheek. She had seen Finn's eyes frost with cold disdain when he'd realised the truth of who she was, how she'd deceived him. Her touch would no longer be welcomed.

After Tristan had headed off towards another guest and left her alone with Finn, his expression didn't warm into anything less forbidding. Yet for all the shock of encountering him so unexpectedly, and his open hostility—for which she couldn't blame him—she felt an effervescent joy bubble through her. She'd thought she would never see him again anywhere but in her dreams. It was like some kind of magic that he was here, just touching distance away.

Finn. The strong attraction that had made every other man in the room—in the world—disappear from her awareness had not been dispersed by three months of absence. And now Tristan had delivered Finn back to her.

Soon they would be called to dinner. It was unlikely she would be seated near him. And there could be no mischievous swapping of place cards at a palace soirée.

She felt an urgent need to apologise, to explain, to try and salvage something of that memorable time with him in Sydney. But she did not want to be overheard.

'Finn,' she said in a low voice. 'I don't think we need an audience. Shall we move over to that corner of the room?'

He nodded and followed her away from the main body of guests towards the windows that looked over the lake, closed to the chilly November evening. It was only a few steps away but it gave them some breathing space without being so private that her tête-à-tête with a handsome man would give rise to gossip.

The heavy gold brocade curtains had been pulled back to give a dramatic view across the lake, with the full moon reflected in the dark water, gleaming on the permanent snow high on the jagged peaks of the mountains. Finn admired the view with what seemed like genuine appreciation. In other circumstances it would have been romantic.

But romance was, sadly, not on the agenda. This was more akin to a confrontation.

An uncomfortable silence fell between them. Finn was the first to break it. 'I keep telling myself there must be a rational explanation for your deception,' he said.

'Rational?' She took a deep intake of breath. 'There was nothing rational about how I felt about you,' she said in a voice that wasn't quite steady.

He frowned. 'What do you mean?'

'Meeting you in Sydney was so unexpected and...and wonderful. I had never felt like that about a man. I told you—you made the wedding magic for me. Logically, I should have said goodnight when the wedding wound up. But I simply couldn't bear to shake your hand and thank you for your company as I should have. I was desperate to cling on to every possible minute with you. But I had given my word not to reveal my identity to anyone.' She hesitated. 'Also, I wondered if you would treat me the same way if you knew who I really was.'

'That was my decision to make,' he said. 'You didn't give me the opportunity to make it. Yet you trusted others with the truth.'

'I didn't know you. I had to be cautious. You could have been a reporter for all I knew.'

But she had trusted him enough to want to make love with him. And had spent the last three months regretting that caution had kicked in.

'I trusted you to be who you said you were. But it was just a game to you.'

'No. It wasn't a game. I...I really liked you.'

But she hadn't been honest with him. *'Alla prossima,'* he had murmured, and she had translated, knowing it was a lie, that they would not meet again. Since then she had had plenty of opportunity to reflect on how he must have felt when he'd discovered she had gone without any explanation or goodbye.

She looked up at him, registered the shock he must have felt on seeing *her*, not the Natalie he had known. Maybe she had done too good a job on that disguise if he was having such difficulty reconciling the two aspects of her.

She tried to make all the regret she felt for treating him so thoughtlessly show in her eyes. 'Finn. I'm sorry for—'

His dark brows drew together. 'Sorry for what? Choose an option for your apology—you have several.'

He held up his left hand and ticked off her options finger by finger with his right hand. *Beautiful hands that had felt so good on her body.*

'Option one—lying so thoroughly about your identity. Option two—standing me up by disappearing off the face of the earth with no explanation. Option three—

making me go through that charade just now of guessing your identity.'

She swallowed hard against a lump of anguish. He thought so badly of her. 'I...I plead guilty to options one and two, but I'm innocent of option three,' she said. 'I expect you must be angry, but you can't pin that one on me.'

'Did you really not know I'd be here tonight? Or was that another game for the amusement of you and your brother?'

'I had absolutely no idea you would be here. Tristan had not informed me. I was so shocked I thought I was going to faint.'

His mouth twisted into a cynical line she hadn't seen before. 'You understand I might find it difficult to believe a word you say ever again?'

His words hit their target and she flushed. 'I get that,' she said. 'But I really didn't have a clue you would be here tonight—or indeed that Tristan was doing business with you. I don't know why he didn't tell me. Especially as he wants me to attend some of his meetings with our Montovian business people. I can only think he wanted to surprise me because he realised we'd met at the wedding.'

'He certainly surprised *me*,' he said, with a wry twist to his mouth.

'Me too—and I wish he'd told me. Although for me it was a pleasant surprise. I...I'm happy to see you again, Finn, in spite of the way it's happened.' She looked up at him, but his only response was a grudging nod. 'Possibly Tristan thought springing us on each other might be simpler than having to explain who I really was. Remember, he doesn't know about...about what happened after the wedding?'

'Perhaps,' he said—with, she thought, a slight thawing of his frosty demeanour.

'As Crown Prince and heir to the throne, Tristan is working hard to modernise the royal family and some of their really stuffy old ways of doing things. It's a big job and he's getting both Gemma and me involved in it. He's also become an active advocate for our country's exports. I wasn't trained in business, but I'm doing my best to help with the trade side of things.'

Finn frowned. '*He* was trained for it but not you, even as second in line to the throne?'

'It sounds very old fashioned, I know, but I was brought up to make a strategic marriage to a man of noble birth. Tristan studied law. My older brother studied economics. I was sent to a strict Swiss finishing school. However, once I'd graduated, with straight As in deportment and how to manage servants, I insisted I be allowed to follow my own interest and study architecture in London.'

'So there's no career in fashion?'

Again, there was that cynical edge to his voice. Again, she couldn't blame him.

'Well, not in the retail sense. However, I do work very hard on my fashion auctions, so that isn't a total fib.'

'Fashion auctions?'

She was pleased to see genuine interest. 'You haven't heard of them? I don't suppose you would have. As Princess of Montovia, I'm the patron of several charities—including my own favourite, which works with an international foundation to support the education of girls in developing countries. Long story short: a lot of designer clothes and accessories are only worn once or twice by people like me and my privileged friends. As a fundraiser, I organised an online auction of donated items which was so successful it's become a regular thing and it's getting bigger and bigger. We get both donations and bids from all around the world. The charity has really benefitted, way beyond the scope of regular donations.'

'That sounds admirable,' he said.

'I'm proud of it,' she said.

'It seems you should be.' He paused, searched her face. 'I'm still struggling to make sense of you being a princess. For instance, what do I call you? Natalia? Princess? Your Highness? Is bended knee required?'

'Natalia is fine. Or Natalie would work too. I *am* Natalie, Finn. Or I was in Sydney, where I was *allowed* to be her.'

She couldn't keep the wistfulness from her voice. It had been a taste of a different life. A bright, flaming light interspersed between various shades of grey, with Finn being the most brilliant of flames.

'Natalie Gerard told me she was single. What about Princess Natalia?'

'Notorious for being single. In spite of a lifetime of grooming for wifedom.'

'Notorious?'

She sighed. 'Now that you know who I am, I'll save you the trouble of looking up media reports about the "Heartbreaker Princess", or the "Bachelor Princess". I make great copy for the European gossip magazines because I've rejected the proposals of six palace-approved men. Actually, seven now. I've knocked back another one since I got home from Australia.'

'Wait. You can't choose your own husband? He has to be approved?'

Put like that, no wonder he sounded incredulous.

'Until recently Montovian royalty could only marry spouses with noble blood.'

'No "commoners" allowed?' he said, using his fingers

to make quote marks and his voice to let her know just what he thought of the term.

She realised how insulting the word was. Another anachronism for her and Tristan to work on.

'That's right. But then Tristan used his considerable legal research skills to search the royal archives and discovered that any reigning King could amend that rule. My father was persuaded to change it—the restriction has not made for happy marriages in our family, including that of my parents—so Tristan could marry for love. As it turned out, Gemma discovered she was distantly related to both the English and the Danish royal families, so the change in rule was not needed. I remain somewhat of a test case.'

'So you're allowed to marry who you want to?'

'In theory, yes. In practice, my parents still want me to marry a well-born European aristocrat. In fact, they have to give their permission, whoever I might want to marry. I am, after all, second in line to the throne. You may not know that my older brother Carl was…was killed in a helicopter crash, along with his wife and two-year-old son.'

Her voice hitched. It was still so difficult to talk about the accident, even to acknowledge that it had happened. She didn't think she would ever get over the loss of the brother she'd adored, his precious little son Rudi, or poor Sylvie, too young to die. One day Carl had been there, acting the bossy big brother, and the next he'd been gone. She didn't think she'd ever be able to come to terms with it.

'I'm sorry. I did read about the tragedy in my research on Montovia.'

Natalia took a moment to collect herself. 'Everything changed. Losing Carl meant I moved up to second in line to the throne. And Tristan had been quite the party boy until then. He had to step up to the responsibility of being Crown Prince and the future King. My parents threw a cordon of protection around me. Suddenly it seemed as though I'd been thrown back to the nursery.'

'If that was the case, how were you allowed to swan around Sydney by yourself?'

She shrugged. 'I wasn't. I could pretend I had absolute freedom, but my bodyguards were always close to hand.'

His dark brows rose. 'Your bodyguards?'

She nodded. 'That waiter at the wedding who was hovering solicitously nearby?'

'I thought he fancied you.'

She shook her head. 'Just doing his job. As was the chauffeur of the hire car. Both Montovian bodyguards.'

Finn ran his ran through his hair. Natalia ached to smooth it down for him but didn't dare. She wasn't sure what kind of reception she'd get.

'And at your hotel?'

'They shared the adjoining room.'

Finn's disbelief and horror was to be expected. 'You mean they could hear what was going on in your room?'

'Probably.'

She couldn't meet his eyes. She had asked her bodyguards not to mention that she'd had a visitor to her hotel room. They liked her. She sometimes thought they felt sorry for her, for the restricted life she had to live in spite of her wealth and privilege. There had been no adverse reports back to her parents. As far as they had observed it had been entirely innocent.

He swore under his breath. 'It just gets worse.'

'What do you mean?'

'My recollection of that day is vastly different from yours. It's like we were operating on two different levels of reality.'

'I'm still *me*, Finn.'

He shook his head. 'I don't know you, Princess Natalia.' He made a credible attempt at a bow. 'I knew Natalie. I liked Natalie a lot. She was gorgeous and she was fun. Things moved fast with me and Natalie—until she put on the brakes. That was frustrating, but it was her prerogative. We arranged to meet the next day and I went away a happy man. Then I turned up at her hotel, to take her sailing as arranged. Only to find she had checked out very early that morning. She didn't leave me a message at the desk to explain. No. She just disappeared. Standing there in that lobby, when I realised I'd been stood up in a spectacular manner, wasn't my finest moment.'

She cringed at the pain on his face. 'I really am sorry, but I can explain—'

'Can you?' He shrugged. 'After I got over my annoyance—and I admit my intense disappointment—I figured Natalie was a tourist, looking for some no-strings fun. She ran out of time and ran out of town. I'd been played. I should have known better.'

She gasped. 'It really wasn't like that.'

But that was how it must have appeared...

'So, what's *your* version of events?'

She shifted from one stilettoed foot to the other. 'I...I couldn't bear to say goodbye for real. I was scared I would break down and spill the truth about myself. Which would have got me into big trouble. I know I'm twenty-seven years old, but my parents aren't just my parents. They're the King and Queen of my country and their word is law. Our private jet was there to take me home with Tristan and Gemma. I was obligated to go with them. I wanted to part on good terms with you. So I didn't tell you I was leaving. It...made it easier.'

She closed her eyes at the image of Finn asking at the hotel reception desk for her, only to be told she'd gone. How must he have felt?

'Your definition of parting on "good terms" seems to translate as leaving after lie had been piled upon lie.'

'Guilty as charged,' she said, feeling inexpressibly sad.

She couldn't tell him about all that had motivated her without giving away her entire story. She was still a virgin. Her situation hadn't changed. To make love with him would have come with risks and consequences that hadn't changed in the three months since she'd kissed him goodbye at the door of her hotel room. Maybe now she might take those risks on board if she got the chance, but maybe duty would still win out.

She realised she could apologise all she wanted for the Natalie Gerard deception, but he would never forget what she'd done.

He would never again believe a word she said.

He looked down into her face, as if searching it for the answers he might sense she wasn't giving.

'Loss of face is important to me. You made me look foolish. Not to mention gutted at losing Natalie, who had made quite an impact on me.' He paused, took a step back from her. His expression hardened. 'But what happened in Sydney wasn't really that significant. It wasn't even a day of my life—or yours, for that matter. You've apologised. I've put it behind me.'

'I see,' she said, feeling as though she had lost for ever something of immeasurable value.

She saw from the set of his jaw that Finn the businessman had taken over.

'That's as far as it goes,' he said. 'There's nothing in the contract I've signed with your brother that necessitates me spending extended time with you. The business meetings are necessary, but there's no need for the guided tour. I just want to finalise my business with Tristan and get the hell out of here.'

Mutely, she nodded. 'Of course,' she finally managed to choke out.

She looked up at him and recognised the marvellous man she had connected with in Sydney. *Finn.* Every moment she had spent with him was seared on her memory. But he looked at her and didn't see Natalie. He saw a stranger who had lied to him, who had made a fool of him. She had hurt him. And he didn't want anything further to do with her.

She was in a room filled with other people, and the murmur of conversation was rising and falling around her, yet she had never felt so alone.

Finn felt bad at the Princess's shocked expression. There was hurt there, too, in those beautiful blue eyes. But he could only get his head around this very odd situation he found himself plunged into by thinking of Natalia as someone he didn't know.

She wasn't the woman he had fallen for in Sydney. Not fallen *in love* with. Of course not. For one thing, he was not a believer in love at first sight—he'd confused infatuation with love with Chiara. But his meeting with the woman he'd known as Natalie Gerard had been something bigger than just a casual hook-up at a wedding.

The fact she lived in another country had been cause enough for him to put the brakes on. However, his time with her had come skidding to an abrupt halt before he'd even had a chance to think about the wisdom of taking things further. This woman—Princess Natalia—was absolutely out of bounds in too many ways to count.

It wasn't just that she lived on the other side of the world from him, hers was a world where he was considered a 'commoner', lacking in status or authority. How could trying to rekindle those Sydney feelings go anywhere? For him a serious relationship—one day perhaps marriage—was all about a partnership of equals, working together to enjoy life together and then, when the time was right, raising a family. Like his parents, his grandparents, his friends like Eliza and Jake.

The sooner he put Natalie/Natalia behind him, the better.

He followed her to the football-stadium-sized dining room, noting the sexy swing of her hips. The sway was not quite the same as the one he'd seen before from her alter ego, as the Princess was wearing a restrictive long gown, but it was every bit as enticing.

He was still having difficulty getting his head around the fact she was 100 per cent Natalie, but the sway when she walked was undeniably hers. The way she'd looked so different in Sydney was a kind of witchery, a modern sleight of hand, magic performed by hairdressers and make-up artists and a princess who was a mistress of the art of dissembling.

The grand Montovian royal dining room, with its soaring moulded ceilings, was decorated like a museum, with priceless antiques, masterpieces on the walls, crystal chandeliers and gleaming gold place settings. Very formal…very European. Wealth beyond the bounds of imagination.

He was not seated next to Natalia, for which he was thankful. He had no desire to revive memories of the last time they had shared a table. It hurt too much to remember how happy he'd been in her company.

Man, had that Kerry woman got her predictions wrong. Her so-called psychic powers hadn't picked up on a false identity.

Princess Natalia was seated on the opposite side of the table. Close enough so he could observe her, not close enough to talk to her. She was so elegant, so poised, her smile so charming. The lights picked up the diamonds glittering at her ears and her wrists. A real princess. Yet she seemed subdued—as if someone had dimmed the lights on Natalie to result in Natalia.

He noticed she pushed the food around on her plate with her fork, scarcely a bite reaching her mouth. It wasn't the fault of the food, which was superb. No wonder she was so slender. Natalie had had a hearty appetite.

He would go crazy if he kept comparing them.

His mind finally grasped the fact that Natalia was indeed Natalie, but she seemed like a diminished version of the woman he'd met in Sydney.

He was seated near Tristan, alongside his cousin Marco and his wife Amelie. Over dinner, they talked about their time in the Montovian military, where service was compulsory for all young people.

Tristan had served, despite his royal status, and Marco— a count and high-ranking officer—had met his doctor wife Amelie—a Montovian commoner—while deployed on a peace-keeping force in an African country. They had only been able to marry because of the change in law Tristan had brought about.

It was such a different world to the one Finn had experienced growing up. Again he had the sense that he had fallen into a movie set. Perhaps even a different century.

Just before dessert was to be served, Finn found himself in private conversation with Tristan.

'Natalia tells me you have politely turned down her services as tour guide,' Tristan said.

'Yes, I have to catch up on some work between meetings.' It was as polite an excuse as he'd been able to come up with on the spot.

'Would you consider changing your mind?' Tristan asked.

The guy was a prince and Finn was a guest in his palace. Was this a lightly veiled order?

'I suppose I could...' he said slowly, not certain where this would take him.

'I would appreciate it if you'd spend that extra time with her,' Tristan said. 'You see, we're worried about Natalia. All the family have expressed their concern.'

'Concern?'

Tristan sighed. 'She is not herself since she returned from Australia. Almost as if she has disengaged from her life in the palace. She does her duty—Natalia is nothing if not dutiful—but she's lacking in zest, showing no real enthusiasm for anything, except perhaps her auctions. That's not like her at all. You must have noticed how thin she has become? That is in spite of Gemma organising special meals to tempt her appetite.'

An unexpected terror struck Finn's heart. 'You think she's unwell?' He choked out the words.

Her lies, the deception, his loss of face—all seemed suddenly insignificant now he was faced with the possible loss of this woman who had moved him to the edge of both love and hate.

'Perhaps... I don't know. I can't ask her doctor. Even the Crown Prince can't do that. My sister is an independent person.'

'But how do you think spending more time with me would help?'

'It has struck me that the last time I saw my sister laugh was when she was dancing with you at Eliza's wedding in Sydney. Perhaps you can make her laugh again?'

CHAPTER SEVEN

FINN HAD ARRANGED to meet Natalia, via an exchange of stilted phone conversations, early the next morning at the high, locked wooden gate that opened on to some stone steps leading up to the external walkways and corridors of the castle. As he approached he could see she was already there, her back to him, looking out to the lake below.

She was dressed in sombre colours: dark grey trousers, black boots, a thick wool light-grey jacket, a silver-coloured scarf. Her dark hair swung straight and loose to skim her shoulders, gleaming in the mid-morning sunlight.

Against the backdrop of the towering walls of the castle, the vastness of the lake, she seemed fragile and alone, and Finn remembered Tristan's concern. He thought about his own realisation that she might be suffering from depression, and felt a surge of remorse at how harshly he'd spoken to her the previous day, when she had tried so hard to be honest with him.

She needed kindness and understanding, not condemnation. He needed to tell her that. Explain his perhaps over-the-top reaction to the startling news about her identity. Make his own apologies.

As he walked towards her his shoes crunched on the crushed stone pathway. 'Natalia!' he called.

Startled, she turned to face him.

Her first expression on catching sight of him was, to his immense surprise, delight—quickly covered by a schooled indifference. She was aloof, but not in the manner of a princess—rather in the manner of a woman who had been told that the passion she'd shared was of no importance, easily forgotten.

Inwardly, Finn cursed himself for his thoughtlessness. And his dishonesty. He hadn't meant a word of it. He'd used those words to hide his battered pride and hurt that she had walked out on him without notice.

'You called me Natalia,' she said, after he'd reached her and stood hand-shaking distance apart.

'Yes,' he said. 'There's no point in arguing over semantics. Natalia is your given name. Natalie is the anglicised version of your name. I have a Chinese name—Ming-tun—which only my grandfather uses. What I'm trying to say is the name doesn't matter. It's the person.'

'Thank you,' she said. 'I like Ming-tun. What does it mean?'

Her cheeks were flushed pink with the cold and her eyes shone blue. She was every bit as lovely as a brunette as she had been as a blonde.

'It means intelligent. My grandfather had high hopes.'

'Seems to me you've lived up to your name. He must be proud.'

'I've done my best,' he said.

But how intelligently had he dealt with the revelation of her real identity?

He had studied hard at school and at university because it had been expected of him. His immigrant grandparents and father set great store on a good education. But all he'd ever wanted to do was to dive head-first into the family business. Although without his degree perhaps he would not have been able to drive the business forward so successfully, so quickly.

She looked up at him, her head tilted to one side, blue eyes narrowed. 'What made you change your mind?'

'About your name? I decided it was pointless thinking

of you as two different people when Natalia and Natalie are one and the same.'

'I didn't mean that. I meant you being here this morning. Last night, you seemed so sure you didn't want me to show you around. You said that we would meet at the chocolate factory.'

It's because your family are concerned you're depressed and it shocked me.

Tristan hadn't exactly said that, but his concerns about Natalia had immediately raised flags for Finn. One of his mates in high school had had an undiagnosed depression that had ended in a funeral after he had taken his own life. Finn had beaten himself up for not having been there for his friend.

His school had insisted that the boy's classmates attend extensive counselling, and ever since he'd been alert for symptoms of depression in the people close to him. He'd been able to get help for them when he'd seen the signs. He'd recognised them in Tristan's description of Natalia.

'Why did I change my mind? Perhaps the fact I don't speak a word of Montovian?' It wasn't the world's best excuse but he decided to run with it. 'Your cousin Marco warned me that many of the townsfolk don't feel comfortable speaking English, even though they study it in school, and that Montovian is a language almost impossible for a foreigner to learn.'

'It *is* a difficult language,' she said. 'However, Gemma is becoming fluent in it so it can be mastered. But that doesn't really answer my question.'

He squirmed just a little under the gaze of those perceptive blue eyes. 'I guess it doesn't,' he said. 'Truth is, I realised I'd be crazy to knock back the services of a guide who's a member of the royal family, who must know so much about Montovia.'

'It's true we've been around for centuries,' she said drily.

'That's exactly my point,' he said.

'I appreciate your worthy explanation, Finn. But I suspect the real truth is that Tristan coerced you into it.'

'Not true.'

She raised her dark eyebrows. 'Really?'

'Well, possibly true. Not coerced. He asked me to reconsider. He's concerned about you. Thinks you're unhappy. He thought I might be able to cheer you up. That I seemed to have the touch.'

She smiled—a slow, curving smile that was a ghost of her usual dazzling smile but still very appealing, with a hint of sensuality. He realised that she was remembering, as he was, just how he had kept her entertained back in Sydney.

'Tristan has no idea about you and me at the wedding, does he?' she said.

'Not a clue,' he said. 'He and Gemma left before the end, I believe.'

'So he didn't see us kissing behind the orchids and no one reported it to him, either. Gemma has certainly never mentioned it.'

Memories of the incident flooded his mind. How wonderful she'd felt in his arms. Her scent. Her taste. How sensual and exciting her kisses had been.

How much he'd wanted her.

'We were discreet,' he said, his voice suddenly husky as he looked down into her face.

'Fortunately for us they were very big planters of orchids.'

As they shared the moment of complicity her lips parted without her seeming to realise they were doing it, or that it looked like an invitation to kiss her again.

'How could I forget?' he said, wrenching his gaze away from her lips. He knew she knew he wasn't talking about the orchids.

'If Tristan knew—if my father knew—that you had come back to my hotel room, you would be languishing in the dungeons right now.'

He wasn't sure if she was joking or not. Not in this movie set of a home of hers. 'You have dungeons?'

'They're not part of my guided tour, but, yes. Genuine dungeons—damp, dreary and complete with medieval instruments of torture.'

'Don't tell me—some of them are specifically designed for men who compromise the virtue of Montovian princesses?'

'Indeed,' she said, with a hint of that mischief he'd liked so much. 'Custom-made to fit the crime.'

'*Ouch.* Dancing with a princess in those days really meant living dangerously.'

He grimaced and she laughed.

He'd made her laugh.

It made him feel good to see her laugh.

'Don't worry too much,' she said. 'The torture chambers are intact but they haven't been used for a long, long time.'

'Still, it might be wise to keep Tristan in ignorance about the extent of our time together in Sydney,' he said.

'Yes. He obviously likes you and trusts you. I don't believe he'd want to torture you just to defend the honour of his sister.'

'I sincerely hope not, if we're to do business together. He saw that you enjoyed dancing with me—that's all he needs to know.' He paused, not sure how far he should go in case she clammed up. 'He tells me he hasn't noticed you enjoying yourself much since.'

All traces of laughter vanished. Her mouth set in a

tight, unapproachable, distinctly unkissable line. 'That's probably true.'

She went to turn away, and he sensed her closing up on him. 'Natalia…' He put a hand on her shoulder to turn her back to face him, then dropped it immediately when she complied.

There could be no more touching—even through the thickness of a coat. Not now he truly understood the situation. He was careful. They were not completely alone on these battlements. There was a party of gardeners in sight, and no doubt they'd encounter other people.

'Is Tristan right? *Are* you unhappy? I've noticed how different you are from your time in Sydney. It's not just the hair colour—which I like, by the way. But it's as if… as if your light has dimmed.'

'That could be because it's winter.' She didn't quite carry off the light-hearted retort.

'Perhaps…' he said. 'You've lost a lot of weight, too.'

'Isn't there an old saying that you can never be too rich or too thin?'

'If you want to be thin, that's okay. But you do seem different. Not as vivacious.'

She closed her eyes tight for a moment, as if to give herself time to think. Or to look back into her past.

'I wasn't happy before I went to Australia. My personal life didn't seem to be my own any more. Not since Carl died and everything changed. That's why I wanted so desperately to go there. To be anonymous. To maybe find what was missing.'

She sighed—a sad sound that struck at Finn's heart. He wanted to take her in his arms to comfort her, but thought better of it.

'You saw me at my best. I was riding a high. I loved the

independence and the freedom to be myself. Of course it all came crashing down around me when I got back home.'

'Did you seek any help to deal with that crash? Because—'

She put up her hand in an imperious gesture to stop him from going any further. 'I don't want you feeling sorry for me, Finn. Because there's nothing to be sorry about. And I don't need help.'

'I don't feel sorry for you at all. I'm just concerned.'

She took a deep breath. 'That's very sweet of you. But I can deal with my…my unhappiness.'

'In other words—"butt out, Finn"?'

'Exactly.'

Finn detected the wobble of her lower lip and realised she might not be as composed as she wanted him to believe.

'I know I'm the girl who has everything. And I'm not ungrateful. But I'm nearly twenty-eight and I don't have my own life. No career—though the auctions have become a real interest. No husband. No children. Everything is about duty and doing the right thing by others. Marrying for the sake of the succession—not for my own happiness.'

'Would your family honestly force you into marrying someone you didn't like?'

He'd been presented to her parents the night before— King Gerard and Queen Truda. They'd seemed more modern and approachable than he'd imagined.

'*Like* being the operative word. *Love* doesn't come into it—and I won't settle for less than love. Tristan and Gemma have set the standard. My own parents have a miserable marriage. My father wasn't allowed to marry his girlfriend—a girl from a good Montovian family but not good enough for a future king. He put off marriage for as long as he could so he could be with her. Then he had to marry my much younger mother. She thought she was marrying for love—until she was sadly disillusioned by finding out that my father had kept his real love as his mistress and still does to this day. After my mother bore my father a male "heir and a spare", and then me, she was free to do what she wanted so long as she fulfilled her ceremonial duties as Queen when required. She was discreet about the lovers she took. And I think my grandmother actually *hated* my grandfather. Theirs was another marriage of convenience. She subjugated her misery into worthy causes.'

'And you were expected to do the same?'

'Until Tristan had the law changed. Before that I just kept saying no.'

'That was brave of you.'

'It wasn't difficult as none of the men appealed in the slightest. I wouldn't even have answered their posts on a dating site, we had so little in common—not to mention a total lack of chemistry. There was only one man who tempted me. He was good-looking, fun, my own age… I thought we might be able to make a go of an arranged marriage. Until I realised the love of his life was his very handsome private secretary—a charming guy.'

'I'm sorry,' he said, not sure what else to say.

'I needed an escape. Australia seemed to offer it. The whole Natalie thing was an adventure and the freedom was exhilarating.' She dropped both her gaze and her voice, scuffed the pathway with the toe of her boot. 'And then there was you. I…I wasn't expecting you.'

'I wasn't expecting you either,' he said. 'But there you were.'

He remembered standing respectfully, watching the wedding ceremony, and then feeling compelled to turn towards the beautiful woman on the other side of the aisle. After that he'd been unable to think of anything but her.

'I…I'd never been so attracted to someone. I didn't know how to handle it,' she said.

'It *was* powerful. The attraction came from out of the blue for me too. And then we hit it off. You were such fun. It wasn't just about how beautiful you were—*are*—it was the way we seemed to click.'

She looked up at him again. 'It was a first for me.' Her eyes were clouded with bewilderment and loss. 'I'm truly sorry for the way it ended. No wonder you're angry with me.'

He hated to see her hurting. 'Natalia, please… You don't need to say sorry again. Last night I should have made it clear that I accepted your apology for the way you left. Now, even in the short time I've been here in your country, I've got a grasp on the restrictions of your royal life.'

'Thank you. It's difficult to understand if you don't see all this.' She waved her hand to encompass the palace, the castle, the lake and the town below.

'I can also see you were telling the truth when you said you had little control over the situation in Sydney—why you acted the way you did.'

'I had to do the right thing. It was agony, watching you walk away, knowing I would never see you again. I can't imagine you believed that at the time, but it's true. I pretended I was ill all the way home on the plane so I didn't have to talk to Gemma and Tristan.'

'I searched for you. But I—'

Just then a buzzer went off on her watch. Startled, Natalia looked down at it. 'Where did the time go? Our window of opportunity for sightseeing is rapidly shrinking. Soon we need to head out to the chocolate factory.'

He wanted to say that the only sight he wanted to see was her, but knew that would be both cheesy and inappropriate—although true. Despite all his resolve, he found himself falling under her spell again. Only this time he knew who she really was—and that the impediments to any kind of relationship between them were insurmountable.

The girl he'd known as Natalie had said she'd lived in England, and his first thought had been that long-distance couldn't work. But distance seemed nothing compared to the chains of obligation tying Natalia to her life as a royal. At least this time around he knew what he was dealing with.

'Right,' he said. 'Lead on.'

'We won't get much more done this morning than an introduction to the castle. Considering our limited time, I'll take you straight to the walkway on the battlement walls. It has an interesting history and an amazing view.'

'I like the sound of that,' he said.

She paused and eyeballed him. 'It can be cold up there on the battlements. I hope you're dressed warmly enough?'

'These are my northern hemisphere winter clothes,' he said.

He was dressed in the warm cashmere coat, hat and gloves that he only ever wore on his frequent trips to Europe. It never got cold enough in Sydney for them to be taken out of his wardrobe. He didn't think he could bear to live in a cold climate such as this.

The large wrought-iron bolt on the gate slid open easily. Finn could only imagine the army of staff it took to keep an ancient monument like this in such good order.

As if reading his mind, Natalia paused as she pushed open the gate. 'There's a full-time architect, an engineer, and an army of stonemasons and tradespeople responsible for keeping the castle standing and in such good order. Fact number one—some of these walls that seem so solid are actually stone shells on both sides, filled with rubble. They were designed to withstand contraction and expansion in extreme weather. Imagine—they knew to do that all those years ago.'

'Clever,' he said. 'And getting the stone up the sides of the mountain must have been quite a feat.'

'A system of levers and pulleys, we believe,' she said.

He followed her up several sets of steep, narrow steps, cut into the side of the mountain, until they emerged onto an external corridor that hugged the solid walls of the castle on one side and a high wall on the other.

'Fact number two—'

'You're a really experienced tour guide.'

She laughed. *Laugh number two.*

'Let's just say it's not the first time I've given a visitor a private tour. But this part of the castle is actually open to the public at certain times in the summer.'

'Okay, so hit me with the next fact.'

'The castle was built as a fortress in the eleventh century.'

He whistled. 'That old?'

'Even older. Fact number three—it was built on the ruins of a Roman *castellum*, which was like a watchtower. This was a strategic place for a fortress. The mountains behind form a formidable natural barrier. They were virtually unscalable—especially in winter. Standing on the battlements above us on the lake side they had a clear view of any approaching enemies.'

'You know a lot about it.' He was surprised by her passion for her subject.

'Is it surprising that growing up here I've developed an interest in architecture and a passion for history? Over the centuries the original fortress building was extended to give us the castle we see now.'

'You sound like you've memorised the guidebook,' he said.

'I actually wrote the guidebook,' she said. 'In four different languages.'

'I'm seriously impressed,' he said. 'So tell me more.'

'You're not bored?'

'I'm fascinated.' *As if he could be bored by anything she said.*

'If you're sure?'

He looked down into her face. 'I'm sure,' he said. He didn't intend to say anything further but could not resist adding, 'Sure I've never met a more fascinating woman.'

She blushed high on her cheekbones. 'Thank you.'

'I thought it when we first met and I think it now. I like the way you're so passionate about your heritage.'

'I always have been—ever since I was a child. And as I got older I spent quite a lot of time in the palace archives.'

He could imagine her as a studious little girl and the image was endearing.

'Tell me more about the castle.'

'Fact number four—the south wing, where the palace is, was built not so much as a show of strength but to display the wealth of the royal family.'

'Where wealth equals power of a different kind of strength?'

'Exactly.'

For a moment he might kid himself that she was just a guide, parroting facts from a preset script. But there was no escaping the fact that she was a high-ranking member of the royal family, and that its wealth and power still existed today. Her role brought with it privileges, but also restrictions.

He was beginning to realise what being second in line to the throne actually meant. What it might mean to *him*. If he wanted to see more of her he couldn't just call her and ask her to the movies.

He looked around him with awe. 'The castle is indeed ancient and imposing. To think what these walls must have witnessed over the years…'

'It's mind-boggling, isn't it? This is actually the oldest part of the castle. Let me show you something rather special.'

'The entire place is special,' he said.

'I never take it for granted,' she said. 'I love my home and I love my country. It's just that when I was in Sydney I began to wonder if that was enough.'

For a long moment they didn't speak. He looked into her face, trying to read her expression of thoughtful sadness. 'Is that part of your unhappiness?' he asked.

She flushed pinker. 'Yes. No. I really don't know.' She looked down at her watch again. 'But what I *do* know is that we're running out of time. Follow me.'

She stopped just before the path started to widen and put her hand reverently on the thick wall. 'This is what remains of the most heavily barricaded area of the fortress. Fact number five: those slits were where arrows were fired from.'

'No boiling oil dropped down from above?' One of the computer games he'd enjoyed as a teenager had used that particular device to destroy the enemy. He'd always thought it particularly gruesome.

'That too,' she said, very seriously.

Not just for computer games, then.

'And cannonballs came later.'

'Your ancestors must have been fierce and formidable. And there were the dungeons with the torture chambers too.'

'Exactly.'

They kept walking as the pathway followed the contour of the mountain. It opened up to a lookout comprising several high-arched windows set in a stone wall facing the lake.

'Those arched lookouts came much later than the barricades we just saw. It's always been a popular place.'

Finn stared in wonder at the magnificence of the view framed by the windows. It looked out on not just the vast lake but further, to the system of smaller lakes it adjoined and then the jagged snow-capped mountains reflected in their stillness. Down below, the town, with its cobbled streets, looked like a toy town. The slightest of breezes chased wisps of white cloud across the brilliant blue sky. He found it mind-blowing to think this was her home... her heritage.

'This view is famous,' she said. 'And it's a favourite for postcards. Now it's famous in the family too, for being the place where Tristan proposed to Gemma. You mustn't repeat that, of course,' she said, putting a warning finger to her lips.

'Another secret for me to keep?' he said.

He realised that the castle and the palace were not just ancient monuments to power and tenacity, the seat of a ruling family dating back centuries, but Natalia's home. And that there would be no place there for a boy from Sydney, no matter how wealthy he might be.

If only Natalia was who she had first appeared to be— an ordinary English girl who could choose what she wanted to do with her life. Someone with whom he could—if he so desired—contemplate a relationship of equals.

Instead he'd met a princess. A woman with loyalties and obligations to the monarchy of which she was part. And that, he suspected, would come before any personal relationship.

It would probably be wise of him to cut his ties with Montovia. Forget the contract with Tristan. Cancel his remaining meetings with the good burghers of the kingdom. Fly home and forget Princess Natalia.

Trouble was, he couldn't forget her. He hadn't forgotten her in the three months between meetings. Possibly he was under some kind of enchantment—he would believe anything in these mythical, medieval surroundings.

The buzzer on Natalia's watch sounded again—a twenty-first century intrusion. She was organised and efficient—something he appreciated.

'Does that mean the tour is over?' he asked.

'Just this part of it,' she said. 'Next on your schedule is our meeting with Franz Schmid, master chocolatier. Montovian chocolate is, as I'm sure you know, a luxury product.'

'The platinum standard of chocolate—that's how I hear it described. The world's best. And that is what interests me about it as a product for import...not just for Australia, but for new markets in Asia.'

'There are a number of chocolate producers in Montovia with whom you'll be dealing, but Franz's business is the largest. It is also very dear to our hearts, as when we were children and started to make official appearances with our parents the chocolate factory was our favourite. Be warned: the scent of chocolate is intoxicating—from the large pods that hold the beans to the pralines and the truffles made from the chocolate butter. And then, of course, there is the taste...'

The chocolate factory was set on the shores of the lake, some miles outside the old town. Behind the façade of a centuries-old stone farmhouse was a small modern factory devoted to the creation of superb chocolate. It was spotless, with the production team—mainly women—wearing white overalls, head-coverings and surgical masks. Although he didn't understand Montovian, Finn could sense the buzz of excitement from the factory floor because the Royal Princess was on the premises.

The chocolatier, Franz, was as jovial as Finn would have expected from someone whose passion was something as delicious as his chocolate. Finn asked lots of questions, as the more he knew about the product the better he could sell it. He wasn't disappointed in the chocolatier's replies about fair trade single-origin cocoa beans, and the use of cream from cows grazing on local pastures. All were part of the story.

Finn was impressed with Natalia's knowledge and business acumen. Had Tristan asked her to lead this meeting because he saw her as his future liaison? If so, he wasn't sure how he felt about it. He could never see her as just a business contact.

When they reached the end of the tour Natalia asked if she could show Finn a project she had developed with Franz. 'I'm hoping you can help expand the market for it,' she explained.

Curious, he agreed.

She took him to a display of chocolate bars in distinctive pink wrapping. 'It's a premium milk chocolate, studded with freeze-dried Montovian raspberries,' she said. 'Quite irresistible.'

'Princess Natalia designed the packaging—it's the Princess Bar,' said Franz.

'All profits go towards the promotion of girls' education,' she said. 'So, you see, the more we can sell around the world, the better for girls.'

Finn spoke to her in an undertone. 'You say you haven't got a career? I think the entrepreneurial talents you've applied to your fundraising proves otherwise.'

She beamed, and again he realised how happy it made him feel to see her smile.

CHAPTER EIGHT

NATALIA WASN'T SURE which she dreaded the most—the summons to her mother's office for a queenly reprimand, or the summons to her mother's private rooms in the Queen's apartment for a mother-daughter chat.

Not long after she'd returned from her lunch meeting with Finn and the Chocolate Makers' Association, she had been invited by her mother to what she'd hoped would be the second kind of meeting. As soon as she saw her mother she suspected it might evolve into one of the queenly reprimand kind.

Her Majesty, Queen Truda, patted the place next to her on a gilded and upholstered love seat. The valuable antique was placed in front of French doors that opened to a balcony and looked down to the rose garden below. The roses had finished their autumnal flush of flowers, and now just a few frostbitten blooms were hanging on to their stems.

Her mother kissed her on both cheeks. She was elegant, blonde and had had a considerable amount of subtle surgery to keep her looking ageless.

On Natalia's twenty-fifth birthday she had suggested that Natalia was at the right age to start some preventative cosmetic work, with injectables and fillers. She had hinted that her daughter might have already left it too late to arrest wrinkles.

Natalia had politely declined. Her mother had warned her that she might regret not getting started with work on her face as soon as possible, and Natalia had gritted her teeth in an effort not to give a caustic reply.

The Queen's eyes were the same colour blue as the eyes Natalia saw when she looked in the mirror. But no amount of cosmetic surgery could erase from them the underlying sadness of being married to a man who did not love her and of having lost her firstborn son and grandson.

Right now they were narrowed—as much as her mother was able to narrow her eyes because of her frequent muscle-freezing injections. Natalia had been expecting an interrogation since the reception the night before. She was not to be disappointed.

'The Australian. Finn O'Neill. Tristan's new business associate. I saw you spent quite some time alone with him last night.'

'Yes, Mother.'

'Any longer and it would have been inappropriate.'

'Yes, Mother.' She'd learned young to agree with her mother whenever possible.

'I saw the way you looked at him.'

'What do you mean?'

'He's a very good-looking young man.'

'Yes, he is.'

'Is he the man you danced with at the wedding in Sydney?'

There was no use fibbing, or even prevaricating. Her mother would have read the bodyguard's reports. 'Yes.'

'Do you want him? In your bed, I mean?'

'*What?* Mother!'

'Well?'

Again she couldn't lie. Her mother knew her too well. 'Yes.' She couldn't lie to herself any longer, either.

'You know you can't have him?'

'Why not?'

'Because he's not suitable as a husband and you're not allowed to take a lover until after you're safely married.'

Natalia gritted her teeth. '*Why* is he not suitable for a husband? Under the new law I'm not bound to marry a royal. Finn is educated, successful, wealthy,' she said. Not to mention great company and a sensational kisser.

'*Very* wealthy. And he's squeaky clean when it comes to his finances. No criminal record either. Not so much as a parking fine.'

'So where is your objection?'

'I can't see that your marriage to someone like Finn O'Neill could work. You—*we*—live a rarefied kind of life that people not born to it might find difficult to adapt to.'

'Gemma and Tristan are perfectly happy.'

'They're the exception—and Gemma has had some teething problems. Not the least of which is giving up her life in Australia. But, without being sexist or elitist about it, it's a rare man who is going to be happy having a wife who is far superior to him in social status.'

'Of course that's being sexist and elitist, Mother,' Natalia said, unable to let the comment go. 'Surely it would depend on the individual's attitude?'

'Or a princess could renounce her title and all that goes with it.'

Natalia gasped. 'What are you saying?'

'It's an option—although not a desirable one.' Her mother took both her hands in hers. 'We *are* talking theoretically here, aren't we, my darling?'

Natalia couldn't help a heartfelt sigh. 'Yes. Purely theoretically. There's nothing between me and Finn.'

Her mother attempted to raise her perfectly arched eyebrows. 'Nothing at all?'

Natalia sighed again. 'Okay, so I kissed him at the wedding. But that's as far as it went.'

'You're sure about that?'

'Very sure.'

'You know there are good reasons for a Montovian princess remaining chaste before her marriage? I rather like the way that British Princess put it: she "kept herself tidy".'

'I know,' Natalia said.

The words had been quoted at her before. But that British Princess had been nineteen at the time. She was twenty-seven, for heaven's sake.

'The cute young Duke... You're sure you don't want to see him again?'

'"Young" being the operative word, Mother. He's sweet, but he's only just started shaving. Besides, I suspect he's in love with his seventeen-year-old sister's best friend and is waiting for her to come of age. And, before you suggest it, I have absolutely *no* interest in meeting his uncle—the hip replacement High Duke.'

'Don't call him that. He's a very charming and cultivated man. Handsome too. He thinks you're way too young for him. Besides, he's a widower and not looking for a new wife. A discreet relationship with a mature woman closer to his age would be more appropriate.'

'Mother! *You* like him!'

'And he likes me. Who knows what might happen?'

Her mother deserved some happiness—although she was bound to her father until one of them died.

'I'm happy for you,' Natalia said.

The Queen's face softened. 'Above all, Natalia, I want you to be happy in your marriage.'

'Happy with a palace-approved man, you mean,' said Natalia. 'That's never going to work for me.'

'I want to give you the best chance to make it work,' said her mother. 'There's no divorce for the royal family, as you know.'

'I know,' Natalia said.

She could recite all the rules and regulations that governed their lives. So could her mother—who was trapped in a miserable marriage. Sometimes Natalia felt she should hate her father for what he had done to her lovely mother. But he and his mistress truly loved each other, and had done since they were teenagers. They should have been allowed to marry. It was one of the reasons her father had agreed to change the law.

'I see Tristan has included you in his business meetings with the Australian. Not his wisest move. Be careful. Try not to be alone with him. Don't encourage him.'

'Mother!'

'I mean it, my darling. Even if the law says you can marry him, I don't see how it could possibly work. Your differences are too great. And you can't have him as a lover. I don't want to see you heartbroken.'

'I don't know where this talk of marriage comes from. Certainly not from me. There is nothing between me and Finn. I hardly know him.'

Her mother's grip on her hands tightened. 'You might *say* that, my darling, but I saw the way you were looking at him last night. And the way he looked at you. Nip it in the bud. That's my advice to you as your mother and your Queen.'

An hour later Natalia sat with Finn in her favourite chocolate shop and tea room in the heart of the old town. It was ornate and old-fashioned and hadn't changed at all in her lifetime.

'The three of us loved coming here as kids,' she explained to Finn, who was opposite her at a small round table.

He looked around him at the array of premium Montovian chocolates, the displays of cakes and pastries, the splendid samovar. 'My sister and I would have thought we were in heaven.'

'We did too. Our parents were strict. And our nannies followed their rules to the letter. But a visit to this place was our special treat—a reward for good behaviour.' She paused. 'I miss my brother Carl most of all when I'm here. Carl was a chocoholic before we'd ever heard the word. He was always negotiating increases in our chocolate allowance. Never just for himself, though. Always for all three of us. He was a born leader.'

'Tristan had big shoes to fill?'

'Yes. And he's filling them remarkably well. Having Gemma as support has really helped him, I think. It was such a dark time for us when we lost Carl.'

'Did you have grief counselling to help you come to terms with his loss?'

'You sound like a counsellor yourself when you say that.'

'I just wondered. Sudden change… Unresolved grief… All could contribute to your unhappiness.' His gaze on her face was intense. 'I don't like seeing you unhappy.'

Just sitting here with him, close enough so she could reach over and touch him, was making her feel happier than she'd felt for a long time—three months, to be precise. 'I'm not as unhappy as I was.'

'Why is that?'

'Who could be unhappy sipping the best hot chocolate in the world?' *With you.*

On her trip to Australia she'd found what was missing in her life. A relationship with a man who excited her. *Finn.*

'Good point,' he said.

'Nip it in the bud,' her mother had commanded.

Natalia had no intention of doing any such thing. She had never met a man like Finn and she intended to spend as much time as she could with him. If there was a chance to be alone with him, she would grab it. If there was a chance for her to go through with her original plan to lose her virginity to him, she would. She had a plan.

Of course it remained to be seen if Finn wanted to be any part of it.

She looked down at her watch. 'I've got my tour guide hat on again. The sun sets by five, and I would like to show you around the old town and through the cathedral while it is still light. I don't want to rush you, though. The town is beautiful, and you'll want to be able to divert down a cobbled lane or into a market square if something interests you. Our clock tower dates back to the sixteenth century. When the clock strikes the hour, medieval figures appear in rotation to strike the bell. It's quite a tourist attraction.'

'Another one of your favourite things about your home?'

'It never fails to fascinate me.'

'I look forward to seeing it. We Australians are interested in old buildings because we don't have many of our own.'

'So that timing suits you?'

'Yes.'

'Then this evening you will dine in Tristan and Gemma's private apartment at the palace. It will be much less formal than the soirée last night. And it goes without saying that any food Gemma serves will be superlative.'

'Will you be there too?'

'Of course.'

Finn leaned over the table to be closer to her, so their heads nearly touched. He lowered his voice to barely above a whisper as there were curious onlookers at other tables in the tea room. 'Will there be a chance for us to spend time alone together?'

'Is that what you want?' She also kept her voice to a whisper.

'You bet I do.' Her heart leapt. 'What about you?'

'Oh, yes,' she said, perhaps too fervently. 'But I will have to work around a directive from the Queen that I must avoid being alone with you.'

He frowned. 'Why is that? Does she think I can't be trusted with you?'

'I believe she thinks it is me who can't be trusted with you.'

'What the hell—?' he said, forgetting to keep his voice down. 'I mean, what the hell…?' he whispered.

She laughed.

'Laugh number three,' he said.

'What do you mean by that?' she asked, puzzled.

'I'll explain later,' he said.

She drew back from the intimacy of their heads nearly touching, made a show of pulling out her phone and scrolling through it, then spoke in a normal tone of voice.

'Tomorrow, according to your timetable, Tristan has you scheduled for morning meetings in our administrative capital of St Pierre. Tristan will accompany you for those. On your return to the palace you will be placed once more in my hands.'

Finn gave a discreet, suggestive waggling of his eyebrows, with just a hint of a leer that made her smile. 'I like that idea very much,' he said.

'Me too,' she murmured, trying not to think about what she would like to do to him with her hands. 'There's a visit to an artisan cheese producer. Then I'd like to take you out of town to visit our family's mountain chalet. It's our ski chalet in winter, but we often don't get good falls until January. A visit at this time of year will give you a taste of traditional Montovian rural life and an opportunity to hike. If we're lucky, there might be a dusting of snow.'

'I like that idea very much,' he said. 'But how—?'

She leaned over the table again. 'I'm working on how we can spend time alone. Trust me.'

'Can I really trust you?' he whispered with a wicked grin.

'Oh, yes,' she said.

At that moment the middle-aged woman Natalia had been expecting arrived and headed towards their table. Finn immediately got up from his chair.

She greeted her guest briefly in Montovian and then switched to English for introductions. 'Finn O'Neill— Anneke Blair.'

They shook hands.

'Anneke, Finn is here from Australia on a brief business trip and I've been charged with showing him around.'

Finn gestured around the tea room. 'Natalia has brought me here to chocolate heaven. What an excellent idea.'

'It is indeed,' Anneke said with a big smile.

'Anneke is married to Henry, who is originally from Surrey in the UK. He has been my English tutor since I started to speak. Anneke also speaks excellent English, and she knows more about the old town, its stories and secrets than even I do. So she will be joining us for our tour.'

'Thank you, Anneke,' Finn said. 'I appreciate you taking the time to do so.'

Her mother could have no complaints about her inclusion of Anneke. It would divert the Queen's focus from her and Finn, and it would send her the message that Natalia was, once again, being the dutiful royal daughter.

But not for long. She had plans for the chalet. *Plans for Finn.*

CHAPTER NINE

SEATED AT TRISTAN'S very hospitable dining table that evening, Finn was able to relax for the first time since he'd arrived in Montovia. The reason? He and Natalia were the only guests. And, as Gemma and Tristan were in the know about Natalia's visit to Sydney for Eliza's wedding, that meant he didn't have to hide the fact that he had met her before his visit to the palace.

Of course the extent of the time he and Natalia had spent together was still a secret shared only between them. As far as the others were concerned Natalia had danced with Finn and some of the other guests before waving the bride and groom off on their honeymoon when the wedding had wound up. Then Natalia and Finn had gone their separate ways.

That they had done nothing of the sort was a deliciously private secret between them that bubbled under their conversation and heightened the awareness between them with every glance.

Natalia sat across the table from him. She looked regally beautiful in a deep ruby-coloured velvet dress with long, tight sleeves. Adorning the creamy skin revealed by the V-neckline was an antique pendant of pearls, diamonds and rubies—no doubt a priceless family heirloom. Her hair swung loose, one side fastened over her ear with a pearl-covered hairpin.

She looked every inch the Princess, but warm and approachable too. Was it his imagination or did she look a little happier since he'd been able to make her laugh? He'd now lost count of the number of times he'd enjoyed the sound of her laughter.

To call the Crown Prince's private quarters an 'apartment' was clearly an understatement. Over two levels, it was more like a mansion. However, in contrast to the other parts of the palace Finn had seen, the design was sleek and contemporary. Natalia had whispered to him that Tristan had had the apartment gutted and redesigned after he'd inherited the Crown Prince title from Carl, to eliminate sad memories of his beloved older brother's tenure.

Wherever Finn was in the palace he was aware of the immense wealth of this royal family. Even the guest suite where he was staying was luxurious. But tonight's dinner reminded him of an evening with friends at home. Gemma had even cooked most of the meal, although there was a maid to serve and clear up.

And Gemma was obviously delighting in having a fellow Australian to chat to. 'Did you really not recognise Natalia at the soirée last night?' she asked, looking from him to her sister-in-law.

'I honestly didn't,' said Finn. 'It came as a complete surprise to me that the girl who sat next to me at the wedding was a princess in disguise.'

It was good to be able to discuss, even superficially, what he'd bottled up for three months. The way Natalia had stood him up in Sydney had been too devastating for him to share with anyone.

'I thought she looked gorgeous as a blonde,' Gemma said. 'I reckon long blonde hair is your look, Nat.'

'Thank you, Gemma,' said Natalia, smiling. She and Gemma were clearly good friends. 'But it was way too much upkeep. I'm happy to be back to my natural colouring.'

'I like it too,' said Finn, careful to keep the compliment

discreet and respectful. She would look beautiful which-
ever way she did her hair.

'What would you have done if you'd *known* she was a
secret princess?' Gemma asked.

'Probably not have dared to speak to her, let alone
asked her to dance,' he said.

'And that would have been a shame,' Natalia said
lightly.

'Natalia tells me your business meetings have gone
well?' Tristan said.

'Very well,' said Finn. 'And I enjoyed my tours of the
castle and the old town.'

'Thank you, Finn,' Natalia said, doing a good job
of appearing not to show any personal interest in him.
'Tristan, that brings us to our schedule for tomorrow.
After Finn's visit to St Pierre with you, we have a visit
to our favourite artisan cheese producer scheduled. As
it's on the way to the chalet, I plan to take Finn up to the
chalet afterwards. That area is a great showcase for rural
Montovia without us having to go further afield.'

'You might be cutting it fine in terms of daylight,'
Tristan warned.

'You're right. And if it snows those roads could be
dangerous at night... I wonder if we should plan to stay
there overnight? I've invited Marco and Amelie for dinner and they're keen to stay over. Would you and Gemma
like to come too?'

'I'm afraid I can't,' said Gemma. 'Shame... I love the
chalet. However, I have other plans for tomorrow.'

'So do I,' said Tristan. 'But it sounds like a good idea.
It's like the land that time forgot up there.'

The whole place had that air about it, Finn thought.
Though he was discovering that—palaces, medieval castles and quaint towns aside—Montovia was a forward,

prosperous country, and highly successful as a financial centre.

'I'll inform the housekeeper at the chalet you'll be having guests for dinner and breakfast,' said Gemma.

'That's settled, then,' said Natalia, in a very business-like tone.

Finn didn't dare catch her eye. Clever princess. He had no doubt she'd concocted the visit to the chalet to give them some time alone together, without flagging up the fact that there might have been more to the way they'd met in Sydney.

'Well planned,' he whispered to her when he got the chance.

'Even better than swapping place cards,' she whispered back, straight faced.

The dinner had started early and ended early, as Gemma was tired. Natalia, taking her place as hostess, escorted Finn back to his room on the floor below. She didn't have to—he knew the way—but he welcomed the extra few minutes with her.

Perhaps there were security cameras about, or simply observant eyes, but she acted purely within the boundaries of her role. Until she leaned forward for just a second as she shook his hand goodnight and whispered, 'I can't wait until tomorrow.'

Finn didn't know where this thing between them could possibly go. But he was only in Montovia for another two days and he was going to grab any time he could with her without worrying about what might come next.

CHAPTER TEN

NATALIA'S ACQUAINTANCESHIP WITH full-blown insomnia had been well and truly renewed. Last night she'd hardly slept. Thoughts of Finn had relentlessly churned around and around in her mind, keeping her eyes wide open until way into the early hours.

Her obsession with Finn was almost adolescent—what was a twenty-seven-year-old woman doing, getting in such a tizz about a man she'd only known in total for a few days? For all that wedding guest psychic's predictions, and for all her mother the Queen's warnings, not a word about anything serious had passed between her and Finn. *But to her it was a very big deal.*

She had never felt like this about any man. She doubted she would ever feel it again.

The disaster of their parting in Sydney had been forgiven, if not forgotten. She needed to see if Finn saw the possibility of any kind of relationship blooming between them. This sneakily planned visit to the chalet might be the only chance she got.

He returned from his meetings in St Pierre at the agreed time. Natalia had been counting the moments until she saw him again—conscious of how limited they were. They met at the top of the circular palace driveway, which led to the road that twisted its way from the castle down the mountain to the town.

Finn had changed from his business suit and was appropriately rugged up in black jeans, a grey cashmere sweater and a smart charcoal quilted coat. He was as so-phisticated and stylish as any prince or duke, and a heck of a lot more handsome. Just looking at him sent shivers of want through her. But she forced herself to be profes-sional and impartial—as if she were simply dealing with a business contact.

'A four-by-four and a uniformed chauffeur,' he said. 'Interesting choice of transport.'

'The roads can be rough around the chalet. Ice and pos-sible snow can make them dangerous,' she said.

'Not quite what I expected for a princess-mobile.'

'The glass carriage and white horses won't cut it for today, I'm afraid,' she said, with a regretful shake of her head.

'I'm disappointed,' he said, with the grin that had the magic power to lift her spirits.

'But a princess doesn't drive herself around town,' she said. And then added as a murmured aside, 'And this way I get to sit in the back seat with you.'

Her heart was racing—not only at the thought of being alone with Finn but also at the audacity of her plan.

Being accompanied at the chalet by her cousin and his wife—both close friends who wanted to see her happy—might not be quite what her mother had in mind. But she'd had a lifetime of obedience. Her time in Sydney had made her see life with different eyes. Made her realise you had to grab opportunities when they were offered to you. You weren't always given a second chance. She fully intended to seize this one.

'Tell me about the chalet,' said Finn as he slid in next to her in the back seat. Close, but not too close.

He knew what was expected of him in public. But in private…? She shivered in anticipation.

'The chalet has nothing but happy memories for me.

It's high up on the mountain, above the snow line. The building started life as a farmhouse about three hundred and fifty years ago. It must have been a long way from civilisation then. In the old days the farmers were cut off from the town for most of the winter. Those remaining still live a traditional life.'

'I was beginning to think everything was ancient in your country until I saw St Pierre today. That's a very modern city.'

'Our country has one foot planted in the past and the other striding towards the future. I'm very proud of it.'

'And the chalet now?'

'My grandfather had it converted to make a private residence. It's rustic, traditional, built from stone and timber, with sloping roofs because of the snow. Humble in its own way. But the bathrooms are new and the heating has just been updated.'

'I wouldn't expect anything less from one of *your* family residences,' he said.

'Be warned—it's no palace. My grandfather used it as a hunting lodge and it still has that kind of décor.'

'I don't hunt,' he said.

'Neither do we. We only shoot animals with a camera. The land around the chalet is a conservation area now. Some of the animals that were hunted to the point of extinction are coming back. My brothers and I were able to run wild there like we were never able to at the palace—well, our version of running wild.'

'Do you use it for skiing?'

'The chalet is not near any commercial skiing areas. But we use it as a base for cross-country skiing. The trails are wonderful. Do you ski?'

'I like skiing. But I prefer sailing.'

'Er...of course,' she said.

Natalie hoped he wasn't remembering how she'd stood him up for their sailing date in Sydney. Then she wondered if he was a mind reader.

'Just a reminder—you don't need to say sorry again,' he said.

Compassionate. That was the word for the expression in his eyes. He now seemed to understand the challenges that came with the expectations of her privileged way of life, not just dismiss her as a 'poor little rich girl'.

She ached to reach over and take his hand. She knew it would not be wise, and yet some new rebelliousness wanted to draw his head down to hers for a kiss and do what any ordinary girl had every right to do but a princess of Montovia did not.

Instead, she shifted just a little farther away from him and forced herself to stick to the more sensible plan she had already put in place. Though his nearness, his scent, his warmth meant she was in a constant state of yearning for him.

What if he didn't feel anywhere near the same for her?

They had left behind the old town and the newer suburbs on its edge, flown through the cobblestoned villages, and were now steadily climbing the twisting roads up the mountain.

'Everywhere I look is a postcard,' said Finn. 'The land's still so green, with the colour from the trees holding the last of the autumn leaves, the black and white cows. Then there are the rustic houses and the stacks of chopped wood underneath, ready for the winter, the pumpkins piled in baskets. It's like it's all been posed for the camera.'

'Even the three tractors trundling down the middle of the road that we've had to overtake?'

'Even those,' he said with a smile. 'They were actually very smart tractors. Everything is so different from Australia—like a different world.'

'You must have seen a lot of the world for your business?'

'Yes—although I travelled first with my parents and grandparents, to visit family. Hong Kong, then Italy, Ireland later. I had a stake in all those countries—I belonged by blood. But even with our diverse background and urge to travel, we're an Australian family, through and through. Australia was good to my family. It will always be my country.'

'You're as patriotic as I am.' Somehow she hadn't thought of that. Hadn't factored in his own love of his country in her wild dreams about what might be.

'In my own way—as a citizen. As a ruler, you have a quite different relationship with your country. One I'm trying to get my head around. But I understand your connection to your family, because family is very important to me too.'

'Could you see yourself living anywhere other than Australia?' She held her breath for his answer.

'It's where I need to be. My business is based there... the Asian markets are the future for trade. I want to be part of that future.'

Natalia let out her breath on a slow sigh. 'I see.'

He turned to her. 'I had to give all that some thought when I was still at university.'

'What do you mean?'

'In my second year I spent my winter vacation in Italy.'

'Where it must have been summer?'

'Yes. I stayed in the town near Naples where my grandmother's family came from. I worked in a pizzeria, practised my Italian and met a girl. Her name was Chiara. I fell head over heels for her and she for me. I quit the pizzeria so I could spend all my time with her. Then I had to go back to Australia for uni.'

Natalia hated to think of him with another woman. It actually made her feel nauseous. She had to force her voice to sound light and neutral. 'A holiday romance?'

'It was more than that. We were engaged to be married. I thought it was for ever. I really tried to make that long-distance romance work. Once I even flew to Italy for a long weekend, so I could be with Chiara for her birthday.'

'I don't see a happy-ever-after ending to this story...' With a great effort of will, Natalia had managed to keep her voice at an even, conversational tone.

By contrast, Finn's tone darkened. 'Of course it ended. Now I can see it was inevitable. Then I was gutted. She didn't want to leave her family and friends. I had to finish my degree in Sydney. We were too young. Long story short: she met an Italian guy. She ended it with me quite brutally.'

'I'm sorry, Finn,' Natalia said—not sorry at all that he didn't get the girl, but sorry that the experience might have made him wary of long-distance relationships. 'What happened next?'

'From then on I've only dated women who live in Sydney,' he said, looking out of the window instead of at her. 'And I hold a very cynical view of love at first sight. I don't trust that it can work.'

So a girlfriend in Montovia was out of the question. Was that what he was trying to tell her? As for the 'love at first sight' comment—she wasn't sure what he meant by that either.

She decided not to try and second-guess him. Thankfully she could change the subject, as they had reached the small artisan cheesemaker who made some of the most prized cheeses in Montovia.

* * *

The cheesemaker's premises looked like yet another post-card view, Finn thought. The old stone buildings, the incredible green pastures, the mountains in the back-ground—all were breathtakingly picturesque. Natalia brought a flash of colour in a red coat and a soft pink beret and scarf that suited her brilliantly. He liked see-ing her in pink and red again rather than tones of grey.

'Before we go in, tell me again why we're here?' he asked Natalia.

'Matteo, the cheesemaker, prides himself on the qual-ity of his handmade, cave-aged product,' she said. 'His family had always made cheeses here, but on a very small scale for local consumption. The cheese became some-thing of a legend in Montovia and highly prized. There's a saying that good cheese makes milk immortal, and that truly applies here. Since Matteo took over he has grown the business, but still kept it on a small scale. His cheese commands top prices. He maintains exclusivity and that is one reason he doesn't want to export.'

'If he doesn't want to export, why am I seeing him?'

'For your interest,' she said. 'And so that if he ever changes his mind, he will remember you.'

'I follow your way of thinking,' he said, once again appreciating her and Tristan's business acumen.

He also appreciated the fact that the work Tristan did with the export of his country's products was not for per-sonal gain, but rather the promotion of Montovia.

'Although we do get a return in the form of taxes from successful businesses,' Natalia had shrewdly pointed out when he'd mentioned it.

Finn clicked immediately with Matteo—especially after they realised that while Finn's Montovian was non-existent, and Matteo's English basic, they both spoke fluent Italian, as did Natalia. He appreciated yet another side of Natalia as she spoke fluently in the language of his grandmother, complete with requisite hand gestures.

She would fit in with his family.

He shook his head to clear the thought. It was such an unlikely scenario.

Matteo took them through the process of making his cheeses. It started with milk from happy, stress-free cows, feeding on rich alpine pastures that included regional wild-flowers, and ended in cool subterranean cellars, their walls lined with ancient wooden shelving stacked with wheels of prized cheese in various stages of ageing.

Finn was fascinated by it. The cheesemaking he'd seen before had been on a much larger commercial scale. Here, tradition dictated every step. What was it Tristan had said about the land that time forgot? And Natalia was a part of that tradition, bound by customs that hardly seemed relevant to modern life. Yet like this cheese, prized for its tradition, her traditions had shaped the woman she was.

After farewells had been made, Finn headed with Natalia back to the four-by-four, carrying a wheel of Matteo's finest cheese to take to the chalet.

'I actually understand why Matteo doesn't want to lose the essence of his cheese by over-expanding, even though I would very much like to have his business,' he said.

'I liked seeing your passion for the cheese,' she said. 'I understand now why you're so successful in your business—you care.'

Finn saw immediately why Natalia loved the Montovian royal family's chalet. It might have started off as a humble, rustic farmhouse, but it was now every bit the luxurious mountain retreat, in a traditional style of carved timber and stone, leather and wool.

Finn was wealthy, and he came from a comfortably off family, but the extent of privilege enjoyed by the royal family was staggering. The chalet kept a year-round staff, whose brief was to have the place ready at any time for the family to use—which seemed wildly extravagant. Although at the same time, it kept practically a cavalry of staff in employment.

He needed to keep his mind open—not view Natalia's life burdened with his preconceived ideas of what a princess should be.

Natalia introduced Finn to the middle-aged grey-haired housekeeper Hanna, and her husband the caretaker, Bernard. Finn was surprised when she greeted them with warm hugs and rapid chattering in Montovian. The caretakers did not speak English.

'Hanna was one of our nannies when I was young,' Natalia explained when they were on their own, coats off, enjoying a hot drink.

She looked elegant again, in slim trousers and a cream cashmere turtle neck. The room was heated by a blazing log fire in the most enormous carved stone fireplace Finn had ever seen.

'Hanna was loyal to us, and we are loyal to her. She is considered to be—what's the English phrase?—a family retainer.'

Natalia's English was so fluent Finn was surprised at the occasional reminder that it was not her native tongue.

'Hanna seems a nice person,' he said.

'She's warm and kind. Often we were left here with just Hanna and Bernard to look after us. We trust them both implicitly.'

'I've been meaning to ask… No bodyguards for you in Montovia? Or have I just not noticed them?'

'The royal family is loved here. We feel safe in our own

homes, our own country. Common-sense precautions are taken, of course—particularly in crowds.' She looked up at him, a smile dancing on her lips. 'By the way, there are no security cameras here.'

Finn liked the emphasis she'd put on the absence of surveillance. He could hardly wait to have her to himself, even if only for a few minutes, with no thought of anyone observing them together. If things went his way, they would need their privacy...

Natalia had placed him in a comfortable guest room at the other end of the chalet from her room. Her cousin and his wife would stay in the room adjoining hers. Finn wished his room was closer to Natalia's. However, no doubt room placement had to follow protocols like everything else.

'I'm near my cousin and Amelie,' she'd explained. 'But you'll find them sympathetic to our need to spend some time together while never appearing to be on our own.'

'Why is that?' He had met Marco and Amelie at the soirée on his first evening, and had enjoyed their company.

'Until the law was changed they were unable to marry because Amelie was a commoner. They had to keep their relationship secret. I sometimes manoeuvred things so they could be together.'

'So they want to return the favour?' he said approvingly.

Much as he liked the Count and his doctor wife, the Countess, he still wished he had Natalia all to himself. His imagination played with the idea of kissing her, of peeling off her clothes on that densely fluffy rug in front of the log fire, seeing the flickering shadows from the flames playing on her creamy skin.

But then it seemed the staff would always be present, so that was a scenario that was unlikely ever to be played out.

Marco and Amelie arrived, greetings were exchanged, and it was decided that the four of them would go for a hike on the trails through the forest surrounding the house.

'The light is already starting to fade,' Natalia said. 'So we won't go too far from the chalet.'

Finn was eager to get outside after their time cooped up in the car, luxurious as it was. He also wanted to snatch any opportunity to be alone with Natalia. He was only too conscious of the hours ticking away towards the time for his departure from Montovia the following afternoon. There were things to be said, decisions to be made. Non-verbal communication too, of the more intimate kind.

The chalet was not far behind them when Marco said he thought he'd spotted red deer and wanted to peel off from the pathway. Amelie followed him. Not a word was spoken but the message was clear. They were getting away to give them space.

He was alone with Natalia. At last.

CHAPTER ELEVEN

AT LAST. FOR three long months Natalia had dreamed of being in Finn's arms again. Now they were alone. She was trembling with awareness and anticipation. There was every chance it might happen.

It *had* to happen. She would die if it didn't. Not literally—she had never had suicidal thoughts. But her soul had shrivelled that morning she had left Finn behind in Sydney. And in the following months she knew her family had been worried about her mental health.

She'd been worried about her mental health. So much so that she'd sought medical advice. She'd been unable to be completely honest, though—rather she had explained that she'd broken up with an unsuitable man and was unable to come to terms with it.

The doctor had diagnosed situational depression, caused by a traumatic event in her life, and Natalia had done her best to follow the advice given on how to alleviate her symptoms. But it hadn't been until she'd seen Finn again that the cloud had started to lift.

Her life was fulfilling in so many ways. It wasn't that she needed a man to take it to another level. She needed *Finn.* She hadn't known what was missing until she'd met him, lost him and then been fortunate enough to have him fall back into her life. Now she'd been given a second chance to be with him, to get to know him, to discover if what she thought she felt about him was real.

Worth breaking the rules real.

Now she stood facing him under the canopy of a thicket

of spruce trees against a chilly blue sky. The forest seemed
still and silent with expectation.

'Have they gone?' Finn asked.

Natalia nodded, too choked to utter a word. She looked
up at him, thrilled by the intensity of his expression, his
green eyes focused solely on her.

'Good,' he said.

He pulled her into his arms.

At last. Her heart sang.

She was wearing gloves, and so was he, but even
through the layers of both their padded jackets she could
feel his strength, his warmth.

Finn. She sighed her joy and relief. This was where
she wanted to be. It had been three very long months
since their last kiss. She couldn't wait a second longer
for another.

She wound her arms around his neck and pressed her
mouth to his, closed her eyes at the bliss of it, the ten-
derness, the way he tasted of coffee with a hint of tooth-
paste. He'd been expecting to kiss her. Maybe wanting it
as much as she did.

'Finn...' she murmured urgently against his lips.

He kissed her back, his mouth firm and warm on hers,
and there were no further words.

The kiss grew deeper, more demanding, more *thrilling*. Their breathing became more ragged, loud in the
still of the forest. Her knees threatened to sag beneath
her. Holding her tight, he nudged her towards a tree so
her back rested against it. That made it easier for him to
unbutton her jacket, to pull off his gloves and drop them
on the forest floor, to slide his hands, bare and warm,
under her jacket.

She gasped as he tugged her sweater from the waistband of her trousers, slid his hands around her waist. His

hands felt so good on her bare skin. Three months of banked-up desire ignited and flared until she burned for him—more touch, more kisses, *more Finn*.

'You're wearing rather more clothes than when I last kissed you,' he said, his voice deep and husky.

Last time she'd been wearing just a pink lacy bra and tiny lacy panties. She flushed at the memory of it. She was wearing the same now—though in a smaller size.

'You're more encumbered too,' she murmured, as she stripped off her gloves and fumbled with the belt of his jacket, annoyed with herself that she wasn't more adept.

He pulled back from the kiss, panting. 'Any chance we can continue where we left off in Sydney?'

'Yes, please,' she said, scarcely able to get the words out. 'Though it's a tad chilly to get naked out here.'

But if he wanted to make love to her in the forest, if he wanted to lay her down on a bed of pine needles, she'd still say yes. Which was all kinds of crazy. And exciting. And likely to lead to frostbite in uncomfortable places.

'Are there bears and wolves?' he asked.

'Maybe,' she said. 'More likely foxes. And rabbits. Hares, too.'

'Hmm…' he said, nuzzling her neck. 'The rabbits don't scare me.'

'The hares can get a bit scary when they fight.'

'Maybe out here isn't the best place,' he said, releasing her with obvious reluctance. 'And not just because of the dangerous hares.'

'Wise decision,' she said, though her words were tinged with regret.

What if they didn't get another chance?

Her hair had got tousled and he smoothed an errant lock away from her forehead in a gesture that sent pleasure shimmying through her.

'Getting together isn't so easy this time, is it?' he said hoarsely. 'Back then we were two regular people, struck by an instant attraction, and possibilities were opening up ahead of us. We could choose what we wanted to do about them. It seemed so uncomplicated. Now we know how very complicated our situation is.'

'I know only too well,' she said.

'Try not to be alone with him.' Her mother's words hadn't been in the slightest bit ambiguous. *Sorry, Mother.*

He cupped her face in his large warm hands, looked deep into her eyes with an intensity that thrilled her as much as a caress.

'I still want you, Natalia. More than anything, I want you.'

'I want you too, Finn. I never stopped wanting you.'

'Back then I knew nothing about you except that I wanted you. Now I know everything I need to know.'

She stilled. 'Not quite everything,' she said, in a very small voice.

'What do you mean?' His face tightened and his hands dropped from around her to his sides. 'More secrets? More lies?'

She could see the disappointment in the twist of his mouth, hear it in in his voice.

'Nothing like that,' she said.

'No more big surprises—please, Natalia. Finding out you were a completely different person was surprise enough for me. I don't know that I can deal with any more.'

'It's not that. I have no more identities. No more lies. It's just...'

'What?' he said.

'Do you remember that night? In my hotel room?'

He grinned—a slow, sexy grin that sent a shudder of want spiralling through her.

'As if I'd ever forget.'

'Back then I told you I hadn't done that kind of thing before...'

'I remember. I guessed you weren't in the habit of taking a man you didn't know very well back to your hotel room. But it felt like we'd known each other for a long time, didn't it? That we knew each other well enough to—'

'You're right. I had never taken a man back to my room. But you have to understand I—'

'Hell, Nat, you don't think I'd pass judgement on you for that? I'm not in the habit of hopping into bed with someone I scarcely know, either. It was special that night. We both wanted each other too much to wait. We both knew the score.'

She bent down to pick up her gloves from where she'd tossed them on the ground. Pulled them slowly back on, first her right hand, then her left. *Delaying tactics.*

'That's just it. I didn't know the score. I didn't know *anything.*'

He frowned. 'I'm not sure what you're getting at.'

She looked down at the ground. Noticed his gloves were there too. She should pick them up for him. They were good ones. Leather lined with cashmere.

'When I said I hadn't done it before, I meant *any* of it. I...I hadn't done more than kissing.' Finally she looked up at him. 'I...I'm a virgin, Finn. A twenty-seven-year-old virgin.'

He stared at her, incredulous. If it hadn't been so serious she would have laughed out loud at the expression on his face.

'You're not serious? You seemed...experienced.'

She screwed up her face. 'I was learning as I went along. I'd never undone a man's shirt before in my life. You were a brilliant tutor.'

'I wouldn't have known. I couldn't tell. There was no need for tutoring. But why?'

'A Montovian princess is meant to go to her marriage a virgin. It's tradition. Certainty that the husband's heirs are his own is the theory. I should have been married by the time I was twenty. But, as you know, I resisted that idea and I got older and older. I've been waiting longer than was anticipated.'

'Whoa… This is taking some getting used to.' He ran his hand through his hair so it stood up in spikes.

'You don't mind?'

'Of course I don't mind. Why would I mind?'

'It's odd, I know.'

'There's nothing odd about it. It's just unbelievable. Although quite precious in a way. You've really never made love with a man?'

'Not even come close.'

'Surely you've fooled around?'

'No. You've got to understand, I've never met anyone I wanted to fool around with. There was a boy at uni I liked. But as soon as my parents got wind that I was seeing him they paid him off and I never saw him again. Remember, I've always been destined for a marriage with someone of suitable rank. Fooling around just wouldn't do. Besides, me being a princess was a barrier. Before you, there was someone who interested me—but it never went anywhere because he didn't want the spotlight that he knew would be on him if we dated. All I met were those suitable suitors.'

'Who were entirely *un*suitable?'

'You were the first man to see me in my underwear.'

He groaned. She was fascinated by the depth of agony in his groan.

'Don't remind me of how sensational you looked. Pink

lace against creamy skin…your beautiful long legs. How have you endured going without sex?'

'It's never seemed a hardship until now. I didn't feel I was missing out. I'd never met a man I wanted. Until… until you.'

She looked up at him. Her heart jolted at how utterly handsome he was. She still could hardly believe her hot guy from the wedding was here.

'You seemed so willing.'

'I *was* willing. Believe me, I was willing. I intended to lose my virginity to you.'

'You *what*? That night? It was to be your first time?'

'It might sound cheesy, but you woke me up.' She felt suddenly shy, but this needed to be said. 'The first time you kissed me you turned on a switch that flooded me with wants and needs I'd never felt before. It was time.'

'You chose *me*?'

'I chose you.'

He turned away from her, as if to gather his thoughts. Then he swung back to face her. 'I wish you'd told me. It's quite a responsibility for a man to be a woman's first lover. To make sure she enjoys herself.'

'Oh, I knew I was going to enjoy myself. The way you touched me, the way you made me feel…' Her heart raced at the memory of it.

He groaned again. 'Natalia, no. Don't remind me. Not out here, where we can do nothing about it.'

'Sorry,' she said, not feeling sorry at all, and loving the power she had to arouse him as he aroused her.

'But you stopped me. I thought that you'd suddenly realised how impetuous you were being. We were moving too fast.'

She sighed. How many times since had she regretted stopping him?

'The protection thing pulled me back to reality. All that stuff I'd blocked because I wanted more than anything for you to carry me to that bed and make love to me. It brought home to me the seriousness of what I intended to do—the risks I would be taking. But most of all I knew I was going back home in the morning. It was so new to me—to want a man the way I wanted you. To make love with you just the once and never again would have been devastating. It wasn't just about the rules. I was protecting my emotions too.'

He frowned. 'Why didn't you tell me at the time that you're a virgin?'

She took a deep breath. This topic took her sailing back into the troubled waters of her deception. 'Because then I would have had to tell you the truth about who I really was. And I just couldn't. Not then, and not afterwards.'

'And now?'

'Nothing has changed as far as my royal obligations go. But you've come back into my life and I want you just as much. More so.'

'What does that mean for us?' he said.

'You...you're saying there's an "us"?'

He turned. 'Come on, let's walk further into the forest. I need to think.'

'Good idea.'

She stooped, picked up his gloves, caught up with him, handed them to him. He stared at them for a moment, as if he didn't know what they were, before shoving them in his jacket pocket. She realised how difficult, how inconceivable, this—her life, the only life she had known—must seem to him.

He held out his hand to her and she took it. She walked alongside him, steering him in a different direction from the one she knew her cousin and his wife had taken.

He spoke again. 'At the wedding I started to wonder about an *us*—an impossible "us". Because you—so I thought—lived in England, and I'd tried long-distance before and it had been a disaster.'

'I can see that,' she murmured. She thrilled to his words. So he'd felt it too, back at the wedding—not just physical attraction, something more, something real, something life-changing.

'But still I started to think of ways I could perhaps *make* it work. Then… You know what happened next. You disappeared. An *us* was never going to happen because there wasn't a *you*. Then, at the soirée, the impossible, the amazing, the unbelievable happened and you came into my life again—a *you* who both was and wasn't *you*—and I couldn't see that there could ever be an *us*.'

It was a long speech, but Natalia had listened, enthralled. 'And now?'

'All I can think of is how much I want there to be an us. How much I want *you*. When we were admiring those vats of chocolate at the Montovian chocolate factory I was thinking about you, and how wonderful it was to be sharing the experience with you. When I was sampling Matteo's cheeses I was thinking about how much I wanted to have my arm around you.'

'And you are in my thoughts constantly. That you're actually here in Montovia makes me want to dance down the street.'

'The entire way up here in the car, admiring the scenery, all I wanted to do was pull you into my arms and kiss you senseless.'

'Why didn't you?' she asked, breathless.

'Because this is so much more complicated than us simply living in different countries on other sides of the world. You're the Princess of Montovia and I'm an Aussie guy from Sydney. The obstacles are onerous. Not just because you're a princess. Not just because you live on the other side of the world from me. But because when it comes to my personal life, I'm a cautious kind of guy. I don't let myself get involved too easily. Dip my toe in the water before I dive right in. I've steered clear of serious relationships while I've been building the business so rapidly. I don't need the distraction of anyone making demands on me.'

'Oh,' she said. The hot guy she remembered from the wedding had seemed anything but cautious.

'But when I met you at the wedding caution didn't get a look-in. I wanted to jump straight in without hesitation. And was so glad I did because you were amazing. Then I thought I'd never see you again. Now here you are. What a rollercoaster. Man, am I distracted. I *want* to be distracted. But all we had was a few hours in Sydney with no time to develop anything more than initial sparks. Is that enough to be an *us*?'

'It's a start. And what's wrong with a strong start?'

He stopped. Turned to her. Put his hands on her shoulders. Urgently searched her face.

'We need to talk. Because if there is a way ahead for us, now is the time for us to set our feet on the path. If there isn't, then we have to walk away before we really hurt each other and—'

The sound of stamping feet and muffled laughter, of loud rustlings in the undergrowth made them jump apart.

'Marco and Amelie—warning us of their approach,' she said.

She brushed her hair away from her face. 'Quickly. Do I look okay? Will they be able to tell we've been kissing?'

He kissed her again—swiftly, fiercely. 'You look adorable, beautiful...your cheeks flushed, your eyes sparkling.

I want the world to know you've just been thoroughly kissed by me. I don't want us to be skulking around bushes and hiding. We need to talk about our options.'

'We have options?' Could she allow herself to hope?

'Everyone has options. Even the impossible *us*. We need to analyse and weigh them up if we're to find our path.'

'That sounds so businesslike.'

'That's the way I am. I don't trust infatuation as a basis for life-long relationships.'

'Do you think this—between us—is just infatuation?' She didn't doubt what she felt for him went way beyond infatuation.

'I don't know. But it feels like something much deeper. It did from the get-go, if I'm to be honest. But it came from nowhere. Lasting relationships to me are partnerships based on a long getting to know each other process. We haven't been given that. It's like we're in a crucible. Your family doesn't talk dating—it talks *marriage*. Advance to "Go" before I've even got a counter on the board. I always expected there to be time for me to get to know a woman before the word marriage entered into it.'

'You make it sound impossible.' She put her hands to her face in despair.

Gently he took them away, looked into her face. 'Not impossible. Possibilities are what we have to talk about. In the meantime, I suggest you smooth down your hair, wipe that smear of lipstick from the corner of your mouth—here, I'll do it—then straighten your scarf, and by the time we get back to the chalet you'll look like all you did on this walk in the forest was explain to me about the regeneration of the wildlife and point out the eagle soaring above us in the sky.'

'What eagle?' she asked, looking above her.

When the others appeared, with Marco calling out an alert, that was what they found—her talking to an attentive Finn in her best tour guide voice.

'And that very eagle, represented with a sword in its beak, is on the crest of the royal family of Montovia.'

Clever Finn for thinking on his feet. For making her laugh. For making her think about possibilities.

But was what they had enough? Was it just infatuation? The thrill of the forbidden? Could she trust whatever had ignited so quickly between them?

When there was a ticking clock on the amount of time they had together how did she know he could give her what she wanted? True love. The kind princesses got in fairy tales, with happy-ever-afters, but the kind that had always seemed elusive to her as a real-life princess.

CHAPTER TWELVE

USUALLY THERE WAS nothing Finn enjoyed more in cold weather than a hearty meal and a good red wine enjoyed in a room lit by a roaring fire. It was the stuff of fantasy for an Australian boy from subtropical Sydney.

Hell, this whole situation he found himself in was the stuff of fantasy.

He was falling for a princess.

But he didn't know if it was real. He didn't have anything to compare it to except that long-ago romance with Chiara, which had seemed real enough at the time, but certainly hadn't felt anything like this.

This intensity, this overwhelming longing to be with Natalia, was something powerful and compelling. He recognised it as the most important emotion he had ever felt. But it was a recognition tinged with caution. He didn't trust sudden flames that could die out as quickly as they'd flared. Those flames had not been enough to sustain a relationship with Chiara.

The strong marriages in his family were based on partnerships. Didn't that require a slow burn, a getting-to-know-each-other before any commitment was considered? He wanted certainty. Could he get that with Natalia? He had no idea where such powerful feelings could drive him. But he knew he could not dismiss them.

He was seated next to Natalia at a long wooden table designed for way more than four, but cosy enough just the same. She wore a long purple velvet skirt and a long-sleeved scoop-neck silk knit top in silver—her version of informal dress. His black jeans and black cashmere turtleneck seemed more than appropriate.

At the table, he was being careful to keep a respectable distance apart from her, but she occasionally slipped her hand into his under cover of the tablecloth. Amazing how the simple act of holding hands could be so thrilling when it was with the woman he wanted almost beyond reason.

He didn't want to let her go.

'Did you enjoy our menu based on traditional home-style favourites?' she asked in her best hostess voice. But her eyes showed more than a hostess should to a single male guest. Did anyone else notice?

'The cabbage pie was delicious—something new for me. And the roast was superb—I really liked the warm potato salad.'

They were talking about potatoes!

He smiled and surreptitiously squeezed her hand. This single male guest probably wasn't doing a great job of masking his feelings, either. He suspected Marco and Amelie were aware of what was brewing between him and Natalia, and were complicit without actually coming out in the open with their approval.

The housekeeper was a different matter altogether.

'Hanna keeps glaring at me,' he murmured to Natalia. 'Do you think she's on to us?'

'No doubt she suspects something—she's fond of me and she wouldn't want to see me hurt. Her generation is fearful of any transgressions of the rules.'

'And you?'

'I need to know which rules I'm prepared to break,' she whispered. 'And the repercussions I'm prepared to suffer.'

His grip on her hand tightened.

They had to talk.

The evening passed very pleasantly, although all Finn

wanted to do was speak to Natalia on her own. He was scheduled to leave Montovia after a mid-morning business meeting the next day, which she was chairing on behalf of Tristan. The clock was ticking down on the time they had together.

It turned out that Marco and Amelie were just as good companions at dinner as they had been at the soirée. Finn learned a lot about living in contemporary Montovia, where young people were testing the old, traditional ways. And they, in turn, were curious about Australia.

'I would love to visit Sydney,' Amelie said.

'You and Marco would be most welcome as my guests if you do so,' said Finn. 'I have a large house on the harbour with several guest rooms.'

'And you, Natalia—you have always wanted to see Sydney, especially after Tristan found his beloved wife there,' said Marco.

Natalia choked on her chocolate pudding but quickly recovered herself. 'Yes, it is a dream of mine. I might even find myself a husband there.'

It was Finn's turn to choke on his pudding. He quickly downed a glass of Montovian spring water, drawn from a well on the property.

Amelie frowned. 'Is there something allergenic in this pudding? Please tell me before I try it...'

'Not to my knowledge,' Natalia said in a faint voice, fanning her face with her hand. 'Just...just the sauce is a little hot.'

Finn wished he could be open and honest about how he'd met Natalia. He wasn't accustomed to lying. Sooner or later he would blunder and make some indiscreet comment that might let the cat out of the bag.

Not long after dessert Marco asked permission for himself and Amelie to leave the table and retire to their room.

'He has to ask because I'm higher in rank than he is,' Natalia explained, after they'd said goodnight to the Count and his wife.

She led Finn to the adjoining room. Three large, comfortable brown leather sofas were arranged in front of another toasty fire. Stacked firewood was shelved on both sides of the fireplace and large metal fire tools hung from a rack. The fire gave a warm, inviting glow to the room, and the only other lighting was from table lamps.

'You have to give him *permission*? Even though he's your cousin...your friend?'

'We're so used to how things work, we don't question it,' she explained. 'I'm not sure that is something Tristan would be able to convince our father to change—not quickly anyway.'

Natalia sat on the sofa facing the fireplace and patted the seat next to her.

'I don't have to ask your permission to be seated?' he said.

She laughed. 'Of course not. You're a foreigner.'

He sighed, and knew it sounded heavy with the weight of his concerns. 'No wonder I find it difficult to get a handle on how it all works.'

'I understand how difficult it is for one not born to it. Gemma found it a steep learning curve. She says she still has much to learn. Not just about being royal, but also about being Montovian. But she's very happy with Tristan and has become a remarkable Crown Princess.'

Finn took his place next to Natalia on the sofa, sitting a polite distance away from her. If someone were to come into the room unexpectedly they would see nothing untoward.

Hell, Natalia's experience with men seemed so limited he wondered if the King and Queen posted surveillance on her dates. He shifted a few inches farther away from her, just to be sure, then angled his body towards her in an entirely acceptable conversational manner.

'Talking of Gemma—what is it about her and Amelie both wanting to go to bed so early?' he said. 'Don't they ever want to party? Is that a Montovian thing?'

'I suspect it's a woman in the early stages of pregnancy thing. Didn't you see Amelie's horror at the prospect of something harmful in the pudding?'

'A mere male wouldn't notice such a thing.'

'Women are attuned to notice such things in their friends. But we also respect the fact that women usually don't want to make any announcement until the pregnancy is safely established.'

'You think Gemma might be pregnant?'

'I suspect so—though we're such good friends I'm surprised she hasn't shared the news with me. I can't help but be concerned that something might be wrong, but I suspect she's simply being cautious.'

'If she and Tristan had a baby wouldn't it kick you down the line of succession? Perhaps she's worried that might upset you?'

'Upset me? I would be glad to be demoted in such a way. It would make my life so much easier.'

Hanna entered the room and Natalie had a quick exchange in Montovian with her. Then she turned to him. 'Hanna wants to know if you would like anything further. A camomile tea, perhaps?'

Finn shook his head. 'Nothing for me, thanks.' He looked up at Hanna and thanked her in Montovian. The older woman beamed at him before she turned to leave the room.

'Finn! You spoke in Montovian. When did you learn that?'

'Don't get too excited. I asked Tristan to teach me how to say "please" and "thank you" before we went into our meetings in St Pierre. Just to be polite. I think I've mastered it.'

'Your accent was perfect. Well done.'

He was glad she was pleased. Montovian would not be an easy language to master. But, as his mother often said, the first new language was the most difficult. The more languages you learned, the easier it became.

He watched as Hanna's back view faded from sight. As if by mutual agreement, he and Natalia both stayed very still and listened for sounds from the next room.

'When Hanna finishes in the kitchen will she go to bed too?' Finn asked.

'House servants in the royal households are obligated to be on call until the family and their guests have retired.'

'So if we stayed up all night, until sunrise, she and Bernard would have to stay up all night too?'

'That's how it works,' she said.

He frowned.

'You're aching to say something, aren't you?' she said.

'No. These are your ways and I'm not one to criticise. Where do they live?'

'Their home is a large, comfortable apartment beyond the kitchen.'

'What if we want to contact them for camomile tea?'

'There's a buzzer connected to their apartment. But I can't remember how long since it has been used. It might even need a new battery.'

'What do they do while they're waiting for the battery-less buzzer?'

'I have no idea. Perhaps watch television in bed?'

He smiled. 'And that's how you work around "how it works".'

'Tristan and I have our methods of getting around the old ways.'

'Which brings us back to us.' He looked around. 'Can we talk privately here?'

'As long as we keep our voices down.'

'I have no intention of shouting. But I *would* like to kiss you.' He kissed her on the cheek—a sweet, simple kiss. 'That's for being kind to your old nanny.'

She kissed him on the mouth. Just as quick, just as sweet. 'That's for you being you.'

He caught her hand, clasped it with his. 'Why do we have to skulk around? If I was here longer, couldn't we date? Your family want you to marry someone they consider suitable, but now there's no law against you choosing who you want to have in your life. This is such an artificial, pressure cooker situation.'

'As I told you, you're the first man I've been seriously attracted to. I guess I'm not sure how to handle it. I could scream and yell and defy my family—insist I want to be with you. Then you'd go back to Sydney, I'd never see you again and I'd have a lot of bridge-building to face with my family.'

'I want you. I like you. And I'd like to get to know you—not as a princess, with all the complications that comes with, but as a woman. Like we did at the wedding. I asked you on a date in Sydney. Have you ever wondered what might have happened if you'd spent that day with me on my yacht?'

'Many times…over three miserable months.'

'I searched for you for weeks, you know?'

'You must have been furious with me. Yet you searched for me?'

'Furious, yes—but worried, too, that you might have come to some harm. My male ego wouldn't let me accept that you could just walk away from the magic we'd shared simply because you didn't like me.'

She gasped. 'You *know* it wasn't that.'

'I know now. Back then I wanted an explanation for how you could just disappear. I thought you might have been kidnapped. Bundled into a boat. Thrown overboard from a ferry. I had all sorts of insane ideas. Anything but face up to the fact you'd played me. That for some reason you'd got me enchanted with you—got me believing you might be just a bit enchanted with me—and then callously dumped me.'

'I was actually very taken with you. That's the thing with enchantments. They entice and snare both ways.'

He kissed her again. So what if they were seen? He almost wanted them to be seen so they could be open about what was happening between them. But he suspected Natalia would suffer the consequences. Would she always be under the thumb of her parents because they were also her King and Queen?

'My next thought was it had to have been a scam. I checked my credit cards—perhaps when I'd gone to the bathroom you could have scanned them—but, no. My bank balance remained intact. My identity hadn't been stolen.'

She smiled. 'I don't exactly need the money.'

He smiled back. He'd appreciated her sense of humour from the get-go. 'Finally, when my desire to know more about you overcame my reluctance to admit my humiliation, I asked Eliza. The first person on her doorstep after she returned from her honeymoon was me, begging for details about Natalie Gerard.'

'Eliza? But she—'

'She kept your secret. She's loyal.'

'Good,' she said, with visible relief.

'I can still see my friend, standing there with her hands on her hips. *"I told you Natalie might not be who she said she was."* Her pity, and her righteous indignation that I hadn't listened to her, rubbed salt into my already stinging humiliation.'

'Poor Finn,' said Natalia.

'Poor Finn?' He snorted. 'I didn't get any information or sympathy from Eliza. *"I tried to warn you"*—that was all she said. Not one more word could I get out of her. Except yet another offer to fix me up with the world's most boring woman—Prue, whose place card we switched at the wedding.'

'Eliza called me at about that time,' Natalia said thoughtfully. 'Asked me if I remembered you. Of course I stuck to the script and said I'd danced with you at the wedding and we'd had coffee afterwards, but that was as far as it had gone. Mind you, while you were trying to find *me* I was frantically looking *you* up on the internet. Of course I found everything you'd told me about yourself was the truth. While all I had done was lie. I was a mess—couldn't eat, couldn't sleep…just torn apart by regret.'

'I had some crazy ideas about what had happened to you. But none nearly as crazy as what turned out to be the truth.'

'And yet you've forgiven me?'

'Because I've never met a woman who attracts me like you do—first as Natalie, now as Natalia. The more I know you the more attracted I am, and the more I find to admire in you.'

He was rewarded by her lovely smile, which lit up her eyes. 'I feel the same about you. I've really enjoyed our time working together.'

He leaned over to kiss her.

Natalia put up her hand to stop him. 'You know we really can't be caught kissing in here… We can't risk Bernard coming in to check if the fire needs another log, or to stoke it, or whatever one does with fires. Or Hanna coming in just wanting to keep an eye on me.'

He pulled back from her. 'Why? These constrictions seem unnecessary. We're both single. We're not hurting anyone by getting to know each other. Or kissing each other. And this fire is kinda romantic. Guy-type romantic, I mean. Forget the flowers and the girly frills. This is what does it for me. A warm rug, the flickering flames, cosy dark corners…and you and I snuggled on that rug needing nothing more than each other to warm us—'

'Stop it,' she said. 'That scenario does it for me, too. I want you Finn. It's torture sitting next to you on this sofa not being able to kiss you, touch you, explore you.'

He shifted in his seat, groaned. 'I can't believe you don't know what that kind of talk does to me.'

'I might have an idea, because I'm feeling the same way.'

She took a deep breath, which only succeeded in focusing his gaze on the swell of her curves in her snug-fitting top.

'Best then, I guess, that we're not distracted,' she said. 'No kissing…no touching.'

'But only because we've decided we don't want the distraction. Not because someone else has put strictures on us.'

'Agreed,' she said.

She turned to face him, their knees nudged and she didn't move back. Again he had the feeling that he'd fallen into a fantasy. It was as if she had conjured up this room— the blaze of the fire, the fresh smell of pine, and his beautiful dark-haired virgin Princess wrapped in her flowing long skirt like a woman in a medieval manuscript...or a movie...or a game.

He wanted the fantasy to be real.

He shifted away from the distracting contact, determined to move things along before Bernard appeared to tend to the fire, or the ancient metallic clock on the wall struck midnight and he was left on his own with only smouldering ashes, longing for one of the most unattainable women in the world.

'In my world, where we could date and get to know each other, and see if what we feel is infatuation or something deeper, I wouldn't be mentioning marriage so soon. But it seems your family want you on a fast track to marriage. No time for feelings to develop. No time for compatibility to be established. No time to be sure it's going to work.'

Her mouth turned down and her eyes clouded. 'We are a family who lost our heir—a beloved son, brother, husband, father—and his son.'

Finn wondered, not for the first time, why both heirs had been travelling together in one helicopter.

'Perhaps, as a result, my parents have become a little obsessive about ensuring the line of succession. Their great fear is the throne going to my uncle's branch of the family—who are dissolute, to say the least. That's not Marco's father, by the way, it's a different uncle. They want my children to be in line as back-up, I suppose.'

'Even though they would come after Tristan, and after his children and then after you? It's not likely they'd ever inherit the throne.'

'Not likely—but possible.'

'But even before your brother's death, you resisted an arranged marriage?'

'I believe in love and only love as a basis for marriage. Don't you?'

'Of course I do. A love that grows based on compatibility and shared interests and proves to be real. A partnership. After a long engagement. That's how it works in my family. My grandparents and my parents are happily married. Each anniversary is a big deal to be celebrated.'

'It's the total opposite in my family. I've told you about my parents and my grandparents. But it was my brother's marriage that really made me wary. Carl was introduced to Sylvie as a potential bride. She was beautiful and vivacious and he fell for her as she seemed to fall for him. But she didn't love Carl. She loved the idea of being Crown Princess, with all the wealth and status that came with it. She was demanding and capricious and she made his life hell. Once she'd had Rudi I don't think they even shared a bed. Poor Carl was so unhappy. Seeing that, I decided I'd rather stay single than marry a nobleman I didn't love. And then Carl died.'

He had to ask. 'Why were they all travelling in the same helicopter?'

'Because Sylvie insisted she didn't want to fly with Rudi behind Carl, in what she saw as a lesser helicopter not befitting her status. And, as he did so many times, he gave in to her to avoid a tantrum.'

'I'm so sorry,' he said. 'Such a tragedy.'

He pulled her to him in a hug and she did not resist. He wanted to protect her, this woman who was usually protected by two bodyguards, to wrap her in warmth and security and take away her pain. To make her laugh every day.

'When Tristan changed the rules more choices opened to me. But my parents can still withhold permission for me to marry someone of whom they disapprove.'

He considered her statement. 'They could make your life uncomfortable if they withheld their permission?'

'*Very* uncomfortable,' she said.

'Would dungeons be involved?'

'Who knows?' She laughed. 'Seriously? Not likely at all. And, apart from needing palace-sanctioned permission, I love my parents and want them to approve of my choice of husband and father for my children. And there can be no other option for me than marriage. Living with a man would never be sanctioned.'

'No doubt I'm not high on the approved list?'

'They believe a royal marriage has a better chance of working if both husband and wife come from the same social strata.'

'Yet that didn't work for Carl,' he said. 'And Tristan chose his own wife—breaking more than one tradition in the way he did it.'

'I could, as a citizen of Montovia, marry without the King and Queen's permission. It's me as a princess who needs it.'

He groaned. 'There's another obstacle around every corner. But I don't want to walk away from you, Natalia. I felt lost without you in St Pierre today.'

'And the palace seemed empty without you while you were away. I was counting the minutes until you returned. I'll really miss you when you leave tomorrow. I wish I could stow away in your luggage.'

'I like that idea. But you live in Montovia, with all the responsibilities entailed in your position as Princess and second in line to the throne.'

'And you live in far-away Australia, where your family is and your successful business.'

The logs in the fire shifted and moved in a shower of sparks. The huge, old-fashioned pendulum on the metallic clock on the wall tick-tocked the seconds away. Finn was conscious of their time together dwindling away.

He slowly shook his head. 'It's never going to be a simple boy-meets-girl scenario for us.'

'No. The stakes are so much higher when it's a princess and a millionaire tycoon.'

'But so are the potential gains,' he said, tracing his finger down her cheek and across the outline of her mouth so she trembled. He didn't care if someone barged into the room and saw them.

'I'm beginning to understand that,' she said, her voice unsteady.

'So we have to think about ways we can make long-distance dating viable.'

'We could just run away—be together somewhere we can just be ourselves, away from expectations,' she said.

'You *know* that's not an option.'

'I so want there to be a chance for *us*,' she said. 'To see if this is more than infatuation.'

'Me too,' he said.

Every minute he spent with her moved him further away from infatuation into something he couldn't yet put a name to.

'So what do you think are the possible options for us?'

Finn put up his hand to count off the options available to them finger by finger. It was a thing he did. 'Option one—we have a secret no-strings affair. I see you whenever I come to Europe. You sneak down to Sydney when you can.'

'I don't like the idea of sneaky and secretive,' she said. 'And I doubt it would make either of us happy.'

'I would rather be open about our intentions,' he said.

'So let's forget that option,' she said.

'So, option two, we date each other openly as best we

can, considering we live on the other side of the world from each other.'

'Which would give you the getting-to-know-each-other period you believe is so important,' she said.

'But it would mean we spend a lot of time apart and we lose our privacy.'

'The media would have a field-day once they got on to it,' she said glumly.

He shuddered 'Horrible. But it would be you they'd be after. I'd get off lightly.'

She shook her head. 'Uh-uh. Once they realise how incredibly handsome you are you'd become a target of the long-distance lens. You've already featured in an *Australian Bachelor Millionaires* article.'

'How did—?'

'I pretty much stalked you for a month after I got back from Sydney. After that… I…it became too heartbreaking.'

'I would have stalked *you* if I'd known who you were,' he said.

She looked so woebegone he could not resist kissing her. Then she snuggled close. He breathed in her scent, already so familiar.

'Still, I like that option,' she said. 'Although the loss of privacy might become an issue.'

'It would become an issue anyway,' he said. 'Because if it worked out between us the next step would be making things more permanent between us.' He put up his hand. 'That doesn't mean I'm proposing. This is a hypothetical discussion, based on the way things work in your family.'

If the day ever came that he asked Natalia to marry him he had strong, traditionally male ideas of how it would happen.

'Of course it's hypothetical,' she said. 'But then—again

speaking hypothetically—we would have to face the biggest of the questions. Who lives where?'

'Which means either you live with me in Sydney or I sell my business and live here?'

'That about sums it up,' she said.

He folded his arms across his chest. 'That would be a really big deal for me. To walk away from the company that was my grandparents' would be very hard in terms of family dynamics. I'm very close to my family. It would be difficult for all concerned if I become only an infrequent visitor.'

She crossed her legs, uncrossed them. 'And then there's my side of the story. I'd still remain second in line to the throne. To leave my country would be very difficult. I would almost certainly have to give up my title and all it entails. I was born to be a princess. I know nothing else. I can't earn my own living. The thought is terrifying.'

'It's *all* a bit terrifying,' he said.

She laughed, but there was an edge to her laughter. 'Can you imagine if anyone could overhear us? What a bizarre conversation. To be thinking so far ahead when, as you point out, we hardly know each other.'

'But the unique position we find ourselves in means we have to be aware of all the options.' He paused. 'Which brings us to option three.'

Natalia mock-cringed away from him into the back of the sofa. 'I don't think I'm going to like this one.'

'I sure as hell don't,' he said. 'Option three—total wipe-out, scorched earth, ground zero. We decide that "us" isn't going to work out.' He almost choked on the words. 'We say goodbye—for good this time—and I go back to Australia and wipe you from my life and, in time, from my memory.'

There was a long silence between them. He could hear

the old timbers in the chalet shift and settle, the sigh of the wind outside.

'And I stay here and make myself forget I ever met you,' she said finally, her voice wobbling. 'Easier said than done, you realise? I've tried and failed at that already.'

He took a deep steadying breath against the pain that surged through him at the thought of not having her in his life in any way. 'I would have to pull out of my contract with Tristan. Have no communication with Montovia ever again. It would be the only way I could deal with it.'

'Me too. It would be too painful otherwise,' she said slowly, wringing her hands in front of her. 'We...we have to be realistic.'

Realistic? Where did being realistic come in to his hopes for a new life in this fairy tale place full of castles and dungeons and magic, with the most beautiful Princess in the whole wide world?

CHAPTER THIRTEEN

NATALIA WAS REELING from the conversation she'd had with Finn. Yet it was a conversation that had needed to occur. So much for dreams and fantasies and longings...

But there was only so far this common-sense type of discussion could go. She felt propelled by an impulse far more visceral, urgent, intensely personal. Finn was in Montovia for only a little more than twenty-four hours—some of that sleeping time. She intended to claim that sleeping time for herself. To claim *him.*

From where she sat oh-so-safely apart from him on the sofa she faced him. They had been speaking in hushed tones. Now she spoke in a normal, conversational tone, using words that wouldn't matter if anyone overheard.

'Thank you, Finn. That's been a most interesting conversation. You've given me food for thought.' For all Finn had urged her to take the reins, she still felt she needed to work within the rules.

He sat up straighter, frowned at her sudden change of direction. 'Huh...?'

She got up from the sofa. Finn immediately did so too. She was wearing flats and he towered above her. Again she was struck by how handsome he was, dressed all in black, with his black hair and the vibrant green of his eyes, those sharp cheekbones, his fabulous body... He was the most gorgeous man she had ever met. No other man could ever match him.

And not just in looks. Enjoying a man's company as she enjoyed Finn's was a revelation. Business meetings became exciting when he took part. She had wanted him from the moment she had first seen him. She wanted him now. If he left tomorrow and it didn't work out she wanted no regrets.

She held out her hand for a formal handshake. 'Breakfast is in the same room as dinner, starting at seven. We have an eleven o'clock meeting. An early start would be a good idea.'

He took her hand in his firm, warm grip for the politely requisite time before releasing it. 'Yes...' he said, sounding puzzled.

She leaned forward momentarily, to whisper in his ear. 'Don't lock your bedroom door. I'll see you in ten minutes.' Then, in her normal voice, 'Goodnight.'

He grinned and winked at her. He *winked*. The Princess of Montovia wasn't used to being winked at and she loved it.

'Thank you again for your hospitality,' he said, very formally. 'Goodnight.'

She was conscious of his gaze upon her as she left the room. Her first impulse was to race to her bedroom. The faster she showered and changed, the faster she could be back with Finn. But she needed to act normally—not to draw attention to herself if anyone were to see her. All her life she had had to be aware of the staff who shared the royal family's personal space. For most of her waking hours she was observed, one way or another.

She forced herself to walk sedately to her bedroom.

Ten minutes later she emerged, enveloped in the luxurious Italian designer dressing gown she kept at the chalet and toasty Australian wool slippers that had been a gift from Gemma.

Cautiously she crept down the corridor towards Finn's room in the guest wing. She wasn't worried about Marco and Amelie. During dinner Amelie had taken her aside and told her how much she and Marco liked Finn and approved of him.

'Go for it, Natalia,' Amelie had said. 'We had to fight to be together. You might have to as well. Finn is wonderful—he's worth it.'

Encountering Hanna or Bernard would be a different story. They would consider themselves duty-bound to report to the Queen what they would see as a breach of royal morality. She was twenty-seven, for heaven's sake, not seventeen. It was about time she took charge of her own future—the first step having been her trip to Sydney.

She reached Finn's room without mishap, to find the door slightly ajar. She tapped so lightly she thought he might not hear it. But he was there within seconds. She gasped at the sight of him in black silk pyjamas with a fine grey stripe. They showcased his broad shoulders, his lean, muscular body. He was as covered up as if he were in trousers and a long-sleeved shirt, but somehow the pyjamas seemed so much more intimate. He was beautiful in an intensely masculine way.

Without a word, he took her by the hand and drew her into the room, then locked the door behind her. With a deep murmur of pleasure, he drew her into his arms and kissed her.

'This is nice,' he said, his voice deep and husky, when they came up for breath. 'I missed you. Even for ten minutes I missed you.'

'I missed you too.' Her voice hitched. 'I…I don't know how I'll bear it when you leave tomorrow.'

'Me neither. As you know, tomorrow I fly to Dublin with Franz, your master chocolatier, to meet my contact from the distillery and discuss the potential for a Montovian chocolate liqueur. Then I'm scheduled for meetings in London for three days before flying back to Sydney. Perhaps you could meet me in London?'

She shook her head. 'I can't. That would be such a red flag to my parents, and I'd rather keep them out of it until we know how it works out for us. Trust me—they will know your schedule and they'll put two and two together very quickly. To my knowledge, they're not aware there is anything between us…although my mother is suspicious.'

'Why is she suspicious? We have given her no cause—'

'She saw the way we were looking at each other at the soirée and drew her own conclusions.'

'Like I'm looking at you now, wondering what you have on under that dressing gown?' His eyes narrowed, gleaming with sensual intent.

'If you'd looked at me like that my mother would have had you evicted from the soirée.'

'And you?'

'I would have gone with you and dragged you back to my apartment.' She reached up to kiss him. 'I'll tell you later what I would have done to you,' she said, her voice laden with promise.

He gave a sensuous growl that both made her smile and sent desire rippling through her.

'I'll look forward to that,' he said. He held her close. 'But in the meantime we continue to keep under the Queen's radar.'

'That's the plan. We need to keep it that way while we figure out how we…*if* we can be together. I don't want my every move to be scrutinised until we invite it. It breaks my heart to say it, because I would love to meet you there, but no London visit for me.'

'Or Dublin or Sydney?'

'Sadly, no.'

He sighed, and she sensed his despair was as deep as hers.

'I won't be able to get back here to see you for another two weeks.' He frowned. 'The dreaded long-distance.'

'I know. I'm dreading it too—which is why I want to make the most of the hours we have left. We don't have much time to take up where we left off in Sydney.' She looked into his eyes. 'And that starts with you helping me out of this dressing gown.'

'Happy to oblige,' he said, his voice husky.

She noticed his hands weren't quite steady as he undid the tie, but they were sure and strong as he pushed the dressing gown off her shoulders, and they felt so good on her bare skin. The dressing gown slid to the floor. She was so new to this. A novice at being naughty.

What next?

She stood proud, wearing only pink lace bra and panties—the same kind as she'd worn in Sydney—and waited for his reaction. Would he notice she wasn't as curvy as she'd been before?

She was not disappointed by his reaction.

'Natalia...' he breathed, his eyes raking over her, gleaming with hunger and admiration. 'I can't believe you wore pink lace. That has figured in my fantasies for three months. You're incredible.'

She was so sure that this was what she wanted—that *he* was what she wanted.

'Not as incredible as you,' she said.

From somewhere came the skill to unfasten his buttons, slide her hands greedily over his chest, revelling in the smoothness of his skin over hard muscle. Such a beautiful man.

'I won't stop you tonight,' she said.

He stilled. 'Are you sure it's what you want?'

'I'm sure. I've thought about it. It's what I want. Is that consent enough for you?'

His hands gripped her upper arms. 'I want you—more than you can imagine. It's just I'm not sure it's right for you just now. The risks and consequences are still the same. If your virginity is such a big deal you were right to be cautious before.' He groaned. 'I must be crazy, holding back. Because there is nothing—absolutely nothing—I want more than to make love with you right now.'

'To be my tutor in living dangerously?' she murmured.

He smiled. 'I'm not convinced you need a tutor in love-making. I suspect you'll have things to teach *me*. You're a sensual sensation just waiting to be unleashed.'

'Really?' she said, thrilled at the prospect.

'Oh, yes. The thing is, it's not about me being the tutor and you being the pupil. It's about learning what pleases both yourself and your partner.'

'Like a...like a two-way learning process?' she said breathlessly.

'Exactly.'

He kissed her again, sliding his tongue between her lips, demanding and getting her response before he kissed a trail down her throat to the edge of her bra until she was melting with want.

'The thing is—though it's killing me to say it—I'm going to have to be the responsible one here. There are other ways—exciting ways—for me to please you and you to please me. I'm sure you know about them.'

'I...I haven't done them,' she said, excited in spite of herself.

'Did you know Tristan wanted you to act as my guide because the last time he'd seen you laugh was dancing with me at the wedding?' he asked.

'I didn't know that.'

With two fingers he tilted her chin up so she would look directly into his face. 'In these last few days I've made you laugh many times.'

'Yes,' she said. 'The dark cloud has lifted from me.'

'I've made you laugh...but I can also make you whimper with want, moan with pleasure, cry out in ecstasy, and then beg me to do it all again.'

She caught her breath as her heart started to hammer

and she throbbed in those places she hadn't known could throb until she'd met Finn.

'Can you?' she choked out.

'Oh, yes,' he said, stroking down the side of her breast, and along her waist. 'And that's exactly what I intend to do—starting right now. But you will leave this room still a virgin. I will not have dishonoured you. I hope you will lose your virginity with me when we make a decision about where we're going. But in the meantime you will in all conscience have done your duty to maintain what seems so important in your world.'

'But I—'

He slid his hand towards the edge of her panties.

'*Oh!*'

So that was what a whimper of want felt like.

'Do you want to talk some more? Or shall we take up where we left off three months ago and I'll pick you up and carry you to the bed?'

'The bed. *Please.* The bed.'

Natalia didn't know how much later it was when she woke in Finn's bed. She was lying naked next to him, her head resting on his shoulder, his arm encircling her and holding her tight. *Heaven.* She breathed in the scent of him. The scent of *them.* She felt relaxed to bonelessness after her initiation into the pleasures a woman could both take and give without technically losing her virginity. Never had she dreamed she could be so uninhibited.

She lay next to him, savouring his nearness, thinking. Thinking about Finn, about how unfulfilling her life had been until he'd reappeared in it.

What was the time? How much longer did she have left with him? *Her man.* Privately, that was how she thought of him.

It was still dark. But the nights were getting long at

this time of year. She couldn't risk being caught in Finn's bedroom.

Not wanting to wake him, she gently raised herself up on her elbow, looked across at the clock on the nightstand. It glowed in the intense darkness that was night at the chalet, without street lighting or any other buildings. It was not yet three a.m. There was still time.

Still time for *more*.

Everything she'd done with Finn had been intensely exciting and satisfying. But it wasn't enough. She still wanted him.

Her movement must have woken him. He stirred. 'Natalia...' he murmured. 'You're here.'

The joy and pleasure in his voice both thrilled and moved her. He turned, reached out for her.

'You're not going yet?'

Her eyes were getting used to the dark and she could see his face. His handsome, handsome face that had become so dear—so *beloved*—so quickly.

He was the one.

'No, I'm not going.' She reached out with newly confident hands to caress him, revelling in the feel of his body. 'I want you to make love to me, Finn. All the way.'

'But we agreed not to—'

'You were doing the honourable thing, and I appreciate your thoughtfulness more than I can say.'

'Not quite so honourable,' he said 'More trying to be sensible. More trying to...to protect you.'

'I'm frightened, you see,' she said, with a little shiver that had nothing to do with the cold.

'Frightened? There's no need to be—'

She took his hand. 'Not about that. I'm not at *all* frightened about that.'

She dropped a kiss on his hand.

'It's the rest of it. Earlier, on the sofa, when we were

discussing our options, I felt so brave—so confident that with you by my side I could reach out and take what I wanted. But in the dark I don't feel so brave. It's difficult to be both a Montovian princess and a feminist, but I do my best. However, it seems to me that when there are decisions to be made it's most often the woman who has to uproot her life. It would most likely be me who'd have change countries. I'm torn. I'm aching to be with you, but I also want to do my duty to my country and to my parents. They have lost one child already and they'd think that me going to Australia would be losing another.'

'I understand,' he said. He picked up a lock of her hair and wound it around his finger, as if binding her to him.

'And, while option two beckons so enticingly, I have to prepare my heart for the fact that option three might be the forerunner. If that's our option, and we have to say goodbye, I want to have been with you in every sense.'

She shifted so she could look right into his face, amazed at how unselfconscious she was about being naked with him.

'You're the one, Finn. No matter how things work out with us, you're the only man I've ever wanted—the only man I have ever imagined I could care for. Please make love to me. Give me memories, if nothing else, that I can carry with me no matter where life might take me.'

'*Natalia...*' Her name seemed wrenched out of him in a harsh, heartrending sob as he gathered her into his arms.

CHAPTER FOURTEEN

BREAKFAST AT THE chalet early the next morning was a subdued event. Amelie wasn't present because she wasn't feeling well. Morning sickness, Natalia suspected. For the first time in her life, she had a flash of concern for herself—what if she was pregnant? She dismissed the thought—Finn had been meticulous about protection. But then she allowed herself the momentary indulgence of wondering what a child of theirs might be like—almost certainly dark-haired, smart, attractive…

She cast a quick, surreptitious look over to Finn. He seemed sombre, with dark circles under his eyes. Neither of them had got more than a few hours' sleep. They'd found better ways to use their time rather than waste it on sleeping.

The intimacy they'd shared had gone beyond the physical. They'd both been in tears when they'd had to say goodbye in the last private moments they would share until heaven knew when. She had never felt sadder than when she'd sneaked out of his room just before dawn.

She'd felt awkward when she'd got to the breakfast table, to find Finn already there making polite conversation with Marco. Had Marco guessed she'd spent the night with Finn? The only evidence was a slight beard rash, but she'd covered that with make-up.

She longed to seat herself next to Finn—her lover!—as close as she possibly could. But that was out of the question. Instead she acted the gracious hostess to both Finn and Marco.

She gagged at the thought of eating—not the delicious bread rolls Hanna had baked fresh, not Matteo's fabulous cheese or even the finely sliced ham and fresh fruit. Black coffee was all she could tolerate. She was too miserable at the prospect of Finn leaving in just a few hours.

She was about to ask Finn and Marco for the umpteenth time if there was anything else they needed, when she looked up to see big fat snowflakes drifting past the window. She alerted the others.

'The first snow!'

She'd never lost the excitement of the first fall, but she wasn't always at the chalet to see it. Was it an omen that perhaps—just perhaps—things might work out for her and Finn?

With Marco predicting the possibilities of skiable snow, and Finn saying snow was a novelty for a Sydney boy, any awkwardness was smoothed over. And the snowfall propelled her and Finn to start their journey back to the palace straight away, as their driver was worried that the roads might be affected.

They needed to be back in plenty of time for their meeting with the Chamber of Commerce.

She and Finn passed their journey back to the palace in much the way they had the journey to the chalet. The only difference was that Finn spent quite some time on his cell phone, for which he apologised.

'I have to check all is okay with my meetings in Dublin and London.' He leaned over to her. 'I'm glad we've got one more business meeting together.'

'Even if it's likely to be the stuffiest,' she said.

'It's a way to extend our time together for as long as possible. No meeting could possibly be stuffy with you chairing it.'

'Thank you,' she said, aching to touch him—even put

her hand on his arm—but knowing it would not be wise. She mustn't risk any hint of scandal—not when they had been so discreet.

Finn was proud of the way Natalia conducted herself at the meeting later that morning. The men and women of the Chamber of Commerce were delighted that their Princess was taking an active interest in local businesses, and Tristan and his savvy sister—Gemma was again absent—worked well together. She would be an asset to any business. To any country.

To him.

It was a kind of torture to play the polite visitor when Natalia was in the room and all he wanted to do was be by her side, claiming her as his own. But he was just a guy from Australia, whose interest lay in the gourmet foods he could import at a profit into his country on the other side of the world.

He was very aware of how deep the roots of this country went. How old the traditions of the people were. How conservative their customs. To uproot Natalia might not be the best option for her.

His grandparents were great gardeners. He knew from working with them that sometimes a plant uprooted from a particular type of soil did not transplant successfully, but rather withered and died. Natalia was the most beautiful flower, adapted to thrive in this fantasy land of castles and dungeons and family retainers. Sydney was an altogether brasher place, and tough in its own way.

Natalia smiled at him from across the room. To chat about chocolate and cheese with her, without acknowledging that she had been in his bed last night, was excruciating.

What he felt for her was so much more than infatuation. It had been from the get-go. He realised that now.

Everything about Natalia felt so right, and just her smile sent his heart soaring to heaven. It had nothing to do with her being a princess, and everything to do with her being the perfect woman for him. Yet there were very real obstacles to be overcome.

He *had* to make option two work. In the next two weeks away from her, he would come up with a plan.

At the end of the meeting he shook hands with her in a formal goodbye that tore him apart. He could tell from the almost imperceptible quiver of her lower lip that she was finding it equally torturous. How quickly he'd learned to read her.

As he made his way to the official car that was taking him and the master chocolatier to the airport, and thence to Dublin, he found every excuse to turn back and see ever-diminishing last glimpses of her.

He had a horrible fear that her family would try to make sure he never saw her again. But he would never let that happen.

That afternoon, alone in her apartment, Natalia missed Finn so desperately it physically hurt. She literally could not think of anything else but him.

She had been premature in believing the dark cloud of gloom that had hung over her for so long had dissipated. It had eased. But it was still like a grey fog that strangled the vitality from her, misted her vision of any hope for the future.

He had gone.

The meeting with the Chamber of Commerce that morning had concluded only too quickly After she'd waved Finn goodbye, with the perfectly calibrated royal wave she had been trained to do from a little girl, she'd had a quick chat with Tristan to review the other meetings she'd had with Finn. Her brother seemed to have a high opinion of Finn, and she had sensed Tristan could become an ally if she ever had to fight for her right to be with a man her parents considered unsuitable.

She had to gather her allies. And Tristan had already fought and won his own battle with Montovian tradition.

After her exchange with Tristan she had pleaded a headache and headed for her apartment in the palace. The perfectly decorated apartment that felt suddenly as lonely as if she were in exile.

Despite thoughts of Finn and their options churning through her brain, she decided to try and sleep, fully clothed on her bed. After all, she had had virtually no sleep the night before. But before she was overwhelmed by drowsiness she phoned through to her mother's private secretary and booked an appointment with the Queen for the following morning.

She was pretty sure she knew what she had to do.

At some stage she awoke and reached out for Finn—only to find cold, empty sheets. Even after one night of sleeping in his arms she knew she wanted him always there—in her bed, by her side, sharing her life. Being with Finn had become more important than anything. This was—at last—love. That elusive emotion she'd feared she might never find. She just hoped—prayed—that Finn felt it too. Because she could never settle for less than his wholehearted love in return.

Holding that thought, she got up and showered, changed and climbed back into bed.

But sleep didn't come easily, and it was late by the time she drifted off again.

She was woken by the sound of her phone, saw it was still early, reached out to her nightstand, fumbled for the phone and looked for the caller ID.

Finn!

She was immediately awake. Then she burst into tears at the sound of his voice.

'Hey, what's going on?' he said. 'Are those tears I hear?'

She sniffed. 'No. Yes. I was just…overwhelmed to hear your voice. I…I think I had a deep fear I might never talk to you again.'

'That's not going to happen. We're talking now, aren't we? And we need to talk some more.'

'Where are you? In Dublin? London?'

'I'm here. In Montovia.'

She thought she was hearing things. 'At the palace?'

'I didn't think I should storm the walls and come and find you,' he said, in that laconic manner she liked so much. 'I'm at the tea room with the chocolate in the old town. Can you meet me here?'

'*Now?*'

'If a princess is *allowed* to do such an ordinary thing as meet a man for coffee.'

'This isn't a dream?'

'No.'

'Then the answer is yes!'

Fired with sudden energy, she quickly fixed her hair and applied make-up with hands that trembled with excitement. No matter how desperate she was to see Finn, the Princess of Montovia did *not* go outside the palace looking less than her best.

She threw on skinny black trousers, a tight black cashmere turtleneck, black boots with a heel that could handle cobblestones, and a gorgeous loose-weave wool short coat in different shades of pink that she'd been too depressed to wear after she'd bought it. Contemporary pink ruby earrings and a bracelet completed the look.

She booked a palace car to take her down to the old town and then ran from her apartment—something that really wasn't done in the corridors of the royal palace of Montovia.

CHAPTER FIFTEEN

NATALIA STILL WASN'T quite sure that Finn's call hadn't been a dream—a manifestation of her longing for him. But there he was, sitting at the most private table available at the tea room. He rose to greet her, darkly handsome in a superbly tailored business suit. Joy bubbled up inside her.

She forced herself to walk to him at a suitably sedate pace, when really she wanted to run and fling herself into his arms. She greeted him with a businesslike hand-shake, then sat down opposite him. This was one place where she would be observed and her behaviour noted by the townsfolk.

He'd ordered her the hot chocolate she'd been enjoy-ing here since she was a child. He had a coffee in front of him—short and black. He offered her a chocolate crois-sant, but she declined.

'It's so good to see you,' he said, his voice hushed.

Hopefully there was enough clatter from the other ta-bles to mask their conversation.

'Oh, Finn, I can't tell you how amazing it is to see you. I...I think my heart is literally jumping for joy. But what are you doing here? How...? Why...?'

'I cancelled my meetings in London, postponed my flight back to Sydney and flew back here from Dublin after the meeting. I stayed last night in a small hotel near the clock tower. Not that I slept.'

'Why didn't you tell me?'

'It was late when I got in. Besides, I needed some time to plan my strategy.' He leaned across the table towards her, his eyes intense. 'You see, beautiful, wonderful, perfect Natalia, I realised nothing was more important in my life than you. *Nothing.*'

'Oh, Finn, I feel the same.'

Her heart soared with the knowledge that he cared for her too. She ached to kiss him, but she knew they had an audience. A discreet, quiet audience, but an audience just the same.

'I wanted a plan for how to put option two into action. But option two without the separation, the long-distance angst. I decided I would come here to live. Not permanently. I thought three months…on a tourist visa. I could find an apartment here in the old town, so I would be near to you in the castle. As long as it had good Wi-Fi, I could work remotely. Then, as we discussed, we could start dating. Three months should give us time to get to know each other better.'

He looked very pleased with himself.

Her heart soared. 'But, Finn, I—'

He put up his hand to stop her. 'Hear me out. I can afford to ease off the pedal on my business for a few months. I've thought about what you said about being frightened. I realised I was scared too—of leaving behind my country and people I love to be a foreigner in a strange land.'

'It *is* scary,' she said.

'But that's exactly what my family did. My father left Ireland for a better life than on the small farm where he grew up. When my great-grandparents emigrated to Australia they left everything—everyone—for the chance of a better life. My Chinese great-grandparents were fleeing persecution…my Italian great-grandparents were fleeing poverty. In their day, there were only letters that took weeks to be delivered to communicate with the loved ones they'd left behind. My Chinese great-grandparents never saw their parents again. My grandparents had to fight prejudice and racism to be together and become the Romeo and Juliet of their suburb. *That's* the background I come from. Why shouldn't I be prepared to emigrate to build a life with you? I want to give it a trial for three months. That is if it's what you want too.'

Natalia laughed a laugh that she knew was tinged with hysteria. 'But I had the same idea. I decided we should try option two without all the long-distance to-ing and fro-ing by me living in Sydney for a while.'

'What?'

'Yes!' She lowered her voice. 'The plan I came up with was that I would come and live in Sydney for six months, so we could spend time together and get to know each other better. But perhaps three months might be more feasible. I would take a sabbatical from some of my charity commitments and work online for the auctions. I have good people to help here while I'm away. I thought of leasing an apartment near where Eliza and Jake live. You wouldn't be far. Perhaps I could meet your family, too? But the idea is to be *near* you, Finn. After our time in the chalet I cannot bear the thought of being parted from you again.'

'I hated being apart from you just that one night.'

He laughed, and she loved the edge of incredulous delight in his laughter.

'I can't believe we independently came up with two versions of the same solution at the same time.'

'Perhaps we can do both,' she said.

'Why not? I'll live in Montovia near you for three months...' he said.

'Then I'll move to Sydney for three months to be with you. I would *love* that. I was going to call you this morning to see what you thought of my idea.'

'And now I'm here to talk to you in person, because I couldn't stay away from you.'

'I've booked a meeting with my mother this morning, to tell her of my plans. But I'll go with you to Sydney anyway—even if she doesn't approve.' She paused. 'Your approval is all I need, Finn.'

'You have it wholeheartedly. We will make the decisions that affect our lives. And, while I'm certain I'll enjoy my three months living here near you, I will love having you in Sydney. I know my family will welcome you with open arms.'

'Oh, Finn, this is just wonderful!'

He leaned across the table and kissed her, his lips firm and possessive on hers. The kiss was short and sweet and utterly heartfelt.

And greeted by a chorus of applause and bravos.

Natalia broke away from the kiss and saw the smiling face of the tea room proprietor—a jovial, elderly man who had known her since she was a child. Everyone else in the shop would know who she was too, and about her history of turning down proposal after proposal, but all she saw were kind faces and goodwill.

She smiled back, unable to contain her joy that Finn was in her life and they could be open about what they meant to each other.

The alarm on her watch went off. '*Ack!* I'm meeting with my mother in twenty minutes. I've got to go—try and head her off before the news breaks that the Princess was seen kissing a handsome foreigner in the chocolate shop.'

'I'm coming too. We'll face her together. Let's start as we mean to continue—as a couple.'

They left the tea room to further applause, and headed for Natalia's car and driver.

'Wait,' Finn said. 'I have a suggestion. Rather than confronting the Queen with a *fait accompli*, why don't we ask her advice on how we can make it work?'

'Good idea,' Natalia said. '*Excellent* idea. You might end up a Montovian diplomat yet.'

Natalia was glad they'd agreed on Finn's strategy. When they entered the Queen's office she could tell by her mother's frosty expression that the news from the tea room had already reached her.

Her mother sat behind her ornate antique desk. She did not offer Natalia and Finn a chair, but rather let them stand. Finn gave a deep bow to the Queen, as Natalia had coached him. He did an excellent job. It was as if he were born to it.

'Your Majesty, Natalia and I beg your forgiveness for our indiscreet behaviour in the tea room.'

'We're in a relationship, Mother,' Natalie said. 'We couldn't help it. By the time you told me to "nip it in the bud" it was too late. This morning I was so happy I forgot I shouldn't be kissing Finn in public. Please take me off the royal matchmaking list. From now on I'm only dating Finn.'

'Where do you think this will take you?' said the Queen.

'To a future together, I hope,' she said.

She cast a sideways glance at Finn, who nodded.

Finn took Natalia's hand. 'We need to spend more time together, Your Majesty,' he said. 'However, that is complicated by the fact that we live in different countries on different sides of the world.'

'So I'm going to spend three months in Sydney with Finn,' Natalia blurted out.

So much for diplomacy. But she had lived by the royal rules for so long—she needed to make a strong statement about how now she wanted to live her life her own way.

With Finn.

'But first I plan to spend three months in Montovia, Your Majesty,' he said. 'We are seeking your advice on how we can best accomplish this. And of course Natalia will want to discuss with you the logistics of her taking some time to spend in Sydney.'

Natalia marvelled at how Finn had got the tone of his speech just right.

'Do you intend to live together?' asked the Queen.

'We intend to maintain separate residences,' he said. 'In both Montovia and Sydney. For three months in each country.'

'The King and I have given this matter considerable thought over the last few days.'

'What matter?' asked Natalia. 'Me and Finn? Mother, what do you mean, you and Father have been discussing it for the last few days? We have only just realised ourselves that we want to be together.'

The Queen quoted a Montovian saying that pretty much translated as telling them that she hadn't come down in the last shower. 'I saw how miserable you were when you got back from Sydney. How that misery lifted once this young man appeared at the palace.'

'Oh…' Natalia said, exchanging a glance with Finn.

'And if you make your living arrangements more permanent, where do you plan to live?'

'I would live wherever is best for Natalia,' Finn said.

'I realise that as second in line to the throne I am obliged to live here,' Natalia said.

She looked around her mother's ornate and exquisitely decorated office and thought about how much she loved the palace and the castle and being Princess of Montovia.

'Or I can make the choice to renounce my title.'

It hurt even to say the words. Renouncing her title would mean alienation from the family she loved. But she wanted to be with Finn—whatever the cost.

The Queen smiled the stiff smile that came from her regular wrinkle-fighting injections. 'Recent events have taken the pressure off you in that regard. Gemma is pregnant—'

Natalia clapped her hands together. 'I *knew* it. How wonderful! I'm so thrilled—'

Her mother raised her hand imperiously. 'Please let me continue, Natalia.'

'Yes, Mother.'

'Gemma is pregnant with twins. A boy and a girl. She has held off from sharing the news because there is a greater risk of complication with twins. However, her consultant has given her the all-clear to make the announcement. What this means for you is that once the twins are born you will go from being second in line to the throne to fourth. I know that will make you happy.'

'Yes, Mother it does.' She felt as though the enormous weight that had been crushing her since Carl's death had been lifted. 'I am delighted for Gemma and Tristan about the twins. And for you and Father. Not just because there will be new heirs, but new grandchildren.'

'It is happy news,' the Queen said.

Still there was the sadness of loss in her eyes, but there was also joyful anticipation of new life. The new babies would do much to heal the wounds in her family that had made Natalia's life so constricted.

'The best kind of happy news,' Natalia said.

The Queen continued. 'You should know that if you and Finn decide to marry you have our permission.'

Was she hearing things?

'Really?'

'I told you—I want you to be happy. It is not just the news about the twins that has prompted our decision. However, there is a condition. If you decide to make your home in Australia we would require you to make regular return trips home to Montovia.'

'To fulfil my royal duties?'

'To see your mother and father. We would miss you, my darling.'

* * *

After they'd left the Queen's office Finn asked Natalia to take him up to the arched lookouts, with their magnificent view across the lake.

'We need some privacy and a place to think,' he explained.

As they walked up the steps and along the battlements, holding hands, he marvelled to himself at how the castle, the town, the country that had seemed like a movie set, populated by witches and wizards, was now beginning to seem like home. Because it was Natalia's home.

Perhaps one day she would feel the same about the view from the veranda of his house across to the Sydney Harbour Bridge and the Opera House.

When they reached the middle archway he put his arm around her and pulled her close. In silence, they both looked out at the view. He wondered if Natalia, as he was, was taking some quiet time to process that astonishing pronouncement by the Queen—that she and the King gave their permission for him to marry her daughter.

She wasn't wearing a hat, and a teasing chilly breeze was lifting her hair and blowing it across her face. He turned her to him and gently pushed her hair back into place. Then he cradled her chin in his hands and tilted her face upwards, so he could look into her eyes.

'I love you, Natalia,' he said, his voice hoarse with emotion. 'I already know all I need to know about you and I know I could not imagine a life without you in it.'

His beautiful princess closed her eyes and then opened them again, as if scarcely able to believe she was here with him. Her mouth curved in the most joyous of smiles. 'Oh, Finn, I love you too. I think I fell in love with you that first day in Sydney. Only because I've never been in love before I didn't recognise it.'

'The whole time we've been discussing our three-month plan for option two I've been thinking we don't really need to spend time dating. I don't want to live apart from you. I love you. I adore you. I want to marry you, and have children with you, and wake up every morning to your face on my pillow.'

'Oh, Finn…' She sighed. 'That sounds like heaven.'

He reached into the inner pocket of his jacket and pulled out a small velvet covered box. 'Natalia, will you do me the honour of becoming my wife? I love you and I want to honour and cherish you for the rest of our lives—not because you're a princess, but because you're the most wonderful woman ever put on this earth.'

She put her hand to her heart, seeming almost too overcome to speak. But she managed to choke out some words. 'Yes, Finn—yes. I love you and I want to honour and cherish you too. More than anything I want to be your wife.'

His wife. Two such wonderful words.

He took her left hand and slid onto the third finger an engagement ring magnificent in its simplicity—a large, oval cut white diamond on a narrow platinum band. He'd guessed the size just right.

She held out her hand and splayed her fingers to admire the ring as its facets caught the light and glistened with tiny rainbows. 'It's beautiful. I love it. But how—?'

'My cousin in Dublin directed me to the best jeweller in town. I didn't think I'd get a chance to give it to you quite so soon.'

He kissed her long and sweet and tenderly.

Natalia pulled away from his kiss and leaned back against the circle of his arms. 'You realise this is where Tristan proposed to Gemma?'

'I do. I know how important tradition is to the older Montovians. Why not start some traditions for our generation?'

'When we marry you'll be a Montovian too. You become a citizen on marriage.'

'I'd like us to marry as soon as we can. But I'd still like to do the three months in each country. What do you think?'

'Me too. Only, because we're engaged, we might actually be able to live together. And, in light of your proposal, maybe I should come to Australia first, so we can be here in Montovia for the three months before the wedding.'

'I thought something simple, private...'

She gave a snort of most un-princess-like laughter.

'*Simple?* I am Princess of Montovia and my parents' only daughter. I'm afraid we can't have "simple". Don't even try to fight for it. We'll have a spectacular royal wedding in our beautiful cathedral with all the ceremonial bling. Nothing less.'

Finn realised that his private life out of the spotlight was about to come to a screeching halt. But with Natalia by his side he didn't care nearly as much as he'd thought he might.

'My family will love a big cathedral wedding,' he said. 'What about that glass carriage drawn by white horses?'

He was joking. Natalia was not.

'The horses—yes; the glass carriage—not possible. But there *is* a royal landau. It's an open carriage, so that means a spring wedding.'

'Six months away? Perfect timing. At the end of our time getting to know each other better.'

'I'm going to enjoy every second of it,' she said.

'We have a lifetime together ahead for us, my beautiful wife-to-be,' said Finn, drawing her into his arms.

He couldn't imagine ever feeling happier than he did at this moment, but he suspected that being married to Natalia would mean happiness compounding upon happiness.

EPILOGUE

Six months later

NATALIA COULD FEEL the goodwill emanating from the Montovian citizens who crowded the cathedral square, hoping to catch a glimpse of their Princess in her wedding dress as she alighted from the sleek black limousine with her father King Gerard. There was a media contingent too, with cameras at the ready, so sizeable it had to be kept in check by members of the royal family's personal guard.

There was intense interest in her love story with Finn all around the world. A beautiful European princess marrying a handsome Australian commoner was story enough. But the 'Secret Princess' angle was what had sent their love story viral.

Not long after they had made the formal announcement of their engagement some sharp-eyed person in Eliza's circle had noticed the resemblance blonde wedding guest Natalie Gerard bore to dark-haired Natalia, Princess of Montovia. And when photos of her dancing with Finn at Eliza's wedding were published, Natalia's cover was completely blown.

Now the whole world knew how they had met. But, despite media digging, no scandal had been unearthed. Rather, their story was being celebrated for its heady level of romance.

Natalia alighted from the car, waved to the crowd, then climbed the stairs to the cathedral on her father's arm, her long train trailing behind her.

At the top of the steps her bridesmaids were there to greet her, dressed in exquisite long gowns in gradating tones of pink—Gemma, new mother to the world's most adorable twins, Amelie, heavily pregnant, Finn's beautiful sister Bella, already a dear friend, and three of her close Montovian friends.

They clustered around her to pat her hair into place and adjust the filmy veil that covered her face, anchored by the diamond tiara her great-great-grandmother had worn, before it fell to the hem of her white lace gown. They fussed with her bouquet of indigenous Australian blooms—flannel flowers, white waratah and orchids, air-freighted from Sydney. Then they kissed her for good luck.

Her bridesmaids left her to walk in procession, one by one, down the long, long aisle to the high altar of the cathedral. The same altar where her ancestors, stretching back generation after generation, had wed.

Natalia stood with her father as the organ music swelled and she started her own stately march down the aisle to where Finn waited for her—her husband-to-be. There were gasps of admiration from the congregation as she made her way down the carpet.

She was pleased. She wanted Finn to gasp too. His reaction to how she looked was the only one she cared about. Her dress was made in a similar style to the pink dress she'd worn in Sydney when she'd first met him, only by the original Paris designer, and the silk lace was heavy and luxurious, the design simple in its construction.

Every pew in the cathedral was packed with people who had come to witness her wedding and wish her well. All she could see was a mass of smiling faces.

As she got to the first few rows she recognised her family and friends. The Queen in the ornately carved monarch's pew. Her new family, Finn's parents and his grandparents, whom she already adored. The other Party Queens and their husbands—Eliza holding her baby girl.

And next to Eliza sat her neighbour Kerry, she of the uncannily accurate prediction, who had been high on the invitation list. Her new prediction was for a long and happy life for the bride and groom and their three children yet to be born.

And then there was Finn—her beloved Finn—standing by Tristan, his best man. Her husband-to-be, tall and handsome, in an immaculately tailored morning suit. When she finally reached him, he was obviously too overcome to say anything, but his eyes told her everything she needed to know about how he felt about his bride.

Her father handed her over to the new man in her life and slid back to his pew.

'You are the most beautiful bride I've ever seen,' Finn whispered when he found his words. 'I'm a lucky, lucky man.'

'I'm the lucky one—to have found you,' she whispered back. 'Want to see my "something borrowed"?'

Her 'something old' was the diamond tiara. The 'something new' her gown. The 'something blue' was the sapphire and diamond necklace and earrings gifted to her by her parents.

She held up her right wrist. 'This is my "something borrowed".'

Finn stared at the fine platinum bangle from which dangled the cufflink he had left behind in her hotel room back in Sydney, where it had all started.

'So that's where it went,' he said. 'I was too busy searching for you to look for it.'

'I kept it close to my heart, always hoping I'd see you again,' she whispered.

Every day she fell more and more in love with him.

'We'll never be parted again, I promise you,' he said, taking her hand, drawing her close and facing the archbishop as the ceremony that would make them husband and wife commenced.

After the service had ended—having been conducted in both Montovian and English—Finn sat back in the antique open landau drawn by four perfectly matched white horses that was taking him and his brand-new wife on a ceremonial tour through the ancient cobbled streets of the old town of Montovia. It was a perfect May day.

The narrow thoroughfares were lined with well-wishers waving the Montovian flag, with its emblem of an eagle with a sword in its beak, and the occasional Australian flag. Along with Natalia he waved back, soon losing his self-consciousness at doing such an unaccustomed thing.

Again, he felt as though he'd been plunged into the set of a fantasy movie as the carriage wound its way through the shadow of the ancient castle that stood guard over the town, past the famous medieval clock and the rows of quaint houses that were multiple centuries older than anything in Australia—all to the accompaniment of the glorious chiming of bells from one of the oldest cathedrals in Europe and the cheers of the crowd in a language he was only just beginning to master.

He turned to his bride. 'I love you, Natalia, my wife, for ever and for always,' he said as he kissed her.

The crowd erupted with joyous cheering.

His heart was full of love and gratitude that, as in the best of fantasies, he and his real-life Princess Natalia were being given their very own fairy tale happy-ever-after and beginning their new life together.

* * * * *

THE MARINE'S
FAMILY MISSION

VICTORIA PADE

Chapter One

Emmy Tate took off her soiled leather work gloves, stuffed them partially into the front pocket of her jeans and ran the back of her right wrist over her forehead to wipe the sweat away. Then she pressed both fists into the ache in the small of her back.

Enough for today, she decided.

As she surveyed her progress on the field that had, until two days before, been growing spring vegetables, she fought feeling discouraged and overwhelmed.

Bad enough that the record-breaking hailstorm had wreaked massive destruction on the organic farm on the outskirts of small-town Northbridge, Montana. But why did her progress clearing the damage have to be so *slow*? She'd barely made a dent.

Mandy would have done better, she thought.

Of course, her late sister would have known what she was doing, and that wasn't true for Emmy.

But she was trying—and trying, and trying, for months now—to make the best of a bad situation.

But tomorrow was another day, she told herself, surveying the farm. She looked beyond the field to the apple orchard behind it, where branches were nearly bare of leaves now, where many limbs were dangling or left broken on the ground.

It would have made an effective photograph. One she would have taken long ago when she'd worked for the Red Cross documenting their good works in natural disasters or war zones.

But those weren't the kinds of pictures she took now. Not that she had time for pictures at all lately, with all she had to do. At least cleaning up the field left her out in the open. She was dreading getting into that orchard.

She'd called the only arborist in the area to come and take a look at it. Because he'd known and liked Mandy, he'd come despite the fact that he was overbooked with all the damage in the area. But he refused to deal with anything under ten feet high or to start work before the already-downed limbs and the ground debris were cleared.

He'd assured her that it wasn't anything she couldn't take care of herself. Drag out the downed limbs. Rake the leaves. Use the pole saw and pruner to cut down the broken branches below ten feet.

He'd shown her how to do that, confident that she could manage.

It wasn't that she didn't think she could, it was just that she'd have to be in that orchard to do it. Under those broken branches that could—*would*—fall to the ground, sometimes without warning. If she wasn't far enough back or quick enough to get out of the way, they'd trap her...

It'll be fine, she told herself impatiently, tamping down on the panic trying to rise to the surface. *It isn't the school in Afghanistan, it's a bunch of trees, for crying out loud.*

And she was over what had happened. She was okay now, she insisted to herself.

But still she closed her eyes and took a deep breath,

then exhaled slowly, repeating the process again and again until the panic wasn't looming.

Or at least until it was looming less.

"I don't know how I'm gonna get in there, Mandy…" she confided to her late sister in a whisper.

But cleanup had to be done. She needed the place in perfect condition if she was going to find someone to lease it so she could get back to her everyday life in Denver. Back to what she'd been doing since leaving her work with the Red Cross—taking photographs of happy occasions like engagements and weddings and taking portraits of newborns.

"It's just a bunch of trees," she said out loud this time before she headed for the farm's truck, assuring herself that it was only a matter of time before she could go home to Denver.

Although it wouldn't exactly be back to her everyday life. Not when she'd be taking her three-year-old niece and two-month-old nephew with her to raise.

But even unexpected single parenthood was less daunting than the farming her sister had loved—and mastered. She reached the truck and saw her reflection in the driver's-side window.

She'd never seen Mandy look as bad after a day's work as Emmy did at that moment.

"You're a mess, Em," she told her reflection.

Strands of her chin-length reddish-brown hair had come free of the topknot she'd put it in this morning and fell limply around her face.

She hadn't bothered to put on makeup, so there was no blush on her high cheekbones, no eyeliner or mascara to accentuate her chestnut-colored eyes, no highlighter dusting her thin, straight nose or lipstick on full lips that craved balm at that moment.

But there *was* a dirt smudge across her forehead and a general griminess to her appearance.

Not wanting to get into the truck with too much of that grime, she took the work gloves from her pocket, slapped them against the side of the truck until no more dust billowed out of them, then used them to whack the loose layer of soil off her jeans and faded red crew-neck T-shirt.

Once that was done, she kicked her boots against the truck's running board to clear some of the crusted dirt from them and then climbed up behind the wheel, glad no one but her mother and the kids would see her looking like this before she could climb into a much-anticipated shower.

A shower, after which she would dry off with a clean towel before she put on equally clean clothes fresh out of the laundry her mother would have folded and waiting for her. Then she'd enjoy the nice dinner her mother was making and some time with the kids her mother had taken care of.

For this one last day until Karen Tate left.

But Emmy couldn't think about the fact that her mother was leaving tomorrow. About the fact that she would soon be on her own, not only with the farm and storm cleanup, but also with the house and the laundry and the meals and the kids, who included a colicky baby who cried for hours at night...

No, she couldn't think about it. She was already tired and dirty and hungry, and she just couldn't.

So she pushed everything out of her mind, turned the key in the ignition and started the truck's engine.

"I sure hope you didn't bite off more than I can chew, Mandy," she muttered as she released the emergency brake.

Then she sighed and said, "One foot in front of the other, Em. That's all you can do. Just keep putting one foot in front of the other."

The truck made a cranky noise when she put it into gear and she reminded herself to add auto repair to the list of skills that would be good for a leaser to have. Then she drove down the dirt path that took her to the private drive leading to the house.

It was only once she was on the private drive that she saw another truck ahead of her. A black one almost as dated as the pale blue one she was in.

Company? She wasn't expecting anyone. She and her mother were supposed to spend this evening going over the food her mother had stocked the freezer with and the revolving schedule of babysitters her mother had lined up to help with the kids. Then her mother needed to finish packing. She was leaving early Saturday morning, so Emmy doubted her mother had invited anyone over.

Hopefully it was just someone coming to say an impromptu goodbye to Karen Tate and Emmy could leave them to it while she hit the shower.

The other truck came to a stop near the front porch of the white two-story farmhouse. Emmy parked her own truck, paying little attention to the guest, who she was increasingly sure must be there to see her mother.

Until she got out of the truck.

The other driver had already disembarked and was standing beside his vehicle, facing Emmy, apparently waiting for her.

That was when she realized who her guest was.

Oh no, not him! Anybody but him!

Of all the people who had come to give condolences for her brother-in-law, Topher, in October, of all the people who had come to give condolences for Mandy during the last six weeks, of all the people who had come to visit or help since Emmy had taken over, of all the people in the whole wide world, not *him*.

Declan Madison.

He was her late brother-in-law's best friend. The neighbor Topher had grown up with and considered a brother. The person Topher had gone to the naval academy with, who he'd served with in the marines. He was the person who had been with Topher when Topher died seven months ago, in an IED explosion in Afghanistan that also left Declan wounded.

And if it wasn't bad enough that he was also tied to Emmy's Afghanistan nightmare four and a half years ago, he'd rejected her in the worst way at Mandy and Topher's wedding not long after that.

Emmy had dreaded the thought of seeing him again ever since.

But there he was.

She wanted to get back in the truck and drive as far away from him as she could get.

But he was staring straight at her and making this yet another bad situation she had to make the best of.

Feeling rooted to the spot, Emmy once again took a deep breath, breathed it out, then literally forced herself to put one foot in front of the other to cross the farmyard.

As she did, she took stock of him.

She didn't know exactly how hurt he'd been in the explosion—she'd only heard that he'd survived. But looking at him now Emmy saw no clues as to what injuries he'd suffered.

As far as she could tell, there were no visible scars, no discernible differences in him. He still stood tall and straight—inches over six feet. His shoulders were still a mile wide, and even though he looked slightly leaner, the officer's service uniform he was wearing was still packed with muscle.

It was only when her gaze went above the impressive body that she noticed a difference.

At first she thought it was just that he'd grown out the buzz cut from his black-coffee-colored hair. But a couple of steps closer made her realize that his handsome face had a new gravity to it. A brooding quality. Plus the hint of some weight lost there, too, had carved hollows that made his cheekbones and chiseled jawline more ruggedly drawn, adding an intensity to his exquisitely masculine features.

A few more steps took her near enough to better see the remarkable cobalt blue eyes that had mesmerized her in the past, and there she saw even more change.

There was no sparkle, none of the humor or lightheartedness that she'd seen in them before. Even his supple-looking mouth looked somber. It was as if the light had completely gone out in him.

"Declan," Emmy said in greeting, hearing the chill in her own reception but unable to heat it up as she came to within feet of him and stopped.

"Emmy…" he answered with a heavy helping of his own reservations.

Only in that moment did Emmy remember how she looked herself—awful.

It was bad enough to have to meet up with this guy again, but to do it with no makeup, with stringy hair and all-around grunge? For the second time, she wanted to run the other way.

But she squared her shoulders as if she had nothing to be self-conscious about, thanked heaven that at least seeing him again still hadn't caused flashbacks to Afghanistan and said bluntly, "What are you doing here?"

His clean-shaven chin went up a notch, defiantly, defensively. "I've been in one hospital after another since October and now I'm just out of two months of rehab—I was released three days ago. I thought I'd be coming to face Mandy, but then I got the news that she died?"

The question revealed understandable shock. As far as anyone knew, her sister had been a healthy, vital thirty-two-year-old.

"Apparently she had a congenital heart problem that no one knew about... She died in her sleep two weeks after Kit was born."

"She made it through a second pregnancy, a second birth and then..." His full dark eyebrows arched and he shook his head in disbelief.

"My mom thinks Topher came for her so they could be together," Emmy said softly, wanting to believe that, too.

The mention of Declan's late friend caused those eyebrows to pulse together as if she'd struck a nerve before he said, "I'm sorry for your loss. I liked Mandy. She and Topher were good together."

"They were," Emmy agreed.

A moment of silence followed that before Declan went on.

"So instead I'm here about the kids," he announced.

"The kids?" Emmy repeated.

"I came to see what's going on. To make sure Topher's—" the name choked him up but he conquered it in a hurry "—kids are okay. To do what I can... I'm Trinity's godfather, you know."

And Emmy was her godmother. It had happened in two separate ceremonies—one with Emmy soon after Trinity was born, and a second with Declan when Topher and Declan had arranged leave time a month later.

It had been something Emmy was grateful for so she didn't have to see Declan again then.

"Not long after Topher died, Mandy decided she'd better make a will and name a guardian for the kids in case anything ever happened to her. Nobody thought it would, but…" This time it was Emmy who choked up a bit before she got on top of it. "She named me as the kids' guardian, so…they're mine and you don't have to concern yourself with them."

That beetled his brow again. And seemed to raise a little ire in him because there was an edge to his deep voice when he said, "Topher was no different to me than either of my own brothers. I feel about his kids the way I'd feel about my own blood niece or nephew. I'm going to do what I can for them."

"They don't need you. Or anything from you," Emmy said tersely, her own ire raised at the thought of having to have anything to do with him—and also at the implication she wasn't enough to look after them.

"Look—" he said in a commanding, no-nonsense voice just as the front door opened and her mother came out.

"Declan! Is that you? I looked out to see if Emmy was back and… It *is* you, isn't it?"

Oh nooo… Emmy groaned silently.

She knew how her mother felt about Declan Madison. Even before meeting him, Karen Tate—like Emmy herself—had been grateful to him for saving Emmy's life in Afghanistan.

At Mandy and Topher's wedding—unaware of the memories Emmy feared that the sight of him might cause her—her mother had expressed that gratitude and developed a fondness for him.

What her mother *didn't* know was what had happened later on the night of the wedding.

Or how incredibly confused Emmy's feelings about Declan had become.

Or that he'd walked her to her hotel room, made a date for breakfast with her and then gone next door for a night of what had sounded like very raucous sex with another bridesmaid.

So of course Karen Tate was excited to see him and hurried down the steps of the front porch to give him a hug.

"Oh, honey, how are you?" she asked.

Declan returned the hug stiffly, keeping his solemn, steady gaze on Emmy over her mother's head as if to let her know that they weren't finished with their talk.

"I'm okay," he answered, his tone oddly reserved.

Emmy's mom must have heard it, too, because she ended the hug and linked her arm through Declan's to turn him toward the porch. "Come in. I want to know how you *really* are. And I know you must want to see Kit. And every time Trinity looks at the picture of her daddy, I point you out standing next to him and tell her who you are—she calls you *Decan*. Let's see if she recognizes you in person."

Then over her shoulder, Karen Tate said, "Go on up and have your shower, Em. I'll keep *Decan* occupied."

As her mother urged Declan to the porch steps, Emmy noted his slight limp.

For his part he didn't cast her so much as another glance. Which irked Emmy even more.

She let them get all the way through the door before she followed, thinking about what had seemed like nothing but a generous idea when Mandy had said she wanted to volunteer for the Red Cross mission to Afghanistan that Emmy had been assigned to follow and photograph four and a half years ago.

And how much her sister's life and her own had been altered when Topher Samms and Declan Madison had become their military escorts.

Chapter Two

"You're going to *stay* at Topher's farm?"

Declan was sitting at the kitchen table with his sister, Kinsey, in the farmhouse where they'd grown up. Kinsey had made him breakfast, and while she was at it, he'd told her about his visit to the Sammses' place the day before. About the long talk he'd had with Topher's mother-in-law that had made it clear Emmy Tate needed his help.

"I know you thought it would be fun for us all to be back here," he said. "To stay in the house together one more time before it gets packed up and sold—"

"I keep scheduling times to come and clear it out, but something always interferes. So while we still have it—and it *isn't* packed up yet—I wanted to get married here."

"Sure. But come on—this place will be bursting at the seams by the wedding next week. Me, you, your groom and his mother are already here. Conor and Maicy, and Liam and Dani and the twins are all coming... This place just isn't that big. What difference does it make if I bunk in the workout room downstairs or down the road? I'm just five minutes away. And I need to do what I can for Topher's family. *Whatever* I can. I owe him that..."

"I know that's important to you," his sister admitted.

It was. He felt responsible for his best friend's death, and that meant it was on him to step in on whatever Topher had left behind. Even more than his sister's wedding, that driving need was what had brought him back to the small town where he'd been made to feel like the scum of the earth growing up.

"It's bad over at the Sammses' place, huh?" his sister asked. "It's so strange that the storm totally missed us but decimated them. I guess we dodged the bullet."

"It's definitely bad over there," he confirmed. Karen Tate had described three fields full of spring plants wiped out, the orchard torn apart, the family vegetable garden gone, the roof and one side of the house and the barn shredded, the chicken coop battered and untold damage on the apiaries.

"The farm has been in the Samms family for six generations, and Topher—and Mandy—loved that place," he went on after outlining the problems. "They were dedicated to keeping it in the family, to raising the kids there, to passing it down to them." And had his friend been alive, Declan knew that there was nothing Topher wouldn't have done to meet that goal.

"It can't happen the way Topher and Mandy planned now," he said, hearing the ragged edge that came into his own voice as guilt weighed him down. "The kids aren't going to grow up on the farm—Mandy made her sister their guardian—"

"Emmy—that's her name, right? Mandy's sister? You rescued her in Afghanistan?"

"I dug her out of some rubble when a bomb hit a school she was in taking pictures of kids for the Red Cross," he confirmed.

"You say that like it was no big deal, but you saved her life."

He shrugged that off. "I was just doing my job," he said as if he hadn't been frantic to get her out from under that debris. Because even though it hadn't been the same love at first sight for them as it had been for Topher and Mandy, before that school had been hit, he'd had a few laughs with Emmy, he'd liked her.

But that was water far, far under the bridge now.

"Anyway," he continued, "she doesn't know squat about farming. She lives and works in Denver, and her mother says that's where she plans to take Trinity and Kit. But she wants to keep the farm in the family so the kids have the option of running it when they grow up, which means she's figuring on leasing it. Only nobody's going to take it on until she gets it cleaned up. And she needs an extra pair of hands and someone who knows their way around a farm to do that."

"Are you well enough for farm work?" Kinsey was a nurse and very protective of his health right now.

"I'm fine. The knee is a little stiff, but I'm keeping up on the physical therapy exercises for it. The farm work will just help get me the rest of the way back in shape. I have to wait for my review with the Medical Evaluation Board anyway before I can get the go-ahead to get back to my unit. Might as well be productive in the meantime."

His sister didn't look convinced, but he knew his body. He knew how hard he'd worked in rehab not just on regaining the use and strength of his leg, but with weight training on the rest of his body so he'd be ready and able to return to duty.

"Plus there's the kids," he said then. "Mandy's mom has been staying at the farm, but she told me she's leaving today. Mandy's dad has been holding down the fort at their travel agency, but her mom really needs to get back. The timing is rough. Before the hail hit, there was someone serious about leasing the farm—he was set to take over so Emmy could take the kids to Denver with her mother this weekend. But he backed out once he saw the hail damage."

"So now they have to start all over trying to find someone else?"

"That's what Karen said. She also said that Emmy is good with the kids but she was in over her head with the farm even before the storm, when other farmers were lending her a hand here and there—"

"But now other farmers have to regroup from the hail themselves," Kinsey said.

"Right. So she has to clear the damage, replant the fields, take care of the animals and, with her mother leaving, do all the household stuff and take care of Trinity and Kit, too. Plus Karen said Kit is *colicky*—whatever that is—and he cries a lot at night... There'll be some help from babysitters coming in during the day, but Emmy will be on her own for one sleepless night after another and—"

Declan sighed. "Bottom line—there's a big need for help over there, for more than two hands. So I'm going to work with Emmy to do what I can."

As long as he didn't go over there today and find her standing on the front porch with a shotgun to run him off the property.

It had been her mother—not Emmy—who had told him what was going on. In fact, Emmy had looked like she wanted to strangle her mother when she'd come downstairs after her shower to discover just how candid Karen had been.

And when he'd offered his services, Emmy couldn't have been more against it. She'd flatly and fervently refused his help.

The two women had gone back and forth for a while.

But Karen had held her ground and eventually Emmy had conceded, even to the idea of him moving into the basement so they could trade off nights being up with Kit.

But the whole concession had been so obviously against Emmy's will that he thought she might have only pretended to go along with the plan in order to end the argument, always intending to keep him away once her mother was out of the picture.

It was what Declan was half expecting.

More than half, really. He already knew how changeable she could be.

She'd been friendly when they'd first met in Afghanistan. But after digging her out of that bombed school, she wouldn't even let him visit her in the hospital. Instead she'd sent a thank-you note with her sister. Her sister, who hadn't been inside the school when it was blown up and had escaped injury.

After leaving the hospital, when Mandy and Topher were still keeping as constant company as they could, Emmy had had her sister tell him that she still wasn't up for any visits.

And during Mandy and Topher's lengthy parting at the airport? Emmy had hidden aboard the plane and Declan had been left hanging on the tarmac, not even allotted a goodbye.

Message received—that was what he'd thought. Apparently sharing a couple of laughs had meant more to him than it had to her and she didn't want anything to do with him. Okay, fine.

But then there was the wedding.

She'd been weird toward him initially. She hadn't done anything but raise her chin to say hello before taking off as if her tail was on fire. And she'd kept her distance from him through the rehearsal and rehearsal dinner, through the pre-wedding pictures.

Then at the reception *she'd* approached *him*. She'd said she wanted to thank him again for unburying her from the school debris. She'd even stuck around to chat and that friendly, fun side of her had come out again. To the extent that he'd started to think they might hit it off after all.

They'd spent almost the entire reception together, doing a lot of drinking, dancing, laughing. He'd had a great time with her. But she'd been pretty drunk by the end of it, so he'd walked her to her room. He hadn't so much as kissed her because he hadn't wanted it to seem as if he was taking any kind of advantage.

What he *had* done was make a date for breakfast the next morning.

But by breakfast she'd turned on him again—she'd stood him up, and when he'd happened to run into her in the hotel lobby and asked if she'd forgotten about it, she'd said, "Are you kidding? You really thought I'd have breakfast with you after last night?"

Then she'd turned her back on him, stormed off and not spoken to him the two other times their paths had crossed post-wedding.

So yeah, he wasn't putting much stock in her agreement to his help now. She was a Jekyll and Hyde if ever he'd seen one.

But despite that, he did hope that she accepted his help.

Not because he had any desire at all to deal with her but because helping with the farm and the kids until a leaser could step in or until he passed his medical review and was deployed again was something he could do for Topher.

For Topher he would do anything. For Topher nothing would ever be enough…

"You don't say her name like you like her," Kinsey observed, bringing him out of his reverie.

"I don't *dis*like her," he said, though it didn't sound altogether believable even to him. "I don't know... For some reason things just don't gel between us."

"I've heard that she's really pretty, though. I met Greg Kravitz in town and he asked if I knew her—he sounded interested."

"Kravitz? He's still here?" Declan said through nearly clenched teeth.

"Yeah, he has a landscaping business—mostly I think he mows lawns, shovels snow in the winter... I forgot, you guys really hated each other, didn't you? You were like archenemies."

Kinsey had no idea...

"He's a jerk" was all Declan said. He'd always kept things to himself when it had come to Kravitz. And maybe his own long and ugly history with him was the reason that it rubbed him so wrong to think of Kravitz being interested in Emmy Tate. But it did. It rubbed him really, really wrong...

"I wouldn't wish Kravitz on anyone," he grumbled.

"But especially not on Emmy Tate?" his sister probed.

Declan sighed and shook his head. "You know what happens when everybody in your family finds someone and you're single? They all think they have to pair you up with someone. But let's just put any idea of me and Emmy Tate to rest once and for all, huh? I don't know what makes her tick, but I do know that it doesn't work for me."

Sure, she was great-looking, there was no doubt about that—even when she was as dirty as a farmhand after a day's hard work yesterday he'd still seen that. And then she'd cleaned up and...

Okay, yeah, great-looking.

She had the creamiest skin he'd ever seen and a face like some kind of enticing girl next door, with gorgeous, big, doe-brown eyes, a straight little nose, kissably full lips that he'd never had the chance to kiss and dimples—she had the damn sexiest dimples...

Plus she had smooth, shiny reddish-brown hair that turned toward her chin on the bottom, with a long wisp of bangs that sometimes fell like a see-through silk scarf over one eye in a way that was shy and coy and seductive all at once.

And her body?

Yeah, that was great, too. Trim and tight with just enough oomph in all the right places.

So sure, he'd been interested when he'd come across what had seemed like a little breath of fresh air from home in Afghanistan.

And yeah, she'd been intriguing enough for him to drop his guard again with her when she'd warmed up at the wedding reception.

But those cold shoulders she'd thrown his way the rest of the time—including yesterday? That definitely didn't work for him.

"I'm here because we lost Topher and there are things that have to be taken care of on his behalf," he said firmly then. "And *from* here the only place I'm headed for is where I belong—back to the marines and my unit. So don't go hoping for some kind of romance with anyone while I'm here."

"It might do you some good," his sister suggested with a different tone that he also recognized—the worried-about-him-and-his-state-of-mind-since-Topher's-death look and sound that he'd met from Kinsey and Conor and Liam.

"I'm good enough," he proclaimed, even if he was finding it hard to be the old Declan. "So all you happy love-birds can roost here and I'll go down the road and hope I can do some good there. But don't be putting some other kind of spin on it because it isn't gonna happen."

"Declan..." his sister said, sounding more worried still.

"I'm good, Kinsey," he cut her off, his tone more reprimand than anything. He knew that wasn't going to reassure her, but it was still the best he could manage.

And feeling the weight of his sister's concern heaped on top of what he'd been carrying around since Topher's death—*over* Topher's death—had him thinking that weathering the ups and downs of Topher's sister-in-law was preferable to hanging around here and weathering concern from all three siblings.

At least he hoped it would be.

But with Emmy Tate?

He couldn't be sure of anything.

"The guy whose gorgeous face gave you nightmares, the guy who turned out to be a player, will be moving in with you?" Carla Figarello demanded.

"I don't know..." Emmy said uncertainly. "It's my mother's idea... A really bad one..."

Saturday had been a loss in terms of getting anything done beyond the usual morning chores—water and feed the animals, collect the eggs, milk the cow and the cantankerous goats that gave her fits. Then a babysitter had come in to stay with Trinity and Kit so she could drive her mother to the Billings airport.

The babysitter had had to leave when she got back, so she'd given Trinity lunch, fed the baby and put them both down for naps. And now, while the kids slept and she couldn't be out of earshot, she was indulging herself with a much-needed phone call to Carla—her best friend since kindergarten, her confidante, the only person she'd talked to about what had begun to happen to her in the aftermath of Afghanistan.

"It's not a bad idea when you desperately need help and he's someone who can give it," Carla hedged. "But it sounds like your mother steamrolled you into agreeing to let the guy move into the basement, and what I want to know is if you're going to be able to handle being with him."

Emmy didn't know.

Since the wedding—and until the hailstorm—she'd been sure she was in control of the emotional backlash from the school collapse. Yes, some things had changed for her, but she'd found ways to manage her anxiety pretty well. A lot of people didn't like small spaces, so she wasn't the only one to avoid them, and who wouldn't be afraid of the idea of being underneath something that might fall on them—like the broken tree limbs in the orchard?

For the most part, though, she'd considered herself perfectly fine until seeing the devastation of the hail damage had brought the fear back. Not a lot of it—she took heart in that. But now seeing Declan Madison again did make her worry that more might break through.

"I didn't have a panic attack at the first sight of him," she said, putting as much optimism into her voice as she could.

Panic attacks when she saw him didn't make any sense to her, but soon after her rescue from the rubble, her reaction to Declan Madison had morphed from deep gratitude into the first of that emotional turmoil.

When the bomb had hit the school in Afghanistan, she'd been alone in a supply closet, packing her cameras and equipment. The explosion had flung her, knocking her unconscious.

When she'd come to—before she had any conception of what had happened or where she was—all she'd known was that both of her feet were trapped under a lot of weight. She'd worked to get them out, and when she had, bricks and mortar had crumbled with the movement, enclosing her even more.

She'd been left with her knees to her chest, in a space about the size of a barrel. There was no room to move—when she tried, more debris fell on her.

It had been pitch-black except for a speck of light that she'd been able to see above her, and that had given her hope that she'd somehow ended up near to the outside.

She'd shouted for help, not knowing if there was aid available or if she'd be rescued by friend or foe.

For four hours she'd been entombed, and all she'd known was that periodically her surroundings would shift, crumble and fall in, closing the space around her even more. She'd been terrified that at any moment the whole thing would collapse on top of her.

Then her shouts brought a voice from outside and the sounds of digging in to reach her.

When that dot of light had finally grown bigger, the first thing she'd seen had been Declan Madison's face.

Relief had flooded her, followed by more stress as he tried not to cause a cave-in while working at opening a space to pull her through.

He'd been diligent, assuring her that everything was going to be okay, that he'd get her out.

He'd barely made a two-foot gap in the wreckage when something overhead shifted more drastically. Acting quickly, he'd shoved his upper half in to grab her under the arms and had yanked her free just as a collapse did occur, dragging her out of harm's way a split second before she would have been crushed.

As he'd helped load her onto a gurney, then into an ambulance, she remembered thanking him—again and again and again—before she was rushed to a hospital. It was only later, after she'd been treated, after she'd been diagnosed with a concussion and had been given a bed so she could be watched overnight, that her appreciation had been eclipsed by something new and terrifying.

Declan had shown up at the hospital, and at first she'd only heard his voice asking where she was. That alone had caused uneasiness in her, but when she'd glanced in his direction and had actually seen him, the simple sight of that face had mentally thrown her back into the dark, dusty cranny amid the crumbling rubble.

And rather than associating Declan Madison with the relief of being freed, instead, in her mind, he instantly became a fast ride right back into the heart of her terror.

Mandy—who had been outside the school with Topher and Declan and hadn't been hurt—had been with her in the hospital, at her bedside. Emmy hadn't wanted her sister to know what she was feeling. In fact, she'd been ashamed of it—children and teachers had died in the attack, others had been scarred or maimed for life, there were little kids in beds around her stoically accepting their irreversibly changed lives, while she'd suffered nothing but a headache and a few cuts and bruises. Yet she was ready to crawl out of her skin with one look at the very person who had saved her. Thankfulness should have been the only thing she'd felt, and instead she was fighting terror.

Hiding it, she'd told her sister that she was tired and needed to rest. She'd asked Mandy to leave and take Declan with her.

So Mandy had left without knowing about that first distress, and Emmy had kept every other incident of it to herself ever since—except for telling Carla.

"So that's stuck—no panic attacks when you saw him at the wedding and none yesterday either," her friend said.

The wedding had been six months after the bombing. By then Emmy had reset her career. She'd talked poor Carla's ear off about her nightmares, her problem with small spaces, the flashbacks and anxiety, and she'd been doing much better. But she hadn't been sure what would happen if she had to see Declan Madison's face again.

Then she had. And while it had raised some memories, it hadn't made her hyperventilate, it hadn't caused all-out panic. In fact, worrying about it had been worse than anything that had happened when she had actually seen him.

Partly in order to celebrate that, and partly to control the worry that the panic still might hit, she'd had a whole lot to drink—beginning with champagne while the wedding party dressed and continuing at the reception. The more she'd had to drink, the calmer she'd felt, until she'd found the courage to approach Declan, to thank him again the way she knew she should have before leaving Afghanistan.

"No, no panic attacks yesterday either," Emmy confirmed.

"No symptoms of the PTSD at all?"

"I hate when you call it that. That isn't what it is. I've taken pictures of the kinds of things that cause PTSD—they're big and devastating and life changing, they aren't just a few hours being scared until somebody finds them and everything is okay again."

"I know that's how you see it, but—"

"That's how it is," she insisted, refusing to accept her friend's opinion. "What I have is just fallout from a bad experience, and it hardly ever even happens anymore."

"Okay—it hardly ever happens anymore, you're over the Afghanistan thing and seeing Declan Madison at the wedding and again yesterday didn't cause anything bad," Carla repeated as if she was temporarily conceding to Emmy's arguments. "But what about what *did* happen at the wedding? Do you want to be under the same roof with a guy who seemed interested in you and then spent the night with somebody else right next door to you?"

"That's definitely the other half of why I was hoping I might not ever have to see him again. But I guess going into this knowing I'm not his type is something," she said facetiously.

"So spending time with him now won't send you out into the arms of another Bryce?" Carla pressed.

Emmy laughed humorlessly. "There definitely won't be another Bryce. *Ever.* And as for this guy? I'm a whole lot tougher and smarter than I was four years ago at the wedding. He will *not* get to me."

Not even with those incredibly blue eyes or that face that could have been carved by the gods or that hella-hot body.

Besides, this wasn't a Las Vegas wedding, with wine flowing and inhibitions discarded. Now there was Topher's death. Mandy's death. Now there was the farm and hail damage. Now there were two kids she was suddenly a single parent to, and she had so much to wade through, to get used to. She was in no mood for anything but getting some control and order back into her life.

And unless she was mistaken, the changes she'd seen in Declan Madison made her think that he wasn't in any mood for anything either.

They'd just do what needed to be done and then move on in separate directions.

"I know we have some weird history—" she said then.

"I'd say," Carla agreed. "All good and cheery in Afghanistan at first, then really, really not good. Then sort of good again for a while at the wedding, until you were thinking one thing was going on between the two of you and—"

"It wasn't. Like with Bryce…" she added derisively. "But it's *all* in the past and this is now," Emmy concluded.

"And you think you can just do the *now* without any of the past poking in?"

Emmy sighed and wished she was in any other position. But she wasn't. "I hope so," she answered her friend honestly. "I know I can't do everything here on my own."

"Then I guess you kind of have to take him up on his offer of help," Carla said. "At least the faster you can get the hail damage cleaned up, the faster I can hopefully find you a new leaser and the faster you can come home."

"Oh, that would be good…" Emmy said earnestly.

"So that settles it."

"Yeah," Emmy agreed.

But for some reason she still didn't feel at all *settled* when she thought about letting Declan Madison anywhere near her.

And not only because there was a bit of nervousness that being anywhere near him might bring to the surface more of that bombing backlash.

There was also no denying that his looks were potent.

Or that, when he tried, he could disarm her with his heady charm.

Or that, at the wedding, he'd somehow managed to get her to let down her defenses when she shouldn't have.

Only for her to end up feeling like a fool…

"Tell Declan good-night," Emmy encouraged her niece as she tucked the three-year-old into bed.

Emmy had suggested that Trinity let Declan read the bedtime books she'd chosen. But Trinity had denied him that privilege. She'd granted him only permission to listen to Emmy read them.

Dressed in combat boots, a camouflage-print shirt and

pants today, he'd stood in the doorway of Trinity's room to do that and was still leaning against the jamb.

"Night, Decan," the little girl said in answer to her aunt's prompting.

"Night, Trinity. Sleep tight. I'll see you tomorrow," he responded.

"Decan'll be here too-morrow?" Trinity asked Emmy.

"He will. He's staying with us. In the basement," she explained, trying not to sound negative despite her own lack of enthusiasm for it.

"Okay," Trinity said, accepting it far more easily than her aunt.

Trinity's honey-colored hair was cut into an easy-to-care-for bob just long enough to cover her ears, with bangs that came to her eyebrows. Emmy smoothed them away from the child's forehead so she could kiss it.

"Goodnight, my sweet-thing," she whispered.

"Night, my Em," Trinity said in a sleepy voice before tugging her stuffed monkey to her side and closing her big brown eyes.

Emmy gave her a second kiss, then turned off the bedside lamp and headed for the doorway.

Since Declan had arrived just after dinner tonight, they'd had the kids as a buffer between them. Trinity had been standoffish toward him the day before—she hadn't seen him for over a year and didn't remember him despite her grandmother pointing him out in the photograph.

It had taken some time for the little girl to warm up to him tonight, but eventually she'd stopped hugging Emmy's leg and glaring at him, tentatively letting him in.

When that had happened, Emmy had had the chance to teach him how to hold Kit, heat a bottle, change a diaper and burp the baby. She'd taught the jiggle-and-walk to use when Kit was unhappy, and she'd even tutored Declan through Kit's bath in the kitchen sink.

Because Trinity fancied herself an expert on her brother she'd added her instructions wherever she'd thought Emmy had overlooked anything. And when it came to Emmy teaching him Trinity's routine, the three-year-old had insisted that she could do everything herself.

"At least she *tries* to," Emmy had told Declan, humoring the little girl. "But sometimes she needs a little help," Emmy had stated, demonstrating when it came to taking clothes off and putting on pajamas, reminding to go potty and brushing teeth.

But now Kit was asleep and Trinity was in bed, and it was just Emmy alone with Declan Madison.

And while no, she hadn't had any flashbacks or anxiety, she also wasn't comfortable being with him. Her stomach was tied in knots. Between that and their history, she knew she was not being very welcoming. But it was the best she could manage. And honestly, she didn't think he had any right *expecting* anything more from her.

And his solemn and withdrawn attitude wasn't making things any easier.

Not that any of it mattered. One way or another she just had to get through this. They both did.

"Now I can finally show you the basement," she said as she joined him in the hallway, closing Trinity's door all but a crack, hoping he would go down there and not come up again until tomorrow.

"I nearly grew up here. I know how to get to the basement and what's down there—unless Mandy changed things up."

"Oh sure…" Emmy said, feeling stupid for having spent the evening being a bit of a tour guide throughout the house. So why *hadn't* he pointed that out to her at the get-go? she thought, not appreciating what seemed misleading by omission.

But all she said was "I wasn't thinking about you knowing the place probably better than I do."

Declan didn't say anything as he waited for her to lead the way downstairs to the main level.

As she did, she wondered if being here was actually the reason for his somber attitude.

"It's gotten better, but when I first moved in after Mandy died, it was hard—to me, this was her house, her furniture, where I've seen her most for the last four years... But for you... I guess I wasn't thinking about all the memories you must have of this place...of being here with Topher."

"Mandy redecorated. It doesn't look anything like it did when we were kids," he answered without any inflection.

"Still, it's where you grew up with Topher, and now... it can't be easy."

Declan didn't respond at all to that. It left Emmy wondering if she was right. Or not. At any rate it didn't seem as if she'd hit on the root of whatever was going on with him.

The silence felt awkward, though, so as they reached the entryway she felt the need to fill the gap.

"Since they built the new garage, Mandy was turning the old one into a guesthouse. She wanted a place for me or for Mom and Dad to stay when we came. It isn't quite finished yet and there isn't any furniture, but you could stay out there if you wanted..."

They were passing in front of the sofa where she'd slept for two weeks. She hadn't been able to bring herself to sleep in Mandy's bed until she'd rearranged the room. Seeing the couch made her remember that.

As much as it pained her to make the offer when she really wanted Declan to vanish into the basement as often as possible, she forced herself to say, "If it will bother you to use the basement bedroom, you could sleep on the couch…"

"I stayed in the basement bedroom the last time I was here," he said, again flatly.

And again he left dead air as they passed through the living room and moved on to the kitchen.

Emmy struggled for something more to say. "Later on I'll have the guesthouse—that's what Mandy called it—finished, so maybe I can bring the kids for weekends or on vacations to spend some time here. I want the farm to be familiar to them, for it to seem like home as much as it can when I'll have them living in Denver. Maybe Mandy and Topher won't mind so much that the kids won't grow up here if I can at least bring them for visits…"

Declan had been a great conversationalist when they'd initially met in Afghanistan and again at the reception. Even when he wasn't talking, he'd seemed engaged and interested in everything she had to say. But now it was like she was talking to a brick wall. It only made being with him worse. *If he doesn't want to be here, why doesn't he leave?*

But she didn't say that. She reminded herself that she needed his help. Damn him anyway!

When they reached the kitchen, Emmy opted for abandoning the small talk and simply returning to instruction—maybe he saw himself as her employee. If that was the case, fine, they'd just talk business.

"Mom and I have been trading off nights walking Kit—I know, since he's sleeping now, it seems like he'll just stay that way till the morning, but he won't. He'll wake up for a bottle somewhere between ten and eleven and after that he'll be fussy and he won't go back to sleep. And he won't even be happy just being held. He has to be walked and rocked and patted and jiggled until he's hun-

gry enough to take another bottle—which will be somewhere between 2:00 and 3:00 a.m.—and then he'll fall
asleep again."

"Yeah, your mom told me that. I said I thought I could
take her shifts so you could sleep every other night the
way you were with her here."

He could have said that before she went into the whole
spiel.

Again, she wondered if he liked making her feel dim.

Emmy didn't say anything, though. She merely finished what she'd been about to tell him. "Mom took last
night and let me sleep, so I can take tonight. That'll give
you tomorrow to get more used to handling him before
you have him on your own."

"Okay."

One word.

"I have to clean the kitchen, but if you want to go down
and unpack and get to bed early or something—"

"I can help."

"With the dishes? But you came after we'd finished—
you didn't even eat."

He shrugged a broad shoulder. But said nothing.

She just wanted him to go away despite the fact that
he was eye candy. But without waiting for instruction, he
merely went to the kitchen table and picked up the dishes,
then took them to the sink.

Emmy tried not to sigh and gathered the rest of the silverware and glasses.

"I do have to get Kit's formula ready for tomorrow—
I guess you could learn how to do that," she said resign-
edly. She lapsed into silence of her own as she rinsed the
dishes, loaded the dishwasher and then got out what she
needed to mix the infant formula and fill bottles.

She had no idea exactly how long they went without

talking, but it seemed like forever before he said, "So how are you going to follow around the Red Cross to take pictures and raise two kids?"

"I don't do that anymore," she said, just about as flatly as he'd answered her questions earlier. And without offering additional explanation the same way either.

"Really? You said you loved that job—that it was better than when you were a freelance photographer taking pictures of the destruction of war or natural disasters because you got to take pictures of people trying to do good, getting things done."

She *had* said that. And it had been true. For a day and a half more after they'd had that conversation.

"After the school bombing I...I just decided... I don't know... When I first started my career, it was exciting to be in the thick of things—that's why I chose photojournalism. But a few years of that and I wanted to look through my viewfinder and see more positive images—so I went to work with the Red Cross. But I was with them for almost six years and..." She shrugged as if the latest career alteration wasn't a big deal. "Then I wanted to see and be a part of things that weren't anywhere near the thick of anything. When I got home from Afghanistan, I just... stayed. Now I take mostly wedding photographs with a few engagement or retirement parties thrown in, and the occasional shoot for a new baby."

"Pretty pictures."

"That memorialize the happiest times in people's lives rather than the—"

"Ugliest."

Like everything else he'd said since yesterday, his tone was matter-of-fact. But still it somehow irritated Emmy, making her feel guilty and embarrassed. And weak.

She was on the verge of defending herself when Declan

said, "Lucky for Trinity and Kit—now you'll be around for them. Mandy probably wouldn't have been able to make a guardian of someone like me, who's halfway around the world for who-knows-how-long at the drop of a hat."

So he hadn't been judging her, she'd just done that to herself. She was glad she hadn't launched into the justifications she'd been about to fire off.

Instead she merely muttered, "Yeah, lucky. If I hadn't quit before, I would have had to now."

"How do you feel about…you know, instant parenthood?"

"I'm okay with it," she said succinctly. "It's strange—I'll admit that. But I love those little buggers and…" She shrugged again. "I'm adjusting. I'll always do my best for them."

"Just like that?"

"Yes," she said with resolve. Not that it had been so simple to accept such a huge responsibility. But she'd promised her sister. So she didn't allow herself to think about the way she used to envision her life.

"Even while Mandy was still alive, my course changed suddenly. Again…" she added. "I needed to…embrace that and make new plans—"

"For your career again?"

"No, for my personal life." But she wasn't about to say more on *that* subject. "Then this happened and…now the kids will be a part of everything I do from here on. And when it comes to them, now that Mandy and Topher are gone, I wouldn't have it any other way."

She thought she could feel his eyes on her, and as she finished prepping to make the formula, she stole a glance to see if she was right.

She was. He was staring intently at her.

Then he said, "Thanks for that."

There was genuine gratitude in his tone that surprised her.

"I wouldn't have it any other way," she repeated, meaning it.

Then she turned to making formula and tutoring him, explaining that anything left after twenty-four hours—even under refrigeration—had to be thrown out when he asked why they didn't make a larger quantity.

Once the bottles were filled, he put them in the fridge while she cleaned that mess and started the dishwasher, both of them silent again.

Into that silence he said, "Tomorrow is Sunday. I don't know if you go to church or—"

"No, but if you want to, feel free."

"Church attendance is an 'only in the right time and place' thing for me and Northbridge is *never* either of those," he said acerbically.

"You don't like Northbridge or you don't like the church here?"

"Both." His tone was flat again, definitive, but he didn't explain why he disliked his hometown—and the church here. Instead he went on without revealing anything. "I need to see all the damage to the farm so I know what we're up against. Why don't we do that tomorrow?"

"Sure. But we'll have to take the kids out with us—Sundays are the hardest time to get babysitters and Mom couldn't set up one for tomorrow."

He was back to making no comments, but he did raise an acknowledging chin.

That seemed to be the end of his efforts because he took a breath, exhaled and said, "If there's nothing else to do tonight, then I think I'll turn in."

Emmy again gave what she was getting and only nodded, watching him as he went toward the door to the basement.

And while the first thing she thought was that he still had a great butt, the second thing to register again was his limp.

"Uh…" she said.

He stopped and turned halfway around to look at her.

"Are there things you can't do around the farm?" she asked with a slight lowering of her gaze to his leg.

"No."

Once more his tone was flat, definitive, and this time with a warning not to ask him that again.

So okay, she wouldn't explore it.

She only said a curt "Tomorrow, then."

And for that she received nothing, not even another raise of that sculpted chin of his before he went to the basement door and finally disappeared down the stairs.

Oh, this is going to be loads of fun, Emmy thought, trying all over again to resign herself to living and working with the guy she no longer had even the slightest illusion of any rapport with.

Which was good.

No illusions that he liked her was good.

So why did the reality of that rub her so wrong?

Chapter Three

"Em... Em... Em... Em..."

Emmy opened her eyes only a slit. "Oh, Trinity, it's waaaay too early. Even Kit isn't up yet," she complained when her niece appeared at her bedside to wake her as the sun was only beginning to rise.

"The Decan-guy says he can gives me breaksfuss and you can sleep s'more. He says is it okay."

"Declan is already up?"

"Uh-huh."

"You could get into bed and sleep a little longer with me..." Emmy tempted.

"I wan breaksfuss."

Emmy was sooo tired. Kit had kept her up walking the floors until 3:30 a.m. "Is it okay with you if Declan makes it for you?" she asked her niece, thinking that Trinity might not be comfortable enough with him yet to agree.

But she surprised her. "Uh-huh."

"Really?"

"Uh-huh."

"Okay, then."

The little girl padded out of her room and Emmy closed

her eyes again, certain that she would fall instantly back to sleep.

But thoughts and images of Declan invaded her head. The same way thoughts and images of him had kept her constant company last night when she was up with Kit.

Wasn't it bad enough that Declan was here, living in the basement? That she was going to have to see him every day? Work side by side with him? Eat her meals with him? Couldn't he at least be out of sight, out of mind?

But no, apparently not, because even when she desperately needed more sleep, there he was. Again.

In her mental images of him, sometimes he was dressed in the combat gear he'd had on when they'd first met, looking rugged and powerful.

Sometimes he was in the dress blues he'd worn for the wedding—tall and broad shouldered, his narrow waist wrapped in that white belt, his wide chest adorned with ribbon bars and stars and medals.

Sometimes he was in the civilian clothes she'd seen him in the morning after the wedding—simple jeans and a gray hoodie that no one had ever looked as good in...

And that stupid face of his!

No one man should be that hot.

Somehow that broody thing he was sporting now only made it worse. It made him look all dark and mysterious, with that coarse, sort-of-wavy hair that cupped his head close. Staring out from under full eyebrows with eyes too blue to be real. His just-right mouth a straight line that was still intriguingly sexy. That mouth that he'd never even *tried* to kiss her with...

That should have been your first clue that he wasn't interested, that you were reading him wrong, she told herself.

Luckily it hadn't gotten as far as it had with Bryce, but

with Declan *and* with Bryce, she kept trying to figure out why. Were they intentionally leading her down the garden path and she was too gullible to see it? Or had she been imagining things that weren't really there?

She didn't know.

But Declan and Bryce weren't the only guys she'd ever dated—there was a feeling, a sense, an intuition when things were clicking with someone, and she'd been so sure with both of them that that had been the case. And then been wrong. Soooo wrong with Bryce.

So wrong that she didn't trust her own instincts anymore.

Although with Bryce it hadn't been *only* her instincts—he'd told her he loved her, had alluded to a long-term future for them.

With Declan she just didn't know whether he'd been toying with her or whether she'd genuinely misunderstood.

All she knew was that ultimately with both Declan and Bryce she'd ended up feeling the same way—disillusioned and foolish. Hurt.

And she wasn't going to let it happen again. Not with any man but certainly not with one she'd already learned to be wary of.

But given that newfound caution, why couldn't she stop thinking about Declan?

It wasn't as if she was interested in him. Sure, she recognized that he was hands down the hottest guy she'd ever laid eyes on. But that meant only that she wasn't oblivious. It didn't mean she cared. It didn't mean she was attracted to him.

Was she failing so utterly at putting him out of her mind because his rejection of her made him a challenge?

She'd never been like that before. Why would she be that now?

Usually when she discovered she wasn't someone's type, she'd just accepted that. No one was *every* guy's type.

And apparently Declan's type was loud Brazilian bombshells in stiletto heels and Lycra dresses with plunging necklines that exposed four inches of cleavage.

And actually, the fact that someone like Mandy's friend Tracy appealed to him made him not *Emmy's* type.

She wanted substance in her men. And a guy who was on board for a one-night stand with a bombshell didn't shout substance.

So again, *why* was Declan stuck in her head?

Could it be a rebound thing?

She'd had more than three years with Bryce—who she'd rebounded *to* when Declan had left her feeling about as attractive as a mud fence—and that relationship had only ended this last December.

Maybe she was ping-ponging, she thought, feeling as if she was finally getting close to understanding what was going on with her.

Thinking that she'd hit on an answer to why she was so fixated on him suddenly—that it was just a belated rebound from Bryce—she felt better.

And really, it was better that nothing *had* happened between them at the wedding. She'd still been reeling from the school bombing. She'd been drunk. If he *had* kissed her, she might have invited him into her room. She probably would have slept with him just to prove to herself that she was over her reaction to the sight of his face, that she was over the consequences she'd been fighting against for months.

And then she would have woken up the next morning—

sober—and regretted it. And been ashamed of herself for a whole new reason.

So really, he'd done her a huge favor by *not* being interested in her.

And now that she had it all sorted out, she could just stop thinking about him.

She turned onto her side and tried to fall asleep again.

But her lengthy thought process had her too awake now.

Still, that didn't mean she had to get up and go downstairs to him.

Trinity was okay having him make her breakfast. Kit was still asleep, and even if he woke up, helping with the kids was what Declan had volunteered for. So why not get up, take a leisurely shower, shampoo her hair, even put on a little makeup?

And not—absolutely *not*—because of Declan Madison. Only as the kind of confidence booster she *should* be indulging in so she *didn't* find herself looking to a man for it.

And since they were going out only to tour the hail damage today rather than clear any of it away, she was going to wear what she might if she was in Denver, going for brunch with Carla—a pair of her good jeans and a lightweight high-necked pink sweater.

Between funeral clothes for Topher's services, end-of-the-relationship-grieving sweats after Bryce, more funeral clothes for Mandy, then work-on-the-farm clothes and clothes that could withstand spit-up, it had been a long time since she'd worn anything that had made her just feel cute and feminine. And not only did she think she'd earned it, she decided it had medicinal value to put her on the road she *should* be on to healing any ego bruises left by both Declan and Bryce.

A little self-pampering was exactly the right thing to do for her own sake.

And *not* because afterward she'd be going out to some hot, dark, mysterious man who she'd just love to show what he'd missed.

"Oh geez, you went all over me!"

Emmy had had her shower, done her hair, dressed, applied makeup and was finally coming out of the master bedroom when she realized there was activity in the nursery. She stepped into the doorway just in time to hear Declan's exclamation.

And to see what had prompted it.

She couldn't help laughing. "I warned you about boy babies..." she said in a bit of a singsong.

"I didn't even get the diaper partway off and he got me."

"He got you good," Emmy observed.

"It's even on my chin," Declan said in horror. One big hand was on Kit's stomach to keep the infant safe even as Declan reared back to a full arm's length, his appalled and revolted expression making Emmy laugh again.

"Can you finish this so I can take another shower?" he asked.

"I can," she said, stepping up to take over.

Her not-so-adept helper rushed out of the nursery, calling along the way, "Trinity is in the kitchen. She's supposed to be eating, but I can't make any guarantees."

Emmy wasn't sure what that meant. But once he was out of earshot she bent over, kissed the baby good morning and whispered, "Atta boy!"

Thinking about Declan's over-the-top response made her smile again as she diapered Kit and replaced his pajamas. Then she picked up the fussing baby, who was gnawing at his fist, hoping that Declan had thought ahead to take a bottle out of the refrigerator to warm.

But not only hadn't he done that, he'd also turned the kitchen into the kind of disaster that stopped her in her tracks.

When she'd finally gotten Kit down in the middle of the night, the only thing out of place in the kitchen had been the baby bottle she'd left soaking in the sink.

Now it looked like a cyclone had hit the place. There were pans on the stove top, dishes and bowls in the sink, eggshells, cereal boxes, uneaten toast and crumbs on the counters. The butter dish was out, and Trinity was sitting on her booster seat at the kitchen table with a little of everything all around her, along with an overturned glass of orange juice.

"I spilt juice," the three-year-old confessed matter-of-factly when she saw her aunt surveying the damage. "I wan some milk."

"Oh dear…" was all Emmy could say.

Carrying Kit in one arm, she started a bottle warming, then she took one of Trinity's plastic cups with a lid and straw and filled it with milk. After bringing it to the three-year-old, she did just enough damage control to keep the juice mess from spreading to the floor. Where there was already cereal and crumbs.

"Your poor grandma worked so hard to leave this place clean and now look at it," Emmy said more to herself than to Trinity. Then to her niece, as she tested Kit's bottle and sat at the kitchen table to feed him, she said, "Have you actually eaten anything?"

"I wanna mossed egg."

"Let me feed Kit and I'll make you one."

But she'd learned that the little girl could be—and needed to be—occupied with small jobs, so when Trinity started to entertain herself by slapping at the puddle of juice, Emmy said, "Look at all those cereal boxes... Can you maybe put them back in the pantry for me?"

The three-year-old slipped down from her booster seat and went to do Emmy's bidding.

Luckily Kit took the first bottle of the day the fastest, so it wasn't long before Emmy had him fed and burped and could set him in the bouncy seat on the floor.

About that time a freshly showered Declan came up from downstairs, a nice soapy smell coming with him.

"I was going to clean all this before you could see it," he said, casting a discomfited glance around.

Gone was the sweat suit that Kit had anointed, replaced with a pair of jeans and a short-sleeved dark green crew-neck T-shirt. And his hair was damp.

But Emmy didn't want to pay enough attention to him to note details like that, so after a quick look she, too, let her eyes follow the line of kitchen destruction. "Yeah... what happened in here?"

"I don't know," he said, sounding frustrated. "When I was a kid, I ate cereal for breakfast, so I thought that would work for Trinity. I got out the cereal boxes so she could show me which one she wanted. She started eating out of the boxes and said she wanted a *mossed egg.* I got the egg part, but *mossed*? I tried to figure out what that was—"

"It's a scrambled egg—it took Mom and me a while to translate. We think maybe it's the way she says *mashed* and she might be saying she wants a mashed egg..."

"I went through the whole list of eggs—boiled, fried, scrambled—she just kept saying *mossed.* So I started cooking eggs—including a scrambled one—but she wouldn't eat any of them. Then she said she wanted cereal. But the cereal was right there—well, it was also all over the table and the chair and the floor by then. But I thought maybe she wanted it in milk. Wrong again. I finally figured out that she wanted hot cereal. But she wouldn't eat the malto-something-or-other she said she wanted—"

"Did you make it with butter and salt?"

"Butter and salt? No, I put milk and sugar on it."

"She likes it with butter and salt."

He sighed in exasperation. "Then I found some other hot cereals and she wouldn't eat those either, and we were back to the damn *mossed* egg thing."

"I wanna damn mossed egg," Trinity said.

Emmy made a face even as she fought a smile. "You have to be careful about bad words. You'll never get one past her and she'll repeat it every time."

Chagrin filled Declan's handsome face. "Sorry," he muttered.

"And she doesn't get juice—I know there's a bottle in the fridge, but that was here for Mom. Juice isn't good for kids—too much sugar. Trinity only gets milk or water. And in a plastic glass with a lid on it—always a lid or—"

"I spilt it," Trinity supplied.

Declan just shook his handsome head in defeat.

"Remember I showed you the drawer that's hers…" Emmy reminded him.

"I thought that was a drawer she played in—when you showed it to me, that's what she started doing," he said defensively.

"She does play in it, but it's also got her bowls and dishes and cups to use."

At least he had found Trinity's miniature silverware in the silverware drawer. Emmy supposed she should give him a point for that. If for nothing else.

"I've liberated whole towns and villages from insurgents with fewer problems," he said then, his frustration still showing. "And you're probably thinking this is worse than having the kids on your own," he added as if he had no doubt she was finding fault with him.

Which she kind of was.

But she needed help and she had to hope that he'd get better, so she resisted the urge to take his monstrous failure and rub it in anymore. Instead she said, "It's harder than it seems sometimes—I keep finding that with the work outside."

He raised his chin to acknowledge her point, but it didn't seem to make him feel any better.

"I should also probably show you how Trinity likes her egg scrambled because you can't just beat it and put it in a pan to cook it. You have to break the egg into the pan and use a spatula to just sort of break the yolk and fold that and the white a couple of times so that there are still some all-white and some all-yellow parts. If there aren't, she doesn't believe it's an egg and won't eat it—probably why she didn't eat the one you scrambled for her."

"She's finicky."

"She's three—she wants things the way she wants them."

"Or else."

"Kind of," Emmy confirmed. "But it does make a good egg, especially with some cheese added just toward the end, which she also likes. I'll show you," she suggested then, taking an egg and some already-shredded cheddar cheese out of the refrigerator.

It took only a few minutes and the egg was ready. She slid it onto a plate, put it in front of her niece and Trinity ate it without complaint.

"Yeah, that is *not* how it went for me," Declan grumbled.

"Did you eat?" Emmy asked.

"Yeah, most of what she wouldn't so the food didn't go to waste," he said. "Why don't you have something while I get started cleaning this mess."

Emmy made herself an egg, too. As she did, she said, "Trinity was awake earlier than usual this morning, and you were already up?"

"With the sun."

Except that the sun hadn't even been up yet.

"Is that a military thing?"

"I was a farm boy—it started there. Chores before breakfast."

Chores...

Emmy had been so involved in thinking about Declan, about what to wear, about using a little blush and high-lighter, eyeliner and mascara, and lip gloss, that she'd lost sight of the fact that she still had to go out and do the morning chores. In her good jeans and nice sweater.

It was something she'd had to do every day for the last six weeks, so it should have been a habit by now. How could she have so completely forgotten about it?

She could have kicked herself.

"I do those after the kids are up and fed," she said as if she'd remembered the chores all along.

"If you walk me through it today, chores are probably something I can take over without making a disaster of everything."

He was willing to take over the morning chores?

Emmy wanted to jump for joy. Mandy had loved animals—she'd become a veterinarian to make them her life's work. Before meeting Topher, Mandy's dream had been to work in the country, to care for large animals, to have a working farm and eventually also a sanctuary for animals that had been abused or abandoned or were handicapped.

Emmy had admired that dream. Supported it. And when Mandy had met Topher—a small-town farm boy himself who aimed to return to his family's long-held farm and convert it into all organics after he finished his tour of duty—Emmy had agreed with her sister that it seemed like a match made in heaven.

But Emmy herself was a city girl. Through and through. And while she'd been doing her best to take care of the farm and the animals without complaint for Mandy's sake, the truth was that she didn't relish any of it.

The thought of being spared the daily tasks with the animals bought Declan a full pardon for demolishing the kitchen with breakfast.

But she wasn't going to let him see how thrilled she was, so she said a simple "That would be helpful."

"That's what I'm here for—believe it or not so far," he added facetiously.

"Although you might want to do a little sleeping in yourself after a night with Kit," she said. They should probably trade off the morning chores the same way they were planning to trade off the night duty.

"I don't sleep in," he said as if it was unfathomable to him.

"Even if you're up until three thirty in the morning the way I was last night?"

"Since the day my mom married my stepfather—who was a retired marine—I've been up at the crack of dawn. Hugh's main objective was to get me and my brothers ready for the marines, and early rising was part of that—regardless of what time we'd gone to bed the night before. I have an internal clock that's more reliable than any alarm you'll ever buy."

"Well, I love to sleep in and I *don't* love to collect eggs or milk cows and goats—especially the goats. So if that's a job you want, go for it. I'm happy not to do it for however long you're around," she said. And it was good to find this difference between them, she decided. The more things they *didn't* have in common, the better.

She was glad that the morning's turmoil was making him talk more, though.

When she and Trinity had both finished their breakfast, Emmy cleared enough space on the table for the three-year-old to color, then pitched in with the kitchen cleanup.

As they cleaned, she was discouraged to note that whatever had inspired Declan to speak more than a few words at a time had apparently waned. He was back to speaking in short, terse phrases—and only when spoken to.

Once the kitchen was back in order she suggested Declan get started collecting the eggs while she dressed the kids. Again with no more than an "Okay" from him, they parted ways.

After that, with Trinity in tow and Kit in the stroller, Emmy showed Declan the hail damage to the barn and the structures near the house.

In a lean-to behind the barn was a tractor that Declan recognized from his youth. He marveled that it was still around.

"Mandy used it, but I don't know how to operate it and when one of the co-op guys tried it a couple of weeks ago it wouldn't start," Emmy explained.

Declan didn't comment on that. But after lunch, when she'd put both kids down for naps and was pulling the shade on Trinity's bedroom window, she saw him go back out to the tractor and begin to work on it.

He stayed out there while the kids slept and Emmy did laundry and preliminary preparations for dinner, and by the time both kids were waking up again, she heard the tractor start.

For the remainder of the afternoon—with Kit either strapped in a sling or sitting in the stroller—she showed Declan the rest of the hail damage, ending with the orchard.

They'd been side by side for everything else, but when they reached the outskirts of the orchard she said, "Go ahead and check it out. I'll wait here. I'm not sure how stable some of the branches are and I wouldn't want the kids in there if anything broke loose."

Declan didn't seem to find that curious, and as he surveyed the work that needed to be done there, she wondered if she could delegate that job to him alone.

They had done a lot of walking, and as they returned to the farmhouse, Emmy noticed that Declan was limping slightly again.

She didn't say anything about it, and through their beef stew, biscuits and salad dinner she filled his silences only with chatter about the kids and the farm.

But once the kids were in bed and Emmy again found herself alone with Declan in the kitchen—supervising as he tried his hand at making formula—she needed something else to talk about. And since she was not only curious about his injuries but needed reassurance that he was capable of the work that needed to be done, she decided to broach the subject that he'd obviously avoided the previous evening.

"When Mandy was notified about Topher, she asked about you. They said that you were badly hurt in the explosion, too. But there weren't any details..."

She thought that should have been enough to prompt him. But as usual, he wasn't forthcoming and said only, "No?"

"No."

Still nothing from him.

She didn't actually want him to go back to being the charming guy he'd been in the past because she didn't want anything to disarm or mislead her. But come on! Had he lost the capacity for simple conversation?

Then something else occurred to her and she said, "You seem a lot different... You don't talk much..." Or ever smile or do or say anything that showed his personality was intact. "Is that from the explosion?" And if so, was she expecting too much of him?

He frowned at her. "Are you asking me if I had a brain injury?" he said, cutting through what she was trying to address with some sensitivity. Then, before she could answer his question, he glanced back at what he was doing—measuring infant formula powder—and said only, "No, I didn't have a brain injury."

Even that was delivered so emotionlessly it didn't seem as if he really cared. But clearly if she didn't ask him outright he wasn't going to say more, so she said, "How *were* you hurt?"

"A hidden IED went off under the right front tire of the Humvee I was driving."

"No, I meant what parts of your body were hurt," she qualified, unsure if he'd genuinely misunderstood her or was intentionally skirting an answer.

She didn't think he'd genuinely misunderstood her when silence was what followed.

Again.

It was getting aggravating.

"Are you giving me the silent treatment?" she asked suddenly. "Is that what's going on here? Because I didn't do anything to *you*."

"I didn't do anything to you either," he said with another frown, not missing the inflections in her voice and seeming confused.

Emmy couldn't deny the truth in that—he hadn't done anything to her. That neglect at the wedding had just left her feeling spurned because it had seemed as if more was going on between them.

She decided to use his own tactic of skipping over something he didn't want to talk about and ignored his comment. Instead she said, "So if you haven't had a brain injury and you aren't giving me the silent treatment, *talk* for crying out loud!"

He seemed unaffected by her annoyed outburst, but at least he finally did answer her question about his injuries.

"There were cuts, bruises, three broken ribs. My arm and hand were broken, too. And my leg was nearly crushed. It was touch and go for a while with the leg—there was a lot of talk about amputation. But I had seven surgeries to keep it, to get me here, and—like I said before—I've been in hospitals and rehab until a few days ago."

"Wow..." she responded. She'd had no idea how much he'd gone through. Maybe *he* had PTSD.

Whether or not he did, though, she could see that what he'd been through would have dampened his disposition— especially coupled with the loss of Topher in that same explosion—and she felt guilty for being impatient with him.

The issues she'd brought back with her from Afghanistan had sometimes made her short-tempered and nervous and fearful and edgy. She'd kept it under wraps when she was with her family or in a professional setting, but it had come out with Carla.

Carla had ridden it out with her, though. Her friend had never been annoyed or irritated. Now maybe it was time to pay that forward with Declan. Regardless of their missteps in the past.

So with less hostility than she'd shown up to then, she said, "Don't get me wrong, I need help around here and

I'm grateful that you want to give it, but…after all that and just now coming out of rehab, it doesn't seem like what needs to be done around here is anything that you should be worrying about."

"The most important thing to me is that I get back where I belong—to my unit, to being a marine. I spent the last two months in rehab, recuperating, but I was also working out every minute they'd let me—and sometimes more than that on the sly. I did it to be duty-ready. I'm actually stronger now than I was and certainly capable of doing farm work."

"But the limp…"

"It happens. The knee stiffens up. But I'm still doing physical therapy exercises for it and it isn't weak."

Emmy wasn't sure if she should believe him. But desperation—and the fact that he'd gotten the tractor working and knew how to use it—made her not argue.

"A little pain here and there is nothing," he added in a way that made it sound as if he thought he deserved that—which started her wondering about something else.

"They said that Topher was in the passenger seat of the Humvee. That you dragged him out of the wreckage—how did you do that in the shape you were in?"

"Needed to be done."

"He was still alive then?" Emmy ventured despite the strong sense that Declan did not want to talk about this.

And he didn't for several more silent moments before he seemed to concede and said in a very deep, very quiet voice, "He was moaning but he wasn't conscious. He didn't get back to being conscious. I kept telling him to hang on, to stay with me, but I don't know if he even heard. He was gone before the rescue team reached us. They said they wouldn't have been able to save him even if they'd gotten there earlier… He was just too messed up…"

There was suddenly such a heavy pall in the room that Emmy regretted bringing it up. And for a while neither of them said anything at all again.

Then, thinking this time about his mental state, she said, "Have you had counseling?"

"Now you sound like my family," he grumbled.

Emmy hadn't had any herself. Carla had tried to convince her to, but she'd been determined to handle her problems on her own.

"While I was in the hospital, my brother Conor sent in shrinks and spiritual guidance people right and left," Declan went on. "So I've had that shoved down my throat. And in order to get the hell out of rehab I was *required* to sit through group therapy sessions. But I don't have flashbacks. I don't have nightmares. I'm not jumpy or agitated, and there's nothing in me that isn't ready to go back to what I came out of. I haven't had the need to self-medicate with booze or drugs—I haven't even taken most of the pain medication they want to load me up with. I've seen PTSD. I've lost people to it. Luckily I don't have that and every professional I've had to meet with about it has given me an all clear."

"And your family—"

"Is still not convinced. They watch me like hawks— I think they're figuring I'm going to crack at any time. But I'm not. Am I different than I was before this? Yeah, I am. I lost one of the most important people in my life. It wouldn't have been any worse to lose either of my own brothers, including my twin. And I was driving…" he said with a heavy dose of self-condemnation. "But that's what life is, isn't it? Things happen, we cope. But we don't always come out the same person we were."

Emmy couldn't argue with that. Since Afghanistan there were changes in her, too. And while the fearfulness of things like the orchard weren't good changes, she still felt as if some other changes in her were—she had a stronger sense of what was important, which she was convinced was helping her to more easily accept sudden parenthood and the life-altering it was requiring of her.

When it came to Declan, Emmy could understand if his gloomy detachment alarmed his family. But it didn't matter to her. In fact, she thought it might make things easier. The old Declan had been funny and charming—and ultimately insincere. Maybe with this new, more serious version, they could rebuild some trust and actually have a productive working relationship, taking care of the farm and the kids.

But she did feel the need to tell him some things, so she returned to what they were talking about before she'd posed the counseling question.

"When Topher died, Mom and Dad and I started trading off weeks to come here to stay with Mandy so she wouldn't be alone. The last week I was with her, just *before* we lost her, she said she was going to try to find out how you were, where you were, so she could thank you."

"Thank me?" he said as if that was a ridiculous notion.

"From the start she was glad you weren't lost, too. She was just too deep in grief to reach out and tell you so. But she knew that you tried to save Topher. She knew you would have done anything to save him. Mandy never—not for one single second—blamed you or held you responsible—"

"I *was* responsible."

Emmy recognized anguish when she saw it because she was no stranger to it. She'd photographed it too many times. She'd felt it herself after that last trip to Afghanistan.

"Being the driver doesn't make you responsible," she said. "The person who put the bomb there was responsible. You were as much the victim as Topher was."

"Not quite as much. I'm here, in his kitchen. I can see his kids. Hold them. Play with them. He can't."

This guy was definitely carrying some baggage.

Baggage that made her problems with him seem small in comparison. Petty, even. And while they were enough to keep her from any kind of romantic illusions, she knew for sure then that she had to compartmentalize her problems, to shield herself with them while not letting them bleed into her interactions with Declan. To really give him the patience Carla had given her.

"You're wrong," she said simply then.

"Am I?" he said, his tone letting her know he believed she was the one who was mistaken.

"Do you think Topher had more right to live than you do?"

"No. But he had a wife and kids who needed him."

"And it wasn't you who took him away from them. Instead you're here trying to do something for his kids. If you had died, too, they wouldn't have that."

Declan just shook his handsome head, denying what she was saying.

She went on anyway. "You can—you should and you need to—mourn the loss of your friend. But there's no place for guilt or taking responsibility in that just because you were driving the dumb vehicle. Believe me, I was with my sister while she was working through her grief, and when she reached the anger part of it, you weren't involved at all. She was as mad that you'd been hurt as she was that Topher had been lost. There was nothing about you being blamed for his death. So stop doing that to yourself."

"Yeah, okay, sure, done," he muttered facetiously.

"I know—feelings are weird," she said. It wouldn't do any good to tell herself to stop what she was feeling about going into that orchard. Telling him to stop blaming himself couldn't have much impact either. But still she said, "Not only didn't Mandy blame you, but I also can't imagine that Topher would have."

Declan didn't respond to that at all.

Emmy took that silence to mean that he knew she was right. Even if it didn't alleviate any of what he was dealing with.

Then he said, "Doesn't matter whether Topher would have blamed me—"

"Because you do," she finished for him. "And you can't give yourself a break?"

"No."

"Maybe you should work on that. I didn't know Topher as long as you did, but it seems to me that he'd have gotten kind of mad at you for holding on to that guilt. Sometimes Mandy would get angry at something and hang on to it, and Topher would say—like it was one word—*letigo*."

The short, quick breath Declan let out was almost a chuckle—humorless but still, almost a chuckle. "Yeah, he loved to say that."

"So maybe that's what you should start trying to tell yourself—*letigo*. Sometimes I say it to myself..." Although she had to admit that in the throes of things like her fear of going into that orchard, it didn't have much effect.

"Yeah, maybe I'll try that," Declan said without conviction.

Emmy had the sense that his words were more to shut her up than a vow to actually give it a shot.

But she didn't know what else to say to him, so this time she just let the silence stand while he filled the baby bottles. As he finished each one, she capped it, and then she passed it back to him to put in the refrigerator.

When that was done, Declan leaned back against the

stainless steel door and stared at her with those blue, blue eyes. "Still think it's better to talk?" he challenged.

She was standing basically in front of him, not far away, and leaned a hip against the edge of the counter. "Better than the silent treatment," she said.

"I wasn't giving you the silent treatment," he argued.

"Still."

"Okay, if that's what you want," he conceded, sounding only the tiniest smidgen more cordial. But he didn't bother to smile.

Still, Emmy realized that she'd gone as far as she should talking about Topher's and Declan's injuries, so she dropped it and went on with something else.

"Do you think you can handle the overnight with Kit tonight?" she asked him.

"You made me practice the diaper thing all day, so yeah, hopefully I can do it without getting spritzed again. And I've given him two bottles—I got him to burp better than you did the last time," he reminded.

"I get him to burp just fine," Emmy defended. "What about the walking?"

"I'll do whatever he needs."

"If it gets to you, you can sit with him. You just have to sort of do a fast rock with your body and still jiggle him—"

She tried to demonstrate, but it wasn't easy standing up and without a baby in her arms.

And while Declan still didn't smile, something in his chiseled face seemed to ease up slightly, as if somewhere deep down it amused him.

She stopped. "You get the idea."

"No. Show me again."

He might be miserable but he could still be bratty.

She arched an eyebrow at him, shook her head and said, "You'll figure it out."

"Most likely," he agreed, and there was almost a hint of the sparkle she'd seen in his eyes in Las Vegas.

That sparkle that had drawn her in and convinced her that he was going to kiss her.

She'd been sooo ready for him to...

He was great-looking. He had a sexy mouth. Who wouldn't have been wondering what it would be like to kiss him?

She was wondering it right then. Again.

No illusions! she silently commanded herself.

And yet, even without them, she was still wondering what it might be like.

And if he was any good at it...

Emmy pulled herself out of those thoughts, took a deep breath and said, "You can nap on the couch until Kit cries or just wait for it, but he didn't let me have much sleep last night, so I'm going to bed."

Declan nodded.

"If you can't handle him—"

"I'll knock on your door. But we'll be fine," he repeated.

"Good luck," she said flippantly, pushing off the counter's edge with her hips and catching when his glance dropped to them.

But she would *not* read anything into that any more than she'd read anything into that flicker of a sparkle in his eyes, she told herself.

And as for those dumb thoughts of kissing him?

Over and done with.

Now and forever.

"

Chapter Four

"Bye, Decan."

"Bye, Trinity," Declan responded late Monday afternoon to the three-year-old as Emmy buckled in the little girl to the back seat of a small SUV.

Kit was already strapped in. Emmy was taking the kids to town for an appointment with the local doctor. The doctor was convinced that Kit was having problems adjusting to formula after having been breastfed. Since the latest attempts to help him hadn't improved the situation, the doctor wanted to see him.

The plan was for Emmy to pick up hoagies for dinner when she finished with the appointment. While she was busy in town, Declan needed to make a visit to his own family's farm.

He was behind the wheel of his late adoptive father's old truck and had started the engine before Emmy got into her own driver's seat, so he left ahead of her. As he went past the SUV, Trinity waved to him.

He waved back, and on the way out to the main road he said, "She's a sweetheart, Topher. I'm sorry you aren't here to see that. You should be..." Battling the clench in his gut that that thought gave him, he added, "Damn it all to hell..."

Then the weirdest thing happened.

In his head he heard Emmy's voice from the night before saying, *letigo*.

That had been Topher's favorite thing to say since they were seventeen.

Letigo...

"Easier said than done," he grumbled.

But it wasn't something he'd thought of since Topher's death, and he had to admit that that funny reminder of his easygoing friend was preferable to the thought of his friend not being there.

Thanks for that anyway, Miss About-Face...

And Emmy *had* done another about-face on him.

Since meeting up again here she hadn't been outright hostile, but she had given him the distinct impression that she was barely suffering his presence because she needed his help.

Then last night she'd done another one of her about-faces.

He'd actually seen her pause as he was talking. Rethink something. And then alter her attitude toward him.

She hadn't turned instantly warm and cuddly, but she had mellowed out and stopped acting as if she hated him.

Definitely another about-face. But the ones that made her more pleasant to be around were better than the ones that made her difficult.

Hey, it wasn't much, but it was a little bit of progress.

Not that he was looking to make progress with her. He just wanted things between them to be civil enough to get the job done. Animosity would slow things down. And his goal was to get in, get the job done, get out. They didn't have to like each other, they just had to work together.

Which was what they'd done today.

And he had to give her credit—as rotten as she was at

farm work, she tried damn hard. She *worked* damn hard. And without complaint even though it couldn't have been more obvious that she was out of her element clearing a farm field.

Of course, who knew—by tomorrow maybe that would be different, too. Maybe she'd sit alongside the field and do her nails or something.

The point was, he knew to be leery of her. Not to trust that what he saw from her one minute would be what was there the next.

And seeing her make another about-face last night had made him wonder about something else—what if she was as inconsistent with the kids as she was with him?

And if she was, shouldn't he be leery of her as Trinity and Kit's guardian, too?

He might not know much about kids or raising them, but he did know that the last thing any kid needed was a caretaker who ran hot and cold. They needed someone they could rely on, someone they could trust to be consistently caring day after day.

He wasn't altogether convinced that that person was Emmy Tate. It sure as hell hadn't been the Emmy Tate he'd experienced.

Not that he could fault her handling of the kids so far. Everything he'd seen of her with them was patient, low-key, loving. It was just with *him* that she was all over the place.

But between having seen her swings before, then seeing one again last night, he thought he'd better keep an eye on her when it came to Trinity and the baby.

And if he saw her display those mood swings with them?

"I'll take care of it, Topher. I won't let you down.

Again," he swore out loud to his late friend. "I won't let anything get in the way."

Like the way Emmy looked…

Because damn, but it was hard to ignore that, he admitted to himself.

She had those chestnut eyes with caramel-colored flecks in them. And those dimples that flashed at the slightest upturn of those luscious lips of hers. And yeah, even out in the field today, with her hair in a ponytail and dressed like a farmhand, he'd still caught sight of her compact little body and that butt that just begged to be cupped by his hand rather than to be used for wiping the dirt off hers…

Enough of that! he told himself, forcing into his mind the images of her in cold-shoulder mode instead. Of those eyes glaring at him. Of that mouth turned down at the corners and the dimples gone.

That helped.

Until what jumped into his head was the picture of her after her quick shower before taking the kids into town just now.

Hair all shiny and smooth. Her high cheekbones sun kissed into a healthy pink. Dressed in jeans and a simple white blouse fitted just enough to show off a couple of other things his hands wanted to cup…

Frown lines between her eyes…

Her chin raised at him in contempt…

Talk! she'd snapped at him last night just when he'd thought things had been going fairly well…

Yeah, that was enough, he thought as he pulled up in front of his family's farmhouse. Erratic was not a turn-on, and since the last thing he wanted was for her to turn him on, he was good with that. As long as she was only erratic with him.

Feeling more in control than he had all day, he turned off the truck's engine and got out, cringing slightly when he put weight on his injured leg.

But he immediately rebounded from that cringe. He'd worked that leg, that knee, hard in the last twenty-four hours—hiking around the farm yesterday, walking Kit for nearly four hours last night, resting it only a few hours before *essersizing* it—as Trinity had called what he was doing when she'd joined him this morning to mimic his workout. And then he'd worked in the field all day today.

A night's sleep and he'd be good again. He had to be. There was no way he was letting it stop him from getting back to duty.

And as far away from Northbridge again as he could get.

"Hey, I just came for the clothes that were in the wash when I left," he called when he went in the farmhouse's front door.

"I'm so glad you're here! I need to talk to you," his sister called back with more enthusiasm than he'd expected. "I'm in the kitchen."

Declan found Kinsey sitting at the oblong table reading a piece of mail and smiling.

"Good news?" he asked as he sat down, too.

"It's from our lawyer. The DNA results confirmed that Mitchum Camden was our father. We *are* Camdens."

So...*not* good news. At least as far as Declan was concerned.

His sister must have read his feelings in his expression because when her eyes met his, she stopped smiling. He felt a pang of guilt but pushed it away. She knew he'd been so against her pursuit of being accepted by the Camden family that he'd refused to submit his own DNA for testing.

Not that it had mattered—Liam had let her have his and Liam was Declan's identical twin.

But no matter what the DNA said, Declan believed they were better off ignoring the whole ugly subject of the secret relationship their mother had had with one of the richest men in the country—a man who had already been married when he'd fathered the four of them in a years-long affair. They'd been the dirty secret, openly sneered at by half the town for not having a father until their mom finally married Hugh Madison a few years after Mitchum's death. To Declan, Hugh Madison—who had adopted them and raised them as his own—was their one and only father. The genetics didn't matter, and Mitchum Camden and the rest of his family could keep them. Not that the ten legitimate Camden children—all of them around the ages of Declan, Liam, Conor and Kinsey—didn't seem to be decent people. They were known for their philanthropy, for their good deeds. But that didn't change Declan's feelings about them. Or about his sister's desire to be embraced by them as part of the family.

"The letter is from your lawyer, not from the Camdens themselves," he pointed out.

Lonely after the deployment of her brothers and intrigued by their mother's deathbed confession of the name of their biological father, Kinsey had become determined to pursue a relationship with the grandmother who had never claimed or acknowledged them, and with the half siblings and cousins who made up this generation of Camdens.

Initially Kinsey had gone to GiGi Camden—the matriarch and grandmother of the legitimate family—with the letter from their mother, describing the affair. The elderly woman had appeared shocked and unaware of their existence before that. But she also had not instantly taken

Kinsey into the fold the way Kinsey had hoped she might. Instead she'd initiated an investigation into the claim and then demanded DNA evidence.

Now there was proof. But it still wasn't GiGi Camden or any of her other grandchildren approaching them. This was merely a formal letter from an attorney relaying the test results to Kinsey—test results that presumably were also being relayed to the Camdens.

Declan didn't want his sister reading too much into what was merely a relaying of facts. Even though Conor and Liam had let her have their DNA for testing, they weren't much more enthusiastic about Kinsey's quest than Declan was, and all three of them were worried that she was setting herself up for an enormous disappointment.

"No, the letter isn't from the Camdens," she acknowledged. "But now I know they know the truth. And so do we."

"And do you think that's going to make us any less excluded from that family?" Declan asked gently. It had been different for Kinsey—and for Conor and Liam— than it had been for him. Yes, they'd all been looked down upon, but for the rest of them it hadn't been as overt—or as brutal—as it had been for Declan at the hands of a bully. He didn't ever want Kinsey to feel the things he'd felt and he was worried that now that she knew they really were the offspring of Mitchum Camden, not being allowed into the inner circle of Camdens might cause that.

"Maybe," Kinsey said hopefully.

"Have any of them RSVP'd to your invitation to the rehearsal dinner or the wedding?"

"Not yet."

"This is Monday, Kins. The rehearsal is Friday, the wedding is on Saturday."

"It doesn't matter. I included them in the head count.

So if they come, there will be seats for them and enough food."

"That isn't what I'm worried about," he persisted.

"They're probably getting this information today, too, don't you think?" she reasoned. "They probably didn't want to jump the gun and RSVP before they knew for sure. I think it's a good sign that they didn't just say no."

"And what if they don't show even now? Are you gonna be so disappointed that it ruins your rehearsal, your wedding?"

"No," she said but not with conviction. "It would just be nice, is all, if they came. If the whole lot of us could be brought together by my wedding."

Declan saw that she wasn't going to budge from her optimism and decided that this might just be a hard lesson she had to learn. He couldn't protect her from it.

"I need to talk to you about something else, though," she said then, changing the subject. "I have a real problem—my photographer went mountain climbing, fell and broke both of his legs. He had to cancel!"

"Don't look at me, I can't take a decent picture to save my life."

"But your friend…"

Friend?

Declan didn't know who she was talking about. He sure as hell didn't have any friends in Northbridge. Not with Topher gone.

"Topher's sister-in-law," Kinsey clarified. "You met her when she was in Afghanistan as a *photographer*…"

"She's not a friend," he countered, a little too quickly.

But it was true. Emmy couldn't be considered a friend. Sometimes she even acted as if they were enemies.

"But she *is* a photographer," Kinsey said. "Do you think maybe she'd pinch-hit for me?"

"I don't have any idea," he said honestly. "I guess she does do that kind of photography in Denver now. But—"

"Would you ask her for me? There isn't a photographer in Northbridge, and even if there was, hiring someone now, for this coming weekend? There's no way."

So he would be asking a favor of Emmy?

That didn't sit well with him.

It was one thing to be doing what he was doing on the Samms farm and with Kit and Trinity—it wasn't for Emmy; he was doing it for Topher. But to ask Emmy to do something for him? He could never be sure how she might react to anything. Even if she said yes, could he count on her to follow through?

Plus it was another *wedding*.

After what had happened at Topher and Mandy's wedding, he wasn't thrilled with the idea of being at another one with her. What if it set off that Jekyll and Hyde thing again? Now, rather than going to separate hotel rooms, they'd be going back to the same house, needing to take care of the kids, to go on dealing with the farm. And if she turned into Hyde like she had the morning after Topher's wedding? No, thanks.

"I don't think that's a good idea, Kins. There's the kids and all the work that needs to be done on the farm. Plus, at the rehearsal and at the wedding, I'll be busy even though there isn't a formal wedding party, and if she's the photographer, she'll be swamped. What would we do with the kids?"

"This is Northbridge, Declan—it's a small town and people pitch in. Especially to hold a baby or keep an eye on a three-year-old. And we'll pay her what we were going to pay Kevin," Kinsey went on. "Pleeease? I'm in such a bind…"

Not a good idea. It is not a good idea for us to be at another wedding, Declan thought.

But how could he say no to his sister?

"I guess it would have to be up to her," he said as if conceding to torture.

"Will you call her right now and ask her? Then maybe I could talk to her and we could get things started?"

His reluctance showed in the slow-motion way he took out his cell phone and hit the button to dial her.

And as he waited for Emmy to answer, he knew with cold certainty that being at another wedding with her was as big a mistake as inviting the Camdens.

"Bad goat!"

"Bad Billy!" Trinity added from near the barn door.

"Ooh, stay there, Trinity. Stay with Kit. Don't come over here," Emmy cautioned in a panic.

There was never a need to watch the clock to know when it was time for evening chores. The chickens clucked and the goats all started crying a warning that they were hungry.

That noise had greeted Emmy when she'd arrived home from Kit's doctor's appointment. Declan wasn't back yet, so Emmy had put Kit in the stroller and taken him and Trinity with her to do the chores—beginning with the complaining goats.

The largest male always gave Emmy fits. But tonight he was apparently particularly peeved because rather than eat, he'd lowered his head and come at Emmy with his horns in charging position.

Emmy had left the kids near the barn's door, and although Trinity loved the goats and the goats loved her— including the largest male—she didn't want the little girl coming closer for fear that the animal might turn on the three-year-old, too.

For the moment he had only Emmy in his sights—but unfortunately, he had her cornered with no way around him to escape. The goat was staying a few feet back but lunging threateningly—head down, horns pointing like spears—whenever Emmy moved.

She'd tried a soothing voice to calm him. She'd tried cajoling. She'd tried firm commands.

When none of that had had any effect, she'd tried stomping her feet, clapping her hands—anything to seem intimidating enough to scare him into backing off.

But none of that had worked either.

"Aren't you hungry?" she said seductively. "Go eat your dinner…"

"Iss good…" Trinity added, again trying to help.

The goat didn't move.

"This is ridiculous!" Emmy said in frustration, wondering how her sister could have loved this life so much. She then put that frustration and anger into loudly shouting, "Get out of my way, you stupid, stupid goat!"

It didn't faze the goat.

"Yeah, uh, name-calling doesn't really bother goats."

Emmy's eyes shot to the barn door, where Declan had come up behind the children. A quick survey seemed to enlighten him as to what was going on, and he actually cracked the tiniest of smiles. It infuriated her—not only because it was at her expense, but because even in her current predicament she couldn't help noticing that it made him more appealing than that brooding frown he usually sported these days.

"Whatcha doin'?" he asked as if it wasn't obvious.

"They were out here hollering for their dinner when

I got home, so I fed them. But this one would rather terrorize me than eat."

"I talkted nice at him bu he's bein'haive bad, Decan," Trinity contributed.

"He's bein'haive *really* bad," Emmy confirmed.

"Sooo, do you have this under control—shall I go ahead and take the kids in and give them dinner—or do you need some help?" Declan asked.

Oh yeah, he was definitely enjoying this.

Emmy kind of wanted to wring his neck for being so complacent while she was still being held at horn-point by the goat. And no, she didn't *want* his help. Not when he was making it seem like she was some damsel in distress. That was just galling.

But what else was she to do?

Still, she couldn't be gracious about it and countered with "Do you want pictures taken of your sister's wedding?"

He was no more fazed by her threats than the goat had been.

"Hmm…now that you mention it, this might be the time to negotiate the price," he goaded as he went around the stroller and Trinity to saunter over to Emmy and the goat, looking smug and all too handsome in boots and jeans and a navy blue hoodie.

"Or maybe we could do some bartering," he suggested. "Free wedding pictures in exchange for hostage negotiations with old Billy here…"

Emmy sighed, not getting anywhere near the kick out of this that he was. "Just get this thing to let me out of this corner."

"You're gonna owe me…" he warned, sounding as if he relished that idea.

"Yeah, what else is new?" Emmy shot back, her sarcasm provoking the goat and buying her another lunge that came dangerously close to winning her a horn in her jean-clad thigh.

Declan used a booming, authoritative voice to order the goat away, and that was all it took to get the animal to comply.

"Really?" she muttered to the stubborn goat.

"Hey, he's just doing his job," Declan defended. "This is all your own fault."

"It's *my* fault that that goat is mean?"

"He's not mean, he was just letting you know he's boss in this barn. These goats have been raised around people. They consider people to be part of their pack. He was putting you in your place."

"He's alpha goat?"

"He's alpha to the rest of the pack and he sees you as one of them. Unless you show him that you're dominant, he'll keep at you."

"How am I not dominant? I'm bigger and smarter... I'm the human!"

"You could try handing over your credentials but he'd probably just eat them. You have to *show* him that you're boss."

"And how do I do that?" Emmy answered, unsure if he was playing a joke on her.

"You have to get next to the big bad goat, reach under his belly, grab his front and back leg at once, and pull him down to his side."

"You want me to roll around on the ground with a goat?" she said, her distaste evident.

"If you end up rolling around with him, you'll be doing it wrong," Declan said. "And it's up to you, but unless you physically dominate him, he'll go on trying to keep you in line."

Emmy glared at Declan to let him know he was in trouble if he was just messing with her.

"Did you do this when I wasn't looking?"

"Didn't have to."

"But I do?"

"Nope, you don't *have* to. But if you don't..." He shrugged one of those broad shoulders, leaving the decision to her.

Emmy did *not* want to do it. But still, she sneaked up to the side of the goat and did as she'd been instructed. Or at least she *tried* to. But her attempt was inelegant, and while the goat toppled onto his side, so did she.

They both shot back onto their feet and the goat cast her a look that said stalemate.

It was something else that made Thus-Far-Gloomy-Gus Declan smile—if only slightly. "Wow, no wonder he's got you bullied," Declan said. "Try again."

Determined to best the goat—and to squash Declan's amusement—Emmy did. Four more times she was forced to sneak up to the animal while he ran at the first movement she made toward him. But finally only the goat went down. Not easily, though, and the minute his side hit the barn floor he scrambled to all fours again.

By then Declan had wheeled in Kit's stroller and lifted Trinity to sit on a hay bale and the three of them were watching as if they were a rodeo audience. But Declan and Trinity did clap for her when she finally succeeded.

The trouble was when she turned to take her bow. The goat apparently decided to regain his authority because the next thing Emmy knew she'd been butted from behind and was flat on her face on the barn floor.

Which Trinity found hilarious while Declan seemed barely able to contain himself.

"Yu'r funny, Em," her niece told her.

Luckily the horns hadn't pierced her jeans or her skin, but still Emmy had felt the blow to both her posterior and her ego.

She got to her feet, rubbing the abused body part, and again she leveled a glare at Declan. "This isn't really what I'm supposed to do, is it? You're just putting me on."

"It really is the only way that goat will stop getting *your* goat," he assured. "Give it another try and make sure you're not shy about it."

She didn't want to give it another try. But not only was she determined not to let the goat get the best of her, she wasn't going to let Declan believe she was too much of a wimp to pull this off.

So she went on to rounds six and seven, finally toppling the animal with a modicum of grace and receiving a disdainful—but more leery—look from the goat, who turned his tail up at her and walked to the opposite side of the barn.

"Tell me I win," she demanded of Declan.

"Queen of the goats!" he decreed with a full-blown smile.

And for just a split second it was almost worth what she'd had to do for that praise.

And to see that smile.

After wrestling with the goat, Emmy needed another shower, so Declan finished the chores and fed both kids while she cleaned up.

She was again inclined to do a few extras with hair and makeup afterward, but the trip into town and then the goat had taken up too much time already. So after throwing on yoga pants and a simple gray T-shirt, she blew her hair dry using a round brush to put some turn into the ends, applied a quick bit of eyeliner and then hurried out of the master bedroom. It was already time to get Trinity through her bedtime routine while Declan put Kit down for the first half of the infant's night.

It was only when all of that was finished that Emmy could think about eating, and she was surprised to find that Declan had waited rather than having his sandwich when he fed Trinity.

It was nice, though, not to just be left to wolf down her hoagie and chips standing over the sink by herself. To instead find after she tucked Trinity in and went to the kitchen that Declan had their food set out on the table, complete with napkins, a cold beer for himself and a glass of the flavored sparkling water stocked in the fridge for her.

"How's your goat butt?" he asked when she first appeared in the kitchen, smiling yet another small smile at his oh-so-hilarious question.

The wordplay of it almost seemed flirtatious. But she reminded herself that she'd also thought they'd done a lot of flirting with each other at the wedding and, in retrospect, believed she'd been wrong.

So rather than answering with some wordplay of her own, she merely muttered, "Stupid goat." Then she added, "There's a bruise but I think I'll live." Although she did feel it when her rear end hit the hard wood seat of the kitchen chair.

Declan must have seen her flinch because that made his smile grow slightly.

"It isn't funny," she said, although it surprised her how much she liked seeing his expression lighten.

"Believe me, it was funny," he said, smiling even bigger.

Emmy didn't want him to know how much she liked his smile—so much that she didn't mind that it was at her expense—so she rolled her eyes before she changed the subject. "You didn't have to wait to eat," she said as Declan sat across from her.

"That would have been just plain bad manners," he countered. "What did the doctor have to say about Kit?"

So not only had his sober side taken a rest, he was also putting some effort into talking tonight without her having to demand it. That made things smoother.

"We're trying a different formula," she answered. "Kit hasn't lost any weight—in fact, he's gained a pound—so that's good. But until he adjusts, there isn't much hope for a quick 2:00 a.m. feeding and getting him right back to bed—which I guess is the ideal for babies this age."

"Maybe the new formula will do the trick."

"Maybe."

They ate in silence for a moment. Then, thinking about the phone call from him and his sister that afternoon, Emmy fell back on what she'd learned about him in the past and said, "So your family... Are your twin and your older brother still in the military?"

"Nope, they've both opted out in the past year."

"I didn't know you have a sister, too—is she military or civilian?"

"Civilian all the way. Our adoptive father was a retired marine and he tried to get her on board with the rest of us, but Kinsey wouldn't have any of that."

"You and your twin were adopted?" This was the first she'd heard about that.

Declan shook his head. "Hugh adopted the four of us kids when he married our mother."

"Ahh," Emmy said. "What happened to your real dad?"

"Hugh was our real dad." There was some defensiveness in that that also seemed to slam the door on giving her any more information.

It left Emmy curious, but since it wasn't any of her business she didn't pursue it and instead asked, "So the Madison brothers all went away to the military and your sister stayed in Northbridge?" It was a reasonable assumption since his sister was getting married on what Emmy had been told was the family farm at the end of the week.

"No, Kinsey left, too. She lives in Denver."

"Are your parents still here? Is that why she came back to get married?"

He shook his head again while he finished a bite of sandwich, then said, "My mom died at the end of last year. Hugh went two years before that. We're planning to sell the old farm, but it's been tough for the four of us to get together to go through the things in the house so we can prep it to put on the market. Since it's still ours she wanted to come back here to have the wedding. No way would it have been my choice, but—"

"Because you don't like Northbridge," Emmy recalled. "I know sometimes people who grow up in small towns can't wait to get out of them, but Mandy and Topher loved it here. And I've never seen such an... I don't know what to call it except an outpouring of sympathy and support and caring and help, both when news of Topher came and when we lost Mandy. It's been amazing."

"Yeah, that's a small town for you."

"And you hate that?" Emmy asked.

"There are good things about a small town. And there are bad things, too. I was miserable growing up here."

"Was it claustrophobic for you? Were you just aching to spread your wings, find adventure?"

She said that with a smile, but he didn't seem to see the humor in it. He stared at the tabletop, sober and solemn again. He ate some potato chips. He drank a few swigs of beer. But he didn't answer her, and Emmy thought, *Great, the return of Gloomy-Gus...*

Then he took a breath, sat up straighter and looked at her rather than the table. "One of the bad things about a small town is that it's hard to keep anything private. Pretty much everyone around here knows my family's history, so you might as well hear it from me. My mom wasn't married to our biological father."

"So...what? She and your father lived together without getting married and because it was a small town that didn't go over well?" Emmy asked.

"That would have been so much better. Instead my mother was Mitchum Camden's longtime mistress," he said flatly. "He'd come to town for visits—always meeting our mom in secret, trying to make sure no one ever saw them together—and then he'd go home to his wife and kids in Denver. And as of today, DNA says that he was definitely our father."

Emmy was confused again. "You just learned that today?"

"When my mom died, she told Kinsey who had fathered us all—"

"Not before?"

"Not before. Camden—and a lot of his family—died in a plane crash when Mom was pregnant with Kinsey—"

"*Camden*... Like Camden Superstores?" Emmy was just trying to get the details straight.

"Yeah, Camden as in Camden Superstores." More contempt. "Mom married Hugh when Kinsey was two, Liam and I were three, Conor was barely seven. Hugh adopted us—"

"But you still called him by his name? Not Dad?"

"We called him Gunny. That's what he was in the service—a gunnery sergeant—and that's what he liked to be called. Outside home we called him our father, but Mom always referred to him as Hugh when she was talking to us, so when we refer to him that's what we've all called him, too. Either Hugh or Gunny."

"But you were still close to him? You still grew up thinking of him as your father?"

"Him and no one else. And he was our dad in every way that counted—he legally adopted us right away, took over the farm, supported us, raised us. He was the only father we knew, and whenever any one of us asked who our real father was, Mom would shut it down. She'd say that it was hurtful and disrespectful to Hugh to bring up anyone else when he was so good to us."

"Wasn't it a little weird? I mean, she wouldn't open up about who your real father was, but still she made it clear that your adopted father *wasn't* your real father by only calling him by name with you?"

"Yeah, I guess it was."

"Did it always leave you wondering who your real dad was?"

There was another long, heavy pause before Declan said in a quiet, deep voice, "I didn't have to wonder. I knew. I never told the rest of my family, but from kindergarten on, I did."

"Kindergarten? How did you learn something like that when you were so little?"

"Greg Kravitz," he said. And if ever Emmy had heard hatred in a name, it was then.

"Greg Kravitz," she repeated, knowing the name but unsure whether to reveal that knowledge.

"See, that's what can happen in a small town," he went on. "A scandal can go underground when it's over, when a tough marine comes along and makes an honest woman of someone who has four bastard kids with some rich player. But even if the scandal goes underground, even if a majority of the townsfolk start to overlook it, to put it in the past, there are still some people who hang on to it— just more quietly. Some people who talk about it around their own kids—"

"Their kindergarteners?"

"Well, yeah," he said scornfully. "They need to do that when they find their kid in the same class with one of those town bastards and they want to make sure their kid doesn't go anywhere near him."

"Oh, that's so ugly," Emmy said.

"It's definitely not pretty," Declan agreed.

"But how did it only affect you and not your twin?"

"School policy was to separate twins into different classes. Liam and Topher were in one class. I was in the other."

"With Greg Kravitz."

"Who, by the third day of school, got me alone in the boys' room to tell me what his parents had told him— that I was the bastard kid of one of the Camdens, that my mother was his whore."

"Oh. Wow. Someone said that to you in kindergarten?" Emmy said with even more incredulity.

"Yeah. I didn't know what a bastard or a whore were but it was pretty clear they were *bad*." He sighed and shook his head once more, but this time in such a sad way that Emmy's heart went out to the little boy he'd been. Then, in a quieter voice, he said, "So I went home, asked my mom and made her cry…"

The ongoing weight of that was evident, and Emmy felt even more sorry for young Declan.

"She and I were alone when I asked her," he went on. "Her face went ghost white, her eyes got really big…" Declan's own eyebrows arched and Emmy could tell that the image of his mother's ashen face was vivid in his mind.

Then he said, "And all she said was that those were bad words and I was never to repeat them to anyone." And she must have said it sternly and with some defeat in her tone because that was how Declan spoke now.

"Seeing what those words did to her…" He shook his head yet again. "I loved my mom. To me she was a great lady, and…man, I didn't want to make her cry! I still didn't know what those words meant, but I knew enough to know that they had to be kept secret. So I never mentioned them again. In fact, I've never told anybody about the hell Kravitz put me through until right now."

"Not even your brothers?"

Declan let out a humorless chuckle. "*Especially* not my brothers. Or Kinsey. How could I tell them what I was hearing about our mother? Even after we were grown, do you really think I was going to talk about how people around here considered our mom a *whore*? No way."

"So you just kept it inside?"

He shrugged his answer to that as if there had never been any other course for him.

"How did you handle that?" she asked, knowing it had to have been a huge burden for him.

"I didn't handle it all that well," he said with some chagrin. "I kept to myself unless I could be with Liam or Topher—which got me the reputation as a loner."

"But you did trust Topher?"

"His mom was my mother's best friend, so…I don't know…maybe she just accepted the affair that produced us all. One way or another I trusted that whether or not Topher knew, it wasn't an issue with him or his family. But otherwise I stayed strictly to myself, on the sidelines."

"Did that make Kravitz leave you alone?"

"Nah. I think it actually made it easier for him to get to me *because* I was alone. When I was with Liam or Topher, he stayed away."

"So you were the only one he tortured—his pet project. But it went on from kindergarten?" Emmy asked.

"Oh yeah, he took his last shot the day we graduated high school. Around here—at least then—unless a parent or a teacher wants a change, the class you start out in in kindergarten is the class you're in until middle school. So through fifth grade, Liam and Topher were in one room while I was stuck in the other."

"But in middle school that changed," Emmy said, looking for some hope.

"Yeah, Kravitz and I had some classes together from then through high school, but not all of them. We were still in the same small school, though. And by then he was just so good at it..." Declan said. "He was a devious SOB. And God, but did he know how to make himself look innocent. He knew he'd get in trouble if anyone heard him using that kind of language—not to mention, he'd have to deal with my brothers and Topher if they realized what he was doing—so he made sure that he only taunted me when no one was in earshot. At least, no one but people who were already on his side. I certainly wasn't going to report him—telling anyone would mean calling my mother a whore, even if it was just to repeat what he'd said. As we got older he learned to have his friends as backup—they'd be grinning from behind him—"

"So there *were* other kids he told."

"Hey, you can't keep it to yourself," he said facetiously. "He was discreet enough to stay out of trouble, but his crew definitely knew."

"And again, how did you handle it?"

"I tried to ignore it, ignore him. I tried to stay away

from him. But he just *loved* that he had something so juicy that always got a reaction out of me. When we were little and I'd reach the point where I couldn't take it anymore, I'd ram him to the ground, we'd roll around until somebody pulled me off him. When we were older, I'd throw the first punch, he and his friends would pile on, and..." Another shrug. "And I'd usually get my ass handed to me. There were so many fights that after a while I was not only the loner, I earned the title of troublemaker, too."

"How were you the troublemaker when it was all of them jumping on you at once?"

"Like I said, I was always the one to throw the first punch. And how could I defend myself when teachers or the principal or cops broke it up? I couldn't tell anybody what was going on, so I just looked like the hothead with a grudge against a more popular kid."

"And at home...they never knew why you were in so many scrapes?"

"I'm not really sure. I only know that I never faced any consequences at home for the fights. But neither Mom nor Hugh said anything, and I didn't say anything either."

"Did your stepfather know that Camden was your father?"

"I honestly don't know that either. Behind closed doors Mom might have confessed the truth. Or maybe she never volunteered the information and he respected her enough not to ask. I have no idea. And I don't know if he knew why I was fighting—but I do know he never punished me for it."

Declan shrugged again. "Hugh was all about toughening us up—me and Liam and Conor—to get us ready for the military. Could be he thought the brawls were just good training," Declan said with some amusement finally showing through.

Until he sobered again. "All I do know is that from kindergarten on I couldn't wait to get the hell out of North-bridge. And as happy as I was to go, Northbridge was probably just as happy to see me leave. I'd imagine that when they heard it was me who drove Topher to his death, they all just said *that figures*..."

"No, you're wrong about that," Emmy said. "I under-stand why you couldn't wait to get away from here. But whenever I've heard your name mentioned with Topher's, it hasn't been negative. Not at all. Everyone just seems relieved that if it had to happen, at least only one home-town boy was lost."

His laugh this time was so harsh it was almost hard to hear. "Don't try to tell me anyone around here claims me as a *hometown boy*. I may have been born and raised here, but the academy was the first place I ever felt like I wasn't a full-grade outsider. It was the first place where I was truly treated like I belonged. The marines are my home. The marines are what I can't wait to get back to. This place? I'm just here to do what needs to be done and then I'll be happy to put it behind me again."

"I still think you're mistaken about how the town sees you," Emmy said, even though she could see that he wouldn't be convinced. "I think whatever went on with you here in the past is forgotten. You were only a kid after all."

"Even so, if my sister has her way things are going to get stirred up again—she's thrilled to be a Camden and she's invited the whole clan to her wedding. As you can imagine, they've been...less than thrilled to learn Mitchum was a long-term cheat. They refused to believe it was true, but now we have DNA that proves it. Not sure if that changes anything. But whether they show or not, she's opening the lid on that old scandal. And I don't want any part of what happens after that."

"I can't say I blame you," Emmy said quietly, wondering why he'd chosen her to tell this to for the first time.

It had probably just been a fluke, she reasoned. Or just a convenience—he'd received the confirmation of his birth father today. Maybe he'd needed to unload a little, and she just happened to be there when that need peaked.

He finished his beer and took his plate to the sink.

Emmy saw that as the signal that he was finished talking about this. She'd long since stopped eating, so she took her own plate around the counter, too, just in time for Declan to reach for it to put the plate in the dishwasher with his.

"So tonight's your night walking the floors with Kit," he said then. "You worked hard today... Are you up for it or do you need me to take a second night?"

"That wouldn't be fair," she declined even though she appreciated the offer. "Besides, I've been doing this for a while now—every other night. I'm used to it."

"If you're sure..." he said with an inflection that she thought might have been respect.

He closed the dishwasher and rested a hip against the counter's edge, crossing his arms over that broad chest of his. "And then tomorrow we have a beekeeper coming to check out the hives and tell us what to do with them?" he said.

Emmy nodded. She was standing not far away, squarely in front of him, and looking up into eyes she still couldn't believe were that blue. "Late tomorrow afternoon," she confirmed. Then, to get her mind off those eyes, she goaded him a little. "You'll have to wear the suit, you know?"

"So will you, won't you?" he challenged.

"Yeah, but I know *I'm* gonna rock it..."

He chuckled, clearly not having expected her to say that. "Well, since I haven't seen you in anything that you haven't *rocked*, I think you'll probably do wonders for bee suits, too."

Emmy had been joking, not fishing for flattery.

Not that she didn't like hearing it. Or seeing him genuinely smile again.

She liked the compliment and the smile too much, so she bypassed both and went on with her joke. "But you…" she said, sighing tragically. "I'm just worried that you'll look silly."

He lifted his chin to scratch the evening's stubble. She'd been trying to keep herself from thinking about how sexy he looked unshaven, but there was no *not* thinking about it when he did that.

"Nah… I'm pretty sure I'm gonna rock it, too" was his cocky comeback.

"Oh, you are, are you?" she challenged.

He finished rubbing his chin and lowered his eyes to hers, the sparkle that had been only a scant flicker the night before finally there in full force. "Pretty sure," he confirmed brashly. "In fact, I think I'm gonna rock it more than you are."

Emmy laughed. "We might have to have the beekeeper rate us to make sure there's no question."

His smile turned into a grin and that brought Emmy's gaze to his supple and sexy mouth. "Hey, bring it on," he said.

There was more insinuation in his tone than there had been before, and when his gaze dropped to her mouth and stayed there, their topic of conversation became a fleeting memory to Emmy. Instead the only thing on her mind was the idea of that mouth of his kissing her…

His smile was softer now.

His eyes were warmer.

Was he leaning forward the slightest little bit?

She thought he was.

She thought it to such a degree that she raised her chin, fully ready to accept the kiss that was about to happen.

Unless she was imagining it...

Oh right. She probably was.

That was her pattern after all, she reminded herself. Her imagination got the best of her and she believed things were different than they were. Especially with this guy.

But there's nothing going on between you, she told herself firmly, spinning around suddenly so her back was to him before he could realize the mistake she'd almost made.

"I left the sample of the new formula powder in my car," she announced in a hurry. "I have to go get it. The doctor said to finish out today with the old stuff and start the new tomorrow. You might as well go to bed. I can take care of that, too."

Then she left the kitchen and went out the front door without another word to Declan. She paused for a few minutes in the chilly night air to take some deep breaths and clear her mind of this crazy tendency to see things one way when the reality was completely different.

Because the reality *was* completely different, she insisted to herself.

And she absolutely would *not* let go of her hold on reality with this guy.

Chapter Five

"Hi, honey. I was going to call you tonight to see how things are going—did you read my mind?" Karen asked when she answered Emmy's phone call early Tuesday morning.

"No, no mind reading. I'm just taking out your Mexican casserole so it can thaw in the fridge today. But you didn't write the cooking temperature on this one. I thought I'd catch you before you go into the office so I'm prepared when I cook it tonight. Plus I have a favor to ask."

Her mother gave the cooking direction and with that out of the way, Emmy explained that she'd accepted a job taking wedding pictures for Declan's sister and asked if her mother would pack her cameras and equipment and express ship it all to her.

After taking extensive notes of what Emmy needed and assuring her she and Emmy's father would ship it the following morning, her mother said, "Where are the kids?"

"I just gave Kit his morning bottle, so he's in the bouncy chair right here, and Trinity is downstairs doing Declan's physical therapy exercises with him before the sitter gets here."

"How are things going?" Karen asked.

"You were right," Emmy conceded. "Having Declan here is a big help. Yesterday we got about three times more done than I would have been able to do on my own."

And that had been primarily due to Declan. In fact, Emmy thought that she'd probably accomplished less herself than she would have working alone because she hadn't had any distractions when she'd worked alone.

But Declan was a major distraction in worn jeans that just loved that divine derriere of his, plus an equally aged chambray shirt that whispered across his muscles. Sleeves rolled to his elbows exposed finely developed forearms, which drew her eyes like a magnet. As did his thick wrists and big hands—two more things that had never caught her attention on anyone else.

And that sculpted face of his shaded under the brim of a cowboy hat? That hair that was perfectly mussed when he took it off? Those forearms or the back of those wrists rubbed across his sweaty brow?

None of it should have had any allure.

But too many times yesterday she'd lapsed into some kind of dazed pause, staring at him gape-jawed.

She'd catch herself, mentally holler at herself and then force herself to get back to work.

Only to do the same thing a few minutes later—all of which had cost her work time.

But *he'd* gotten a lot accomplished.

And thankfully never caught her ogling him.

"Are you getting along with Declan, then?" her mother asked.

"Well, sure. I've never not *gotten along* with him."

"That's not exactly true…" her mother said the way only a mother could. "You know Mandy didn't understand what was going on with you when it came to Declan. She said you seemed to like him before the bombing and then wouldn't even let him visit you after it. Then at the wedding reception it sure *looked* like you liked him, but the next day…you were really rude to him. *Embarrassingly* rude to him."

This again, Emmy thought.

She'd been through this more than once with her sister and with her mother.

"I told you, I just wasn't up for visitors after the school deal. I wanted to get home and put it behind me. And I don't know why you guys made such a big deal out of dancing a few dances with him at the reception. It was basically just a best man/maid of honor courtesy thing—"

"The only dance you didn't dance with Declan was the one dance you danced with Daddy. And the two of you sat at the same table—"

"The table for the wedding party," Emmy pointed out.

"But instead of him staying on the groom's side, he moved to sit next to you and you didn't seem to mind… through the whole reception."

"I'd had a lot to drink," Emmy said, repeating the excuse she'd given before. "I would have danced with the waiters and the cleaning crew, too, if they'd asked."

"But then the next day—"

"I was hungover. And there was no reason for Declan and I to have anything to do with each other by then, so I'm sure the fact that I wasn't cheery couldn't have mattered less to him either." Especially after the night he'd had next door with Tracy…

"But you're being nice to him now, aren't you?"

"Of course," Emmy assured. "I'm treating him like I'd treat any coworker—because that's what we are here, just two people working together."

It was exactly what she'd told herself every time she fell into that trance looking at him.

Which wasn't *only* out in the field. There was a time or two around the house, too. Like when he first came upstairs after a shower, smelling all clean and outdoorsy, his hair damp, his face freshly shaven.

Or other times...

Stubbled and scruffy.

Just after his workout.

Coming in from morning chores.

When he was gently roughhousing with Trinity or cradling Kit in those muscular arms.

Almost any given moment for no reason whatsoever...

Why does he—of all men—have to be cologne-ad hot? she silently grumbled.

"It just worries me, is all," her mother was saying, interrupting Emmy's wandering thoughts. "For whatever reason, I've never seen you be as snarky as you were with Declan after the wedding. And living with any man now, after everything that happened with Bryce, must be hard."

"I'm not going to punish Declan for Bryce—if that's what you're worried about," Emmy assured her mother.

And she meant it. But what she was doing was using what had happened with Bryce as the glaring reminder to take everything with a grain of salt when it came to Declan. To make sure she did not see the budding of a relationship where it didn't exist.

Like last night. When Declan had confided who his birth father was.

Instead of believing his choice to share the story with her was something significant, she'd made sure to keep in mind that he'd told her only because his sister was determined to let the world know anyway. *That* was the significant part and she'd made sure to note it. She couldn't let herself think that sharing a confidence like that made her something special to him. He'd probably just needed to vent. It wasn't like he could tell his family. It had to be frustrating to learn that what he'd suffered in order to protect his family from knowing about their mother was now something his sister wanted to rejoice in.

And if he couldn't tell his family, who else in Northbridge could he tell? Emmy recognized that she was a third party without any connection to any of it—not the town, not his family, not his history. She was just like a stranger on a train—someone safe to air his grievances to, someone safe to reveal an old wound to. But that was all there was to it—a stranger-on-a-train thing.

And the fact that it had occurred to her that they had something in common when it came to keeping a big secret and trying to bear that secret without burdening their families? She'd refused to see that as a foundation for any kind of bond between them.

They were two people with nothing but a superficial connection, caught up in circumstances that put them together for the time being. If, during that time, they got to know things about each other, it was just something that was bound to happen. It didn't go beyond that, and she could not, should not, would not view it as having the potential of developing into anything substantial.

Period.

To think anything more, to expect anything more, was just asking to be brought up short again.

"So the two of you are getting along?" her mother asked, interrupting her thoughts a second time.

"We're getting along just fine."

"I think he's a good man," Karen Tate said, changing to matchmaker mode.

"I'm sure he is," Emmy agreed as if it was totally unimportant to her.

"So maybe you should give him a chance…"

She *had* given him a chance. And he'd passed it up.

But she was too proud—and embarrassed—to tell her mother that. Instead she said, "Let's see… Clean up an entire farm from the damage of one of the worst hailstorms this town has ever seen. Replant fields—something I haven't the foggiest idea how to do. Take care of two kids. Lease this place so I can move those two kids back to Denver with me and be their mom. Find someplace for us to live that can't be my tiny apartment. Restart the business I've had to leave hanging while I've been here. *And* try to hook up with a career military man who won't even be on this continent as soon as he can arrange it. All just months after being dumped by the guy I thought was going to marry me? That does seem like a good idea, Mom."

"See? You can be snarky," her mother said lovingly.

"I can also not deal with any more than I already have."

"I know that's true," Karen conceded. "It just seems a shame when there you are, with such a good man—"

Who prefers Brazilian bombshells…

"I have to go, Mom. I can hear him and Trinity coming upstairs and I need to get the kids dressed," Emmy said, thrilled to have a reason to end this conversation.

"I just feel so much better that you aren't there alone, that you have help."

"Me, too. Don't forget the cameras and stuff."

"I won't. I'll check in with you in a day or so, but call me if you need me," Karen said and hung up.

None too soon, as far as Emmy was concerned.

Because as difficult as it was to ignore Declan's physical attributes, as difficult as it was not to feel closer to him after an evening like the last one with him, where it had felt like a barrier between them might have dropped a little, as difficult as it was to end that evening imagining that he might be on the verge of kissing her—and having to fight the crazy wish that he would—the last thing she needed was her mother or anyone else pointing out more about him that was appealing.

It was hard enough to remember that, when it came to her, he wasn't interested.

She didn't need more reasons to forget that she wasn't interested in him either.

"Kiss 'n make it better." That was Trinity's recommendation.

Emmy and Declan had continued clearing the hail-damaged fields until late that afternoon when a beekeeper from the co-op came as scheduled.

All three of them had suited up for the beekeeper's visit so they could survey the damage to the hives and so the beekeeper could teach Emmy and Declan what to do to repair that damage and keep the hives going.

During the course of that, Emmy had apparently not completely secured the veil of her headgear and she'd been stung on the back of the neck.

The initial pain was severe, gradually turning into a dull ache. But she knew she wasn't allergic, so she hadn't made a big deal of it.

As the evening wore on, though, the sting began to hurt and burn much worse, and she could feel it swelling even more.

The last thing she wanted to do was ask a personal favor of Declan. But the sting was in a place she couldn't see. So once Kit was asleep and Trinity was choosing her bedtime book, Emmy gave in and asked him to look at it.

"Huh… That looks like it hurts…"

She was bent over the sink in the bathroom connected to the master bedroom where the light was brightest. Declan was standing next to her, his height an advantage. But he was close enough for her to feel the heat of his body, to smell the clean scent of the soap he'd used to shower before dinner, and she was unnerved by what those two things did to her. So she was relieved when Trinity joined them.

She just wasn't quite as pleased with the three-year-old's kiss-it-and-make-it-better idea.

Especially when Emmy found herself the tiniest bit inclined for him to do it…

"Maybe we shouldn't have trusted an eighty-two-year-old with half-inch-thick glasses to tell us there wasn't a stinger," Declan mused. "Because I think there's one in there. I'm gonna need some tweezers."

Emmy straightened up, opened the door to the medicine cabinet and found the tweezers. Then she handed them to him.

"Is this like a thorn?" she asked. "Do you have to dig for it?"

"Not sure—I've never done this before. But I think I can grab it… Just hold still."

Back in position—with Trinity now observing from her seat on the closed toilet lid—Emmy said, "Okay, do it."

Declan placed a big hand on one of her shoulders.

There was nothing to the gesture but to brace himself or maybe to hold her steady, but still she was abundantly aware of the feel of that hand on her, of the size and strength of it. Even through the T-shirt she was wearing, his touch sent what felt like a warm electrical charge to her nerve endings.

Which maybe had a good side to it because she was thinking so much about his touch that she didn't even feel what he was doing with the stinger before he said, "Got it!"

He didn't take his hand from her shoulder, though. He left it there while he took another look at the back of her neck.

"I think you'd better ice this—it's pretty red and about the size of a golf ball."

"Kiss 'n make it better," Trinity insisted as if they were overlooking the easiest cure.

There was just enough of a pause from Declan to make Emmy wonder if he was considering it.

Or maybe that was just wishful thinking.

That theory was confirmed when he swept Trinity off the toilet seat and held her up behind Emmy. "Go ahead, kiss it and make it better," he instructed the little girl.

Sweet Trinity did just that.

And Emmy wondered if the bee venom was affecting her powers of reason because she felt a wave of something wash through her that almost felt like a letdown.

"Better?" Trinity asked after the kiss.

"Oh, much better," Emmy lied.

"Now read a book?" the little girl asked.

"How about I read your book tonight," Declan offered hopefully, "so Emmy can go put that bag of frozen peas I saw in the freezer on her bee sting?"

"Em reads, you watch," Trinity decreed, still resisting altering her routine.

"Then I'll get the peas and bring them up," he said, taking the rejection in stride the way he had every other night so far.

While he went downstairs, Emmy took Trinity into the bedroom and got her situated in bed. Then she sat beside her niece on top of the covers with the picture book Trinity had chosen tonight.

Declan was back with the frozen peas just as Emmy was about to start.

"I brought you an antihistamine, too," he informed her, handing her the bag, a small pill and a glass of water. "I think you might be having a little reaction to the sting."

Emmy didn't argue. She took the pill.

But when she tipped her head back to swallow it, her gaze went to the ceiling. "Uh-oh—is that water coming in over there in the corner?"

It had been raining for about an hour—not hard enough to cause her to worry about the hail-damaged roof. But one look at that dark spot on the ceiling and that worry started.

"That's what it looks like to me," Declan agreed. "I'll go up in the attic and check it out."

Emmy was suddenly happy that Trinity had again chosen her to read the bedtime story, leaving Declan free to head to the attic. Just the thought of that small space made her uncomfortable.

Trying to ignore it, she read Trinity the book, then tucked her niece in, kissed her good-night and left the room.

Only to find Declan just coming down the steps that led to the attic.

"There's a pretty bad leak we'd better deal with," he said when he saw her.

We?

Emmy felt her entire body clench. "On the roof?" she said hopefully, far, far preferring the idea of climbing onto a slippery rain-soaked roof in a storm to the thought of going up into a cramped attic.

Declan looked at her as if she'd missed something. "We can't patch the roof in the dark, in the rain."

"I'll find you a bucket, then. You can put it under the leak for tonight," she said, searching for any solution that would keep her out of that attic.

"It's coming in too fast for that. There's some scrap plywood up there. I'll need you to hold it in place and I'll nail it up. Just let me get the hammer and the nails—"

"You're sure you need me?" she said, working hard to keep the anxiety that was running through her out of her voice.

"I'm sure," he said, his confusion at her hesitation clear. "It won't be hard. You just need to hold up the wood while I nail it."

What was she going to do, refuse something that sounded so simple? Tell him that in almost four and a half years she hadn't taken an elevator and instead chalked up always using the stairs to a good cardio workout?

In a moment of what she considered truly stupid fear she actually considered getting Trinity out of bed and having her hold the plywood for him.

But she knew she couldn't do that either, so she said, "Okay, get the hammer and nails," and hoped she could use the few minutes he'd be gone to get a hold of herself.

Declan went downstairs, and Emmy began to take deep breaths, to exhale them slowly, to put all she had into calming herself down.

She told herself that she could do this. She'd gotten so much better. She hadn't had any problem seeing Declan at the wedding or again here in Northbridge. It had been more than three years since she'd had a panic attack. Surely that meant she was over those initial problems she'd had right after the explosion.

She told herself that it was natural to be worried that the attic might set her off again—but being worried about it didn't mean that the worst would happen. It hadn't with Declan, she kept reminding herself. If she stayed in control, kept breathing, focused on what she needed to do, reminded herself that she wasn't trapped, that within minutes she would be able to leave the attic, maybe she'd be okay...

She heard Declan coming back up the steps and opened her eyes.

You can do this...

"Why don't you grab some towels to sop up what's already come in so it doesn't keep soaking through to Trinity's room," he said.

"Sure," Emmy agreed, eager for even that much of a delay.

Once she had the towels, though, she didn't have a choice but to follow Declan up the stairs, knowing she wasn't faring well when she didn't even care that she got to see his great derriere up ahead of her.

You can do this, she silently repeated to herself at the foot of the steps.

She took another deep breath and climbed the first stair, her knee actually wobbling when she put her weight on it.

Come on, she chastised herself with disgust, holding on tight to the railing as she forced herself to climb the rest.

Her head poked through the attic floor first and she paused to take stock of the space.

The slope of the roof made it too small for Declan to stand upright anywhere but in the center. There was a small window at either end, but it was too overcast outside for even moonlight to come in and give the sense of the outside. The only illumination came from a single bare bulb.

That light was way more than she'd had in the school cave-in, though. So that was better...

Another deep breath and she went all the way into the attic, trying to ignore the tightness that seemed to wrap around her rib cage, trying to ignore the sound of her heart pounding hard and fast in her ears. Trying harder not to think about being knees-to-chest in that other confined space...

"Just hold it," Declan said when he had the plywood in place.

Emmy dropped the towels and managed to do as she was told, listening to the rain, trying to picture herself out in it, in the open air where she could breathe...

Except that there was such a heaviness in her chest that she wasn't sure she could.

And suddenly she was so dizzy, so light-headed.

Her hands were tingling, her palms were so damp she wasn't sure she could keep her grip on the plywood.

And those sloped walls...they were closing in on her.

And just about the time Declan had pounded in the third nail, she couldn't catch her breath.

"Are you okay?" he said, ceasing his hammering when she started gasping for air.

His scrutiny only made it worse.

She couldn't talk, but she didn't seem to need to for him to realize what was happening.

Suddenly his voice was quieter, softer, and that big hand that had been on her shoulder earlier was on her back, firm and strong, pressing in just enough to ground her as he said, "It's okay. You're okay. Cup your hands over your nose and mouth, purse your lips and breathe through them..."

He gave her a moment to do all that and she complied, desperate to have this end.

"Feel the floor under your feet," he went on then. "Know there's plenty of air, just let it come in. In and out. Slow and easy..."

His voice meant everything to her right then. Calm. Deep. Comforting. The way it had been that day long ago.

"It's okay," he was saying. "It's okay… You're okay…"

He repeated that over and over again, and Emmy mentally held on to it like a lifeline until breathing into her cupped hands did begin to stop the hyperventilation.

When Declan could tell she was breathing more normally, he said, "Come on, let's get you out of here."

Oh God, how she hated herself for letting this happen! For letting him see it!

But the same way she couldn't have gotten out of that rubble in Afghanistan without him grabbing her and pulling her free, she couldn't get out of that attic without him leading her to the stairs, helping her down into the hallway.

Total humiliation took over then and with what air she now had in her lungs she said, "Go! Go!" and motioned toward the attic.

"It'll wait," he assured, still in that soothing tone.

Emmy shook her head vehemently to let him know she just wanted him to get back to it.

"You're sure?" he asked.

"Go!" she said again, wanting those blue eyes off her.

He still didn't move for another long moment, watching her. Then he finally took her at her word and went back into the attic.

Apparently the three nails that Declan had pounded into the plywood before she'd gone to pieces had been enough to keep the board in place because the sound of more hammering came while Emmy contended with the remnants of her fright.

She bent over and braced herself with her hands on her bent knees, letting her head hang.

Little by little she shed the terror, reveling in the fact that she could breathe without difficulty again.

The cold sweats stopped and so did the racing of her heart.

When she could, she took a really deep breath, held it for a minute and then exhaled, unsure what was worse— the panic attack or the fact that Declan had witnessed it. But there was nothing she could do about it now, so she stood up straight again and returned to the bathroom connected to her bedroom.

She filled her cupped hands with cold water and splashed her face over and over. Then she took a hand towel from the cupboard under the sink and patted her face dry.

She felt drained. Exhausted. And she just wanted to hide so she wouldn't have to face Declan.

But even if she locked herself in her bedroom now, she couldn't stay there past the morning. She couldn't hide forever. Might as well get the conversation over with now.

She dropped the towel to the counter and looked at herself in the mirror.

Her cheeks were flushed. Her hair was mussed, so she ran a brush through it—mostly in an attempt to give her a feeling of control.

Then, knowing she was going to have to answer for herself, she went back out into the hall.

The door that hid the attic stairs was still open, and although the pounding had stopped, she could hear Declan moving around up there.

Rather than just waiting for him in the hallway, she opted to go downstairs.

If it hadn't been raining, she would have gone outside, into the open air. But since it was storming, she went through the kitchen to the mudroom in the back and opened that door instead, standing at the screen to be as close to the outdoors as she could get.

That was where she was when she heard Declan coming downstairs.

"Emmy?" he called quietly.

"Mudroom," she answered without much force.

A few more minutes lapsed before Declan joined her. He leaned a shoulder against the door frame, looking at her profile while she steadfastly stared out the door, only seeing him peripherally.

"Just a splash of whiskey," he said, holding out a small glass to her. "I thought maybe you could use it."

Looking at the glass rather than at him, Emmy accepted the drink and took a sip. "Thanks," she said, watching the rain again.

"I was thinking about that little boy at the school in Kandahar," Declan mused then, out of the blue. "The one who had a crush on you. I was thinking about how he kept trying to get you all to himself. How he took your hand that one day and pulled you into that tiny little closet with him and wouldn't come out until his teacher made him."

Emmy recalled the four-year-old but only raised her chin a notch to acknowledge Declan's words.

"Being in that tiny little closet didn't bother you at all. But that was before the explosion…"

So that was his lead-in.

Emmy didn't respond to it. She merely went on watching the rain.

"I've seen PTSD, Emmy."

"A lot of people don't like small spaces," she rationalized. "That doesn't mean they have PTSD."

"Okay," he said as if he accepted that. "I know you had your sister thinking you're okay—when you wouldn't see me before you left Afghanistan, I had Topher ask Mandy how you were doing. Word always came back that you were good, so I'm betting she never saw what I just did."

"I had an experience that changed a few things for me, is all," Emmy said. "Other people have been through worse. Kids even."

"So…what? You don't think you *earned* PTSD?"

"I don't have PTSD," she said more firmly.

"Well, you don't seem to have lost interest in things, and you also don't seem withdrawn or detached—not with your mom, not with the kids. As far as I can tell, you sleep all right…don't you?"

"I sleep great."

"You don't have any problems concentrating," he went on. "You aren't jumpy or jittery—if you're not in an attic…or other small spaces?" The end of that was probing.

Emmy ignored it and challenged, "Let me guess—those are the signs and symptoms of PTSD and you think you're an expert on it?"

"No, not an expert," he said patiently. "But I told you I've been evaluated for it myself—more than once. Maybe I couldn't write a book on it, but I could write a pamphlet."

She tried to muster up a smile at his joke because it was a pretty good one.

"How about nightmares? Are you having those?" he asked.

"For a while I did but not anymore," she answered honestly.

"Anything else—besides the small-spaces thing?"

"I wasn't sure what it might be like to see you again at the wedding," she admitted. "Hearing your voice at the hospital—I could hear it when you first came and wanted to visit afterward, even though you didn't know it—hearing your voice again then was the first time I freaked out so I wasn't sure if seeing you, hearing your voice at the wedding, might be a reminder. But I did okay through that. And since then I've made a few adjustments—"

"Okay… And what about counseling—you asked me if I'd done that. Have you?"

"I've talked to my friend Carla. I don't need to talk to anybody else."

From the corner of her eye she saw him nod before he said, "Does any of your family have any idea?"

She shook her head.

For a moment neither of them said anything and Emmy had the sense she was being evaluated. She braced for his conclusion and for the argument she was ready to mount to defend herself for not having sought out therapy or other avenues of treatment.

But then he said, "Well, I've known guys who can't get through half a day without problems. Some who can't function, who are wiped out by emotional and mental stuff. Just having an occasional event…that would be a huge win for them. I still think you can call what's going on with you PTSD, but it isn't as debilitating as a lot I've seen. Not by a long shot. So it doesn't seem like you're doing too bad with it."

That wasn't what she'd expected. It wasn't even what she got from Carla—who fretted about the fact that she had any lingering effects at all.

And Carla hadn't seen what Declan just had.

It was strange, though, because listening to what he had to say—knowing he knew about the real thing—and having him take what he'd just witnessed in stride, was a relief of sorts.

And it provided a kind of support she hadn't found even with her friend because it confirmed what she thought about herself.

Yes, she hated what had happened to her, hated that it

had changed her at all, hated that she had these fears now
and could be thrown into a panic attack. But she honestly
didn't feel as if she had any life-changing emotional issues from it—she didn't find any less joy in life or in her
family or the kids or even in the happy occasions her clients invited her into to photograph.

Yes, at first she'd been overwhelmed by what had happened and what had followed it. But time had taken care
of some of that, and she'd done a lot of reading about anxiety, a lot of research. She'd put everything she'd learned
into practice. She hadn't buried any of her feelings—
despite the fact that she'd concealed some of them from
her family. She'd talked and talked and talked to Carla.
And she'd gotten better.

She just wasn't completely home free yet.

But she had hope that in time the rest of the lingering
effects would resolve, too. And here was someone who
seemed on that same page.

It was also freeing that Declan knew now what was
going on and he wasn't alarmed. He was acknowledging
that she hadn't come out of the explosion unscathed and
unaffected, but he wasn't making anything a bigger deal
than it was.

The muscles in her shoulders unbunched.

She took another small sip of the whiskey to help things
along.

"But that couldn't have been fun for you upstairs,"
Declan said then.

It would have been silly to deny that, but he went on
before she had the chance to say anything.

"All you had to do was tell me you didn't want to get
up into that attic, you know?"

"I was hoping I could just push through it."

"Yeah, but if you had told me ahead of time, we could

have taken it a little easier getting you up there, and maybe then you *could* have pushed through and conquered it. One of the things I've seen that really works is to take it a step at a time when something potentially triggering comes up. Kind of inch into it."

When she thought about it, that was sort of what she'd done with him at the wedding. She'd kept a great distance from him at first, only furtively looking at him from across the expanse. Then she'd looked a little more directly at him. She'd moved in slightly. She'd maneuvered herself into a position of being able to eavesdrop on him just so she could test what the sound of his voice did to her.

Passing each trial without incident had given her the courage to take things a little further until she'd felt as if she really could see him, talk to him and not have the reaction she'd had initially.

Still, what he was suggesting—that she could have opened up to him even before the panic attack—was something she'd done only with Carla. Carla, who she trusted, who she could confide in. But this was Declan Madison—someone she'd learned to keep at arm's length. *Not* someone to trust or confide in.

"So I should have *told* you?" Emmy said skeptically.

"Yeah, you could have. There's no judgment here," he said. "I was there, you know? I know where you were, I know how bad it was for you—hell, I was scared silly I wasn't going to get to you in time. Or that you'd be trapped under something I wouldn't be able to move. Or that in the middle of getting you out everything would cave in… I get that it was a thousand times worse for you and it makes perfect sense to me that you came away from that with some aftereffects."

She hadn't thought of that experience in terms of having shared it with someone, but she guessed that she had. And it helped to realize that, too.

"I understand that you don't want to make it into something more than it is," he went on. "But sometimes you make a problem worse by *not* just airing it out. So if something else pushes a button for you, let me know and we'll work through it."

The orchard came to mind.

But still she was hesitant to confide in him of all people. It was one thing to accept his participation with the kids and the farm—he'd been like a brother to Topher, he was Trinity's godfather and he *actually knew how to farm*. She had no problem admitting that he was a huge help and that he had every right to be there.

But when it came to her personally? That was a different story.

And yet as it sank in that he—unlike anyone else—understood what was going on with her and viewed it the way she did, she began to wonder if he might be the one person other than Carla who she *could* trust with this.

Maybe.

What if she kept it very clear in her head that trusting him with this didn't change anything between them on any other level? What if she kept it very clear in her head that there was nothing romantic in any of this? That it was like seeing a doctor for a wart—no relationship existed beyond that. When she put it in those terms, it didn't seem *im*possible.

And it might even be beneficial. Especially with the work on the orchard looming.

"Okay," she said then, a belated agreement to his suggestion.

"So *is* there something else you can give me a headsup about before we get into another sticky situation?"

"The orchard," she confessed in a voice that was almost inaudible because she still so, so hated admitting it.

"What about the orchard?"

"I'm not sure I can go in there under those broken branches. Every time I even look at them I think about them falling on me…"

From the corner of her eye she saw him nod. "Okay. I could probably take care of it myself, but when we get to that, how about we try to get you in there? See if we can't work you through it? If not…you can leave it to me."

So no pressure. There was also relief in knowing that if she *couldn't* do it, there was another option. That he could and would. That the burden and responsibility wasn't solely and completely hers.

Just knowing that gave her a bit more courage. "Okay," she agreed.

"Is there anything else?"

"No," she said honestly.

Silence fell then and there was only the sound of the rain as the whiskey helped Emmy calm down until she didn't even care that Declan was studying her from the side. In fact, she was beginning to completely unwind.

"I'm a little curious about some other things," he said then.

"Like what?" she asked, relaxed enough not to be daunted by whatever he wanted to know.

"When you wouldn't let me visit you right after the bombing… Every time Mandy delivered the message that you weren't up for it, she still swore to me that you were doing well, that the concussion was mild, none of the cuts were deep. She said she didn't know *why* you weren't up for it, but you swore you weren't. I couldn't help wondering if I'd done something wrong… But it was that the sound of my voice gave you flashbacks?"

"You didn't *do* anything except get me out of that rubble, and I was grateful for that," she said as confirmation. "But yeah, I couldn't stand to even hear your voice," she reiterated quietly. "It didn't make any sense but the sound of it... I heard you ask where I was that first time you came to the hospital, and then I looked out and saw you and... I knew it should have been all good. The sight and sound of the person who had saved me? How could it be a bad thing? But something about you just shot me back into that hole in the rubble—"

"Flashbacks," he repeated as if the light was dawning for him.

"I didn't mean to be rude, but—"

"I was a trigger," he finished for her. Surprisingly, he sounded as if he liked that explanation, though she couldn't imagine why that would be the case. "But you got over that by the wedding?"

"I didn't know if it would happen until I actually did see you."

"And it didn't."

"No."

"Did it not happen at all or did you keep it from happening by drinking?"

That sounded like another testing-for-symptoms-of-PTSD question. "It didn't happen at all. So I was drinking to celebrate that—along with the wedding—because that was the first really big sign that I was on the mend."

Another nod from him. "You were getting back to the real you then. At the wedding."

That seemed like a strange thing to say and she didn't know how to respond. She settled on the most obvious reply. "I've always been the *real* me. The explosion just caused a few glitches."

"Were there any at the wedding?"

The only glitch then had been his. Or maybe hers when she'd misread him. But either way they'd gone through enough tonight, and Emmy didn't want to get into the wedding stuff now, too. So she merely said, "I actually felt like the wedding was a sign that I was getting on top of the explosion aftershocks because there *weren't* any glitches. I'd promised Carla that if seeing you caused a panic attack, I'd see a psychologist. When it didn't, even she relaxed a little on that and started to believe that I was doing okay."

He nodded again and let another moment go by with only the steady patter of the rain.

Then he said, "You're a tough little thing, aren't you?"

He said that as if he intended it as a compliment. But *tough*? That didn't seem too flattering.

She felt better enough to turn her shoulder to the screen and face him. Better enough to meet those intense blue eyes with her own. "I've never thought of myself that way."

"Not everyone could do what you're doing—with your 'glitches,' with the kids, the farm... Even though you're just flying by the seat of your pants, you still jump in, plow ahead..." And yes, he'd gone on in a tone that said it was all something that impressed him.

That sexy mouth of his only got sexier when he smiled the way he was right then—more with one side than the other.

It caused Emmy to lose her train of thought for a split second so the only response she could come up with was a shrug before she said, "I really am just flying by the seat of my pants—that's true."

"There's a fearlessness to that—no matter what attics or broken branches do to you," he commended.

Tough and *fearless*—again she wasn't sure those were how she wanted to be described.

But then she reminded herself of what was really between them. They were partners in dealing with the farm and the kids—but nothing more.

Since she had to resist falling into thinking anything else, maybe it was good that his flattery was so utilitarian.

Still, there was an intensity in the way he was looking at her that made it hard to believe there wasn't a little something more in it.

And when his eyes slowly drifted down to her mouth, she didn't know what he *could* be thinking about except kissing her.

Okay, this is where it gets dangerous, she told herself.

He'd been great in the attic and in the time since then. When he was thoughtful enough to bring her a drink. When he was being supportive and offering more understanding, more solace than she'd found even with Carla. When he was being sweet and kind.

Now here he was, this gorgeous man, looking at her with something almost simmering in those eyes. It all chipped away at her resolve, at her certainty that he wasn't interested in or attracted to her. It sure *seemed* as if all of it might be leading to a kiss...

No, she couldn't think like that. She'd promised herself that she wouldn't.

Eyes wide open. No illusions...

And yet it occurred to her that when she'd thought he was going to kiss her last night she'd told herself she was imagining it.

But she didn't know that for sure because she'd turned tail and run away from him. The only way she would have known for sure was if she had waited to see how it played out.

And tonight she was going to do that.

So she stayed where she was, she drank in the sight of that hella-handsome face that was all sharp angles and masculinity. She breathed in the scent of his cologne mingling with the rain. She could even feel the warmth coming from his big body.

And no, she didn't think she was imagining the electricity that seemed to charge the air around them.

But maybe she was, because he didn't kiss her. He just raised his eyes from her mouth and said, "How's the bee sting? I should take a look at that, see if it's better now that the stinger is out."

So no, he hadn't been going to kiss her and she *had* been imagining things.

Stop setting yourself up for this!

"It feels better," she managed to say, wanting to kick herself for building anticipation of a kiss only to face another fall.

"Let me take a look anyway," he insisted.

Emmy returned to facing the screen and dropped her head forward while she focused on the evening air coming in and cooling her off, wondering once more why it was that every time she thought things were going one way with this guy, they went another.

Wondering when she was going to figure him out so she could stop doing this to herself.

He bent forward enough to see the sting and studied it. "It's not as bad as it was but I still think it needs to be iced. I brought the frozen peas with me when I came down and put them back in the freezer—I think you ought to take them with you when you go to bed."

"Sure," she muttered, trying to sound casual to make it seem as if nothing about the last few minutes had been anything more than friendly to her.

But if the sting looked all right, why was he still bent over her?

Then she felt his hand on her back again, the way it had been in the attic but different. He wasn't bracing her, it was just there, lightly, making contact, connecting them.

And then he did kiss her—on the nape, nowhere near the bee sting, at the very base of her neck. Gently, his lips barely making contact. His breath was a warm brush against her skin, and still it sent a rush of pleasure from that spot all through her.

It was there for only a brief moment before he was gone and all that was left was a tingling where his mouth had been.

"Just wanted to follow Trinity's advice to make it better," he said facetiously in a husky voice, finally standing tall again and rearing back, away from her.

Emmy wasn't sure what to make of that, so all she could think to do was play along. "That definitely did the trick—I'm healed," she joked.

She straightened up and turned to face him again, willing him to do more than that. To kiss her for real. On the lips.

But he merely pushed off the doorjamb, took the empty glass from her and suddenly it was business as usual.

After the wedding reception, she'd been sure that he was going to kiss her good-night and he hadn't.

Now he *had* kissed her, and she still felt as if she'd been left hanging. A little buss on the back of the neck just didn't cut it. It only served to whet her appetite.

And leave her wondering about him yet again.

Had the kiss really only been playful, nothing but a joke based on Trinity's kiss-it-and-make-it-better insistence? Or had it been something more?

But there were no answers to be had, so Emmy closed

the back door and followed Declan into the kitchen, where he was rinsing the glass and putting it in the dishwasher.

"If you need help with Kit, wake me," she said as she passed through.

"Sure" was his completely bland and benign response before she took the bag of peas from the freezer and they exchanged good-nights. As if nothing had happened.

Because maybe it *had* been only a joke.

It just hadn't seemed like it.

And again with no answers she headed up the stairs to her room, still thinking about that kiss on the neck, still unable to tell for sure what was going on.

But knowing without a doubt that until she had some certainty, she had to protect herself. She had to not get sucked in.

And yet even after she'd made her way to bed and was resting on her pillow with the frozen peas on the bee sting, she was still thinking about Declan.

Still feeling his lips on her neck.

And as much as she willed it not to be true, it was still the feel of Declan's lips on her own that she was itching for...

Chapter Six

"I didn't know if I'd ever be saying this, let alone so soon, but yeah, I think you'll pass your med eval—and not just for limited duty. I think they'll clear you."

The words were music to Declan's ears.

On Wednesday his older brother, Conor, had arrived at the Madison farm with Conor's old-flame-now-new-bride Maicy. After putting in a full day's work at the Samms farm, Declan and Emmy had left Trinity and Kit with a second babysitter for the evening. Later on, they planned to attend a meeting of the organic farmer's co-op in Northbridge.

But first they'd made a stop at the Madison farm so Declan could see—and be examined by—Conor, who combined his medical degree with his overbearing-eldest-brother nature to fuss over Declan like a mother hen. While that was going on, Emmy was meeting with Kinsey to plan the wedding pictures.

"Your range of motion is surprisingly good," Conor continued. "There's no swelling. If the pain isn't enough for you to take a pain reliever even after a full day of hard labor—"

"And after walking with a crying baby for hours last night," Declan put in.

"Then yeah, I think you could actually get back to your unit—if that's what you want."

"That's what I want," Declan said resolutely.

In fact, knowing he and Emmy would leave here to go into Northbridge—where he would see people he'd known and loathed while growing up—made him all the more eager to be back on the job. The idea of facing those people who had disliked and looked down on him was about as appealing to him as getting shot.

But apparently that didn't show because his older brother frowned curiously at him and said, "Seems like you're in better spirits, too."

"Does it?" Declan countered, wanting—as always—to avoid another conversation about his emotional state.

Still, his brother's observation did make him think about his mood lately, and it struck him that he might be in a slightly improved frame of mind.

He wasn't quite sure why. There was nothing about losing Topher that had gotten any easier for him. Walking with Kit in the dead of night was actually an exercise in mental and emotional torture—every room he went in and out of brought memories of times there with the friend he'd lost. Every bounce, every jiggle, every whisper to that tiny baby boy in his arms reminded him that Topher had never gotten to hold his own son.

And yet, in spite of that, he realized that his feelings of guilt, his remorse, even some of his grief, weren't as constant as they'd been before. That he was weighed down a little less…ever since he'd talked about it with Emmy.

Nothing she'd said had made him feel absolved. But thinking about Topher's *letigo* motto had eased some of his depression. And he guessed that maybe it did help to know that Mandy hadn't blamed him—that she didn't seem to think Topher would have blamed him either.

"This is the first time in eight months that you seem more like yourself," Conor was saying. "The first time that it doesn't seem like you're just barely plugged into what's going on around you."

Declan shrugged.

"It's a big deal, Dec," his brother insisted. "You're not making me worry about where your head is. You haven't just figured out how to hide it better, have you? You haven't reached some kind of decision..."

That last part sounded ominous and it caused Declan to chuckle. "Wow, that was a fast trip from thinking I'm better to thinking something worse is going on."

Conor was studying him now. "To go from as down as you've been to calm isn't always a good sign," said the professional in his brother.

"I haven't made up my mind to do harm to myself—that's what you're getting at, right? I know for some people, making the decision can bring on a kind of peace, but that's not what's going on here."

"What *has* happened, then?"

"Emmy has said a few things and... I don't know... But I do know that you don't have to worry about me. The body, the leg, are coming along and I'm ready to get back to where I'm supposed to be, to do what I'm supposed to be doing."

"So Emmy—the photographer, Topher's sister-in-law, who's now his kids' guardian..." Declan and Conor were alone in the kitchen, Emmy was in the living room with Kinsey, and Conor inclined his head in that direction. "You've talked to her about...things?"

Declan shrugged again. "It's come up" was the most he would admit to.

"And that had more impact than any psychiatrist or psychologist I sent around?"

"Maybe it was just the right time for me to actually listen? I don't know, Conor. I just know that you don't have to worry about me. I'm doing okay."

"Because of the pretty little redhead."

"I wouldn't call her a redhead. Her hair is just a little reddish, mostly in the sun."

Conor nodded his head sagely. "No denial that she's pretty, though."

"Why would I deny what's obvious to anybody who looks at her?"

Another perceptive nod. "Hey, I'm just good with anything that's helping you."

Declan couldn't deny that Emmy fit that description, so he just didn't say anything at all.

"But you still want to go back to your unit?" Conor asked.

"Hell-bent on it," Declan confirmed.

"Okay, if you say so."

"I say so."

Conor's smug smile rubbed him the wrong way but Declan decided the best option was to change the subject. "Did Kinsey get any RSVPs from the Camdens?"

That sobered Conor considerably. "No. But I suppose you know there was a DNA match."

"She told me."

"I wish there wasn't," Conor said somewhat under his breath.

"You and me both," Declan agreed.

"But I guess Kinsey is happy about it."

"God, I wish she'd just left it alone!" Declan said, thinking again about going into town from here, about the stigma of their past and the potential for having it brought to the surface again, about how his only escape from it years ago had been to the marines, and how—now that Kinsey was intent on stirring it up—he just wanted out of here all the more.

Although oddly that nagged at him a little, and when he explored what he had going for him here, he realized it was Emmy who came to mind. That he didn't like the idea that putting this town behind him again meant putting her behind him.

It was weird.

It had to have more to do with Kit and Trinity and the farm, he reasoned. It had to have more to do with wanting to do something for Topher.

Didn't it?

Yeah, that must be it. It wasn't about the quiet time he and Emmy spent together after the kids were in bed. It wasn't about wanting to hold her last night when she was upset. It wasn't about wanting to kiss her so damn bad that he hadn't been able to control it, although he'd restrained himself to kissing her neck.

No, it wasn't about any of that. He wouldn't *let* it be about any of that.

"I guess if the Camdens don't show and Kinsey bottoms out, at least we'll all be here with her. *For* her," Conor said, cutting into Declan's wandering thoughts.

"Yeah," Declan agreed vaguely, still half thinking about why he should be in any way reluctant to say goodbye to Emmy.

Conor glanced at the wall clock just then and stood. "I was supposed to wake Maicy from her post-travel nap twenty minutes ago. I'd better go do that."

"Yeah, sure, you better."

"I brought a new beer that's brewed in Denver—help yourself," Conor suggested as he headed for the door.

"I will," Declan answered, thinking that a drink before going into Northbridge was literally just what the doctor ordered.

He took a bottle out of the fridge, read the label before closing the fridge and twisting off the bottle cap to toss into the trash. Then he turned around and leaned back against the sink to take a drink, opting to stay in the kitchen rather than join Emmy and Kinsey's wedding-pictures discussion.

But he was still stuck on the thought that had been distracting him—why the possibility of something prematurely calling a halt to his time with Emmy bothered him.

It wasn't as if this was some kind of romantic rendezvous that he didn't want cut short. They were just temporarily working at a common goal. There wasn't anything else going on.

Okay, a little maybe—what with wanting to hold her and kiss her last night. What with having trouble ever keeping his eyes off her. What with having trouble *not* thinking about her, day and night, too.

But even so, it didn't mean anything beyond a passing attraction. Certainly nothing that should give him any kind of reluctance to say goodbye to her.

Especially when he still had reservations about her.

Because he *did* still have reservations about her.

Although…

Learning about her panic attacks last night did explain a few things. It canceled out his concern that he'd done something wrong in Afghanistan to make her refuse to see him. And it left him with more sympathy for her. Sympathy and understanding—of course she would have refused to see someone who caused her flashbacks.

So no, he didn't have any more reservation about her based on how she'd acted that first time they'd met.

But there was still the wedding.

Of course he also understood that she would have been scared as hell to see him again, worried that he'd still trigger her.

But once she'd known it wasn't going to happen, she'd warmed up to him only to do a complete one-eighty the next morning for no reason.

At least no reason he knew about.

But he hadn't known what was going on with her in Afghanistan either. Maybe he was in the dark about something that had happened at the wedding, too.

And if he was, then maybe he was judging her too harshly.

Maybe now that he knew the truth about Afghanistan, he should back off a little with what he'd been thinking had happened at the wedding. Maybe it hadn't been unaccountable capriciousness and instead had a logical reason, too.

On this third go-round together her disposition had been pretty steady, he admitted. Yeah, she'd been cool toward him at first but maybe that was for the same reason she'd been initially standoffish at the wedding—maybe she'd still been afraid that seeing him, hearing his voice, would upset the applecart. When it hadn't, she'd progressively warmed up. Like at the wedding.

And maybe she'd just continue to warm up this time...

It took him a moment but he mentally stomped out that thought.

Emmy had enough going on in her life already, and so did he. He wasn't going to complicate things any more than they already were by kissing her.

Conor had just told him he was doing well enough to pass his medical evaluation, so as soon as that happened, he could get back to where he belonged.

Emmy was on a completely different trajectory and

what she needed—what she deserved—was someone who could be a real and present partner for her. And he couldn't muddy the waters they were in now just because he might be attracted to her.

Okay, not just *might be.* There was no question that he was attracted to her and it got worse all the time—like last night when she was in the throes of that damn panic attack and he'd watched that indomitable strength of hers struggle to fight it rather than just cave into it.

He'd had the impression that she hadn't cared for his description of her as tough. But for him, seeing that in her only made him like her more.

Add the things he was learning about her pluck and feistiness to that silky hair and that face he couldn't get enough of, to that body his hands were itching to touch, and yeah, he was attracted to her.

But he couldn't let it run wild, and he wouldn't.

So maybe it would be better if he *didn't* give her a second benefit of the doubt, he thought wryly. If he hung on to thinking she was just some prickly, unpredictable prima donna who could change on a dime for no good reason.

No doubt that would be a whole lot easier for him to resist. And as it was, he wasn't completely confident that he *could* resist what was going through him.

But still, to be fair, he knew he had to reserve judgment on her day-after-the-wedding gear-switch now. Even if it did make things harder on him.

Emmy just had more to her than he'd realized either of the times their paths had crossed before.

And he had to remember that while what he was discovering made him like her even more—which made it harder on him—those things would serve Trinity and Kit well. It was just too bad that everything he liked about her made it harder to stop himself from touching her. He had to suck it up and keep his hands off her.

Suck it up, keep his hands off her, get done what needed to be done here and then get back to his unit.

And if the thought of putting her in his rearview mirror suddenly bothered him a little?

He just needed to suck that up, too.

"So... First a standing ovation and handshaking at the town meeting and then more handshaking at the end of the co-op meeting afterward... I didn't know I was going to be with a celebrity tonight," Emmy teased Declan as they left Northbridge's courthouse.

"Yeah, what was that?" he said, clearly still as stunned by his reception now as he had been when it had all happened.

They were walking along a nearly deserted Main Street, headed for the ice-cream shop.

"I'm pretty sure it was what that old guy said when he announced he was proud of the man you'd made of yourself. I think they were letting you know that nothing that happened when you were a kid is being held against you anymore. That they appreciate you for who you are now and what you've done is all that matters."

"Not to Greg Kravitz," Declan said as if that refuted her opinion. "I spotted him the minute we walked in— he was the guy slouching in the faded red sweatshirt just to the right—"

"I know," Emmy said, cutting him off. She decided now to let him know that she wasn't a stranger to his bully. "I know who he is. I've been going to the co-op meetings, and he has a problem with the organic farmers—"

"Something about organic farming interferes with his lawn-mowing and snow-shoveling business?"

"He doesn't like that the organic farmers don't use pesticides. He thinks not using them basically causes more bugs on his bushes."

Declan laughed wholeheartedly at that.

Lately he was smiling more readily, more easily, but that was the first time she'd heard such a spontaneous and genuine laugh from him. And as good as his smile was, his deep barrel-chested laugh was even better.

"Bugs on his bushes?" he repeated. "He didn't really put it that way, did he?"

"No, but that's what he gripes about in a nutshell. The point is, the guy is just a jerk all the way around. He actually thought it was a good idea about a month ago at a co-op meeting to tell me everything he didn't like about what my sister and Topher had been doing as organic farmers, and then—as if that would make me want to go out with him—he asked me on a date."

"A date…" Declan said, not sounding as if he approved of that idea. "Did you go?"

It almost seemed as if there was a tinge of jealousy in that.

Emmy nixed that notion, telling herself if was ridiculous, and said, "No, I didn't go. I could already tell he was a jerk. But tonight there must have been eighty or ninety people at the town meeting and I only saw three not stand for you. Plus there was all that handshaking… No matter what you say, that was a warm welcome and I don't think you should let a jerk tarnish it."

"Yeah," Declan conceded with a lack of vigor.

He was clearly still embarrassed by the attention. But there was something else in his tone that said he wasn't buying into the admiration without reservation either and it was that that Emmy addressed.

"You don't think the warm welcome was sincere?"

He shrugged. "I'm just thinking that the reception would have been different if the whole Camden thing was getting a fresh airing out—the way it will if Kinsey has her way and publicly connects us with them."

Emmy understood that he had old scars from that. But especially after seeing what she'd seen tonight—through eyes that weren't viewing it with the haze of distrust—she wasn't as convinced as he was.

"Or it wouldn't change anything now that you're recognized on your own for what you've done," she persisted.

Declan's lack of response to that relayed the message that he wasn't so sure, but since they'd reached the ice-cream shop he had a reason not to say more.

Contrasting the rest of Main Street where most everything was already closed, at the ice-cream shop they ran into a bit of a crowd.

Some were people they'd already encountered at the meeting but some weren't. And while Emmy sensed Declan tense up again and knew he was wondering if he still might meet with negative reactions, he was again only greeted warmly.

There were more condolences for the recent loss of his mother. More gratitude for his service. More concern for his health—stemming from a common knowledge that he'd been seriously injured. There were also more reassurances that while everyone mourned the loss of Topher, they were glad he had survived.

Then Emmy and Declan were back on Main Street with their ice cream, and while Emmy was tempted to point out once again that things here were different now, she decided to just let it all sink in on its own.

Instead she said, "I have to say, I can see some of the reasons Mandy liked it here. I know you don't really agree, but I think it's a nice little town."

"Good and bad," he answered.

"You were right about the ice cream—it's great," Emmy said, enjoying her fudge-swirled chocolate. "So what's bad—not counting your own private hell years ago?"

He handed her one of the napkins he was carrying.

"Do I have ice cream somewhere?" she asked, assuming that was the reason and stopping to use a store window as a mirror.

Granted it wasn't a sharp image but all she saw was what she'd seen in the mirror at home before they'd left—clean jeans, a crocheted tank top peeking from behind the plunging V-neck of her lightweight red sweater, all ice-cream-free. She didn't have anything dribbling down her chin either, and noted that the extra attention she'd paid to makeup tonight still served to make her look far better than she had after her day in the field. Even her hair had kept the bounce she'd put into it by carefully blow-drying it.

Declan had stopped behind her, and since he was taller he was in the reflection, too. She saw him slowly shake his head, his smile sly. "Take a look at the napkin," he instructed.

There was a phone number on it.

"What's this?" she asked.

"Mindy Hargrove's number."

Mindy Hargrove was the woman who had scooped their ice cream—Declan had introduced them.

"She wouldn't give me the time of day when we were in school," he went on. "But she slipped me that when you turned your back and whispered that she's still single. The dating pool in a small town is limited and it can make for some dog-eat-dog competition—that's definitely not a good thing about a small town."

Emmy almost thought that what she felt in response to the ice-cream scooper giving Declan her phone number might be jealousy.

"Huh. *Dog-eat-dog* is a little nicer than I might put it," Emmy commented. "For all she knew we could be a couple."

But she didn't want Declan to know just how miffed she was. In order to appear as if it didn't bother her, she said, "Of course you *will* need company at your sister's wedding. Unless you're just counting on another bridesmaid…"

Oh, that wasn't the tack to take, she thought after the words had slipped out, hating all over again how much his rejection of her that night had stung, telling herself once more that it shouldn't have.

"I don't know what I'd be counting on a bridesmaid for…" Declan said as if he was confused by the remark.

What he did with Tracy is none of my business, she told herself firmly. Any more than it was her business what he did with the ice cream scooper's number.

"I never liked Mindy Hargrove," he said then, moving on from Emmy's comment. "But you wanted to know what's bad about a small town, and one of the things is that the social scene can get pretty stagnant for anyone who sticks around. You end up with Mindy Hargroves slipping their numbers to people they shouldn't slip their numbers to, and Greg Kravitzes pouncing on newbies. So be glad you live in Denver, where you have more options."

Emmy chose not to say anything to that and instead handed him back the napkin—which he tossed into the nearest trash receptacle without a backward glance as they finished their ice cream and headed for the truck they'd come into town in.

But once they were pulling out of the parking lot with

Declan driving, he said, "So *do* you have better dating options than Greg Kravitz in Denver?"

"I haven't dated for a while," Emmy answered with an edge to her voice.

"No?" he asked. Then, as if it had just dawned on him, he said, "I don't know why but I've just been figuring that you're single... Maybe because I am... I mean, you haven't mentioned anyone or been talking to somebody waiting for you in Denver or... But look at you—of course there's a guy already in the picture so you don't have to date..."

"There's no guy in the picture at all. Not anymore. Not since December."

"Sore subject?" he asked.

"Aren't most breakups?"

"Not in my experience," he said. "But this one of yours didn't end well?"

"It didn't end where I thought it would," she said with some self-reproach.

"Do you want me to shut up or can I know about it?"

It sounded as if he *wanted* to know, so Emmy considered telling him.

It wasn't a secret, she decided, so she said, "His name is Bryce Hutchinson—as in Hutchinson Industries."

"Bigwigs?" Declan asked as if the name didn't ring a bell.

"Definitely. Bryce liked to say that there wasn't a building in the state that didn't have one of their nuts or bolts in them."

"Rich bigwigs like the Camdens," Declan said as if that similarity alone condemned her ex.

"I don't know how the math matches up, but I'd guess yes, like the Camdens."

"And both families are in Denver?"

"Right."

"So when you were dating him, did you hang out with the Camdens—like at the same balls and galas and whatever it is the rich do?"

"No. I mean, the Hutchinsons and the Camdens probably were at a lot of the same functions, but I never went to those. Which should have been a really big red flag but I didn't see it," she said with more self-criticism.

"A red flag for what?"

"For the fact that I wasn't going to *make the cut*." The contempt in her tone then wasn't aimed at herself.

"To be a Hutchinson?" Declan clarified quietly.

"Yes. That's what he said anyway. His birthday was December 1 and he said that since he was turning forty, he needed to settle down, get married, start having kids to carry on the Hutchinson name."

Emmy fought not to let the lingering hurt from those words echo in her voice. When she thought she had more control she went on, "But he said he'd thought it over and he couldn't do those things with me because I just didn't make the cut. He needed someone with experience in the same circles, with a higher pedigree—"

"Like a dog?" There was outrage in that.

"That's what I said." And it was slightly comforting to have someone else react the way she had.

"He'd told me he wanted to have a special dinner that night, to dress up…" Emmy went on, unable to completely keep the hurt out of her tone. "I was so clueless, I thought he was going to propose. Instead the dinner was to cushion the blow—*one last hurrah*, as he put it—before we needed to halt our relationship so he could really get down to the business of finding a wife."

"Are you kidding?" Declan said.

Emmy didn't feel the need to assure him she wasn't.

"Where did you meet this guy?"

"At a bar one night not long after the wedding…" Carla had suggested they go to help Emmy stop obsessing over the ego bruise Declan had given her. "Bryce was tall, good-looking, smooth, suave, easygoing. And very attentive—he made me feel like I was the only woman in the whole place." Which had probably been the first thing that wasn't the way it had seemed.

"And the two of you were steady? Exclusive?"

"By the end of that first night he'd asked for my number and I'd given it to him. I didn't know if I'd hear from him or not, but he called five minutes after Carla and I left the bar to ask me out for the next night. And he kept calling. After about a month it was very steady and he said he wanted us to be exclusive, yes."

"He was hot for you," Declan said with an edge to his voice this time.

Emmy shrugged. "That was the impression he gave. For over three years…"

"Were you hot for him, too?"

She thought about that. She'd grown to care for Bryce. To hope for—then count on and look forward to—a life with him. At the very start, though? No, she couldn't say she'd been especially hot for him. But the fact that he was hot for *her* had been exactly what she'd needed to prove she still had it after Declan had cast her aside for the party girl next door.

But she wasn't going to let Declan know that his actions had played such a big role in the start-up of her relationship with her ex, so she said, "We had things in common, shared interests, opinions, likes and dislikes—"

"That's not being hot for someone."

"Still, we clicked," she contended. "And it was nice…" Very nice to be wanted. And although before that she'd been a cautious dater, never jumping into anything with anyone too quickly, she'd thrown herself into the relationship with Bryce.

Unfortunately she'd been so enthusiastic that she'd also been oblivious to the warning signs.

"So he swept you off your feet."

"He did," she agreed. "With Bryce it was roses once a week, every week we were together—oh yeah, and a huge bouquet the day after he dumped me. The consolation prize, I guess. It was front-row seats to concerts and plays and sport events. It was wining and dining, being whisked around in expensive cars or limousines. It was—"

"Dating that took you about as far from disasters and devastations and school bombings as photographing weddings takes you from what you used to photograph."

That gave Emmy pause. She hadn't made that connection before.

But when she thought about it she had to concede. "You're kind of right," she said in a voice that was barely audible and echoed with a bit of surprise. "Still, it wasn't as if the splashy stuff was all there was between us or the reason I was with him. We could talk for hours right to the end of the relationship. He made me laugh. He said he never felt as good as he did when he was with me—those were actually some of his parting words. So it wasn't as if there wasn't more to the relationship than the perks. But we never fought and yes, dating Bryce couldn't have been more pink and pretty—no chaos or conflict at all…" she admitted, suddenly seeing it through different eyes.

She'd blamed Declan's night-of-the-Brazilian-bombshell for her getting into the relationship with Bryce—a rebound of sorts.

She'd compared misreading Declan's intentions toward

her at the reception with her much worse belief that she and Bryce were going to have a future together.

And she still felt those beliefs were valid.

But she'd completely missed the fact that dating Bryce had been so picture-perfect that it *had* helped distance her from things she'd experienced, from the repercussions she'd been dealing with after the bombing. Almost exactly like looking through her viewfinder at brides and bouquets and five-tiered cakes helped keep her miles away from images of flooded cities and buildings reduced to piles of bricks and people battered by war. She'd completely missed that being with Bryce had been another escape...

"How was he with the post-Afghanistan stuff you've been dealing with?" Declan asked then.

It almost embarrassed Emmy to say, "He didn't know about it."

Declan took his eyes off the road just long enough to glance at her again. "He didn't know about what? The issues you've had or—"

"For a while he didn't even know what happened. I told him about being a freelance photographer and then switching to the Red Cross after that. I said that after the last trip with the Red Cross I'd decided I wanted to stay in Denver to work, so I'd opened up shop to do wedding and special-event photography."

Declan's eyebrows were arched in what looked to be more surprise. "Is that how you put it? You didn't tell him any more than that?"

"That was exactly how I put it."

"You didn't tell him you'd been in a bombing?"

"No. But of course my family knew and eventually Bryce found out through them. That was it, though—I told you, I only told my friend, Carla, about my *issues* and she's kept my confidence, so no, Bryce never knew that part."

"You didn't tell the guy you were involved with—for *years*—that you were going through some bad stuff?"

"No."

"And he didn't figure it out?" Declan asked as if he found that hard to believe.

"If I was having a bad day I made something up and canceled whatever plans I had with him. And usually called Carla."

But now Emmy found herself questioning her big omission from a relationship she'd thought had a future. Still, in fairness to Bryce, she added, "Anyway, I was better by the time I met him—that was *after* the wedding. I did tell him I was a little claustrophobic—he knew that much— but he didn't know that it stemmed from Afghanistan. Otherwise...Bryce was all about the future not the past, which was fine by me. I wanted to put the past behind me." And she'd thought being with him helped accomplish that. But now? Now that Declan had given her this new view she said, "I guess it might have been less about sparing him and more about using being with him as a way of separating myself from it."

"If I was that guy I'd hate that you were in the thick of something serious and kept me in the dark about it."

"He kept me in the dark about the pedigree thing," she said defensively.

"So how close of a relationship was this really?" Declan asked kindly.

"Yeah, okay, I can't argue with that because even though I *thought* we had a future together, I was obviously totally wrong. I left out the ugly details of what I was working through. Meanwhile, he was misleading me, because even though there *were* signs I should have read, there was also him telling me he loved me and that he never wanted to be without me and—" Her voice cracked. She didn't want to reveal more about how she felt she'd been deceived.

Declan seemed to know that because he didn't push her for more of those examples and instead said, "What kind of signs did you miss?"

"That he *didn't* ever ask me to the fancy galas and balls and charity things that he was probably at with the Camdens," she said.

"That does seem strange when otherwise you had all kinds of spectacular dates with him."

"He said he was doing me a favor, that the charity events were snooty and boring and tedious. He said he had an obligation to put in an appearance but I didn't. That if he went alone he could drop in, make sure the people who needed to see him saw him and duck out— which was what he always did because he'd show up at my place afterward in his tux, get comfortable and we'd still have time together."

"But now you think he was deliberately keeping you separate from that side of his life."

"Yes. I was only introduced to friends of his who *weren't* rich and *didn't* run in those circles. And even though I met his family, it was just a few times and I wasn't ever with them at the country club or at any of those society things. It all should have told me that I wasn't going to *make the cut* when it came to him picking a wife. But I missed it…"

"Yeah…" Declan agreed but he didn't sound totally convinced. "I could see how you might miss it, though. It seems like he was riding the fence—you and his not-rich friends on one side, his family and social obligations on the other. It doesn't sound like you should kick yourself for not knowing which side he would come down on when push came to shove—especially when he made it look like the other side *wasn't* what he was devoted to."

"But obviously he wasn't *devoted* to me either and I let myself believe he was," she insisted. "If he was actually going to share his life with me, he would have included me in the whole thing. But I didn't see that his keeping me away from it all was a message that I didn't fit in."

Declan turned onto the road that led to the house. "So you didn't look for ulterior motives. You weren't suspicious. You trusted him. Those aren't bad things, Emmy," he pointed out.

"I was gullible," she claimed firmly. "I wanted so badly to believe that I'd found Prince Charming that I only saw what I wanted to see."

"I think you're being too hard on yourself."

She didn't agree with that. After all, she'd made the same mistake with him—choosing to believe that he wanted her when there must have been signs she'd missed telling her that it wasn't true. It had left her feeling like a fool. With Bryce, she had wasted more than three years of her life because she hadn't realized they'd never had the same dream for the future.

Declan pulled up in front of the farmhouse just then and she let that be the natural end to their conversation as they both got out of the truck and went inside.

The babysitter gave them the report on the kids, who were both asleep, and then Emmy and Declan walked her to the front door.

After she'd left, Declan closed the door, leaned a shoulder against it and smiled a thoughtful smile at Emmy before he said bluntly and conclusively, "The guy came down on the wrong side of the fence."

Emmy merely shrugged. That sentiment from someone who also hadn't chosen her gave his words less impact.

But there wasn't any more to say on the subject, so she let her shrug speak for her.

It was late by then and evening's end was in the air. But Declan didn't move from that stance against the door. And he was studying her intently enough that it was clear he wasn't ready to say good-night.

Then he proved it by saying, "I had a long talk with Kit last night—man to man."

Emmy wasn't really ready to end her time with him either so she played along. "How did that go?"

"He listened up," Declan claimed. "I told him that tonight, when he needed to be walked around, you'd be coming in from the big date I was taking you on—an evening on the town—so he should go a little easy on you."

"Did he agree?"

"Well…" Declan raised his eyebrows dubiously. "You know how he can be—a little cantankerous. But I kept at him and eventually he said he'd try not to be *too* difficult tonight."

"I really hope he keeps his word. I mean, a night on the town in Northbridge? Who *wouldn't* need rest after that?"

"Yep, yep, yep…" Declan agreed. Then his expression, his tone, turned less joking, more genuine. "I did have a good time tonight, though…"

"Sure, you were the man of the hour," Emmy said with a laugh.

"Nah, that didn't have anything to do with it. It was the company," he added pointedly, his stunning blue eyes on her. "I figured I'd eventually have to go into town, face everybody. But…" He shook his head for effect. "You don't have any idea how much I hated the thought of seeing those people again, and going into it with you beside me? It helped. But even if the meeting had been a disaster, I think it still would have ended up being a good night just because of you…walking, talking, a little ice cream…" He smiled sweetly but devilishly, too. "That's the part I enjoyed and I don't think it would have made any difference if I'd had rocks thrown at me."

Emmy tried not to like hearing that, tried to take it with a grain of salt, but it was still nice to hear, and it still did please her.

Even so, she worked to hold on to her reserve. "I'm just glad there *weren't* any rocks thrown—that it turned out the way it did. I would have hated to have to go in there and kick some Northbridge butt for being mean to you," she joked.

Declan laughed wholeheartedly, genuinely, spontaneously—the way he had earlier, the way she hadn't heard since the wedding—and the sound of it gave her goose bumps of pleasure, which she couldn't explain.

"I was counting on you, though," he said, almost sounding as if it was true and he'd relied on her because he couldn't take care of himself.

Which he so obviously could, standing there towering above her with those enormous shoulders and the muscles that tested the limits of his white polo shirt.

"Anyway," he said in a voice that was suddenly quiet, "thanks for tonight."

Emmy merely laughed a little and shook her head as if he was being silly to think there was anything to thank her for.

And then when she least expected it, his hand snaked up to the back of her head and he partially pulled her to him, partially leaned forward himself and caught her mouth with his.

Their first kiss—at least the first on the mouth rather than on the nape of her neck.

But it wasn't anything like any other first kiss she'd ever had. There was nothing shy or tentative or hesitant in it. It was a solid kiss from the start as his lips parted and he kissed her like there was no tomorrow—deeply and as passionately as if the kiss had been pent up in him for a long, long time and had finally broken free.

He came away from the door to wrap his other arm around her, to pull her up against that expansive chest, to press a big hand to her back as his mouth urged hers to open. As his tongue found its way to hers.

It was a lot for a first kiss. And yet there was nothing in Emmy that balked. Instead it was as if that kiss unearthed something in her, something she'd buried long ago but hadn't quite managed to smother, and the only thing she did was raise her hands to that glorious chest and greet his tongue with her own.

On and on it went, that kiss from heaven—or hell—because at the same time it delighted and aroused, it also robbed her of the ability to consider consequences, or even think about anything else. Anything but Declan and how incredible his kiss was, how incredible it felt to be in his arms, how nothing else mattered in that moment *but* this kiss and this man and being in his arms...

Oh, he was good at it...

It was everything every kiss should be. Everything and more...

Until he seemed to get a grip on himself just about when Emmy got enough of a grip on herself to realize they should stop.

But even as tongues retreated and lips parted, met again more chastely, then parted for good, he didn't let her go. His arm stayed around her, his hand still braced her head while he dropped his forehead to the top of it and said in a craggy voice, "Spiked ice cream?" It was half joke, half offer—a chance to give them something else to blame that kiss on.

"Must have been," Emmy agreed softly.

"Should have brought home a gallon," he muttered under his breath before he raised his head from hers, straightened up and slowly let go of her.

Emmy forced her own hands away from him, too. "I better go get into floor-walking clothes before Kit calls," she said, needing to put some distance between herself and Declan. It was all she could do to fight the impulse to reach for him and restart that kiss.

Declan merely nodded, his eyes continuing to devour her as if he wanted every detail of her face engraved on his memory.

Then he said, "The orchard tomorrow," and that cooled her off some. "Are you gonna give it a try?"

She didn't know why but the thought of facing it with him made it easier. It even made her willing to attempt what had seemed impossible just days ago. "I am," she said with some bravado.

He nodded again, making her feel warm inside because it was laden with approval. "Okay then," he said.

But he still didn't take his eyes off her and she had the sense that he wanted to kiss her again.

As much as she wanted him to.

But in the end, he didn't.

He stood a little taller, a little stiffer, and said, "I'll see you in the morning."

Emmy took a turn at nodding and watched him go—filling her own memory with the sight of the backside that was as good as the front, and then appreciating one last view of his oh-so-handsome, oh-so-sexy face when he looked back over his shoulder at her before he disappeared around the corner.

Which was when Emmy reminded herself that she needed to go upstairs and change clothes, get ready for the long hours of trying to comfort a crying baby.

And when she also reminded herself that she was not supposed to be kissing Declan Madison.

Despite the fact that everything in her was screaming for her to do it again.

Chapter Seven

"Okay, we'll take it a step at a time."

It was a promise made in Declan's deep, confident voice as Emmy stood with him on the outskirts of the apple orchard Thursday morning.

"If you feel yourself start to take shallow breaths, take a couple of deep ones before you get all the way to hyperventilating."

Just thinking about going into that orchard had put her on the verge of hyperventilating already, and Emmy wasn't sure if he'd noticed or was only giving what he thought was preemptive advice. Either way, she immediately took a deep breath.

It helped. And so did knowing that she wasn't in this alone.

"I'm gonna start work on that nearest tree—" He pointed to it. "I want you to come as close as you can without triggering anything and pay attention to what happens—see that even when I cut a broken branch, I have time to get out of the way before it hits the ground. That I have some control…" He paused. "Try to ride out the anxiety when it hits…"

Again he seemed to realize that merely talking about what she was afraid of was causing her some issues.

"Look up at the sky, look around—see that there's plenty of clear space, plenty of space to move to. Feel the open air all around you..."

This time his tone was intentionally calming, comforting.

He gave her a minute to deal with what was going through her. Then he said, "If and when you feel like you can, move closer. But know all along that anytime you need to step back for a minute—or call this quits altogether—you can. You're only taking baby steps here. Don't do anything at a pace that upsets you. If you start to feel overwhelmed, let me know and we'll deal with it."

Emmy nodded. "Okay..."

"It will be okay," he countered more strongly than she'd been able to. Then he said, "Deep breaths," as he went to the first tree in the orchard.

This still wasn't easy for Emmy. What she really wanted to do was run the other way. But she knew that avoidance only postponed the fear until the next time, it didn't cancel it out. And she honestly did want all the fears she'd taken with her from Afghanistan to end.

Now or never, she told herself, knowing that she was lucky to have Declan to walk her through this.

As he worked, he explained what he was doing, what he was seeing and hearing, how he could test for dangers and maintain his safety if he saw any. It wasn't unlike what he'd done in Afghanistan as he'd worked to get to her, and at first she worried that that similarity might be enough to give her flashbacks.

But in Afghanistan there had been an underlying urgency even in his assurances that he was going to get her out. They'd both known she was in real danger. Now there was none of that awareness of a genuine threat. His tone was casual; he even made jokes.

It also helped that it wasn't only his voice coming to her, she had a visual to focus on as well, and that visual added some distraction. How could it not when, dressed in jeans and a chambray shirt, he was all muscles and masculinity at work?

Plus, even though she would never let Declan know it, he provided an additional element to her drive to overcome her fear.

Yes, she hated what had been happening to her since the bombing and she wanted it to go away. And she certainly didn't want to have the potential for relapses like the panic attack in the attic or the anxiety she'd been suffering over the mere thought of the orchard.

But deep down, she also hated having Declan see any weakness in her. And she liked—more than she cared to admit—when she saw his approval for what he considered her strength.

As he worked without incident, keeping up a dialogue with her, she felt herself relax slightly and was able to move a few steps closer.

"How're you doing?" he asked when he saw that.

"I'm feeling guilty for just standing here watching you work and not pitching in," she confessed.

"You have a job of your own to do," he argued. "Just focus on that."

It took hours, and determination, but over time Emmy was able to move close enough to what he was doing to actually grab and haul away a few of the branches he left lying on the ground outside the perimeter of the tree.

As it turned out, physical activity also aided the cause of clearing the panic from her mind. Dragging the limbs to the pile Declan had been creating, she decided that it didn't matter if part of the reason she was so determined to conquer her fear was to please him. It only mattered that it worked.

It was midafternoon before she thought she was ready to actually venture underneath one of the trees. When she told Declan that, he said, "Are you sure?"

No, she wasn't sure. She hadn't been sure about any of the moves she'd made, and the thought of standing beneath the cover of those far-reaching branches did require more effort to regulate her breathing again, to avoid the panic that threatened to rise up and devour her.

But with each of those baby steps she'd taken today, she'd had to wade through those same doubts, so she said, "I'm just going to try it."

As if he knew she needed a little extra bolstering for this step, he took off one of the heavy leather gloves he was wearing and held out his bare hand to her.

Instead of replaying the terror or panic from memories of Afghanistan, she flashed back to that kiss from the night before, feeling that same hand in her hair, his other hand on her back. The memory helped her accept the offer as she slipped her hand into his.

Concentrating on the warmth, the strength of it, made it easier not to think about the broken branches. But it did leave her unsure of whether the fast beat of her heart was due to the feel of his hand around hers or to the anxiousness. Still, she decided that that uncertainty was better than the knowledge that what was going through her was fear and fear alone.

"Open your eyes, Emmy," he suggested when she'd drawn a short ways under the tree and toward him.

She hadn't realized she'd closed them. But she did open them then, feeling a rush of fear at the realization of where she was, at the fact that the tree limbs blocked the sky from view, at the sense of being more enclosed than she'd been all day long.

There was a gasp of air drawn into her lungs and then she heard Declan saying, "It's all right. Take a deep breath. Nothing is coming down on you. You're okay. You're safe…"

Her arms erupted in goose bumps but like the increase in her pulse, she wasn't sure if that was because of the fear or the rich honey sound of his voice. But she did take the deep breath and then another and another—the way she'd been doing all day—and she began to feel the now-familiar calming coming in stronger than the fear.

Still, she was holding on to Declan's hand for dear life.

It didn't seem to bother him. He held on tight to hers, too.

"How are you doin'?" he asked.

"Okay," she said unenthusiastically.

"Do you want out?"

She did. But she shook her head no.

She forced her head back, forced herself to look up at the dense cluster of tree branches not nearly as far from her as she wished they were. At the sight, she needed to control her breathing again but she managed it with Declan continuing to reassure her. He seemed to know when she'd reached her limit and said, "Enough?"

"For now," she confirmed.

"Okay," he answered without any criticism. Instead he gave more encouragement when he said, "You did great!"

Then he released her hand so she could get out from under the tree. As much as she wanted to get away at that moment, she also regretted losing his touch.

"The hand-holding was good, though. That helped," she heard herself say.

"Then we'll do it again the next time you want to try this."

And that, she thought, was more incentive than he knew to get her under another one of those trees.

"Decan can read a story tonight," Trinity announced at bedtime.

"He can?" Emmy said in surprise. "You *want* him to?" she asked to make sure she was understanding.

"Wan Decan t'do it. You go 'way, Em," the three-year-old persisted in impossible-to-predict three-year-old fashion.

"Okay, I'll go get him."

Because Trinity hadn't yet agreed to have Declan read her bedtime story, Emmy and Declan had settled into a routine that left Emmy reading to Trinity while Declan gave Kit a bottle and put him to bed. Emmy wasn't sure why her niece was switching things up tonight. She knew it was a win for Declan, but it hurt her feelings slightly to be banished and she worried a little that Trinity might be becoming attached to someone who wouldn't always be there for her.

It was her own fault, though, she realized. She'd been offering Trinity the option since Declan's arrival here; now that the three-year-old was making that choice she had to let it play out. So she went to the nursery next door.

It had been a long day in the orchard. Since the babysitter had left as soon as Emmy and Declan returned to the farmhouse, they'd taken turns wrangling the kids while the other showered.

Declan had gone first so Emmy could get dinner started, then he'd readied the barbecue while she took a little longer showering and shampooing her hair, applying a little mascara and blush afterward. Then she'd slipped on jeans and a pink U-neck T-shirt over a plain white tank top that served to fill in the lowest dip of the U.

Declan had also dressed in a pair of clean jeans and a T-shirt, though his T-shirt was a navy blue crew neck with the letters *USMC* framed by two massively muscled pectorals, which the T-shirt rode to perfection.

Through dinner and the kids' baths that evening, Emmy hadn't really seen the rear view of him. But when she arrived at the doorway to the nursery it was the rear view she was presented with. Declan was standing at the side of the crib, cradling in his also-massively-muscled arms the tiny bundle that was Kit.

From her vantage point she had an angled view and Emmy wasn't sure what was the best part of it—the slightly-more-than profile of Declan's broad shoulders narrowing to his waist and his to-die-for derriere, or the peek she was also getting of the baby in his arms while he said, "It's my night for floor-walking duty, so what do you say, little man? Sleep through?"

But regardless of which part was the best, Emmy reminded herself not to take any of it to heart. Declan wasn't there for her viewing pleasure—no matter how much pleasure it gave her—and the fact that he'd been doing as much as he had with both kids was for the kids' sake, for Topher's sake, not for her.

Don't build things into anything bigger than they are, she warned herself yet again, knowing that was particularly important after their kiss last night and the day she'd spent with Declan being patient and understanding and caring and just all-around good to her.

Despite his wedding fling with Tracy, Emmy had come to accept that he truly was a good man—a hero, even. He was someone who wanted to help her overcome her fears. Someone who saw a problem he could fix and dived right in. She told herself that he would do the same for anyone in need, that it had nothing to do with *her*.

And that kiss last night? A weak moment, maybe? His reception in town before that hadn't been anything like what he'd been expecting. And while he might not admit as much, it must have opened up a soft spot in him. The standing ovation, the heartfelt sentiments and welcome-homes that had gone with many of the handshakes and hugs would have done that to anyone. *She'd* been moved to tears more than once, and none of it had had anything to do with her at all. How could he *not* have been touched, even if he *was* a tough-guy?

But being a tough guy, he hadn't given in to the emotional impact at the time, and maybe instead it had come out later, with her, and—for some strange reason—turned into an impetus to kiss her.

That seemed not only possible but likely, she decided. And she stuck to her resolve not to read anything more into it. No matter how hot that kiss had been.

And now, seeing him so sexy and appealing and, at the same time, so loving with Kit, needed to mean nothing more to her than an attractive tableau. She could appreciate it like a visitor to an art museum without having any claim to it.

After his request that Kit sleep tonight, Declan held the tiny bundle up higher and kissed the infant's forehead. Then he told him to sleep tight just before laying Kit in the crib and smoothing his wisps of hair.

Seeing that big hand so affectionately rubbing that tiny head got to her a little more.

But she mentally sidestepped it, not letting it take hold, and—not wanting Declan to turn and catch her watching him—she finally went into the room as if she'd just arrived there and said, "You finally made the roster tonight— Trinity wants you to read her a story."

Declan straightened up and turned toward her, his eyebrows arched. "She does?"

"She doesn't even want me around—she told me to go away."

"Oh...that's kind of rough."

"It's okay, my feelings aren't *too* hurt. I don't think three-year-olds are known for their tact."

"I'll bet it was the maple syrup I put in her oatmeal this morning—I thought I got a few points for that," he said as if to blunt Trinity's rejection of Emmy.

"I don't think it was any one thing—you've just gotten better with both kids. I've noticed that Trinity has been warming up to you more and more. I think she's just finally gotten comfortable with you," Emmy said, not only because she wanted to acknowledge that he'd been working hard at improving and that his childcare skills *had* grown, but also because she didn't want him to use more maple syrup to curry favors. "But whatever the reason, you're in demand and I've been exiled, so I'll finish up in here and you go do that."

"Sure," he said, heading out the door with an obviously pleased smile on his face, leaving her to turn on Kit's sound machine and night-light. She took a peek at Kit, found him already sound asleep and then left the room, too.

The faint sound of Declan's voice reading Trinity's favorite bedtime story followed Emmy as she went down to the kitchen, where she made Kit's formula for the next day and finished the last bit of dinner cleanup.

It was still reasonably early by then and the warm spring day's temperature had lost only a few degrees even with the sun down. So, with a little time on her hands and the evening air beckoning, she decided to go out onto the front porch and enjoy it.

On a whim she bypassed the wooden swing once she'd gone out the door and sat on the porch's top step, letting the peace and quiet take away the last of the day's stress. She sat in silence, thinking again about what she'd accomplished in the orchard and allowing herself the same sense of success that she'd felt when the sight of Declan hadn't given her flashbacks at the wedding.

"Hey," Declan's deep-voiced greeting announced from behind her just then.

"Hey," she parroted with a glance over her shoulder.

"Want to be alone or can I come out, too?" he asked.

"Come out," she invited.

He pushed open the screen and joined her, sitting beside her on the step angled slightly toward her, his back against the post of the porch's railing. He bent the knee of his uninjured leg and rested a forearm on it, stretching the injured leg out in front of him. The pose made her think he was feeling some pain tonight even though he wouldn't admit it.

"What're you doing out here?" he asked.

"Just winding down."

"From the orchard still?"

"A little," she said, repositioning herself so that she was looking at him now, too.

"I think you did great," he praised. "What do you think?"

"I think I did okay, too," she said, unable to keep a hint of pride out of her voice. "I couldn't have done it without you, though—so thanks for that. Maybe you should think about being a therapist or a trauma counselor or something."

"Nah," he said, laughing wryly at the idea. "I may have picked up a few techniques by watching professionals, but that's as far as I'd ever want to go with it."

"Too bad—you're good at it."

He shrugged away the flattery. "I'm just glad it worked. I was a little afraid I might do something wrong and make things worse."

Emmy shook her head. "You didn't. Having you there, doing what you did, only helped." Although she'd had the added secret incentive of wanting to impress him, so for all she knew his technique might not have been as effective with someone else. But then, who *wouldn't* want to impress him?

For a few minutes they sat there silently before Declan said, "So...ever since we talked about what was going on with you after the bombing and why you wouldn't—couldn't—see me again then, I've been wondering about something else..."

"What?" she said when he paused.

"I've been wondering if there was some other upshot from it that happened at the wedding that I don't know about."

"My issues from Afghanistan didn't come into play at the wedding—that was the good part."

"Okay," he said with some confusion. "So what the hell happened between when I left you at your hotel room door after the reception and the next morning, when we were supposed to have breakfast?"

"Really?" she asked in astonishment at his question.

"Yeah, really," he persisted, looking all the more confused.

"Did you not know that the walls in that hotel were thin?" she said incredulously.

He shrugged. "What if they were?"

Emmy shook her head in disbelief. "I heard you meet up with Tracy just outside my door. And I heard everything else that went on the rest of the night in the room *that was right next door to mine,*" she said, her last words overly enunciated to bring home her point.

Declan's expression went from an extended moment of even more confusion to light dawning. And when that happened, he burst out laughing.

Humiliation rushed through her. He thought it was funny that she'd had to listen to him bouncing around in bed with someone?

Emmy did not. And as much as she'd come to like the sound of him laughing since he'd arrived here all brooding and solemn and sad, she didn't appreciate it in response to this.

But she also didn't want to reveal just how angry and upset she'd been—or how hurt she felt by his laughter now—so she took the tone she sometimes used when Trinity was being outlandish and said, "Of course it was none of my business, but I thought it was poor form. I didn't want to sit across the table and eat pancakes with someone who was fresh out of another woman's bed. If you even showed up—because I had my doubts that you would after that."

That made him chuckle. "Well, sure," he agreed. But there was something gallingly superior in the way he said it. "Tell me exactly what you heard."

"Oh gross! Does that give you some kind of charge or something?" Even if he didn't realize how out of line he was being, or how wounded she'd been by having his rejection shoved in her face, this was still crass on a level she really wouldn't have expected from him.

"Just tell me what you *think* went on that night," he amended.

Was he trying to find out if he had any deniability? Because he didn't. And to make that clear, she said, "I heard you meet Tracy outside my door. I heard your conversation taken into her room. And then I heard...everything..."

He grinned. Maybe at the memory?

"So you think I dumped you at your door and high-tailed it to some other woman's bed."

Dumped was definitely how she'd felt.

But there was no way she was going to let him know that. She held her ground with nothing more than an arch of one eyebrow at him.

"All this time you've been thinking I'm a great big fat sleazeball?"

There was nothing fat about his body, but Emmy didn't want to think about that now. In fact, it occurred to her that this was a good conversation to be having after a day full of focusing on his terrific body as a distraction from her anxiety. A good conversation to be having after that kiss last night, when she'd had her hands on his pecs and had then taken to bed the memory of that to relive again and again.

This was a reminder to her of just what she *needed* to be remembering.

That helped her to show nothing but the cool, aloof attitude she wanted to have about this. "I've been thinking that you're a guy who doesn't pass up a one-night stand with anybody who offers it. And that that's your business and none of mine."

He grinned as if he saw through that and repeated, "A great big fat sleazeball."

Emmy shrugged one shoulder, as if she was indifferent.

Declan shook his head and said, "You have that all wrong."

"Okay, you're not a great big fat sleazeball," she said as if it didn't mean enough to her to argue about.

"I'm not, actually—because while I *did* meet that other

bridesmaid in the hallway just after you closed your door, I also ran into the guy she was with. I don't know who he was but she was wa-aay out of his league and he knew it. The guy looked like he couldn't believe his luck, to the point where he didn't seem to care that she was flirting with me while he stood right there. He didn't even say a word as we talked. But I did what you *saw* me do the rest of the night—I pretended I didn't know she was coming on to me, we agreed it was a nice wedding and I left them to go into her room. So whatever you heard after that point did not involve me," he finished.

Was that possible?

Sound had traveled better through the door than through the wall. While she'd definitely heard Declan talking to Tracy in the hallway, nothing Emmy had heard had been distinct once the couple went into Tracy's room. A male voice. A female voice. It *could* have been Declan and Tracy in the hallway, and Tracy and another man in the room.

Or Declan could just be thinking fast and inventing a plausible lie.

But she remembered that he *had* ignored or rebuffed Tracy's advances earlier that night. And that seemed to lend credence to his claim that her flirting hadn't gotten her any further with him in the hallway than it had previously.

Emmy stared at him, seeing how completely unflustered he was—nothing like she would have expected from a guilty man—and it made her wonder if she'd jumped to a mistaken conclusion.

It had been a logical one, given what she'd heard, she consoled herself. But still…

Was it possible that she'd misconstrued something

again? This time taking it to an extreme negative rather than an extreme positive?

"You *didn't* take the Brazilian bombshell up on what she was offering?" she said dubiously because if he was lying, she didn't want to seem too easily swayed.

He laughed lightly. "The *Brazilian bombshell*?"

That had been a slip of the tongue. Emmy had only ever referred to her sister's friend like that to Carla, and it was a little embarrassing to have Declan hear it.

She didn't know quite how to handle that, though, so she merely gave another indifferent shrug. After all, the name really did fit Tracy—who was from Brazil and most definitely had the body and the fashion sense of a Las Vegas showgirl.

It worked because Declan went on to answer her question. "No, I did not take the *Brazilian bombshell* up on her offer. I wasn't interested before I left you at your door, and I wasn't interested after either."

He said that as if it was a plain and simple fact, without any desperation to convince her. Which gave his words more of a ring of truth.

Emmy was uncomfortably aware of her penchant for letting her imagination run away with her. And as she sat there studying him, she thought about how perplexed— and slightly peeved—he'd been when they'd encountered each other in the hotel lobby the next morning. About his questions as to why she hadn't shown up for their breakfast date. About his claim that he'd waited for her for over an hour.

Even at the time she'd been surprised to learn that he hadn't lingered with Tracy for too long to make the date.

It made more sense that he *hadn't* had an all-night romp and had merely left his own—empty—bed in time for breakfast.

It also made sense that he hadn't slept with Tracy after the way he'd failed to show any interest in her despite her flirting throughout all the wedding events.

Plus Emmy couldn't say that there was anything leading up to that muffled encounter outside her hotel room door, or anything after it, that pointed to Declan being the kind of man who would say good-night to her and then hop into bed with someone he'd been shunning the rest of the evening. Nothing that said he was any kind of a sleazeball, let alone a great big fat one.

"You really didn't spend the night with her..." Emmy said, more statement than question.

Still, Declan answered it. "I really didn't spend the night with her. Or with anyone else. I went up to my own room and hit the sack—*alone*, and looking forward to breakfast with you..."

Simple, clean, no more to it than that. But as was her pattern—the pattern she was trying so hard to break—she'd taken it much, much further than that in her own imagination. And thanks to the way she'd jumped to conclusions, she'd missed out on having breakfast with him.

You pay some high prices for building things up in your mind, Em, she silently said to herself.

Then it occurred to her that *he'd* been the one not to do anything wrong, which meant he hadn't earned the rude rebuff she'd dished out when they'd met in the lobby after *she'd* stood *him* up...

"I guess I owe you an apology," she said with a bit of embarrassment.

"For leaving me hanging for breakfast? Yes, you do," he responded lightly, clearly without any lingering offense.

"I'm sorry for that," she said by rote.

"And for thinking I'm—"

"A great big fat sleazeball for four years," she finished for him, knowing where he was headed.

He grinned. "And how about that crack you made last night? Something about how maybe I should take Mindy Hargrove to Kinsey's wedding—unless I'd just be looking for another bridesmaid... That was a jab at what you thought I'd done with Tracy, wasn't it?"

"Kind of."

He nodded knowingly. And waited.

So she sighed, once more took a tone of forced patience that she might use on Trinity, and said, "I'm sorry for the jab, too."

"Apologies accepted," he decreed.

Emmy wanted to change the subject and avoid any more talk of the wedding and her mistake, so she said, "Now I have a question for you."

"Shoot," he said as if he had nothing to hide.

"Last night when you asked me if Bryce was a sore subject and I said *aren't most breakups*, you said not in your experience..."

"Yeah..." he said.

"Does that mean that your breakups *aren't* sore subjects?" Because she couldn't help being curious about his past relationships—and if they weren't sore subjects for him then maybe she could do a little digging.

He shrugged both of those brawny shoulders. "I don't know why they would be."

"Because breakups can be painful and ugly?"

"I haven't had any of those."

"Come on," she cajoled dubiously.

"Okay, I take that back. I did have one bad breakup. My first one," he admitted, sobering slightly. "With Hanna Sandoval."

"Your first love? If you tell me you were in preschool and that that was the only bad breakup you've ever had—"

He cut her threat short. "I was seventeen—old enough that I should have known better," he said ominously.

"Why?"

"By then things between me and the 'good' people of Northbridge weren't all neat and tidy the way they were last night. And Hanna... Well, she was the sheriff's daughter—a cheerleader, homecoming queen two years running, she volunteered with the elderly and at the hospital, babysat the mayor's kids. As much as I was the town devil, she was the town darling. I should have known going in that it was doomed, that being with her could only make things around here worse."

"But you got together anyway."

"She picked me as her study partner in chemistry."

"And study partner turned into first love and she became your high school sweetheart?"

He scowled at that and it delighted Emmy that he hated her putting a sappy spin on it.

"Study partners was where it started and yeah, it grew into more than that," he said, using the terms he obviously preferred.

"It grew into a lot more," she guessed.

"We were hot and heavy. But in secret."

"Why?"

"Because I was the town devil and she was the town darling," he repeated as if that should have been a given.

"Was that the attraction—the secrecy, the forbidden love? Or was it real?"

His eyebrows arched again. "Seemed real. Felt real. Having to sneak around was just...lousy. But her father was the sheriff and we both knew he didn't have any use for me, so we kept it quiet."

"Until?"

"We had a pregnancy scare."

Emmy's delight at goading him disappeared. "You had a baby with her?"

He shook his head. "It was a false alarm, but before we knew that she felt like she had to tell her parents and…" He shrugged once more. "It was definitely ugly," he said, referring to Emmy's earlier comment about breakups. "Even uglier than I thought it would be, to tell you the truth. Her old man didn't just hate me because he thought I was a troublemaker. When Hanna told him she'd been seeing me, he went berserk, threatened to throw me in jail, get me expelled, run me out of town. He said he wasn't letting one of Alice's—Alice was my mom's name—one of Alice's bastards ruin his daughter—"

"He was in the Greg Kravitz camp."

"Apparently so. I knew he didn't like me, but he'd taken me down to the station after fights a dozen times before and never once had he said a word against my mother. I guess he couldn't keep his prejudices under wraps when he thought I'd gotten his daughter pregnant. It did kind of explain why he was always so ready to believe things between me and Kravitz were my fault—he considered me the scum of the earth."

Declan paused, then went on, "Anyway, thank God for Hugh. He threw back as many threats to the sheriff as the sheriff threw at me—abuse of power and unlawful restraint and a lot of stuff that I'm not sure was even real—but it kept me out of jail and in school."

"And when the pregnancy turned out to be a false alarm?"

"Sheriff Sandoval laid down the law with Hanna—she wasn't supposed to ever so much as say hello to me again. But it didn't really matter. She told me that before the scare she'd been about to break up with me. That I was just her bad-boy phase—the gist of it was that she was finished slumming..."

Emmy flinched. "No!" she said, hating that the Camden issue had come into play with his first love on top of everything else it had infected.

"Yeah, made me feel pretty stupid for thinking there was any more to it on her part," he admitted.

Because there *had* been more to it on his part, Emmy thought. But what she said was "It must have hurt."

Declan shrugged that off, too, but Emmy didn't believe it had been easy for him. "I only had about six more months here after that. I went to school, stuck even closer to home the rest of the time... It did make me all the more happy to get the hell out of here when graduation day finally came, though."

"I'm sorry, Declan."

He chuckled. "This is ancient history we're talking about, you know?"

"Still. Do they live here now?" she asked.

"They actually moved out of town a couple of weeks before I left—Sandoval got a job somewhere in Idaho."

"Good," Emmy said.

But hearing about the rocky road of his first love didn't satisfy her curiosity about his adult relationships. In fact, it made her wonder how that rocky road might have influenced them. And since he was intent on not making a big deal out of that long-ago romance, she moved on with her questioning.

"What about once you left here? Have you not let anyone get close to you since then?" she asked, thinking that she couldn't blame him if he hadn't.

"Hanna didn't scar me for life, if that's what you're thinking. There were a couple of girls in college and I've had my share of relationships since then. Just nothing that's gotten too serious."

"Because you haven't let it?"

"Just because it hasn't happened. It's not like I come across a lot of women on a daily basis—there are some that I work with, but there are regulations against fraternizing with anyone under my command. When I do meet someone and something starts...well, about the time it gets going I deploy, and there's a long gap with pretty sparse contact. By the time I might be able to pick things up again there just hasn't been anything left to pick up. Being involved with someone in the military means a lot of waiting around for them."

Emmy couldn't dispute that. "Yeah, sometimes I didn't know how Mandy could do it."

"Topher was lucky," Declan concluded. "And then, too, I can't say I've put a lot of energy into finding anyone who might be interested in making it work. I've always just figured it'll happen or it won't."

"Don't you *want* it to?"

"I've been okay just coasting, I guess. Up until now I've thought of the marines as my family... I mean, along with my siblings. And I guess so far it's filled the bill."

He was looking out at the farm and there was something in his expression, in the almost fondness for the place that she thought she saw there, that made Emmy wonder something else. "There are a lot of past tenses in that— you've *been* okay coasting, *up until now* you've thought of the marines as your family. *So far* other things have filled the bill..." she said. "Are you changing your mind?"

"I don't know. I've put everything into the service, into where it feels like I belong. To tell you the truth, the idea of getting too serious with anyone has always seemed like signing on to answer two masters. I wouldn't want my wife—or kids if I had them—to feel like they weren't my first priority, you know? So instead I've just devoted myself to the marines and enjoyed casual relationships with women. But seeing for myself what Topher had? What he would have come home to?"

He turned to look at her, the small smile returning, his eyes holding hers. "I gotta say—now that I think about it—being here, seeing all Topher had... What I'm going back to doesn't seem as... I don't know, as full, I guess. Or maybe that's just because Topher won't be there..."

He'd been in such a better mood recently, and Emmy didn't want to see his doldrums return, so she quickly moved on from his reference to his lost friend. "You could go back and look for someone willing to wait around for a military man," she suggested quietly, hating the idea of him with someone else but wanting to present him with something hopeful to counter his darker feelings.

It worked, because he laughed the laugh she liked. "I haven't thought about anything but getting myself in shape to go back." But then he was looking at her with something new in his eyes. Something that seemed all about her when he added, "Until lately..."

Emmy warned herself not to read too much into that. But just as she mentally cautioned herself, he closed the small distance between them and kissed her.

He kept his hands to himself and only his mouth found hers in a kiss that was more like a first kiss than their actual first kiss had been. At least that's how it started—lips barely parted and the unspoken question in it that left the opportunity for her to cut him off.

But that was the last thing Emmy wanted to do when she'd spent the past twenty-four hours just wanting to kiss him again.

And now there they were.

So she answered that unspoken question by leaning into the kiss.

And when that was the answer she gave, he took the kiss a step further and once again sent his tongue to play, his hands to cup her head.

She'd tried all day to tell herself that their first kiss might not have been as good as she remembered. But she realized now that she'd only been kidding herself. The man could definitely kiss! And that tongue of his? He rolled it just so and made it a little wicked, enticing her all the more.

Her hands had ached to reach for him again so she did, laying her fingers on his chest until he dropped his to her back, wrapping her in arms that pulled her toward him and urged her arms around him, too.

Not that having his broad shoulders and sinewy back under her palms was a letdown because it so, so wasn't. Any more than having his hands splayed on the flat of her back was.

Those big hands held her with just the right amount of pressure, of command, his long fingers pressing into her in a sublime massage as his mouth opened even wider over hers and the kiss grew hotter and hotter by the minute.

Hot enough to burn away Emmy's better judgment and leave her a mass of quivering, yearning flesh crying out for his hands on more than her back.

Her breasts swelled to the limits of the lacy bra she'd put on after her shower, feeling as if they were threatening to burst through the cups with the hard points of nipples shouting for attention from him.

Even her thighs seemed to have a mind of their own, spreading enough so that when Declan pulled her nearer still and up onto his lap, there was a place for him as she straddled him.

On they went, kissing with abandon. Emmy found the bottom of his T-shirt, sliding her hands underneath it so she could feel not just his powerful back but the warm, sleek skin that contained the muscles that made it so powerful.

That initial meeting of her hands to his skin caused him to groan faintly, a sound of pleasure that made her smile.

And want even more from him.

Which she thought he might give when he took his own turn at sliding his hands under both layers of her shirts.

He delivered, boldly unhooking her bra and bringing both hands around to cup her breasts as if he'd read her mind and knew she wanted him to.

Kissing wasn't his only talent as he showed her the skills of hands that had no timidity, hands that kneaded her flesh and teased her nipples into diamond-hard crests that screamed for even more attention.

And then there *was* more after a moment when he took his hands away, clasped her hips to pull her tight against him and then deserted her mouth and finessed her shirts and bra up above one breast to kiss his way to her nipple.

The cool night air was chilly on her bare skin, adding an even greater component to her arousal. Her back arched and there was a moment's delay before she realized that the moan she heard had come from her this time.

He drew her into his mouth and awakened things even his hand had left sleeping, flicking the tip of her breast with his tongue, nibbling tenderly.

And turning her on until she approached the edge of no return.

The edge she caught herself from falling off as she suddenly asked herself what she was doing. And how far she was going to let this go.

There was no question that her body was crying out for

her to let this go all the way. She just wasn't completely sure she should listen to it.

Maybe her success in dealing with the orchard today had gone to her head. Maybe there was a part of her that was celebrating and causing her to act a bit recklessly. But she didn't want to be reckless and end up regretting it.

So since she couldn't be sure at that moment if this was the right thing to do, she knew she had to deny her body what it wanted so desperately and end this before she did go over the edge.

"Ohhh…we have to stop…" she said, as much a complaint as a command.

"Do we?" he asked as if he thought she might be mistaken.

But she convinced herself all over again that she wasn't and said, "We do."

The tip of his tongue took one more circle around her nipple and then left it to air-dry while his mouth raised up to recapture hers in another kiss that threatened every resolve she'd ever had.

But even as her desires for him made it more difficult for her to pull away, he still did his best to right her clothes, even refastening her bra with a surprising expertise.

He went on kissing her for a while afterward. And she left her hands under his shirt as she reconsidered. It was just so hard to actually make something stop that she really wanted to continue.

But it was Declan who rewound the kiss until it was chaste again. Who moved his hands from her body to cup either side of her face, making the kiss sweetly innocent.

He did mutter a disappointed groan when she forced herself to take her hands out from under his shirt, but other than that he gave her what she'd asked for and finally called a halt to it all, ending that kiss, too.

His hands dropped away from her face then and fell to her hips, lifting her off his lap and replacing her on the porch floor.

He took a deep breath and wilted—as much as the marine in him seemed capable of wilting—back against the railing post, studying her again.

"What's going on with us do you think?" he asked.

Emmy shrugged elaborately, her shoulders going high before dropping back into place, because it was the only answer she could give as she reminded herself that she couldn't leap too far ahead, that she needed to think rationally and avoid jumping to conclusions. She knew there was something about him that made her want to throw caution to the wind, but before she could let that happen she had to be sure they were on the same page, wanting the same things.

He didn't seem to have an answer to his question either and instead just went on looking at her with those penetrating blue eyes.

Then, as if there wasn't an answer to be had, he sighed again and said, "Kinsey's rehearsal and dinner are tomorrow night."

"I know. I'm taking the pictures."

"Will you be my date?"

That surprised her. But maybe he wanted to make sure that things were clearer for tomorrow night than they had been at Mandy and Topher's wedding, than they had been right up to that moment. Maybe this was the first step to letting her know they were on that same page after all.

"I will," she said, liking that clarity.

He smiled another of those small smiles and went on looking at her intently before the smile went devilish and in a gruffer voice he said, "I'm going to sit out here for a few minutes and cool off. It'd probably help if you went in."

"Okay," she agreed. Not that she wanted to because she didn't. But it was getting progressively more difficult for her to be out there with him and not go back to what they'd been doing moments before.

She got to her feet but as she did he caught her hand in his and tugged her toward him. He stretched his torso up enough to kiss her again—another hotter-than-hot kiss that nearly brought her to her knees before he ended it and let go of her hand.

"Maybe you'd better lock your door tonight," he joked.

Emmy just laughed, said, "Good night," and went inside.

But not only didn't she lock her door when she got to her bedroom, she almost left it open.

Until she summoned what little was left of her willpower and slowly, quietly shut it.

Wishing it was as easy to shut off all he'd turned on inside her.

And wondering if even a night's sleep could accomplish that.

Chapter Eight

"Did *you* know that in the years after we all left, Mom and Hugh got that involved here?" Liam asked Declan as the two of them stood in a corner of the church basement watching guests come in through the basement's open double doors.

Liam and his wife and kids had arrived in Northbridge only an hour before the wedding rehearsal. It had been on the hillside behind the Madison family farmhouse where the ceremony and reception were to be held. But the rehearsal dinner was in town. Declan and Liam had given the officiating reverend a ride home after the rehearsal, and during that drive he'd told the two about jobs on the farm that their parents had given numerous townsfolk who were down on their luck. About help they'd given elderly people around Northbridge—before they'd become elderly themselves. About how, once the kids were gone, the Madisons had volunteered to run the local food bank and even quietly initiated and sponsored a program that provided backpacks full of food to be taken home over weekends and holidays by children who usually depended on the school's free breakfasts and lunches.

"I didn't have any idea," Declan answered, as surprised

as his twin to hear that their mother and adoptive father had become such philanthropists when their nest had emptied. "Every time I had stateside leave I either flew them to meet me wherever I was or we met in Vegas. I haven't been back in Northbridge since I left, so no one here could have told me. And not once in any of that time did either Mom or Hugh ever say a word to me about it."

"The part I can't believe is that there was a committee formed to throw this dinner tonight on their behalf, to stand in for them since they aren't here now to do it for Kinsey themselves," Liam went on with the other part of what the reverend had revealed. "Though they're doing it to thank Kinsey along with honoring Mom and Hugh. Did you know that when she moved back to Northbridge to take care of Mom at the end, she also helped out with some home nursing for other people around here without being paid for it? That that's why half the town is expected to come to the wedding?"

"I knew Kinsey had helped out one neighbor when she was here, but I didn't know it went beyond that," Declan said. "Apparently we've *really* been out of the loop."

"I guess deployment will do that," Liam said.

"I guess…"

"Speaking of which, I heard you got a hero's welcome the other night," Liam said then.

"The whole thing is just bizarre," Declan said, embarrassed to talk about that.

He was still finding it difficult to grasp his own reception, let alone to believe Northbridge had taken such a complete turnaround. Was it really possible that the passage of time and some good deeds had redeemed their family from scandal? Or had he been wrong to assume the whole town had been against them all along, rather than just a handful of vocal antagonists?

Uncomfortable with these ideas, Declan changed the subject. "How does it feel being a civilian?"

"It doesn't feel like I'm really a civilian yet—it still just feels like extended leave. I have to remind myself every morning that I actually resigned," Liam answered with a laugh.

"I wasn't sure you could go through with it."

Liam shrugged. "Things just changed for me. Finding out I have kids… Meeting Dani…"

"Any regrets?"

"No," Liam answered, his lack of hesitation also surprising Declan. "I know—if somebody had told me a year ago that I'd be where I am today, I'd have said *never gonna happen.* But it just did. And this feels right for me now. As much as the marines felt right for me before." Liam glanced over at Declan. "How about you?" he said.

"Me?"

Liam tossed a nod toward Emmy, who was taking pictures of the tables, the centerpieces, the people arriving with casseroles and Crock-Pots and covered dishes. "You're keeping pretty good tabs on Topher's sister-in-law—that's how it started with me and Dani…"

"You're imagining things," Declan denied, even though he knew he was guilty of tracking Emmy's every move. He hadn't been able to keep his eyes off her for long all through the rehearsal or since they'd come here.

But she looked so good…

She was dressed in a simple gray-and-white-striped dress that followed her every curve until it flared at the very bottom. The straight-across top was held in place by thin straps that left enough bare skin to have been whetting his appetite ever since she'd walked downstairs tonight. Her hair was a little curlier than usual, a little bouncier, and she had on just enough makeup to accentuate her natural beauty without distracting from it. And he couldn't help enjoying the view.

That was all there was to it, though. Liam was just off the mark.

"The marines are still right for me," Declan said. "I keep wondering how you could opt out—I mean, Conor, sure. He was always a doctor first, military second. But you and me..."

"Things change," Liam repeated. Then he added, "You can't deny that you've made a pretty big change yourself."

"Me?" Declan said, still thinking about Emmy, recalling last night on the front porch and not totally following what his brother was saying.

But now it wasn't Emmy on his brother's mind, Declan realized as he started listening to what Liam was saying.

"I picked you up from rehab and drove you to the airport to get on the plane to come here, remember? I couldn't get two words out of you and there was a dark cloud hanging over you. Now here you are, nearly yourself again. Don't get me wrong, I'm not complaining. But when Conor told me you were in better spirits here I thought he must be joking—you always hated Northbridge, and I thought being around a million reminders of Topher being gone would just make it worse. But here you are..."

Declan was looking at Emmy again before he pulled his glance away to address part of what his brother had said. "There *are* a million reminders of Topher," he agreed. "But most of them are good ones. Actually, being here has helped me remember those and where we all started and why we all wanted to serve—"

"And how Topher wouldn't have blamed you for his death the way you blamed yourself?" Liam prodded.

Declan shrugged, conceding to that. "Emmy convinced

me that Mandy didn't blame me either. And apparently not even Northbridge does," he finished somewhat under his breath and more to himself than to his brother.

"That's because there's no blame to be laid on you," Liam said firmly.

"Still not easy to live with," Declan muttered.

"It's not easy for any of us to live with losing Topher," Liam said solemnly.

"Yeah," Declan agreed. But being here had actually led him to understand that he wasn't alone in the loss—the way he'd been feeling since hitting that IED.

In fact, being here had made him face that that loss was as great or greater to other people—to Mandy before she'd died herself, and to Trinity and Kit down the road when they would grow up without a father. Even to Emmy, who'd turned her life upside down to raise Trinity and Kit and take care of the farm. And she did it all good-naturedly—it was hard to go on wallowing the way he had been in light of that.

He found her again with his eyes, and apparently that renewed his brother's suspicions.

"There you go, watching Topher's sister-in-law again."

"No big deal," Declan claimed.

"She liked you. She didn't like you. She liked you. She didn't like you," Liam said, chronicling the ups and downs with Emmy that Declan had complained to him about along the way. "Do *you* like that you never know what you're in for with her from one minute to the next? Does it keep you on your toes or something?"

"There were reasons for all that," Declan said, going on to explain what he now knew had happened both in Afghanistan and at Topher's wedding.

"All right," Liam allowed when he was finished. "Does

that mean she's okay, then? That you aren't just waiting for the flip side to show up at any minute?"

Declan couldn't say he was 100 percent sure of that. Especially not when he'd come to want her so much that it made him wonder if he was giving her a faster pass to forgiveness than he should. And even with everything explained, she did still run a little hot and cold—he was sure she wanted him, but she kept holding herself back and he wasn't sure why...which was driving him to distraction.

Because he *did* want her. After last night it was damn near eating him alive.

But before he could come up with an answer for his brother, he sensed Liam tense up and followed Liam's gaze to the basement doors again.

"Oh, this will make Kinsey's night..." Liam said for Declan's ears only as the two of them watched a large group of people walk in together.

It took Declan a moment to recognize them from the newspaper and magazine pictures that his sister had shown him along the way.

But after that moment, he knew who he was looking at.

The Camdens had just arrived.

Through her viewfinder, Emmy saw a large group of people file into the church basement all at once for the rehearsal dinner. That wasn't strange—people had been coming in steadily for the past twenty minutes. But it was the quiet that fell over the party room followed by a ripple of whispers that told her something out of the ordinary was happening.

Then she heard the Camden name among the whispers around her, took a closer look at the faces of the new arrivals and realized that they were, indeed, the Camdens that she'd seen in pictures when she'd looked them up after talking to Declan about his family ties.

Emmy knew that Kinsey would be thrilled, so she captured an image of the surprise on the bride's face, the touching smile and tear-filled eyes that followed it. Then she began to take rapid shots of the Camdens themselves to chronicle that arrival.

But at the same time it was really Declan who was on her mind. Declan who she began to inch her way toward even as it changed the angle of her pictures.

She didn't quite understand what was pushing her in his direction at the expense of her photographs—nothing had ever done that before. She just felt a need to get to him, wanting to support him through this moment he'd been dreading.

It was silly because standing together in the corner, Declan and his identical twin brother were a wall of tall human steel that looked as if they could withstand anything.

But she knew that Declan had lived through too many hard knocks over his mother's relationship with a Camden. And even though she didn't completely understand it, she wanted to at least be by his side.

So, continuing to take pictures along the way, that was where she went.

The minute she got to him—thinking of nothing but how to make sure it wasn't obvious—she reached a hand down to his, squeezed it hard and then let go.

He shot her a quick glance, the stone-cold expression on his face cracking into the bare hint of a curious smile that only lasted a split second before it disappeared. And yet in that split second it made Emmy feel as if they'd formed a united front that she could only hope might help him get through this.

From that moment on she made a concerted effort not to be far from Declan's side. She still did her job, documenting the whole event for Kinsey and Sutter, she just never did it far from Declan.

She had more than enough shots by the time the first of the guests began to leave and when she let Declan know that, he used the excuse of needing to get home to Kit and Trinity for them to be among the departees.

As he drove them home he was as solemn and quiet as he'd been when he'd first come to Northbridge. But Emmy left him to it, thinking that he probably needed some time for what had happened to settle.

Once they reached the farm he disappeared into the back of the house while she got the report on the kids from the fifty-year-old babysitter. She and Miss Mona also discussed the babysitting plan for the wedding the next day, including the agreement for Miss Mona to bring the kids home afterward and stay with them until Emmy and Declan were able to leave the reception. Then Emmy paid her and let her go.

Once the front door was closed and locked, Emmy went quickly up the stairs to peek in on the kids, making sure they were sleeping peacefully before she retraced her steps down to the house's first level again in search of Declan.

She found him leaning over the island counter in the kitchen.

He'd removed his sport coat and tie, opened the collar button on his shirt and rolled the sleeves to midforearms. His arms were stretched out to brace him while his hands were flat to the granite.

Emmy eased her high heels off and left them where she knew Trinity would find them in the morning and have fun trying them on. Then she joined Declan on the opposite side of the counter and said, "How're you doing?"

He breathed a short humorless laugh and raised his head from where it was hanging between his shoulders just enough to look at her from beneath his dark eyebrows. "I don't know. I don't know much of anything tonight."

"Strange night," Emmy said. "Not only did you have to be with a lot of the town again, but *all* of the Camdens, too? And there's a *lot* of them."

"Ten who are around our ages, plus their ten spouses, plus *GiGi*—the grandmother—and her husband. That adds up to twenty-two," he said.

"Good thing they all brought food—that would have been a lot of extra mouths," Emmy offered, not sure what else to say.

"Yeah, I was surprised they each brought a dish like everybody else instead of acting like the big shots they are—who I'm sure always get catered to otherwise," Declan said facetiously.

"Maybe they just saw on the invitation that it was potluck so they did what everybody else did because they're more down-to-earth than you thought?" she ventured. That was how they'd seemed to her and she was trying to temper his preconceived notions of them, to maybe open his eyes a little.

Declan didn't respond for a moment and she wasn't sure if saying something positive about the Camdens irked him.

But then he breathed another of those wry laughs and said, "Yeah, I'll give them that—or at least that they're good at making it *seem* like they're real people instead of hoity-toity."

Emmy couldn't help smiling at that term because it

didn't seem like one Declan would use. "Hoity-toity?" she repeated to tease him, hoping to lighten the mood.

It worked because he stood straight and smiled at her. "Do you like *high-and-mighty* better?"

"They all just seemed like everyone else...nice..." Emmy said. "I thought they handled themselves and the situation pretty well, actually. They didn't rush you all at once, they each came over separately to introduce themselves so you had some one-on-one with everyone—and so they had some one-on-one with you. Everybody was friendly but not gushy—I didn't think you'd like it if somebody tried to hug you or something—"

"No, I wouldn't have."

"But all the guys offered their hands when you were introduced. There were a lot of get-to-know-you questions and they seemed sincerely interested in the answers. Your grandmother—"

He made a face. "Don't call her that."

"Okay, the-woman-who-is-*technically*-your-grandmother," Emmy rephrased with an exaggerated eye roll to make a joke out of it, "asked you to call her GiGi the way everyone else does, and gave you and Liam that sweet little talk about how sorry she was that she didn't know you before now, and how she hopes she can make up for lost time..."

"Uh-huh," Declan said guardedly.

"So she didn't *ignore* the fact that she *is* your grandmother but she also didn't try to force anything with you—like some kind of false familiarity."

Declan nodded but didn't say anything to that.

"And they were all really warm to Kinsey—and since it was important to her that they recognize her relationship to them I thought that was good. They could have come but still made you feel like family outsiders, and they didn't do that."

"Yeah," Declan conceded but without any enthusiasm. "I guess for Kinsey's sake it was good. She definitely looked happy—happier even than she did before they showed up. Just one big *happy* family…"

Emmy made a face at his tone. "You don't think it ever will be just one big happy family?" she asked.

She expected a resounding no from him.

But after a moment he relaxed some of his hard shell and shrugged. "I can't say I feel warm and fuzzy about the idea, but I guess anything is possible. And I suppose they did take one hell of an awkward situation and handle it about as well as it could have been handled."

So he was being fair and reasonable despite his own feelings. Emmy liked seeing that. And ran with it. "Maybe it would help if you keep in mind that none of them knew anything about you or Liam or Conor or Kinsey before Kinsey came forward with your mother's letter. They didn't have any more responsibility for what happened than you did."

Only silence filled the air for a moment but Emmy had the impression that he was letting that sink in. And she thought that was a step forward, too.

Then, as if he didn't want to talk about it anymore, he gave her a smile and said, "And were you enjoying playing mama-bear with me tonight?"

"Mama-bear?" she echoed, asking herself if that *was* what she'd been doing.

It sort of was, she admitted when she thought about it. But she wasn't altogether sure it was a title she wanted any more than when he'd called her tough. Mama-bear sounded so frumpy. Which at that moment especially, standing in front of this hella-handsome man, was about the last thing she wanted to be.

"You hightailed it over to me the minute they came in the door, squeezed my hand—" he added a sexy innuendo to that part "—and stayed close by the whole rest of the night. I kept thinking that if one of the Camdens stepped out of line you might take them down."

"That's me—I'm known for tackling little old ladies if I don't think they're behaving themselves," she said with some facetiousness of her own.

Declan's handsome face erupted into another smile. "I can usually take care of myself—even with little old ladies. But Conor had Maicy, Liam had Dani... It was kind of nice to know you were hanging around in my corner..."

Emmy could feel the heat of a blush come into her cheeks, embarrassed to have acted so protective of him. Him of all people. As if he needed it. As if he was hers to protect...

"I was just trying to be supportive," she said to give it a different connotation.

"Still kind of nice," he said quietly, moving from his side of the island to hers, resting one hip against the counter beside her.

Emmy turned to face him and shrugged, deciding she might as well own it after all. "I don't know why I did it. I just didn't like the idea of you being on your own... especially if the Camdens' arrival meant tongues started wagging like when you were a kid... I guess yes, I was being a frumpy mama-bear."

His cobalt blue eyes dropped to give her a bit of an ogle before they rose to her face again. "Who said *frumpy*?" he asked with more innuendo. And a wicked smile to go with it.

"It's right there in the name, isn't it? *Mama-bear?* Mama-bears are all big and hairy and hulking."

He laughed again. "That's you all right—all big and hairy and hulking," he repeated sarcastically, moving a step closer. "And intimidating as hell. Those Camdens had no idea what they might have had to be up against..."

Emmy couldn't help but smile at that. "Don't make fun."

"Never," he vowed. "Especially when it's me who wants to be up against it..."

That one was more than innuendo but he was just standing there, studying her with those gorgeous blue eyes, not making any move at all to prove his claim.

In fact, instead he said, "Maybe you should go up to bed."

"You're sending me to my room?" she half joked.

"Last night has had a hold on me ever since you stopped it," he said in a voice suddenly gravelly. "Now here we are again, this day and night behind us, and that hold is getting stronger by the minute. But I don't want to start something you don't want..."

She *had* been the one to stop things last night. So of course he must have come away thinking that she didn't want to go any further.

He couldn't have been more wrong. It was how much she'd wanted to continue that had scared her off. And worrying that she'd be behaving recklessly if she went through with it.

Except that there he was—tall and macho and masculine, his dark hair just a hint wavy atop a flawless face and eyes too beautiful to believe. And nothing had ever appealed to her less than playing it safe. Particularly when she'd never wanted anything as much as she wanted him. Last night. Every minute since last night. Right now...

And yet she couldn't repeat old patterns, she reminded herself. Those old patterns that turned her into some wide-eyed teenage girl who took a simple *hi* from a cute boy and made it the start of writing *Mrs. Cute Boy* all over her notebook.

With Declan standing there looking as good as he did, telling her he wanted her, she was afraid of giving in and then getting blindsided again when she was the only one who assumed falling into bed meant they'd already started falling in love.

But what if she *didn't* read more into anything than it was? she asked herself. What if she *didn't* expect this to go anywhere except the bedroom? For this one night?

If that was all she expected this to be, then she couldn't be blindsided again, could she? Because then she wasn't letting go of her caution; she was just giving in to the fact that they were two normal, healthy adults finding their way to each other for a night. And as long as she didn't fall into the trap of making more of it than that, then maybe she could have at least this one night…

"I never said I didn't want it," she heard herself tell him.

He arched challenging eyebrows at her. "Then I missed something…"

"Just because I want something doesn't mean I can let myself have it."

He nodded. "Doughnuts, second pieces of pie, three candy bars…" he said as if he understood. "But if I'm the *something*? Just so you know—you have my permission to have as much as you want."

Emmy laughed again. "And nothing changes between us?" she said as if it was a stipulation.

"You call the shots," he assured.

"Ooh, I get to be the boss…" she joked.

Declan merely grinned another of those ornery grins. "I'm game. I just don't want something to start that isn't going to get to end," he warned as if he didn't quite trust her.

"I wasn't teasing you last night. I just…wasn't sure," she said honestly.

He nodded again. "Fair enough." He went on looking at her for a moment longer before he repeated, "So maybe you should go up to bed. And we should call it a night."

If she was still unsure—that was the unspoken part.

Again she offered herself the option of playing it safe. But it didn't have any more appeal now than it had had a few minutes earlier.

"But I have your permission tonight," she challenged.

That hella-handsome face of his erupted into a slow smile. "You do," he confirmed.

"So *you're* sure."

He laughed. "Oh yeah!"

"Maybe I am, too."

"No maybes," he decreed.

He was near enough for her to stand on her toes and kiss him—nothing exotic, just a simple kiss before she dropped down to flat feet again.

"Testing?" he asked.

She shook her head. "Saying yes," she said softly.

"You're sure?"

"Positive."

"Because you know, I've been injured, I'm fragile."

That really made her laugh—he was anything *but* that.

But she played along anyway. "So you want me to be gentle?"

He just grinned more.

"I'll do what I can to take it easy on you but I can't make any promises," she mock warned.

"So that's a yes?" he asked quietly.

She answered that by reaching up and unfastening his top shirt button.

He didn't do more than look down to watch her work her way to his waistband. When she got there she tugged his shirttails free and finished the buttons, leaving his shirt open and finally giving her a glimpse of what she'd only been imagining to that point—a naked chest that could have been on the cover of any athletic magazine.

But he let her have that glimpse for only a moment before he used a crooked index finger under her chin to raise it.

He leaned in to kiss her then but still didn't actually do it. Instead he peered into her eyes and studied her face as if to make it all a memory he intended to keep with him. Or maybe just to make sure that she wouldn't change her mind...

Then he finally did kiss her. As sweetly and chastely as he had to end the evening before, moving his hand to the side of her face where it stayed in a downy caress.

But any doubts he still might have had must have dissolved then because the kiss soon gathered steam, his lips parting, beckoning for hers to, as well. And when they did, his tongue began a leisurely and so-sensual entrance that lured hers into play.

Emmy hadn't unbuttoned his shirt for no reason—she seized the opportunity to slide her hands inside it to his chest.

She relished the feel of his skin over those honed pectorals. She let her hands go where they might, up and over robust shoulders to his expansive back, down bulging biceps so that his shirt came free and hung on his wrists until he let it fall to the floor.

By then the kiss was something more. Mouths were

open wide, parting, returning and toying with the other devilishly as tongues grew bolder and more assertive.

Declan reached around her and unzipped her dress. That sent the spaghetti straps falling and the straight neckline gaping low enough for her to feel cooler air on the upper swells of her breasts above the demi-cup bra. She'd put it on tonight with this in mind—all the while not admitting to herself that this was exactly how she hoped the evening would end.

His hands went to the sides of her waist then, and as if she weighed nothing he lifted her to sit on the island counter just before his mouth moved to those upper swells and he kissed them instead, causing her nipples to stand at attention inside the lacy bra.

But they were in the kitchen. And she didn't want this to happen on the cold slab of the countertop.

So she took his face in her hands to raise from her breasts and initiated a kiss herself before bending to his ear, teasing it with her tongue and whispering, "Upstairs…"

"You're the boss," he said, lifting her from her perch, taking her hand and leading her to her bedroom.

His shoes and socks were the first to go when they got into the space bathed in the cozy light of a bedside lamp.

Then he rediscovered her mouth with his and unhooked her lacy bra, tossing it aside before lowering her dress to her waist and wrapping his arms around her. He held her so that her bare breasts pressed to his bare chest, their bodies so close that the ridge behind his zipper came up against her.

Her arms went around him to bring them even closer together. She let her hands explore every muscle of his back while they went on making a kind of love with their mouths.

But only for a while before he eased them both onto the bed and his mouth went to her breasts again, this time taking one fully into that warm, wet cavern, where he sucked and teased and nipped her nipple into willing submission.

He used one hand to pull her dress off completely, leaving her in only lacy bikinis. Compared to her near-nakedness, his pants seemed like armor. So she unfastened them to let him know they had to go.

He was apparently more than willing, because he deserted her then, took a condom from his pocket with his index and middle fingers to toss onto the mattress, and dropped his slacks and the boxers underneath them to kick across the floor.

As much as she wanted him back on the bed with her, she also wanted to look at him.

Stark naked and definitely something to see, he was stupendous in all his glory, and the proof that he wanted her was awe inspiring.

Then he did come back to the bed to lie beside her and kiss her again while Emmy sent an eager hand to glide along his side and dip forward, enclosing it around him and showing him that she could drive him a little wild, too.

Too wild, it seemed, to go on merely kissing her because his mouth abandoned hers to gasp for air even as his hand trailed a path down her stomach and between her legs, where he slipped an expert finger inside her.

Her grip around him tightened enough to make him moan and then moan again when she did some tantalizing of that steely shaft, until it seemed he couldn't take much more and he rolled away from her to make the quickest work of that condom.

Then he kissed her once again as he came on top of her, slid into her with more than his finger and settled as if he was home and wanted to savor it for a moment.

The kiss was slow and sexy this time. One hand alternated between her breasts, kneading and squeezing, circling nipples, giving them a gentle tug, a pinch, a palm to nestle into and only making her desire for him surge through her.

He pulsed inside her, went in deeper, and that was all it took for a climax to take her by surprise.

But just when it began to pass he went in deeper still then retreated, in and out again. And again. And that peak hung on. Grew.

Meeting him, hips to hips, withdrawing only to meet him again, she matched the pace even as it sped up, taking him in, releasing him only because she knew he'd be back again as need gathered and drove them both, growing and building. The taste of a second climax finally took a full grip on her and carried her into the brightest, most brilliant explosion of ecstasy.

It caught her breath and arched her back and had her clinging to him just as he found his own peak. For a moment, they were both suspended in the embrace of pure bliss while waves and waves of it made nothing as important as their bodies melded together and riding it out.

Until that passion expended itself and receded little by little, leaving Emmy spent in the very best of ways beneath Declan's weight and the perfect union of his body to and within hers.

"I don't think I took it easy on you," she whispered when her breath returned, when she could find the words, suddenly remembering his injured leg and wondering how it had withstood the workout he'd just given it. "Was that too much for you?"

He laughed, the sound gravelly and satiated and sexy all at once. "Too much for me?"

"Your leg...your knee..."

He pushed himself up onto his forearms and kissed her again, a kiss that echoed with all that had come before it, until he ended it and dropped his forehead to hers.

"My leg could have broken in two and I wouldn't have felt it," he assured with another laugh. "Trust me, my leg was not where things were fired up. How about you?"

"My legs are fine," she joked, letting them fall from where they'd wrapped around his massive thighs at some point.

"And the rest of you?" he asked, flexing inside her again. "I mean it feels very, very—*very*—fine to me, but—"

"The rest of me feels pretty fine, too," she assured, tightening her inner muscles around him.

He kissed her once more, this one as alluring and tempting as if he was starting all over again.

Which, to her surprise, Emmy was more than willing to have happen.

Except that just then the sound of Kit waking up came through the baby monitor on the nightstand.

A guttural complaint rolled from Declan's throat and he reluctantly ended that kiss. "Is it that time already?"

"Oh...sadly..."

"Yeah," Declan agreed with emphatic disappointment. Then he said, "I told you that last night Kit woke up, took his bottle and went right back to sleep."

"The new formula," Emmy said as the explanation.

"So how about if I take tonight, too—while you rest up—and we hope it goes like last night did so I can come back?"

Though shocked at how she was already ready for more of him—and thrilled to know he felt the same way about her—she played it cool with a simple "Okay."

"I'll wake you up if you fall asleep," he warned.

"Okay," she repeated, unable to keep from smiling.

Kit was making fussier and fussier sounds, and with a groan of his own, Declan slipped out of her at the same moment he gave her a parting kiss. Then he left the room.

Emmy did close her eyes when he was gone, but there was no way she was going to sleep.

Because while she was sticking to her determination not to think beyond that moment, the fact that she could have more of Declan, more of what they'd just had—at least for the rest of the night—filled her with anticipation.

Anticipation and a warm contentment even though she warned herself all over again that this was *only* for tonight.

Chapter Nine

The weather couldn't have been better for the midafternoon wedding—seventy-five degrees and not a cloud in the Montana sky.

It seemed to Declan that most of Northbridge attended. Plus there were guests from Denver and farther afield, including all twenty-two of the Camdens.

As he stood under the large tent where the reception was set up with food on a buffet, tables and chairs surrounding the dance floor, and a band playing live music against the backdrop of a spectacular sunset, he marveled a little at what he was seeing.

Never, in his wildest dreams, would he have imagined bearing witness to Northbridge celebrating Madisons rather than gossiping about them. And it was happening even after word had to have spread that they were now openly acknowledged as biologically Camdens.

But there it was right before his eyes—his sister dancing with their newfound cousin Beau Camden, her groom dancing with Jani Camden, even Conor dancing with GiGi, all without a single sideways glance from anyone.

"You look tired—are you okay?" Liam asked when he strolled over to Declan just then.

"I'm fine," Declan assured, trying to keep from grinning at the thought of why he didn't seem rested. He'd made love to Emmy until nearly five o'clock this morning and since Trinity was an early riser, very little sleep had been had.

"Did the baby keep you up crying again last night?" his twin persisted.

Declan lost a little of the battle against the grin. "Nah, the new formula has been great. It's been two nights in a row that he just gets up for a bottle and goes back to sleep—that's a world better than hours walking him around."

"But your sleep still gets interrupted. You know I didn't get to know Evie and Grady were mine until they were four years old so I wasn't around for the baby stuff with them. But I can't say I'm sorry that I missed all those sleep interruptions. You're sure you feel all right, though? Your leg isn't giving you trouble and keeping you up nights?"

"The leg is fine, too. If it wasn't, I'd be sitting instead of standing, wouldn't I?"

"I just want to make sure you aren't hiding something that Conor should know about."

While the three of them had been dressing for the wedding, Conor had offered to talk to Declan's doctor about a referral letter that would begin the process of his medical evaluation. The wheels were about to be set into motion for his return to duty.

But what Declan was actually hiding he wasn't going to reveal so he said, "There's nothing to know. Except that you guys have to stop worrying about me—I could run circles around the both of you."

"You could give it a try..." his brother countered with a challenge in his own voice, the way things had always been between the highly competitive brothers. Then Liam said, "What do you think about the Camdens inviting us for a weekend after Kinsey's honeymoon so we can all get to know each other?"

"What do *you* think about it?" Declan volleyed the question back at him rather than admit he didn't have an answer.

Mere days ago he would have railed against the whole idea and ranted against the Camdens.

But now?

Now Emmy had pointed out things that, he had to admit, seemed true about them. They really did seem like nice enough, down-to-earth people. And yes, they weren't any more responsible or guilty for what had happened in the past than he or Liam or Conor or Kinsey were. And Emmy was also right that they were handling this bizarre situation with grace and dignity and a minimal amount of embarrassment to any of them—he had to give them credit for that.

Plus he wanted his sister to have the extended family she'd always craved—after all she'd done to care for their parents during their final illnesses when none of her brothers had been able to lend a hand, they owed it to her. And he didn't want to be the one to throw a wrench into those works for her sake now that the Camdens were giving her the recognition she wanted.

None of that wiped away the years and years of misery he'd endured, so he had mixed emotions. But since he realized those mixed emotions might unduly color things for him, he was inclined to go with Emmy's opinions and observations. And maybe give the Camdens a chance.

As if his twin had read his mind, Liam said, "Maybe we should go to Denver. The whole lot of them did come all the way here for this, for Kinsey. I guess that says something. And we *are* related to them. I keep thinking about Mom…what she'd want us to do…"

"Yeah, there's that, too," Declan conceded.

"So maybe we need to just let it play out, get to know them, go from there…"

"Yeah, maybe."

Their conversation was cut short by Trinity leaving the dance floor, where she'd been doing her own version of a dance with some of the other children. The three-year-old didn't say a word—she merely joined them to slip her hand into Declan's and lean against his thigh.

It was yet another sign that he was making headway with her. The feel of that tiny hand in his, of her leaning against him, gave him a quiet, warm contentment. The same kind of contentment, the same kind of secret satisfaction he found when Kit responded to him now, the infant smiling when he spotted Declan or when Declan made faces and noises at him.

"You doin' okay, Trin?" he asked her.

"Uh-huh," she answered wearily.

"Do you think maybe it's time for Miss Mona to take you and Kit home?"

"Miss Mona's dancin'."

"When she's finished dancing?"

"Uh-huh."

"Can I pick you up so you can rest until then?"

"Uh-huh."

Declan bent over and scooped up the three-year-old to hold on his hip. She laid her head on his shoulder. Which also felt damn good to him.

"She looks just like Topher, doesn't she?" Liam observed sadly then, gazing at the little girl.

"Yeah," Declan agreed, knowing it was true even without being able to see her. It stabbed him every time he noticed it.

Trinity snuggled into the crook of his neck.

"So Topher's *single* sister-in-law inherited everything?" Liam said vaguely and somewhat under his breath, nodding at Trinity to make it clear what he was talking about.

"She did."

"That's a big deal... I don't know if I could have done it without Dani. But Topher's sister-in-law is on board for it?"

"I haven't seen her skip a beat," Declan said, feeling some pride in her that he knew he had no claim to.

"And she knows what she's doing with them? I mean, I was really bad at the parenting thing. It doesn't come naturally for me."

"Yeah, me neither," Declan admitted. Then, with a nod of his own in Trinity's direction, he added, "This is new for me. Nice, but new."

"But Topher's sister-in-law?" Liam reiterated.

"She's great at it," Declan said, remembering back to when he'd had doubts about whether he could trust Emmy with Topher's kids, whether she would be too erratic to raise them.

Now that seemed ridiculous to him. He'd seen that no matter how tired Emmy was, no matter how stressed-out she was—even when she was dealing with deep emotional issues from the school explosion—when it came to Trinity and Kit, she was endlessly patient. She was loving and caring. She was always thoughtful of not only what was best for them, but what would offer some fun for them, too. And though being called a *mama-bear* last night had ticked her off, he saw that streak in her as a big plus for Trinity and Kit.

All of which should have made him feel better about leaving them.

Yet today—ever since Conor's offer of the referral letter to get him back where he thought he belonged—he'd been dreading leaving Emmy alone with them. Hell, just leaving her...

The music ended and the babysitter came over to Declan before Declan could go to her.

"I think we've had enough wedding," Miss Mona announced. "Time to go home."

"I'll help you get them to the car," Declan said, leaving Liam behind to follow the babysitter to Kit, who was being held by a grandmotherly woman at one of the tables.

"You comin' home, too, Decan?" Trinity asked as he put her in her car seat.

"Not yet. Emmy and I have to stay awhile longer. Miss Mona will get you to bed tonight, okay?"

"Okay," the worn-out three-year-old agreed. "Bu' I need yogurt."

Declan laughed. "Hear that, Miss Mona? Trinity needs yogurt before she goes to bed."

"I think we can do that," the older woman said, finishing up with the baby carrier on the other side of the car.

With that settled, Declan kissed the top of Trinity's head and said, "I'll see you in the morning."

"W'ul have maple syrup in our oa'meal, okay?" she whispered as if it was their secret.

Declan liked having that small thing between them that was all their own, and he winked at her. "We will," he whispered back.

Then he closed the car door, said goodbye to Miss Mona and stood there while she drove away before he turned and headed back to the wedding.

The time it had taken to send off the babysitter and

the kids was the longest Emmy had been out of his sight since before the wedding when she'd been with his sister to photograph the dressing of the bride. As he trekked around the farmhouse and up the hill where the reception was going strong, his first order of business was to get a visual on her again.

She'd managed to outfit herself both for the fanciness of the wedding and for work. She had on a sexy-librarian high-necked navy blue lace blouse that gave him peeks at her arms and shoulders before a solid blue underlay blocked those parts he'd gotten to see and explore and revel in last night.

The blouse was tucked into navy blue slacks that caressed her rear end almost as fondly as he had and allowed her to crouch and kneel and bend to whatever height gave her the best vantage point for her picture.

Curling her hair and pinning those curls to her crown also contributed to her festive, feminine look. It struck him when he finally found her in the crowd that if this was the first time he'd ever set eyes on her, he would have rushed to introduce himself.

But as it was he knew she was working, so he merely returned to the tent, ordered himself a beer from the bartender and then settled against one of the tent's support poles to watch her.

And to wonder why it was that the minute he connected even just that much with her, a feeling of calm came over him that wasn't like anything he'd ever experienced.

Which was all the more strange when he kept thinking about Conor's offer to take that first step to get him back to duty. And a reluctance he couldn't explain to accept it…

What the hell was that?

For the last seven months returning to duty was what had driven him. Through pain, through grief, through guilt, that goal had been his single focus—his need to get back to his unit, to his job, to what he was all about, to where he belonged. To the *only* place he'd ever felt as if he belonged. And here it was, within his grasp, and the thought wasn't sitting so well.

Instead the thought that *was* sitting well was that when this wedding ended and he got to take Emmy home, he'd have her to himself again. Maybe they could have another night like last night. And then another and another and another...

Until he had to leave, which—until talking to Conor this morning—had seemed to be in the far-off distance.

But now it was much closer.

And as hard as he searched inside himself, he couldn't find anything that made him glad about the idea of leaving.

He drank some of his beer, watched the dancing couples again—the bride with her groom now, Conor with his wife, Maicy, Liam with his fiancée, Dani.

And for some reason Liam's words came to mind— what his twin had said at the rehearsal dinner about things changing for him.

Things had definitely changed for Declan's brothers. Only months ago they'd both been where he'd thought he was—bent on being career military for years to come.

But in what seemed like the blink of an eye, here they were now, both of them so wrapped up in the women in their lives that they didn't even seem to know there was anything or anyone else outside them.

And here he was more concerned with spotting Emmy through the crowd than rebooting his own military career.

But things had *needed* to change for his brothers.

Conor had become dissatisfied with being an emergency and trauma doctor and had had to resign from the navy to retrain in another medical specialty.

And things had had to change for Liam when he'd discovered that he was a father of twin four-year-olds who'd just lost their mother and stepfather.

But nothing *needed* to change for Declan.

He'd come here to make sure Topher's kids were taken care of. Now he knew they were, and things were finally beginning to fall into place again.

It just didn't feel as if they were falling into the right place.

Because nowhere in him could he find a sense that going back was right for him now.

He looked at the beer in his hand.

It was only his second, he wasn't drunk, so where had *that* thought come from?

Then he looked out at Emmy again and it began to creep into his head that maybe she was the cause. That feelings for her that he hadn't seen coming were rearranging everything about his priorities.

That even though there wasn't a need for it the way there had been for his brothers, somehow things might have changed for him, too.

In Northbridge of all places...

You came for Topher's kids. Just for Topher's kids, he reminded himself.

But the kids were a part of this, too, he realized.

Now he'd walked miles with Kit to get him to sleep. He'd given him more bottles than he could count. Changed enough diapers to be an expert. And when he picked Kit up the baby nestled into his arms, against his chest, as if that was where he was supposed to be, where he felt safe and secure.

Now Declan understood things Trinity said that didn't

sound like words. Now it was no surprise to look up from his morning workout and find her by his side, trying to copy what he was doing. Now he made her breakfast that she would eat and she let him read her bedtime stories and put her down for the night. Now she slipped that tiny hand of hers into his and cuddled up to him.

And it did something to him...something so powerful that the idea of saying goodbye to those kids, the thought of not being around to see them grow up, gave him a kind of clenching pain that was harder to deal with than any of the physical injuries he'd suffered.

Now there was something more to wanting to make sure Topher's kids were okay than what he'd started out with.

And it wasn't coming from the guilt he'd arrived in Northbridge with.

But it *had* come from being in Northbridge.

First and foremost because Northbridge was where he'd found Emmy again.

Talking to her about his belief that he was responsible for his friend's death had led to her showing him a different perspective.

And from that perspective had come memories of Topher in Northbridge, memories of where and when and how he and Topher and Liam had come to their decisions to join the military. Memories of their discussions of the risks, their acceptances of them. Memories that had led him to admit that Topher would never have held him responsible.

Northbridge and Emmy...

Emmy, who he'd believed was moody and temperamental.

But now he thought differently about that, too.

He understood her behavior much better now that he

knew the causes. And since agreeing to accept his help here she'd been on an even keel with him. Even when the ramifications of the school explosion reared its ugly head for her, there hadn't been any signs of her running hot and cold in anything but their physical relationship, where a little uncertainty was natural.

And still, he'd been witness to the slow warm-up that had brought them to last night.

Which had then brought him to tonight, when he felt comfortable in his own skin again—and yet was *not* thrilled with the prospect of exactly what he'd been working his ass off to achieve...

Because what he wanted now wasn't the same thing he'd wanted such a short time ago.

Because he'd actually found something he hadn't thought possible for him—a sense of belonging that wasn't provided by the marines but by Emmy. Emmy and his best friend's two kids.

In Northbridge of all places.

The jury was still out when it came to the small town itself. Things were going well here now and he had to admit that it was nice. And maybe the past would stay in the past and it could go on being nice to be here.

But one way or another that held very little importance to him.

Because as he watched Emmy, as everything and everyone else receded into the background for him the way it seemed to do for his brothers as they danced with the women they loved, as he homed in on Emmy alone and felt that connection to her, even from nothing more than the sight of her, he realized that anywhere that he was with her he felt that sense of belonging.

Without him fully recognizing it, it had happened in every instance that she was by his side or even just within his view. It was the reason why it had been easier for him to face the town that first night at the town meeting. Why it had been easier to speak with the Camdens at the rehearsal dinner. Why it was easier even now, today, at this wedding.

It didn't matter whether the whole town accepted or rejected him. It didn't matter whether the Camdens did. When he was with Emmy, he wasn't an outsider.

And then there were the other times when what he felt was so much more than just that sense of belonging.

Those times when they were alone together. When working with her had shown him her strength and determination, and made him admire and respect her.

Those times when just talking to her had shown him how smart and funny she was, how levelheaded and kind-hearted and fair-minded—those times had made him like her.

There were those times when he saw her with Kit and Trinity. Being a mom to them even though they weren't hers. Loving them, caring for them, never giving any impression that taking on the enormous task of single parenthood was a burden of any kind—that had impressed him, touched him.

There were those times when she was playful and frisky and full of fun. When she was a flirt and teased and goaded him. Those times when she just turned him on so much she drove him wild.

And watching her now, taking pictures of Kinsey and Sutter as the dance ended and they moved on to cut the cake, there was no disputing that she was beautiful and sexy, or that he wanted her so much it was taking everything he had to keep himself under control.

It was in that instant that it struck him like a bolt of lightning that nothing was as important to him as she was.

He needed to be with her. To make a life with her. To share in the raising of his best friend's kids with her and to never again be without her by his side.

He set his barely touched beer on the nearest table and eased his way through the guests standing around the cake until he was right behind Emmy.

He fought not to touch her while she snapped those all-important pictures of the cake cutting, of the bride and groom feeding each other the first bites of it, of them moving out of the way so the waitstaff could cut the rest of the cake to serve.

And that was when he put his hand on Emmy's shoulder, stepped up close and whispered in her ear.

That was when he led her away from the festivities to the farmhouse where he'd grown up.

That was when he hung on tight to the hope that now wasn't the time she proved him wrong and went from hot to cold again…

Chapter Ten

"I don't take breaks during a wedding. If something special happens while I'm gone there won't be pictures of it," Emmy reminded Declan even though she hadn't been able to resist his whispered *I need you* after the cake cutting when he'd whisked her away.

"Everybody's just eating cake," he insisted, keeping hold of her hand as he led her through his family's farmhouse into a bedroom that looked more like a military museum.

Once they got across the bedroom's threshold he closed the door behind them, spun her around and pulled her into his arms to kiss her with the same hunger and abandon that he had shown many times the previous night.

And while it stirred Emmy the same way it had then and instantly made her want to make frenzied, forbidden love right then and there, she let the kiss go on for only a short time before she pushed out of it.

"We can't do this!" she said, assuming that frenzied, forbidden lovemaking was on Declan's mind, too.

But apparently it wasn't, because he let her go, leaned against the closed door and said, "You think I brought you up here to ravage you in my old room?"

"You didn't?" she asked, slightly disappointed and wondering what he *did* bring her up here for if not that.

"It's a fun idea..." he said with a devilish grin. "But no, I just needed to talk to you."

"It couldn't wait for another hour or so?"

"No, it couldn't," he said as if whatever was on his mind was too weighty to be put off.

And yet he didn't say anything more than that. Not right away. He just stood there against the door studying her as if the drive to talk to her was less important than the drive to drink in the sight of her.

She didn't think that boded well for whatever it was he wanted to say.

Was he going to tell her he was leaving? Because she was aware that that could happen at any time, too. It was part of the reason she'd given in to having that night with him—because she hadn't wanted to miss what might be her only chance.

For her, it had been the most amazing night she'd ever had. And after the most amazing night of her life it had been a struggle this entire day not to fall into old habits and think that it had been too amazing not to have rocked him the same way it had her. It had been a struggle for her not to fantasize that it was the beginning of something great. Not to let herself read more into it.

But here she was now, flashing back to that last dinner with Bryce when she'd thought he was going to propose and instead had told her she wasn't good enough for him. She knew Declan wouldn't be so cruel—he wasn't that kind of man. But she'd known from the start that he was leaving, so she'd have to put a brave face on if that was his news.

She braced for it but still found herself suddenly turning to take in all the posters and flags on the walls, all the military-themed old toys and mementos, postponing the inevitable.

"So this is where you grew up," she said, even knowing that she should just get whatever breakup speech he had planned over with so she could put all of this behind her now, too.

He ignored that and instead said, "This morning Conor offered to put in for the referral letter I need to schedule the medical evaluation that could get me back on duty."

Even though she'd been expecting it, there was a catch in her throat that prevented her from saying anything. She just nodded as if it was no surprise.

"And I should have been thrilled," he said. "But I wasn't and I've been trying to figure out why ever since."

She just stared at one of his three marine posters as if it interested her when really she was hanging on his every word.

"It's funny because I just talked to Liam about the changes in his life," Declan was saying. "About how he could ever leave the corps. And then all of a sudden I knew how."

Wait…what? Leave the marine corps—not her?

Emmy slowly turned to look at him. But she still didn't say anything. She just took in every detail of his hair, his features, his tremendous body all debonair in a formal black suit tailored to accentuate his broad shoulders and narrow waist.

He went on to tell her—to marvel at—the change he'd found himself deciding to make. To tell her about how attached he'd become to Kit and Trinity. About how he wanted to help her raise them. About how he'd figured out that despite what being a marine had meant to him, he was ready to do what Topher had planned to do and either accept a medical discharge or resign.

"I know this is kind of out-there," he said, "but what if we *don't* lease the farm? What if we stay on it, raise the kids on it the way Topher and Mandy wanted? Maybe even combine the farm with this property, too, and work something out with Kinsey and Conor and Liam over it? You're getting better every day at the farmwork—that goat loves you now," he added with a laugh.

"I was thinking," he continued, "that since Northbridge doesn't have a photographer, you could set up shop in town and work here rather than in Denver. You might have to add school pictures and maybe sign on to do some work with the local newspaper, but people get married and have babies and want family photographs here, too, so I think you could pick up enough work to make it worth your while. And between that and what the farms could bring in—"

Emmy was confused and not sure she was keeping up with what he was saying.

"Wait," she said to stop him, "you want to stay in *Northbridge* now?"

"I'm okay with it," he said, but unlike the enthusiastic way he'd said the rest, there was marginally less confidence in that in his tone. "You've sort of let me see it through your eyes and that made me see it through Topher's and Mandy's, too. And you may be right that things for the Madisons are different now, that I've been holding on too tightly to old grudges. But even if more Greg Kravitzes come out of the woodwork, I don't really care because somehow, Emmy, being with you keeps me from feeling like an outsider even here. I didn't think anything or anyone could ever make that happen, that anything or anyone could ever top the corps for making me feel like I belong. But you have."

Still not clear what he was suggesting, Emmy said, "So you think we should...what? You should run two farms, I should open a photography studio and we should cohabit to coparent Trinity and Kit?"

He screwed up that handsome face with a scowl. "Oh

God, I'm an idiot!" he exclaimed, laughing wryly at himself. "No! I just skipped ahead into the sales pitch and left out the most important part..."

He crossed to her and took her upper arms in his big hands. "I'm sorry, this is the worst proposal of all time. But believe it or not, that's what I'm really doing here. Today, thinking about maybe getting medical clearance to get back to duty, I realized that something had changed for me and that the marines isn't what I want anymore. That *you're* what I want. You and to be Topher's stand-in dad to the kids."

"So this is a proposal?"

"Absurd as it seems."

It *was* pretty absurd. And coming at her out of the blue in a way that sounded more like some kind of business proposal.

Even so, something in her was right there, ready to say yes. Her mind flashed forward at superspeed into the image of them together for all time, of not bearing the responsibility of raising two kids by herself, of the fact that Trinity and Kit could have a father—the man Trinity was already coming to like and rely on, the man Kit was already responding to as if Declan really was his daddy. The man whose touch brought her to heights she hadn't known were possible. The man she'd come to trust and depend on—with whom she'd formed a workable partnership.

Just that quick Emmy had the image of her and Declan and Trinity and Kit as a family, staying on the farm in the small town she'd come to see more and more affectionately.

She had the image of her and Declan as husband and wife the way her parents were—happy together, partners in life, even in work. She had the image of them growing old together, looking out for each other, caring for each other, solving problems together the way they had been since the two of them had started this.

She had the image of all of it playing out like a storybook, a fairy tale, a flawless romance that had had a rocky start but ended with a happily-ever-after.

But that was not totally unlike what she'd thought would happen with Bryce.

And because she'd been blind to the reality of their relationship, she'd walked right into a whole lot of hurt and disillusionment.

So she took a breath.

And she shoved every fantasy-like image out of her brain.

And she forced herself to look at this realistically.

"I know how awful it's been for you," she said. "Losing Topher. Being the driver. I know you want to do right by him. I know you want to honor his memory. I know you want to make sure his kids are okay. But..." Her voice cracked and she thought that it was no wonder she'd taken refuge in fantasies and romantic images because reality was so much harder.

"I ignored things I shouldn't have ignored with Bryce and I won't do that again—"

"I'm not *Bryce*," Declan said emphatically. "I'm not leading you on. I *am* proposing to you."

"On sort of a whim, I think—"

"I'm a marine. Marines don't act on *whims*."

"But I'll bet they do act on feelings of guilt and responsibility. And it's part of the job to be willing to sacrifice yourself, to give your life for what you believe in."

She glanced around the room, indicating the military shrine they were in the midst of. "Look at this, Declan. You've been all about the marines since you were a little boy. Until this minute I've never heard you say a single word about *not* going back in. You've made it clear that was exactly what you were working for."

She shook her head again. "But now you're willing to live Topher's life? You can't bring him back so you're going to be his replacement instead? That isn't right. It isn't what he or what Mandy would have wanted for you. And adding me onto the plan? I'm just incidental… If I said yes to that…you can't tell me that eventually you wouldn't resent not walking in your own shoes. And there I'd be, just part of what you need to get away from so you can get back to your own life…"

It was Declan's turn to shake his head in denial. "Wow, I've really botched this," he said, an even deeper, more somber frown drawing lines between those beautiful blue eyes.

He pulled her up against him, wrapped his arms around her and just held her there for a minute, her face pressed to his chest where she could hear the beat of his heart.

She had to fight all over again not to let herself believe she could have this—being in his arms, against that magnificent body for all of eternity.

But she *did* fight it. She didn't even put her arms around him; she just left them at her sides.

Then he took her by the shoulders and stepped back, putting that short distance between them again.

"I came at this all wrong. Let me start over…"

She looked up at him, adoring the view but steeling herself against the words she was afraid to believe.

"Last night blew me away. And it seemed so much like you and I being together was…I don't know…a done deal, signed, sealed, delivered…that when I tried to explain what I want for the rest of my life, I skipped over the most important part."

His hands slipped from her shoulders to her upper arms again.

"*You* are the most important part, Emmy. You are *not* incidental, Emmy," he said forcefully. "And this is *not* a way to soothe my conscience—you've already done most of that by opening my eyes to the Topher I'd lost sight of, to the things he thought and believed in. You've already helped my conscience by letting me know how Mandy didn't blame me."

Declan's grip around her arms tightened.

"I do love their kids and want to help raise them. And I *don't* want you to have to do it alone. But those things come second to how much I love you. It's just that what I feel for you is so big in me that it seemed like it's written on my forehead—too obvious to miss. Remember, I'm a jarhead. The same way we don't act on whims, we aren't supposed to be this…this completely taken over by feelings like I am having for you…"

She couldn't help wondering if he was just saying that now.

It must have shown in her expression because he squeezed her arms tighter and said, "I don't think you know how great you are. How beautiful you are inside and out. How smart and brave and resilient. How strong and kind and caring… Lying in bed with you last night was like coming home for me in a way that didn't have a damn thing to do with a place. It sure as hell didn't have anything to do with guilt or remorse or my conscience or Topher or Trinity or Kit. It was all about you. About you and me together. It was all about how right that felt—more right even than the marines have felt to me, and nothing on earth has ever shocked me more than realizing that! I love you, Emmy. I *love* you," he repeated louder and with more intensity. "I want you to marry me. I want to stay here or leave here or go to the moon with you if that's what you want. I want to spend the rest of my life with you. Because with you is where I belong. And I think with me is where you belong. And the *rest* is what's incidental. The rest is just what I thought we could do around that."

Steeling herself against those words hadn't worked but still she was worried about taking them to heart.

She'd spent this entire day telling herself that last night was no big deal, that she needed to take it in stride. That explosive, incredible lovemaking was just that—a few hours of explosive, incredible lovemaking that she could not let herself imagine as anything more than that. As anything that would lead to anything more.

But now here he was saying it *was* a big deal, that he wanted it to lead to more. To so much more.

And she didn't know what to make of that.

Should she just let herself exult in it?

Or should she be wary of it?

This was all happening head-spinningly fast. And what if last night had been *so* good that *he* was getting a little carried away by it?

What if, in a few days or weeks or months he came to his senses, decided he really wanted his old life back?

That seemed possible. Likely, maybe.

And it was on the tip of her tongue to say no again.

But something in her wouldn't let her.

Something in her stopped her and made her think again…

Was it possible that now she was imagining the worst-case scenario and convincing herself *that* was real? Was she projecting the negative instead of the positive and still putting too much stock into it?

Her positive projections hadn't been reliable. But neither had the negative one at Mandy's wedding when she'd convinced herself that Declan had left her and spent the night with Tracy.

So maybe, again, she needed to stay only in the moment...

And in this moment this man was proposing to her and she wanted to accept everything he said, believe in it, believe in him and not worry about the future.

She *did* have feelings for him, she cautiously admitted to herself.

But she'd been fighting those even harder than she'd fought everything else today. And today she'd done a lot of fighting.

She'd been fighting against every inclination to build a fantasy future with him in her mind.

She'd been fighting not to recall every heartfelt talk they'd had, every time he'd taken his turn at opening her eyes to things, every time he'd given her support and comfort and a sense of safety even in the midst of her fears. She'd been fighting not to turn those recollections into images of herself having all of that to turn to from now on.

She'd been fighting not to notice over and over again today how fantastic he looked, how sexy he was and imagine the opportunity to wake up every day to him.

She'd been fighting not to recall every detail of the night they'd spent together, of every touch, every kiss, every climax, and picture it as a wedding night that would be only the beginning of a lifetime of nights like it.

And now was she supposed to stop fighting everything? Stop keeping her feelings for him under wraps, and just trust him and what he was saying?

She was still looking up into that face that had been the first thing she'd seen after being buried alive in the school rubble, and it struck her that she'd trusted him that day to get her out, to save her.

It struck her that she'd trusted him during her panic attack in the attic.

She'd trusted him enough to tell him what she'd told only Carla.

She'd trusted him in the orchard.

She'd trusted everything he'd said to her, every piece of advice he'd given her, every suggestion he'd made.

So why shouldn't she trust what he was saying to her now? she asked herself. Why shouldn't she trust that he knew his own mind, his own heart? That he knew himself well enough to know what he was doing and that it wasn't just guilt or a haze of leftover passion from last night?

Now that she'd allowed herself to begin to consider his proposal, the floodgates were opening and the man she was looking up at was everything for her.

He was big and strong and steady. Tough on the outside but so much more tender inside—enough to sit beside Trinity on her princess bed and read her princess stories. Enough to cradle Kit in those massive arms. Enough to walk Emmy through fears and panic and see her to the other side of them.

He was kind and understanding—more understanding and patient with the school explosion aftereffects than she'd been with herself. And all without any judgment, without making her feel weak or silly. He'd taken the situation in stride and that had helped her deal with it, had helped her feel like she genuinely would be able to get through any more anxiety that might come up. Especially if he was there with her.

And just look at him... she told herself.

It was a face she could look at for the rest of her life. A face she *wanted* to look at for the rest of her life.

In fact, it occurred to her that if she hadn't had the very nebulous start of feelings for him even at Mandy's wedding, she wouldn't have cared so much when she thought he'd spent the night with someone else. It wouldn't have seemed like such a horrible rejection and it wouldn't have affected her strongly enough to send her into Bryce's arms.

Now, here in Northbridge, staying in the same house, caring for the kids together, working the farm together and having him so sweetly comfort her through the resulting aftershocks of Afghanistan, the seeds of those feelings had taken root.

Now they were ready to bloom.

"I do love you, Declan..." she said even as she was just admitting it to herself.

"Then we don't have a problem," he told her confidently, quietly.

"You're sure?" she asked. "About you, I mean..."

"Never more sure about anything. I love you. I want you. Nothing is more important to me than you are."

"I do love you," she repeated with more certainty.

He sighed as if relief was just settling over him. "That's what I needed to hear. That and that you *will* marry me..."

"I will."

"And the rest?"

She thought about it, about all he'd laid out for them.

"I like Northbridge, and between last night and today I've had so many people asking me to take pictures for them that I do think I could make a small business out of it here. Plus I know how important it was to Mandy and Topher to have the kids grow up in a small town, on the farm—and the goat *does* love me now," she joked, filled with joy when she saw Declan smile. "So yeah, I'm willing if you are... Let's give it a try."

"And if it isn't right for us, we'll adjust," he said. "As long as we're together nothing else matters."

She wasn't quite sure where it came from, but she honestly did believe that.

It didn't make any difference that the life they had envisioned didn't look anything at all like what she'd once imagined her future should look like.

Because as he pulled her close again and kissed her so soundly it made her light-headed, she understood what he'd meant when he'd said that being with her had made him feel as if he was home, that being with her was where he belonged.

Now that her own feelings didn't have to be locked up tight, it struck her that being with him made her feel as if she was home, too.

And being with him was most definitely where she belonged, now and forever.

For a future that might be *better* than anything she could have pictured after all.

* * * * *

Thursday 3
October

MILLS & BOON

Coming next month

CINDERELLA'S PRINCE UNDER
THE MISTLETOE
Cara Colter

Imogen could tell Luca's experience with snowballs was limited. The ball was misshapen and did not look like it would survive a flight through the air.

"Yes, Your Highness," she said with pretended meekness, "please remember I'm injured." Then she swatted his snowball out of his hand. Before he could recover himself, ignoring the pain in her foot, she plowed through a drift of heavy, wet snow. She snatched up a handful of it, shaped a missile, turned back and let fly.

It hit him smack dab in the middle of his face.

She chortled with glee at his stunned expression. He reached up and brushed the snow away. But her laughter only lasted a moment. His scowl was ferocious. And he was coming after her!

She tried to run, but her foot hurt, and her legs were so much shorter than his in the deep snow. He caught her with incredible swiftness, spun her around into his chest.

"Oh, dear," she breathed.

"What would an ordinary guy do?" he growled.

Kiss me. She stared up at him. The tension hissed between them.

"Cat got your tongue?"

She stuck it out at him. "Apparently not." Then she wriggled free of his grasp, turned and ran again. And she suspected her heart beating so hard had very little to do with the exertion of running through the snow and what felt like it was a near miss of a kiss!

With the carefree hearts of children, the air was soon filled with flying snowballs – most of which missed their targets by wide margins – and their laughter. They played until they were both breathless. Imogen finally had to stop as her foot could not take another second of this. Though with her hands on knees, breathing heavily, she decided it was well worth a little pain.

He took advantage of her vulnerability, pelting her with snowballs, until she collapsed in the snow, laughing so hard her legs would not hold her anymore.

"I surrender," she gasped. "You win."

He collapsed in the snow beside her and a comfortable silence drifted over them as the huge snowflakes fluttered down and landed on their upturned faces.

Finally, he found his feet, and held out his hand to her.

"We're both wet, we better get at that snowman."

She took his hand. "Before the dreaded hypothermia sets in."

He tugged and she found her feet and stumbled into him. His hand went around her waist to steady her, and he pulled her closer. She could feel a lovely warmth radiating through the wetness of his jacket. She could feel the strong, sure beat of his heart. His scent filled her nostrils, as heady as the mountain sweet crispness of the air around them.

She looked up at him: the whisker-roughness of his chin and cheeks, the perfection of his features, the steadiness in the velvet-brown warmth of his eyes.

They were back at that question: what would an ordinary guy do?

But despite his clothing, he was not an ordinary guy. A prince! She was chasing through this mountain meadow with a prince.

Would kissing him enhance the sense of enchantment or destroy it

Continue reading
CINDERELLA'S PRINCE UNDER THE MISTLETOE
Cara Colter

Available next month
www.millsandboon.co.uk

MILLS & BOON
MEDICAL
Pulse-Racing Passion

Set your pulse racing with dedicated, delectable doctors in the high-pressure world of medicine, where emotions run high and passion, comfort and love are the best medicine.

Eight Medical stories published every month, find them all at:

millsandboon.co.uk

MILLS & BOON

MODERN

Power and Passion

Prepare to be swept off your feet by sophisticated, sexy and seductive heroes, in some of the world's most glamourous and romantic locations, where power and passion collide.

MILLS & BOON
Desire

Indulge in secrets and scandal, intense drama and plenty of sizzling hot action with powerful and passionate heroes who have it all: wealth, status, good looks... everything but the right woman.